Connie Monk grew up in Reading and, following her marriage, lived in the Thames Valley area until 1974, when she moved to Ringwood in Hampshire. After her husband retired they moved to Shaldon in Devon and she began to write. Her first novel was published in 1984. She has since written over fifteen best-selling novels. Two of her books were nominated for the Romantic Novel of the Year Award.

SOMETHING OLD, SOMETHING NEW

Tim and Sue Marshall live in their dream farm on the Berkshire Downs with their young son and daughter and orphaned niece and nephew. When they take in a local boarding-school boy for the summer holidays they watch the shy, bespectacled Quentin change beyond recognition. Quentin begins to see Highmoor as the home he has never really had. But there are big changes ahead not only for Quentin, but for England's farming community and for the Marshall family. History repeats itself as Sue watches her family grow up, fall in love and start families of their own. But she also begins to realise that some things can never stay the same . . .

A multi-generat__al saga se_ __ the 1950s to the present da_

Books by Connie Monk
Published by The House of Ulverscroft:

CONNIE MONK

SOMETHING OLD, SOMETHING NEW

Complete and Unabridged

CHARNWOOD
Leicester

First published in Great Britain in 2001 by
Judy Piatkus (Publishers) Limited
London

First Charnwood Edition
published 2002
by arrangement with
Judy Piatkus (Publishers) Limited
London

British Library CIP Data

Monk, Connie
    Something old, something new.—Large print ed.—
Charnwood library series
    1. Berkshire (England)—Social life and customs—
20th century—Fiction
    2. Domestic fiction
    3. Large type books
    I. Title
    823.9'14 [F]

ISBN 0–7089–9352–4

Published by
F. A. Thorpe (Publishing)
Anstey, Leicestershire

Set by Words & Graphics Ltd.
Anstey, Leicestershire
Printed and bound in Great Britain by
T. J. International Ltd., Padstow, Cornwall

This book is printed on acid-free paper

1

1952

'Throw me the car keys, Sue,' Tim Marshall said as he came through the lobby into the old farmhouse kitchen. 'I'll go and fill up, it'll save you doing it this afternoon.'

There was no need to explain his meaning. That afternoon she was taking Mrs Josh to the optician in Reading and, knowing the old lady's independent spirit, they wanted to avoid stopping at a garage. Leaving her bowl of half-mixed pastry, Sue went to the key rack in the hall. 'I'm glad you remembered. Careful, I'm all floury. Don't forget Mrs Josh's appointment is for half past two so we must eat punctually today. It's only going to be ham and eggs,' then pointing to the pastry, 'this is for supper.'

'I won't be late. Where's Liz? Has she got over being left behind this morning? She can come with me now if she likes.'

'It was only her pride that was hurt. She soon recovered. She's helping Josh, bless him, he's keeping her very busy.'

Josh Hawthorne and his wife had already been at Highmoor Farm nearly thirty years when Tim had inherited it from his uncle and brought his young wife there only a few months after their marriage. When arthritis and age caught up with Josh, it hadn't entered Tim and Sue's heads to make any changes. The heavy work of the farm

1

was beyond him, but still the kitchen garden was his domain and kept both their households in vegetables. To Tim and Sue — and certainly to their family — 'the Joshes' were as much part of Highmoor Farm as the very land. The truth was that, although as a child Tim had loved visiting his uncle during the long school holidays, he had had no first-hand knowledge of farming. Like some of the local lads, he had helped at harvest time until, completing his training as an engineer, he'd become part of the working world and no longer had the luxury of long vacations. After that Highmoor had had no more than occasional visits on his motor cycle. Then, on his uncle's death, he had found himself its owner. The sloping fields of rich pasture had become his own, with a dairy herd, a farmyard noisy with the squawk of hens and the grunt of pigs, nearly 400 arable acres and, mercifully, with Josh Hawthorne. That had been in 1938, a time when farming was in the doldrums. Logic told him to sell out and put any money the farm raised into a property in Reading where he worked and where, just married, he and Sue had been living in a small, up-to-the-minute, utterly character-less home, one of an identical row of bungalows. It had been the best they could afford and had sold itself to them because the front overlooked meadows and there was a footpath that led to the Thames. His uncle's bequest meant that they could look for what they thought of as a 'proper house'. If that's what logic told them, another silent voice urged that for neither of them could a 'proper house' in Reading compare with a farm

2

on the Berkshire Downs. Reason couldn't easily be overcome: making a living from a farm could be no more than a pipe-dream, that's what they'd told themselves. If Tim knew nothing about running a farm, as a housekeeper Sue was a raw beginner even with the assets of an easy-to-run and modern bungalow. Where was the sense in their even visiting Highmoor? Better by far to put it straight into an agent's hands.

It had been in October, a clear Saturday afternoon that believed itself still to be summer, when they'd packed the essentials for a weekend, locked their bungalow and set out, Tim on the motor cycle, Sue in the sidecar. They owed it to Josh Hawthorne to tell him personally what they'd decided to do. If that had been simply an excuse for their making a weekend visit to the farm, they hadn't looked beneath the surface for any ulterior motive. So they'd come to Highmoor, eager for two nights in the country, even discussing which side of Reading they'd look for their 'proper house'. But that first evening, curled up together in an old rocking chair in front of the kitchen range, the old house had begun to cast its spell on them. Their bungalow home, or even the more solid detached property they'd envisaged, belonged in a different world.

'It's as if we've been tossed in the air and have fallen down the right side up,' Sue had murmured, burrowing her face against his neck. There had been no need to explain. They'd known this was where they were meant to be. By the next day their future had found a new shape

3

and when she said, 'Won't our children be lucky, imagine growing up here! They'll have ponies — and Tim, imagine when we have a son how he'll love to learn to look after the land.' Distant dreams from a young bride who had been brought up in the cloistered academic world of Cambridge where her father was a lecturer. But dreams she had never lost as the years went by.

That weekend had changed the pattern of their lives and, a fortnight later, they had moved into the farm leaving their newly built — and none too well-built — bungalow on the market for sale.

Josh Hawthorne had become Tim's mentor. 'Mr Hawthorne' Tim had called him in those first days.

'I can't be doing with too much o' this Mr lark,' he'd been told. 'Your uncle called me Josh, and that'll do me well enough, Squire.' But Tim hadn't found such familiarity easy; even as a schoolboy he'd seen his uncle's right-hand man as elderly — from the vantage point of a schoolboy a man can become elderly ahead of his years.

'Tell you what,' he'd suggested. 'You drop the Squire and I'll settle for Josh.'

That had been the first week and, from then on, it had been Josh and Mrs Josh. But for Josh it had still gone against the grain to use Tim's Christian name, so he had become 'the Guv'nor' while Sue was Mrs Tim.

If Josh had been invaluable to Tim, Mrs Josh — or Ada Hawthorne, to give her her proper name — had saved Sue from many a pitfall.

4

Until she'd married, Sue had never cooked and, in the early weeks while she'd lived at the bungalow she had at least had the advantage of a new gas cooker and shops nearby. Housekeeping at the farm was quite different: she'd had to get used to a solid fuel range, and learn the mysteries of dampers and draughts. It was Mrs Josh who'd taught her to make bread, to scald milk and skim off the cream, to make chutney and preserves, to ensure the crackling on her pork was crisp, and a hundred other things. Now, nearly sixteen years on, Sue had added her own natural attributes to all she'd been taught.

Images of those early days flashed through her mind as she heard Tim drive off in the seldom-used Morris, sensitive to Mrs Josh's need to 'pay her way' and making sure there would be no petrol stop on the afternoon journey. Then, instead of going back to her piecrust, Sue wandered to the open window and leant out. The still air was full of the scent of summer; if she were led here blindfold she would know exactly where she was.

'That's it, duckie,' she heard Josh call to her six-year-old Liz, 'bring it here for me first, then you can turn the tap on.' Dragging the snakelike hose behind her, Liz carefully trod between the lines of runner beans. 'Thank you, m'dear. Now if you can give me a drop of water, not too hard on to start with . . . '

It was easy to take happiness for granted; Sue was determined never to let it happen. But sometimes it was quite frightening how lucky she and Tim were. If everyone's life had a pattern, then why had she been given so much and Elspeth, her elder sister, so little?

Deftly fitting her crust on the gooseberry pie, she let her mind drift back to a time that seemed like a different world. It had been in 1935 when Elspeth had married John Ruddick. Everyone had been so full of confidence for the couple. For John had already been a Captain in the army, following the footsteps of his father, a retired Lieutenant Colonel. When, soon afterwards, John had been sent with his regiment to India, like most other officers' wives, Elspeth had gone too. Sue remembered her own feeling of envy as she'd stood on the dockside waving. Envying Elspeth? We should be glad we can't see into the future! Following the usual custom, Elspeth had returned to England when she was pregnant. That had been in 1939. Sue remembered her coming to stay at Highmoor just after the birth of her twins, Sylvia and Christopher. What a happy month they'd had; looking back it seemed that every summer day had been filled with sunshine, not a cloud on the horizon as Elspeth had looked forward to the babies being strong enough to travel back with her to India. Mrs Josh had taken the two girls under her wing just as easily as she had just one, for Sue had still been learning something new each day, none of it a chore. It had been just the same for Tim, working through his first round of seasons, learning from experience and from Josh. The young couple had been keen to absorb every new thing, so sure were they that, as Sue had said, 'They had been tossed up and had landed

6

the right side up.' As for Elspeth, she'd never so much as picked up a teatowel until she came to Highmoor, but Mrs Josh had taken her in her stride. For all of them, even Elspeth, had remained untouched by the horrors building on the Continent. But before summer was over the world had changed; nothing would ever be the same again. Thinking of it after so many years, Sue was ashamed that her memories of those early months of the war could have been so insular, for what else could she call it? It had taken all her time — and Tim's too — to do a new job well. That neither of them could look on it as drudgery had surely been good fortune rather than selfishness? Tim had never been a soldier, but he had worked every daylight hour — and many more in the milking sheds before the sun was up.

The pie in the oven, Sue dropped into that much-loved rocking chair, thinking of her sister. At the onset of war Tim had suggested Elspeth and the babies should make their home at the farm. It had seemed the most natural thing for all of them. The time they were all together crowded into Sue's mind, not a cavalcade of events so much as an atmosphere that after so many years could still soften her mouth into a smile. Then something that stood alone: John was being sent home after suffering recurring bouts of malaria. There were telephone calls between Elspeth and his parents, all of them waiting anxiously for news that he'd landed safely. Sue gazed unseeingly at the familiar kitchen, reliving the morning when the call was

7

from *him*, to say he had docked. As clearly as if it had just happened, in her mind's eye she could see Elspeth rushing into the room, radiant with joy. 'He's home! He'll be in London by lunchtime. Sue, will you mind the twins? He wants me to meet him there. I said 'yes', I said I could leave them with you all night and we'll fetch them tomorrow and take them with us to his people.' Within an hour Tim had driven off to Reading with her, using precious petrol under the pretext of visiting the agricultural engineer for a set of plough shares after he'd taken her to the station.

If John had arrived a day earlier or a day later how different all their lives would have been. Sometimes it frightened Sue that *she* had been given so much in her own life and Elspeth so little. For weeks London had had no raids, but that night shattered any false sense of security. She and John had both been killed. Any consolation Sue could find after the tragedy came from caring for Sylvia and Christopher. There had never been any question that their home was to be at Highmoor; they were like an elder brother and sister to Paul, Sue and Tim's first child, who'd been born two months after they'd lost their parents.

Standing up from the rocking chair she glanced at the old-fashioned clock on the wall, its swinging pendulum never faltering. Hour on hour, year on year the old clock looked down on them all; there was a comforting continuity in the sound of its loud tick. But, combined with the appetising smell of the almost-cooked

8

gooseberry pie, the discoloured face of the clock told her just how much time she'd been day-dreaming.

★ ★ ★

The tank filled, Tim was on his way home when he remembered that this was the day his friend Maurice and his wife were leaving for their cottage in the Dordogne for their annual holiday. He knew they weren't planning to set off until mid-afternoon; they'd booked one night at their usual hotel in Portsmouth and were crossing on the first ferry tomorrow. He wouldn't hinder them, but he'd just stop and say 'bon voyage' as he passed. Imagine what it must feel like to shut the house and go off for eight weeks! No chance of so much as a week with a herd of dairy cows needing twice-a-day milking, to say nothing of the fields of ripening corn. Therein lay the difference between school-mastering and farming! But, in any case, would he really want to?

Turning in at the open double gate of what the large sign proclaimed to be Merton Court School for Boys Aged 8 – 18, he drove up the long drive to the house.

'Hello there, Barbara,' he called at sight of Maurice's wife. 'I've not come to hold you up, only to say cheerio as I was passing. All set?'

She came over to the car, but there was no smile in her welcome. A tall, striking woman with sleek, almost black, hair and eyes like coals, he'd often wondered whether she ever softened in her approach to the younger boys sent to board at the school. Looking at her that morning, his instinctive thought was that he wouldn't want to be in the shoes of some poor eight-year-old, away from home for the first time. A capable woman, the welfare of the boys would lack for nothing — nothing except warmth.

'All set, you say,' she sounded petulant; today there was nothing of her usual matter-of-fact manner, 'all set to stay in this prison.'

Maurice had seen the car and came out to join them just in time to hear her.

'Come on, now, Barb, I'll get something sorted.'

'Damned school,' she glared at him. 'For nearly eleven weeks we've not had a second to ourselves, surely we're entitled to a holiday the same as everyone else.'

'What's the hold-up?' Tim asked. Usually so calm, he'd never seen Barbara show her feelings so openly.

'You know we have the two McBride boys here, sons of Anthony McBride and Elvira Dereford — '

'All very well for them,' Barbara interrupted. 'Pair of matinée idols, never a moment's thought for anyone but themselves!'

'They're out in the States — ' Maurice tried again.

'They live in a different world from the rest of us,' his disgruntled wife cut in again. 'The screen's ideal married couple, that's what the newspapers call them. It's not what I'd call them! The wretched child is *their* responsibility, not ours.'

'I'll get something sorted out. The elder one, Richard, he's gone off to California to join them, we had him accompanied to Heathrow yesterday. But the younger one, Quentin — '

'Supercilious, dreadful child. He makes me cringe even to see him with that owl-like stare as if he's too clever for everyone.'

'Quentin doesn't join up with his parents, I imagine he wouldn't fit in with their theatrical type of life. Richard does — he hopes to go to RADA when he leaves here.'

'So the young one goes home with friends, is that it? Has something gone wrong?'

There was no humour in Barbara's laugh. 'Friends? What child could stand having him under foot for nearly nine weeks? He's not normal, I tell you. He plays no games, he's always mooning about by himself or reading. If he had a bit of spirit it wouldn't be so bad.'

'Spirit or not, we're lumbered with him until we can get a reply to my cable to his parents. You see, Tim, he usually spends his holidays with his grandparents or, latterly, his grandfather. That's been the arrangement ever since he started here a couple of years ago. Barbara's right about his parents, they have no sense of responsibility whatsoever. Soon after he came here his grandmother died — for years she'd been pretty well blind and, as I understand it, she had an eye operation with no more than a fifty-fifty chance and didn't survive it. Since then he's been sent to his grandfather each holiday. As I said, they've always thought the world of him. Funny really, for as far as Richard was concerned they'd never bothered. This morning we had a phone call from some nurse or other, saying it's not possible to have the boy as Mr Dereford has pneumonia.'

'Just like that!' Barbara glared at the world. 'Not any suggestion that the poor, demented owners of this place have earned their break!'

'I got a cable off to his parents asking for instructions. They'll come up with something, even if it means we have to drop him off at Heathrow Airport we head for Portsmouth.'

'How did the lad take it?' Tim asked.

'There's no way of telling,' Maurice frowned. 'You know, of all the youngsters I've had through my hands, there's never been one who's made me feel so — so — inadequate. That's the truth. Inadequate.'

'Is he mentally handicapped, do you mean?'

'Dear God, no! It's uncanny, but whatever the subject he is top of his class. Whether it gives him any satisfaction God only knows, his expression says nothing at all. Always got his nose in a book, always learning. If only just once I could see him chasing after a ball, or managing to get across a hurdle without falling flat on his face, I might begin to look on him as human.'

'Where is he now?'

'Your guess is as good as mine. Probably hiding in a clump of bushes somewhere with his nose in a book.'

'No, he isn't,' Barbara tugged at Maurice's sleeve, 'I saw a movement over there in the copse.' She shuddered, her movement exaggerated. 'Gives me the shivers. I wish to heaven they'd hurry up and tell us where to pack him off to.'

Tim was fond of them both, but at that moment his sympathies were all with the unwanted ten-year-old. What would Sue say if — ? Even in his mind he didn't finish the question.

'Cable his folk again. Tell them the lad is coming to Highmoor to stay. His elder brother must know where the farm is, he'll be able to reassure them.'

'You mean it? Oh Tim,' this time there was nothing petulant in Barbara's expression, 'I could cry with relief. I was so frightened we'd not get anyone to take him off our hands. I imagined him having to come with us to France — always there, like a spider in the corner. But what will Sue say?'

'Exactly the same as I have.'

'I say, this is damned good of you, Tim. He's a lucky lad,' Maurice opened the car door for Tim to get out. 'Come on, let's go and find him. I can't tell you how grateful I am. He's all packed up ready.' He put an arm around Barbara's shoulder, something Tim suspected he wouldn't have done a few minutes before. 'Better now? We'll get the cases strapped on as soon as he's gone. You take Tim to find him while I get our stuff down ready.'

'This way, Tim,' Barbara, her good humour restored, pointed to the shrubbery, 'he's lurking somewhere in here, probably watching our every move.'

13

'It's not like you talk like that about a youngster.'

'I may not be the perfect wife for the headmaster of a prep school, but most of them I can tolerate fairly well. But this one honestly gives me the creeps. He never gives an inch, never gives an inkling of what goes on in his supercilious, clever-dick mind. No child has the right to make one feel so — so disadvantaged. I sometimes think Quentin McBride bears more resemblance to an all-knowing robot than to a human. But hark at me!' She laughed. 'If I'm not careful you'll wish you'd not been so free with your invitation.' It was easy to laugh now, sure that there would be no suggestion of his changing his mind. 'Honestly, Tim, you don't know just how grateful I am — well, we both are, but I don't think I could have borne it if the holiday had been cancelled. McBride!' she called, her voice sharp. 'Come here, please. Hurry up.'

A rustle in the carpet of last year's leaves and a small boy appeared. Tim had been told he was ten, within a few months the same age as Paul. The lad who emerged looked a good deal less. His dark hair was tidy and well cut, his khaki shorts and white pumps unnaturally clean for a boy of his age, his short-sleeved shirt immaculate. But in that first moment it wasn't what he wore that impressed itself on Tim, it was his solemn expression. Barbara had described him as owl-like and it was easy to see why. He wore spectacles with dark, heavy frames, the lenses seeming too large for his thin

14

face. Whoever chose glasses like that for a child?

'Quickly when I call you, McBride. Right over here.' That Barbara's tone was brusque appeared to make no impression on the boy; steadily he moved to stand in front of her.

'Yes, Mrs Kimber.' Quentin came to within a yard of them. Despite standing obediently still and keeping his eyes downcast, there was nothing timid in his manner.

'This is Mr Marshall, a friend of ours.' Then, with a laugh, 'a very good friend of ours. He is prepared for you to stay with his family for your holidays — or until your parents contact him with further instructions. You know, this really is enormously kind of you, Tim.'

'Not kind at all,' Tim answered, meaning to reassure the boy. 'My lot will be delighted to have Quentin join them.'

Quentin looked up at him then, but still said nothing.

'Well? Have we taught you no better manners than that at Merton?'

'Yes, Mrs Kimber.' Then, to Tim, 'Thank you, sir.'

'Off you hop and collect your things,' Tim told him. 'That's my car by the front door, I'll see you back there.'

Without another word Quentin left them, walking towards the house at a steady pace, his manner giving no hint as to whether he was pleased or sorry at the turn of events.

'Poor lad. Is he always shy?' Tim said when he was out of earshot.

'Shy? That one! Monosyllabic often, but shy never.'

Less than five minutes later Tim and his unexpected guest were heading back to High-moor.

'I live on a farm,' Tim told him. 'You probably know where it is — Highmoor Farm.'

'Yes, sir. I've passed it when I'm allowed out walking. Does the copse belong to you, sir? I've been in there sometimes collecting ferns to take back and look up.'

'You're interested in botany?'

'I like to see things grow, sir. I like to find out about them.'

'I hope your parents will like the idea of your coming to us — I hope you like the idea too?' If he meant it as a question he wasn't to be rewarded with an answer.

'They will be grateful to you.'

'You have very illustrious parents. I under-stand Richard talks of going on the stage too. And what about you?'

Quentin turned to look at him as if the question had been asked in some foreign tongue. 'Me? Oh no, sir,' The way he said it made Tim appreciate what Maurice had meant about feeling inadequate. 'It's all pretend,' Quentin went on, 'I'd hate to have to wear clothes that weren't my own and say things I didn't really believe, just to make a made-up story seem like being true.'

Monosyllabic, had Barbara said? The child didn't seem afraid to express his opinions. 'You called me 'sir'. I'm a farmer, not a schoolmaster.

My name is Marshall.'

'Mr Marshall,' Quentin repeated obligingly.

'Before we get to the farm let me tell you something about everyone so that we shan't completely overwhelm you. There's my wife, you'll like her, I have no doubt about that. Then we have a niece and nephew called Sylvia and Christopher, they're thirteen, twins. They've lived with us all their lives.'

'Live with you, really *live*?' His dark eyes were filled with concern. 'You mean their parents don't want them?' Surely that couldn't have been hope Tim heard in the way he asked the question.

'They were very small when their parents were killed during the war. The twins seem like our own; I only told you so that you'd see why it is they call us aunt and uncle. Then we have a son about your age, that's Paul, and a daughter, Liz, who's younger, she's only six.' Quentin liked the way that when this stranger smiled his face creased, especially around his eyes. It wasn't just a 'smile to be polite' face. 'They all seem to manage to keep themselves occupied during the long summer holiday, on a farm there's never a shortage of things to do. Do you like country things?'

'I think I do. But I don't know really, you see, because I've had no experience.'

'Ah, I see.'

'My parents live in London when they're in England, so when I was too young to go to Merton Court that's where I used to be. Mrs Gibbons lived there to look after me.'

17

'You must be very proud of your parents, there can't be many people in the country who haven't heard of them.' Tim felt it was underhand of him, but he wanted to get some hint of the boy's feelings.

'Oh yes, I'm proud. So is Richard. He's going to be famous too, one of these days.'

'But the stage isn't for you, you say? Well, Quentin, I can understand that, it wouldn't be for me either. We all have to find what's right for us.'

He sensed rather than saw the slight figure settle more comfortably into the seat.

'Here we are, home sweet home. The big kids are all out, it's tradition that whatever the weather they go off with a picnic on the first day they're all home on holiday. But Liz will be glad of some company.'

'Will Mrs Marshall mind me coming? She doesn't even know who I am.' Only minutes before he had made conversation with assurance ahead of his years, but suddenly Tim saw how vulnerable he was. Behind the lenses of his oversized glasses his dark eyes were full of concern.

'I promise you, Quentin, she will be delighted. You don't know her yet, but soon you'll understand what I mean.' He stopped the car in front of the house so that it was ready for Sue to drive across to the farm cottage and collect Mrs Josh in the afternoon. 'Look, over there at the side of the house, there's Liz helping in the vegetable garden. Let's go and see her.'

18

Sue heard him speak as he passed the kitchen window and looked out to see who the visitor was. They weren't coming to the lobby door, instead they were heading for the vegetable garden. Whoever was the solemn little scrap of a child, following Tim along the grass between the plots? Liz was busy picking enough peas for supper, for when the picnickers returned they were sure to be ravenous, but seeing her father she dumped the bowl and came to meet him. Tim said something, his hand on the boy's shoulder; Liz smiled her pleasure at having unexpected company; the boy held out his hand with an almost adult dignity. Used to being looked on as too young to be important, Sue knew just how the little girl would enjoy being shown such deference. The two shook hands then, the first hurdle over, Tim left them to feel their own way towards getting to know each other.

'Who's that you've brought home?' Sue asked as he came into the kitchen to find her.

Briefly he explained.

'Poor little scrap. Well, we'll have to make it up to him. He'll have lots of fun with the others here.'

But then, of course, she hadn't met her visitor. She took it for granted that given freedom to roam, plenty of useful work to help with, an abundance of fresh air to promote a healthy appetite and good food to satisfy it, Quentin's summer holiday was bound to have the necessary touch of magic.

'Perhaps it was fate made you stop at the

19

school. I was thinking this morning about that sort of thing,' she said as she spread the checked cloth on the wooden table. 'Kind fate made us come here instead of putting the farm on the estate agent's books — '

'A comfortable home and a regular salary might have given us fewer headaches.' But she knew from the way he said it that he wouldn't have had things any different.

'Unkind fate chose that dreadful night to be when Elspeth and John were in London. I was thinking about her, Tim, about what a rotten hand she got dealt. I've been so lucky. And why? She and John deserved a life just as much as we did.'

'We get what's dished out to us. And talking of luck . . . ' He drew her close, rubbing his chin against the top of her head. As a child her hair had been silvery fair, now, at thirty-five, it had darkened a little, faded a lot, and was what her enemies (if she'd had any) would have described as 'mouse'.

'Fate is what I was talking about, Tim. What made you call at the school today? They go to France pretty well every holiday and you've never just chanced to call in passing before. There must have been something, some sort of guiding force.'

'I hope you still think so when you've met him. I can't see him careering about with the other three. Even Maurice says — no, I'll leave you to form you own opinion.' He knew she'd do that anyway. Slightly built, only five foot two even when she made a supreme effort, yet she had a will of steel and was a good deal tougher than she looked.

* * *

For the first few days of his stay Sue was disappointed. Like Maurice, she felt herself to be a failure; she'd come no nearer to getting to know him beyond the quiet, polite front. The three older children made no effort to include him. He might be the same age as Paul, but there all similarity ended. Paul was built of sterner stuff, taller, tougher, full of courage and ready for every adventure; just to look at him was sufficient to realise his abundant energy and his fearlessness. Above all else Paul Marshall liked to be out on the farm, but he had no intention of letting his older cousins run away with the idea that because he was only ten he was too young to keep up with them. In fact, such a notion never entered their heads. Despite the unspoken bond between the twins, any outing they suggested was always for all three.

Liz was cock-a-hoop, from being the unimportant too-little-to-be-included one, suddenly she had a companion. Helping Josh had always been one of her favourite occupations; that Quentin liked to help too gave her an added feeling of importance for she was the more experienced, she could anticipate what needed doing. Quentin was ten, vastly grown-up from her viewpoint, yet he chose to stay with Josh and her. Didn't that prove there was nothing second-best about it? No wonder she welcomed her new friend.

21

'Just because you have Quentin here, it doesn't mean you can neglect Daisy,' Tim told her when, two hours' work behind him, he came back to refuel on a large breakfast.

'I don't neglect her, Dad. I rode her,' but she didn't actually say when, 'and she's happy in the paddock with the others, I took her some carrots — '

'When I bought her for you, you promised you would exercise her properly. Taking carrots to the paddock isn't the same thing. Daisy is your responsibility.'

Quentin had listened in silence, looking from one to the other, his pale face wearing an expression Sue couldn't fathom.

'Tell you what,' Paul said, and all eyes were on him, 'why don't you and Quentin ride? You can take Nora, Quentin. She's mine — and I do exercise her, don't I, Dad? — but today me and the twins are on an all-day hike. We're off as soon as we've stoked up on breakfast.'

'Do you ride, Quentin?' Sue asked him.

'No — well, yes — not very well — ' He was biting the corner of his mouth, and kept his eyes downcast. Where was the self-possessed young boy she'd found so hard to understand? Not that the way he avoided her eyes as he stammered his reply made it any easier, but at least she felt she'd taken a step in the right direction.

'It's not Nora I'm concerned about; Paul looks after her very responsibly,' Tim was still talking to Liz. 'But if you're to keep Daisy, I want to see you riding her. Understood?' Liz nodded. Now it was her turn not to look at anyone. She was mortified that he should speak to her like that in front of Quentin, just as if she was still a baby. She was sure her face looked all pink, she could feel how hot it was.

'I'm not very good, Liz, but if you want me to, I'll come with you.'

'Come if you like. It's good fun. Are you any good at jumping? I won a rosette in the gymkhana,' Liz boasted.

'If you take the ponies out this morning, I want a promise from you that you won't jump,' Sue said. 'That's for when we're here. This morning we shall both be out. Mrs Josh is seeing to some dinner for you and Quentin.'

Liz forgot her own embarrassment. Mum and Dad both out was unheard of.

'Out? What, you mean out together? Even dinnertime?'

'We're driving to Oxford,' Tim enlarged on Sue's bald statement. 'We have an appointment with a dress shop. Isn't that so, lady?' How pretty Sue looked, he thought, watching her pour tea from the large earthenware pot.

'You getting a new dress, Mum? Is it for somewhere special? What's it for, Mum?' Liz sounded excited, a new dress for her mother was a rare event.

'It's for being a good lady,' looking down the length of the table Tim's half-wink said more than his words.

Liz's spirits rose. 'Tell you what,' she said to Quentin, 'we'll go to the old Roman road. That's a super place for a good gallop.'

'Buck up with your breakfast, you lot. We want

to be off,' Tim urged them.

'Please, Mrs Marshall, may I leave the rest?' Quentin mumbled.

'Aren't you hungry, love?'

' . . . headache,' he took off his glasses, rubbed them in his handkerchief and pushed them back on his nose.

'Get out in the fresh air,' Tim advised, 'better for you than forcing yourself to eat.'

'Will you excuse me, Mrs Marshall?' The solemn lad pushed back his chair and left the table, going out through the lobby to the yard.

'Bet I know what's wrong with him,' Paul chortled. 'Scared rotten, you could see it in his face.'

'Eat your breakfast and don't talk rubbish,' Tim admonished.

'You're stupid,' Liz told her brother. 'Always think you know everything. 'Course he's not scared. He told us he could ride, didn't he?' She wasn't having her friend made a joke of, and she could see from the way the twins giggled that they agreed with Paul. 'May I get down, Mum? Me and Quentin can go and saddle up.'

'We're off as soon as I can get cleared up, so remember your promise. No jumping. And be back in good time to see if Mrs Josh wants any help getting your meal.'

'Promise. Buy something really, *really* pretty. I ought to help you choose.'

'Off you go,' Tim laughed. 'I think we'll manage.'

There was an air of holiday about the farmhouse, for Tim and Sue to be having a day

24

out affected them all. Liz disappeared, rushing upstairs to change into her jodhpurs, then back again to go outside and find Quentin on her way to round up Daisy and Nora in the paddock. Five minutes later, Christopher carrying a rucksack crammed with sandwiches and home-made lemonade, and all three with long sticks they fancied their all-day hike merited, the other three said their farewells.

'Now it's just us,' and from the way he said it Sue knew Tim was looking forward to their day every bit as much as she was. 'What if I see to the washing-up while you make yourself pretty?'

A rare offer, for at Highmoor there was an outdoors/indoors allocation of duties.

'We'll be on the road by half past nine! Haven't been to Oxford for ages. Hark! Someone's coming back. What have they forgotten?'

'Hey, Mum,' Paul put his head round the kitchen door. 'I guess he wasn't just kidding, he's in the outside doings being as sick as a dog.'

*   *   *

Upstairs in his bed, covered with an eiderdown, Quentin faced his weakness. He had failed Liz; he was ashamed. The others didn't behave like that. How they'd mock him if they guessed what had given him this blinding headache. Well, he wouldn't tell them. They'd probably think he'd got a bilious attack. But what about Liz? He'd let her down. He'd heard the clip clop of Daisy's hooves in the yard below his window and known

25

she'd gone on her own. I'm a coward, just like Father said. I ought to make myself go with Liz. I *can't*, I've got to think of an excuse that won't let her know I'm scared. Scared of a pony! He kept his eyes shut but even behind the closed lids he felt as though they were being pushed into his head.

He heard the bedroom door being gently pushed open, then Sue's voice.

'He's asleep,' she whispered. 'Poor little love.'

'We'll ask Mrs Josh to come over when we go,' Tim whispered.

A long silence . . . perhaps they'd gone. Then Sue's voice again, 'We'd only worry if we left him feeling so wretched.'

At that Quentin opened his eyes.

'No! You're going to Oxford. You've got to go.'

She came across to sit on the edge of the bed. 'We've got lots of days, you mustn't worry about that. Are you feeling any better?'

Tim went back downstairs to finish his unfamiliar task of washing-up.

'My headache was real, it still is,' and she only had to look at the way he couldn't bear to open his eyes properly to know that he was telling her the truth. But his defensive manner confirmed what she'd suspected.

'Do you often get headaches?'

'Sometimes. Usually they go away after I'm sick.' He rubbed his eyes and she noticed how, even when Tim had brought him up to his room, he'd taken off those enormous spectacles and laid them carefully on the bedside table. Now, for a moment neither of them spoke. He lay very still, his face a pale mask. Tenderly she touched his forehead with the palm of her hand.

'If you have a sleep you'll feel better. I shall be downstairs, call me if you want me.'

But as she moved to stand up he gripped her hand.

'Don't know what to do, Mrs Marshall,' he croaked, only with an enormous effort preventing his face crumpling as it would if he gave way to his tears. 'I'm a coward.'

Ah, now she was getting somewhere.

'There are things in all our lives that make cowards of us, Quentin. Tell me' (she mustn't let him suspect that she already knew) 'and perhaps we can think of something together.'

'I wanted to go with Liz, I wanted to be brave enough. Honestly I did. Then my head started, when it does that I can't even see properly. But it was because I'm a coward. Don't tell Liz.'

'We won't tell anyone, Quentin. You don't like riding, is that it?'

'In Ireland at Grandpa's everyone rides. I never liked it, even when I was really tiny, I hated the feeling of it moving. Was awful . . . shouting at me for being a baby . . . jeering . . . laughing. Was awful.' Once started he wanted to tell her everything.

'At your Grandpa's? Isn't that where you usually go for your holidays?'

'That was different. Grandpa never made me go to the stable. You see, Grandma hadn't liked it either. Shall I tell you — I don't know if I can — but shall I?'

'I think you should, Quentin. It's not a good

27

idea to keep things bottled up inside you, not sharing your problems. Usually if we can talk about things they get easier.'

So he started the tale of the last time he'd sat on a horse. It had been when the family had been staying on his grandfather's estate in Ireland, just after his parents had returned from America and the newspapers were full of *Journey Into Destiny*, their latest film at that time. The ride had been arranged as what Sue considered to be a publicity stunt. Photographers had been waiting to watch them set out, reporters at the ready. Quentin had begged not to go, but no doubt the adoring public would relish pictures of the couple in the bosom of their family. The more Sue heard of Anthony McBride and Elvira Dereford the more she disliked them. Quentin had sat on his horse, but the horse had taken its lead from those ahead and his ability was such that he'd been powerless to alter its course. Terrified, he'd hung on as it had galloped across the open country, through a copse, over a hedge . . . even talking about it, Quentin was tense. It was at the hedge that he'd been thrown but by that time the others were almost across the next field. He'd groped around him for his glasses, but they'd been trampled. His face was bleeding and there was an awful pain in his neck, but worst of all he didn't know how to get home, he couldn't see where he was in his misty, unfocused surroundings. The mare had galloped on without him and his father had led it back.

'Couldn't get on again,' he sobbed now, 'he said I was a coward, yellow-livered coward. He was ashamed. But I couldn't. It was awful, I screamed, I could hear me. I remember the way he looked at me when I was sick, sort of disgusted, as if he couldn't believe how awful I was. I don't know what happened after that. When I woke up I was at Grandpa's in bed. The others had gone. But Father was right, I am a coward. I want to be able to go with Liz — but I can't.'

He was sitting up now. Could this near-hysterical child be the same one whose behaviour had put her in mind of an elderly gentleman? She put her arms around him holding him close.

'Paul usually exercises Nora, it won't come up again. But Quentin, if it does, leave it with me. I'll get you out of it. It'll be our secret. And there's nothing to be ashamed of in not riding, most people don't. Between ourselves,' she added with a soft laugh, 'I'm not up to much myself. Now I think the best thing you can do is have a sleep. I'll close the curtains so that the light won't hurt your eyes.'

When she turned back to him he was throwing himself off the bed, his hand over his mouth. She just got the wash-stand basin to him in time.

'Going to feel better now,' he whispered weakly when the paroxysm of sickness was over. 'Glad I told you about it.'

'I'm glad too.'

Leaving him under the eiderdown she went downstairs to Tim. She'd told Quentin his confidence would be her secret, but it didn't enter her head not to relate the story to Tim just as he would have done to her.

An hour later, Daisy back in the paddock and Quentin much restored, the expedition set out. It was to have been a day for the two of them but, right from the moment that Paul had rushed back to call them to Quentin, they had both known in their hearts that they couldn't drive off and leave him.

Mrs Josh waved them on their way, Sue and Tim in the front of the car, Liz and Quentin in the back.

2

Rarely did Sue feel as angry as when, a fortnight or so later, she read Elvira Dereford's letter. That same morning she replied, writing while her fury was at boiling point. Sitting at the kitchen table, she let the words spill from her nib as they rushed into her mind. So engrossed was she that until Tim leant over her shoulder to read her outpourings, she didn't realise he'd come in through the open door from the lobby.

'I feel the same,' he said, 'but we have to think of the boy. It won't do him any good if we upset them; they're more likely to refuse to let him stay here again. And already the kids are making plans for the Christmas holiday.'

'I've never been so — so — knotted up with hate.' She looked up at him miserably.

'Perhaps she meant no harm. Their world's different from ours.'

Picking up Elvira's brief letter, her voice was full of venom as Sue read:

''Dr Kimber has notified us that you are kindly accommodating Quentin. In the present circumstances I hope it will be convenient for you to keep the child until Dr and Mrs Kimber return, when doubtless you will be able to arrange for them to take him back to school early. Enclosed is a card giving details

31

of my theatrical agent; if you will send your accounts to him — weekly, monthly or as convenient — we have instructed him to settle immediately. And may I leave it to you to explain . . . ' and so on. Well, of course we'll break the news. Poor mite. Oh, Tim, he really does seem to have no one.'

Then, even *her* sympathy being overtaken by her anger at the tone of Elvira Dereford's letter, 'I suppose she thinks that all you have to do is throw money at a thing and all the lumps are smoothed out for you. Her own son! What's the matter with the stupid woman?'

'The loss is partly her own. If only she'd spare the time to get to know him, both of them would gain from it.'

'Herself, that's all she cares about! Prancing around being admired and making a fortune for her pains.' She looked down at her hastily written scribble, '' . . . hospitality isn't something we *sell* at Highmoor . . . care and affection can't be bought like the latest fashion or paid for like a face-lift . . . '' Looking up at Tim, she saw the laughter lurking behind his eyes and her own face creased into a smile. 'Well, I feel better for having written it anyway,' she said, screwing it up. 'So I'll tell her we wouldn't dream of accepting payment for having him, he is a delight in the house and wonderful company for the children. I'll even mention Christmas and the plans they're making. Yes, all right, now I've got my feelings off my chest I'll start again. But, Tim, poor little chap. Thank goodness he's here with us.'

Tim ruffled her hair affectionately. 'I'm not so sure about the 'wonderful company for the children' bit,' he teased.

'Having him is salve to Liz's pride when the others don't want her tagging along, even you must admit that much. Anyway, he's a darling. All right, I know he's very buttoned up. But if we'd never had anyone to really love us, would we be any different?'

'Write your letter, lady,' bending over her, he dropped a kiss on the end of her nose.

With her pen on the table she turned towards him, both arms around his waist as she rubbed her face against him.

'I only came in for a crust of bread and cheese while Fred Dawson gets the binder attached. Look what you're doing to me.'

Her eyes shone with teasing love as she looked up at him, the movement of her face making his pulses race.

'The children are waiting . . . it's ten o'clock in the morning . . . must go . . . '

'Ten o'clock or five past, the world won't stop going round,' she stood up, her letter forgotten. 'It can go on without us,' she whispered as his mouth covered hers.

To creep stealthily up the familiar staircase added to the moment. From outside they could hear the voices of the children, the raucous crow of a cockerel, then the tractor engine starting. Only minutes ago Sue had said she felt knotted up with hate; all such thoughts were forgotten as she tore off what few clothes she wore in the heat

33

of summer. The key turned in the lock of their bedroom door, their kingdom was the sun-warmed eiderdown, their world was each other. Lovemaking was a natural and precious part of their lives. With the heat from the sun beating on their naked bodies, their excitement was heightened by the scent and sounds of the summer day wafting in through the open window. Life was moving on, but they were held apart from it; there was a glorious urgency in their need of each other.

So soon it was over; they lay sated and laughing in each other's arms.

'Do I look like a man capable of cutting that top meadow today?' Tim panted.

She chuckled, wanting to hold him back, knowing the day was waiting.

'You look like a man who's made good use of his time. Hark, is that someone coming in?'

'Dad,' came Paul's voice up the stairs, 'aren't you coming? The binder's hitched on, we're all set.'

'With you in two seconds. Tell Fred I got held up, but I'll be right there.'

'OK. Where's Mum? Has she got the food ready?'

'She's about somewhere,' Tim shouted, with a wink at half-dressed Sue, 'look outside in the yard. She just told me she was sending the food over by the youngsters. Hop along back to Fred, I'm just coming.'

Paul 'hopped along', supposing his father had come home for the lavatory. He would have been surprised if he'd been able to see his parents

34

hurrying into their clothes like a pair of conspirators.

★ ★ ★

'Fodder on the hoof,' was what Tim and his labourer, Fred Dawson, called it. Ordinarily, everyone working on the farm went home for a midday break. But there was nothing ordinary about gathering in the harvest, especially when Josh warned them his knees were prophesying rain was on the way. All the morning (or what was left of it by the time they got started) Tim had driven the tractor while Fred followed behind, taking the tied sheaths dropped by the binder and stacking them into stooks. At the same time he managed to make sure he hurled enough back towards the three over-willing young helpers to keep them occupied. When Quentin and Liz arrived bearing the hamper, Tim stopped the engine and climbed down.

'Food time. You take over now, Fred, so that you can sit and eat while you drive,' he said. 'I can wait. I had a hunk of bread and cheese mid-morning, before we started. Don't bolt it, take your time. When you've done, I'll drive again and have mine.'

Leaving two parcels, each containing a home-made meat pie, a bread roll packed with thick home-cured ham and a screw-top bottle of cider, the two younger children gladly handed the hamper over to Paul, Christopher and Sylvia.

'Just about starving!' There was a ring of pride in Paul's voice; he'd been doing a man's job,

35

he'd earned the right to have a man's appetite. He and Christopher led the way, Sylvia just behind and the two younger ones trailing. At Highmoor, helping at harvest time had been a routine part of summer for as long as any of them could remember, but Quentin had known nothing like these last weeks. Sometimes he was almost frightened to think about how much he liked it; it seemed like tempting fate. Today he was more frightened than ever before, for he'd recognised his mother's writing on a letter addressed to Aunt Sue. Aunt Sue, that's what he'd been told to call her, just as though he mattered as much as Sylvia and Christopher.

Liz was worried; her friend had hardly talked to her this morning. Was he getting tired of being at the farm? She tugged at his arm, holding him back.

'Are you fed up with us? Do you wish you could go to your Grandpa?'

''Course I don't. This is the best time I've ever had.'

She beamed, her blue eyes shining with delight. Like her mother, she was slightly built; unlike her mother had been as a child, she had no pale fair curls. Instead, her honey-coloured hair was thick, straight and cut short. It wasn't combed from a parting, but from the crown of her head, and reminded Quentin of a monk's cap.

'That's all right then. Wish I could be older, more like your age.'

'You're fine as you are, Liz.'

'So what's the matter? Have you got a hurting

36

head again, is that it?'

'No. Nothing's the matter. Except — don't tell anyone — it's just that I'm scared it's too good to last.' Even saying the words frightened him. 'My mother has written to Aunt Sue, I saw the envelope this morning. She might say I have to go somewhere else. I never want to leave Highmoor, never, never, never. Don't tell anyone.'

Puffed up with pride at being made his confidante she ran a few steps ahead and threw herself into a cartwheel. By the time they caught up with the others the picnic was under way and Sylvia had poured out five beakers of home-made lemonade.

'Come on, you two. We'll have eaten it all if you don't buck up,' Christopher said, his mouth full of pie. Conscious of his extra years, he was the self-appointed 'man in charge'. 'We've not started the drinks yet, so take whichever you want, you two kids. Oh, damn it all,' a reminder in case they'd failed to appreciate his seniority, 'rotten wasps! Mind your hand, Liz, there's one crawling up your beaker.' For Liz had wasted no time in deciding which looked the fullest.

'Where? Where?' She almost dropped it back on to the ground, flicking her hand around until the offending wasp flew off the beaker only to alight on her arm. There was little that terrified Liz, but a wasp could send her into a frenzy of fear. Now she jumped to her feet, shaking her arms.

'Don't be such a baby,' brother Paul told her, biting into his pie with relish. 'It was only a wasp, not a lion. Anyway, it's flown off now. Good job you're too little to help like we three did, there were mice galore scarpering all over the place.'

She sat down, her face pink with embarrassment. Being the youngest carries great responsibilities if you want to be treated like all the others. He'd called her a baby! Reaching out for her drink she was about to hide her shame in a long draught when the wasp returned and settled on the rim. Rigid with fright she dropped it, the lemonade drenching her shirt and shorts.

'What a daft thing to do! Well, you'll just have to go without,' Paul told her, taking a long drink with extra relish to tease her.

'Don't care. Not thirsty.' But it wasn't true. Worse than that though, if she tried to argue any more she just knew she'd cry.

'Here Liz, honestly I'm not a bit thirsty,' Quentin lied. 'You drink mine.' He moved closer to her, ready to chase the insect off if it came near her.

Her pride was restored. With something almost approaching dignity, she took the beaker he proffered and felt she had the last word when she announced, 'That wasp's in your hair, Paul. Like Mrs Josh says, where there's no sense there's no feeling, expect that's why you didn't know.'

Quentin looked at her; behind the thick lenses his eyes were a mirror to his heart. Materially his life had lacked for nothing, his clothes were from the most expensive stockists, his school bill carried evidence that he was indulged in every 'optional extra'. The one thing he'd needed was someone to love, something that money can't buy. Now he had Liz. Young as she was, she knew with true female intuition that he worshipped at her shrine. So sipping his drink, she smiled at him over the rim of the beaker. His cup of happiness runneth over.

After their picnic they packed the rubbish back in the hamper.

'We must get back to work,' Paul stood up and stretched, proud of his height, proud of his muscles. 'You kids can take this lot home, can't you, there's no weight to it now.'

'Silly show-off,' Liz muttered as she watched the trio rush away down the sloping field. 'Look — that letter. If there's anything you don't want to hear, well, it's no good putting off hearing. Mum told us she's written to tell your lot that you were enjoying it. And perhaps your Mum is just saying she's glad you're here with us. Yes, you'll see. That'll be what it is.' Quentin was less sure. His mother wasn't in the habit of enquiring whether he was enjoying himself.

Except for empty beakers, a no longer clean cloth and screwed-up pieces of paper, the hamper was empty, so Quentin carried it unaided. Running on ahead, stopping for the occasional cartwheel, Liz had already put all thought of the letter out of her head.

'Come on, slow coach,' she yelled when she reached the gate to the yard. 'We don't want to waste the afternoon, we're going on a butterfly hunt, remember.'

She had no idea that he was too frightened to imagine their planned afternoon, too frightened to let himself anticipate happiness that was so intense it sometimes made his mouth feel dry and his tummy hurt. But he mustn't let Liz know or instead of wanting to be with him she might scoff. So with what she mustn't guess to be an assumed whoop of excitement he rushed down the hill to catch up with her. Her chuckle of delight was the only reward he needed.

'Mum,' she yelled as they went through the lobby to the kitchen, 'it was a good picnic. Except that I tipped my lemon all down me.'

'Poor you, lost your drink.'

'Oh, it was OK, Quen gave me his!'

'What a good chap,' Sue ruffled his always tidy hair affectionately. 'There's plenty in the pantry, love. Go and get yourself a drink.'

'Mum,' Liz said and at the tone of her voice he felt himself freeze, 'about the letter his Mum wrote — '

'I'm afraid there's some bad news for you, Quentin, love.'

He whipped off his glasses, rubbed them with his handkerchief and rammed them back, not looking at anyone. He'd known, the moment he'd seen the envelope he'd known! His throat felt so dry and tight that he was frightened to breathe, frightened of the sob that was strangling him. Without looking at either of them, or at anything, he rushed out of the room and up to his room, slamming the door behind him.

'Don't follow me,' Sue told Liz. 'I have to talk to him, poor lad.'

'It's not fair,' Liz grumbled, 'what did *she* have to spoil everything for?'

'Go and change into your other shirt and shorts while I have a talk to him.' Already Sue was on her way up the stairs. Outside Quentin's door she stopped, listening to the muffled sound of his crying. Very quietly she went in, then, knowing how Liz resented being left out of things, she closed the door firmly and turned the key.

'You've guessed what she told me? He'd been very ill, I know it's hard for you, but he'd hate to think he'd made you so miserable.' Wasted words, the child was beyond listening.

'Can't go. Aunt Sue, tell them I'm sick, tell them — tell them — please don't send me away.' His face was buried against the pillow, his body stiff and taut. The only movement was the beating of his clenched fists and, after those few, barely audible words, the only sound his trembling sobs.

First Sue picked up his spectacles which, in his frenzy, had somehow landed on the floor then, sitting on the edge of the bed, she took him into her arms.

'Hush, sweetling,' she whispered just as she used to when the babies had cried, 'you're not going away, your mother is glad you're staying here.' She felt him relax in her arms. 'She asked me to break the news to you, she thought it kinder than writing Quentin, you know your grandfather was very ill, that's why you didn't go to Ireland.'

'You mean it's Grandpa? You mean that's what you have to talk to me about? Is he worse, is that what's the matter?'

41

She shook her head, aware of the silence and knowing that without being told he understood.

'Bet Grandma's pleased to see him.' He struggled to sit up. 'She couldn't see, you know. Do you suppose she can now? Always used to have hold of Grandpa's arm. Then she wasn't there and his arm was empty.' Taking his handkerchief he scrubbed at his tear-stained face. 'He was very kind, he always said I could stay in the holidays. But it was different after Grandma died. It was because he knew that she, well she sort of liked me you know, that he said I could go there. He didn't seem to care much about anything without Grandma.'

'So he'll be happier now,' Sue encouraged the thought, relieved at his almost cheerful acceptance of the news.

'Aunt Sue — about what I was upset about — did she say I could stay? Honestly, she's not going to make me go out there like Richard does?'

'Honest Injun. And I've written back to say we hope you'll be able to be here for Christmas. Of course, I can't promise that your parents won't have other plans, perhaps they'll be in England by then, even.'

'Oh, we needn't worry about that, Aunt Sue. If you say you'll let me be here, they're sure to say I can come.' Well satisfied, he put on his glasses and straightened his crumpled pillows.

* * *

Each August Sylvia and Christopher visited their grandparents, Lucinda and Harold Ruddick, in Gloucestershire. This was a regular school-holiday event, usually a week at Christmas and Easter and a fortnight in the summer, just four weeks which for the ageing couple were the highlights of their year. John had been their only son; when he'd been killed they'd lost everything — or they would have, had it not been for the legacy of his two children. It was Harold Ruddick who paid their school fees, fees that Tim knew he would find it hard to match for his own two. At Highmoor all four children had always been treated the same, and Tim was determined that when it came to schooling somehow he would find the money. Christopher, Sylvia, Paul and Liz, anyone meeting them would have seen them as a family. Yet between the twins was that indefinable union, something nobody could ever take from them. The other two accepted that three times a year they would be taken away to stay with their grandparents. But just as the twins were part of the family at Highmoor, so their grandparents were 'the Grands' to everyone.

In a whirl of bustle and excitement Lucinda and Harold arrived in their shining black Rover; the cases were stowed in the boot, and off the foursome went. No one ever considered that as they were all brought up as one family, it might have been in order to take the others — or at least Paul — along. The Grands, as they were called, belonged to the twins. It was as if that part of their lives was self-contained, had no bearing on the real living that went on at Highmoor. And that's how it might have continued but for something that was said on the afternoon that the Rover transported them home again, its black paint glistening even brighter than usual as a consequence of Christopher's morning's work. At Highmoor, the nearest to resembling a garden was a patch of mossy green in the shade of a sycamore tree and a flowerbed under the sitting-room window. Any other space was given over to more essential needs. Even that one small patch of would-be grass was on the road side of the house but, as the road was no more than a lane leading to Silverdale Farm, it had all the privacy it needed. By the time the Ruddicks' car turned in at the open gate, Sue had erected a folding table in the shade of the tree, spread it with an embroidered cloth and brought out her best bone china tea service, having first sniffed hard to make sure that the air wasn't a reminder of the proximity of the farmyard.

'Molly's got a brand-new calf,' Liz shouted before the engine had been switched off. 'It was born this morning. Me and Quen helped, well, we saw anyway. Paul missed it, he was helping threshing.'

Watching the children rush off towards the field where Molly had performed this miracle of nature, momentarily Lucinda looked wistful. Then she got her face in order, and smiled as Sue held the door for her to climb out.

'I've put the table out here for tea, there's hardly a breath of air indoors.'

Harold Ruddick rubbed his hands together, an expression of his pleasure. 'Lovely, my dear. Four cups — well done, well done. Does that mean we may expect Tim to spare the time to join us?' Retired for fifteen years, but he still looked and sounded the Colonel he'd once been. Not as straight-backed as in former years, his gaunt frame was held upright more by will-power than nature.

'Glad to see you,' and this from Tim himself appearing from the side of the building, changed into decent jodhpurs, a freshly ironed shirt and cravat. For the Ruddicks he always made a special effort. How handsome he looked, Sue thought, her opinion probably coloured by love. The term 'handsome' might be applied to a man such as Quentin's matinée-idol father . . . But Tim? Much of the colour was bleached out of his wiry hair, hair that sprang into waves and, if he didn't go regularly to the barber, curled in the nape of his neck. His blue eyes were clear, his complexion weathered, in his short-sleeved shirt the strength of his arms was patently clear. So used to their being together, it wasn't often they really *looked* at each other. This afternoon Sue feasted her eyes on him. He must have been aware of her attention, for a second their eyes met, his twitched into what only she saw as a wink of recognition. It was one of those special moments, one that would stay with her.

'What about taking me to see this new calf while the ladies get the buns or whatever on the table?' Harold suggested.

Best china, a sponge cake baked that morning,

the prettiest napkins Sue had in her drawer, half an hour ago those things had been important. But with the men walking in the meadow and she and Lucinda in the kitchen stacking the teatray, she felt a warmth of companionship towards the frail-looking Grand.

'It goes so quickly, this fortnight. I dare say it tires us more than we like to own, taking them about, trying to see they haven't time to find it dull being with us.'

'Dull? Aunt Lucinda, as if they ever do!'

'Bless the girl, I may be old but I'm not so stupid that I don't realise there must be limits to how long the young can slow their pace to ours. You'd think we'd go home glad for the peace and quiet but the truth is, the first few days after they've gone the house seems like a morgue. This is where they belong. My dear, you and Tim — you've let them lack for nothing. So often I think about you all, I truly believe that John and Elspeth look down and are thankful. If you and Tim hadn't been here — at the time I could have coped, but each year it would have got harder. And it wouldn't have been fair on them. Yet I love them both so dearly. Not often I say these things — not often we have a few minutes to ourselves.'

'We all love them dearly, Aunt Lucinda. If I say 'as if they'd been born our own' that sounds as though Elspeth and John are forgotten — '

'Not to me it doesn't.'

'We're all family, us, the twins, you and Uncle Harold — ' She broke off, seeing the way Lucinda's bottom lip trembled. 'Here, if I take

46

the tray, can you bring the cake?'

'And they tell me you've taken in another lad for the holiday?'

Sue told her about Quentin, ending up with, 'He's very easy to love. I've written to his parents to ask that he may come to us for Christmas. If they refuse he'll be devastated.'

'Refuse?' The old lady had clearly recovered. 'From what you say they're much too busy carving their names in glory. More likely they'll tie a gift tag around his neck and make a gift of him.'

No more was said about Christmas, it was far removed from that sultry summer afternoon. As the four of them sat round the little table it was Harold who turned the conversation to school fees.

'I see they've put them up again,' he said. 'And it worries me. If I hadn't had this bee in my bonnet that I wanted Christopher to go to his father's old school it would have been more convenient all round to have sent him to Reading.'

What sort of a pension did he have? Two lots of school fees must be a burden.

'Between us, we'll manage. If I can help — ' Tim started.

'No, my dear boy, that's not what I'm saying. Now that Paul is to join him, it's not right that you have this extra drain. You won't let me put a penny in the kitty for their upkeep here, let me do something towards Paul's fees. Humph?'

Sue tried not to glance at Tim. She knew just what a struggle he would find it to meet the new expense three times each year.

'I appreciate the thought, more than I can tell you I appreciate it. But I can't let you. The lad's fees are my responsibility. Maybe I'm stupid, but I get a sense of — yes, almost of satisfaction in knowing that it's my own hard graft that gives the boy his opportunities.'

'Well, the offer stands. But I can understand. We all want to do our best for our children. He'll do well, a bright youngster.'

'Oh he's bright enough,' Sue laughed, 'and tough as old boots. But at heart Paul is a farmer born.'

Conversation drifted comfortably after that and it wasn't until everyone was congregated around the Rover and goodbyes were being said that Sue heard Sylvia say, 'We'll see you after Christmas, won't we, Grandma? We're lucky, we get two Christmases.'

'What do you and Uncle Harold do for the twenty-fifth? Do you go to friends?' Sue said as she held the door for Lucinda to get into the car.

'Oh no, we hold everything back. It's lovely to have some excitement when the twins come.'

Briefly Tim and Sue looked at each other, so briefly that there couldn't have been time for a message to pass. Yet she knew just what he was going to say.

'This year let's make it different. Both of you come here, have Christmas with the family.'

'Yes, oh yes, Grands, do that, please. It would be so much better. Christmas here is magic, you'll love it.' Was it Sylvia or Christopher said it first? Probably both at the same time, their reaction the same.

They don't mean that they don't enjoy what their grandparents do for them; please don't let the old dears be hurt, Sue pleaded silently. They're only children; they just didn't think. She put her head through the open window and kissed Lucinda's thin face. 'Please,' she whispered. 'Families should be together.' She felt rather than saw Quentin standing apart from the others, uncertain whether to go or stay, and put out her hand to him. 'And this Christmas is going to be very special, isn't it, Quentin?'

He moved closer.

★   ★   ★

Maurice Kimber regarded Quentin's request for a bicycle as an improvement on his always mooning about on his own. But it was Tim who took the child to Reading to make the choice, bringing it back in the Land Rover. Despite his aversion to riding a horse, Quentin took to a bicycle with remarkable ease, even the initial tumbles not putting him off. For he had a purpose. The farm was about a mile and a half from Merton Court, no distance by bicycle, but too far for him to be allowed to walk on Saturday afternoons in the short daylight hours of winter. A weekend never passed without his bicycle being propped against the end wall of the cowshed.

That term was Paul's first away from home. Before he'd gone each day to a small

49

co-educational day school in Brindley, just as Liz still did. But Tim and Sue were both determined that somehow they would scrape together the fees so that their own two could go to the same boarding schools as their cousins. So on the 14th of September, without a hint of nerves or tears, he had been deposited at what Sue secretly considered an awesome building in the midst of playing fields in Surrey. The next day they'd made a second journey, that time into Kent to take black-stockinged, gym-slipped and velour-hatted Sylvia, complete with lacrosse racquet and all the excitement of seeing her friends. Only Liz had been left in the back of the Land Rover for the return journey, her usually pretty face wearing a scowl. It really was beastly always being too young for this, too small for that.

But Quentin's bicycle made her life a whole lot more cheerful. Even though he didn't have too many early tumbles, she was still much the more proficient on two wheels.

'Got a trick to show you,' she would tell him, confident of his admiration. She delighted in showing him how she could ride with only the back wheel on the ground or tear down the track at the edge of the top field, riding the bumps with her legs stuck straight out in front of her. If she'd tried to show off to Paul she knew he would have slapped her down. But Quentin never did; she again felt puffed up with pride.

It wasn't long before the Saturday afternoon cycle rides to Highmoor developed into whole weekends, an arrangement that Maurice accepted with almost too much eagerness. For, although Quentin relaxed in the affection he felt at the farm, at school he was still an introverted child, avoided by his more gregarious peers, who saw him as too clever for comfort and no fun at all.

So was formed the pattern that, except on very rare occasions, was to last all through his school life. And never once was Quentin made to feel that he was of any less importance to Tim and Sue than those who were family. At some time during each holiday Sylvia and Christopher went to stay in Gloucestershire with their grandparents. Their visits remained the high point of the elderly couple's year, except perhaps for Christmas, which it became routine for them to spend with the family at Highmoor.

Although their upbringing was the same, their dreams of the future were vastly different. For Paul there could be no other way but to farm. Christopher's ambitions could never be for the land, even though he enjoyed pitting his strength against the men's in the hayfield. For him the army beckoned. Stories of his grandfather's career had always thrilled him and long before the time came for him to leave school he saw his path clearly, something that filled Harold with pride.

★   ★   ★

There was one other person who had an enormous influence on Quentin, and that was Josh Hawthorne. From the viewpoint of a schoolboy, the one-time farm worker with his

51

stooping shoulders and gnarled hands was so elderly that there was a timelessness about him. He was the fount of all knowledge in the kitchen garden.

Tim remembered how on the day he'd first brought the quiet, solemn child home they had talked about the ferns in the copse on the edge of Highmoor and Quentin had told him, 'I like to see things grow. I like to find out about them.' Certainly he never tired of helping Josh. Whether Liz would have been so enthusiastic on her own was unlikely, but to be less than willing to work alongside her friend risked her being looked on as too little to be useful. And she wasn't having *that*.

'You and Sue are damned good to that boy,' Maurice Kimber said as he drove Tim home from a meeting of the parochial church council one evening the following spring. It had been a long session — dragged out by Esmé Bligh, a lady member who doubled as a contralto in the church choir and who was insistent that the ladies should be robed in crimson the same as the boys. Overweight and over-opinionated, she carried all opposition before her, but the result had meant a late end to the meeting. Both men were relieved to be on the road home; the one subject they didn't want to discuss was the meeting. Talking about Quentin came as a relief.

'We've become very fond of him. And he's good for Liz. As long as we know she's with Quentin we never have to worry about her, he's very dependable. They're great friends despite the age difference.' Then Tim laughed, thinking of his young daughter. 'She's mighty touchy if she gets talked down to. Paul is adept at upsetting her apple cart. But Quentin never does.'

'Humph,' a grunt that might mean anything. 'What do they do together, for goodness sake? He never plays a game if he can escape. I'm grateful you take him off our hands at the weekends. He's a loner, never joins in with any of the normal healthy skylarking you expect from a bunch of young lads. And you say your Liz gets on with him? But she's a bundle of energy.'

'A bundle of energy who enjoys admiration,' Liz's father laughed. 'She's a born show-off, bless her. And he's a willing audience. But there's a lot more to Quentin than that. You remember Josh Hawthorne at Highmoor?'

'The old chap who's been there for years. You still keep him on?'

Tim was disappointed in his friend's remark. Josh was part of Highmoor.

'It wouldn't be Highmoor without the Joshes. These days he keeps us all going in fruit and vegetables. I've watched Quentin working with him. You should have seen him straining to turn the clods of earth with the winter digging. He may not have much brawn but he's not short on tenacity. Now he's learning about planting — asking questions, I can tell that just by watching.'

'Oh, he'd ask questions right enough. The boy absorbs information like a sponge absorbs water. If only sometimes I could feel I was getting nearer to him, I could truthfully say that he'd be the most satisfying pupil I've ever taught. Too young to know yet what direction he'll choose for a career. Damn it, whether it's science or the classics he's streets ahead of all the others. Has he too little confidence to let himself join in with the others, is that why he's such a loner? Or does he think himself too bloody superior? Anyway, old man,' Maurice laughed, 'pain though he is, McBride Minor will do credit to Merton Court one of these days — and it won't be in growing spuds, no matter how much he might be learning from your Josh. I foresee Oxford and the classics for him.'

'Sue heard from his mother this morning. They are back in England. Did you know?'

'Richard told me. But anyway it was in the paper. Now Richard, he'll be going to RADA, and it wouldn't surprise me if one of these days he even outshines his parents. You didn't see last year's production of *Richard of Bordeaux*. The boy was magnificent. He just lost himself in the role.'

'Mrs McBride has written that they hope to call on us on Sunday. Are they going to the school?'

'I haven't heard. But I'm sure they'll want to see Richard. She won't take kindly to you if you greet her as Mrs McBride, old friend.' Maurice chortled. 'I can't see your sweet Sue having a lot in common with Hollywood's darling.'

'Thank God for that, unless I'm much mistaken. Anyway, Sue has written inviting them to lunch and she told me not to forget to mention it to you and suggest that Richard joins us.'

'Better you than me, old man. Between ourselves, I think the delectable Elvira Dereford could be a pain in the arse.'

'I shouldn't wonder. But you know Sue, she'll make them welcome with no more and no less fuss than she would if it were you and Barbara or the Joshes.'

'She's a gem.'

'Amen to that. Well, here we are,' as they drew up at Highmoor. 'Time for a nightcap?'

'Better get home.' The flame of his lighter illuminated his face as he lit a cigarette and Tim knew from his eyes that something in his thoughts amused him. 'Poor old Jim Bligh, he'll get a blow by blow account of Esmé's battle of the robes. God in heaven! The woman'll look like a barrage balloon left over from the war, a blood-red barrage balloon. Doesn't it make you count your blessings, man?'

'Beauty's in the eye of the beholder,' Tim laughed.

'Give me a ring when you hear from the gorgeous Elvira and we'll arrange about Richard. It could be they intend to call on you at Highmoor to do their five-minute duty and thank you for taking the runt of the litter off their hands, then collect Richard and take him off to lunch — I don't know, The Leathern Bottle or The Swan. Doubtless somewhere where they'll be recognised and fêted.'

That was on Tuesday night. On Thursday Elvira Dereford's reply came, written in a bold, flourishing hand. It seemed Highmoor was to entertain the darlings of the silver screen.

It wasn't like Sue to feel inhospitable, but on that Sunday morning she felt no eager anticipation as she prepared the seldom-used dining-room table. Today she was out to impress; for Quentin's sake she wanted his parents to approve of all they saw at Highmoor.

'Looks like party time, Mum.' Liz danced round the table with excitement, admiring the gleaming white damask cloth, the silver cruet and the cut-glass wineglasses — wedding presents brought out only on high days and holidays. 'Can I wear my party frock? Please, Mum, can I?'

'Of course you can't, silly. You'll wear your shorts and play shirt the same as you always do.'

Liz scowled. 'Dad's all smart. And he didn't even go to church today.' Then, at the thought of the rare freedom of this Sunday morning she decided she had better things to do with her time than hang around indoors. Usually Sunday morning found her in their regular pew in church, sitting between her mother and Quentin, being watched to make sure she didn't fidget or talk. Talk? It was never more than a whisper, and Mum and Dad whispered to each other sometimes, she'd seen them. But if she did it, she got a tap on her knee and a cross scowl. It wasn't fair. And anyway, it's hard to sit still when your feet don't quite reach the ground. To Liz, Sunday Matins was the longest hour and a quarter of the week.

'Come on, Quen, it's boring in here. Let's go for a ride.'

'Don't forget Richard's coming. Quentin, you ought to be here to introduce him and make him feel at home.'

Was it her imagination or did the skinny young lad stand a little taller?

Half an hour later, as she did up the side zip fastener of her clean gingham dress, she gazed from her bedroom window on to the ceremony of introduction taking place in the yard. Of course she was too far away to hear what was said, but there was no doubting Quentin's proud formality as he did the honours. A smile played at the corners of her mouth as she imagined the correct, almost old-fashioned, dignity he brought to the responsibility given to him. She wished she could have known his grandparents, for surely it must be their influence that had left such an indelible mark.

It was the first time she'd seen Richard McBride. Were ever two brothers so different? Such a handsome boy . . . if he intended to follow in his parents' footsteps with looks like that half his battle was won. Her smile broadened as she watched Tim. The least formal of men but, bless him, he'd taken his lead from Quentin and was shaking their guest's hand as if he were receiving some civic dignity instead of a sixteen-year-old. Clearly Quentin was satisfied; she could almost hear his sigh of relief; he had done his duty, acquitted himself well.

Almost immediately an open-topped, left-hand drive and patently American car, turned in at the open gate. In those first minutes Sue's preconceived ideas of their famous guests were firmly in place. In appearance they were every inch celebrities, Anthony McBride the swash-buckling hero, Elvira Dereford (the delectable Elvira, as Maurice Kimber had described her) as glamorous and elegant in her tailored trousers and silk headscarf as she would have been in a Paris gown.

'Mr and Mrs McBride,' Sue greeted them, the warmth in her smile barely disguising the none-too-friendly intent behind the use of Elvira's married title, 'welcome to Highmoor. Quentin is outside in the yard showing the farm to Richard, so we must make do without formal introductions.'

'How is our young stick?' Anthony asked with a laugh as he shook Sue's hand. 'He writes a weekly letter — they have to, you know, each Saturday morning before they're allowed to enjoy their weekend. His tell us precisely nothing despite the fact that he manages to fill a full page — nothing that matters, I mean.'

'He's a darling,' Sue was immediately on the defensive.

'We're glad to have the opportunity to tell you how good it's been for him to come here,' Elvira said. Honestly? Over-sweetly? Condescendingly?

Sue's natural retort would have been 'And how would *you* know what it means to him? And what would you care, anyway?' But she swallowed her words. Quarrelling with them

58

could so easily rebound on Quentin. So, keeping her smile in place, she ushered her guests indoors.

'You think we neglect him, don't you.' Elvira made a statement; it wasn't intended as a question. 'I can tell you do. And I expect you're right. But Anthony's parents were always besotted with him. Didn't give a hoot about Richard, you know. Right from the day he was born — and so obviously the runt of the litter — his grandmother positively doted on him. And we had very full lives. He was an accident, like most children if one is truthful. At that stage a baby was the last thing we needed.'

'What about Richard?'

'Oh, he's so different. He's one of *us*. He was five when Quentin's arrival could so easily have ruined my career. Five years old and always an asset. Well, if you know him, I don't need to explain. Charm is as much part of him as his amazing good looks. Poor Quentin. Life can be very unfair. It's as if families have just so much to share around, and Richard got the lot, don't you think?'

'No, Mrs McBride, I *don't*. You should hear what Dr Kimber says of Quentin's abilities. But, more important than that, he is sensitive, gentle, dependable. He's your son. Can't you spare him time to get to know him?' She spoke so earnestly. Watching her, Anthony wondered if she had any idea just how pretty she looked in her fresh gingham dress, her face devoid of make-up. An English rose.

'Perhaps we ought to have him stay with us

59

during his holidays while we're in England,' Elvira said. 'But we've tried it before. He really makes himself disagreeable, never tries to be charming. Looks at the world through those hideous great glasses he wears — '

'Are they of his choosing? No, of course they aren't. Lots of children wear glasses, why does he have to have thick dark frames as if he's — he's — '

'The wise old owl?' Anthony smiled. 'Perhaps he is, don't you think?'

'He's wise enough to see through the veneer to the true wood beneath. Please don't take him away at holiday time, not if you're going to be working and you say he doesn't fit in. But, just sometimes, if you'd send him a postcard, a picture of your theatre or a view of somewhere you visit. He'd feel he mattered. He's lost his grandparents — '

'That brings us to another point.' This time it was Anthony. 'We've not seen Quentin since my father-in-law died, but I suppose today I ought to tell him about the will. Not that it will matter to him for years yet. It was his grandmother who made so much of him. Quentin and his nurse made their home there until he was old enough to be accepted at Merton Court. After she died, the old man seemed to lose interest in things. But he was always prepared to put the child up for the school holidays.'

'Yes, Quentin told me.'

'Anyway, in his will he instructed that the house in Ireland should be sold and everything, *everything* be held in trust for Quentin. And

Elvira calls him the runt! Not many runts fall on their feet like that. One of these days he'll be a man of considerable means and without raising a finger too.'

Trying to be fair-minded, Sue reminded herself that if, as parents of two sons, they were resentful, it wasn't altogether surprising.

'How are your shoes?' she asked, her manner suddenly changed, 'can you walk in the yard? Or shall I call them in and say you're here?'

'To the yard,' came Anthony McBride's cry, almost as if he were rallying support for England and St George.

If Sue imagined the visit would run smoothly from there on, she was mistaken. In their presence she saw a new Quentin: aloof, wary, speaking only to reply to the rare direct question, he seemed guarded. The first flicker of a smile was when they were all grouped around the flashy car.

'We'll see you at Easter, Richard. One or two things we have earmarked, people for you to meet. Useful people.' Anthony kissed his elder son in a way that Tim found unnatural. Men didn't kiss; men shook hands.

That seemed to be Quentin's opinion too as he held out his hand, first to his mother, then his father.

'Mrs Marshall says you may spend your holiday here, Quentin. I'm sure you'd prefer that to London.'

And that was when Quentin smiled. He said not a word, but it was as if the tension went out of him.

'Yippee!' Liz yelled as the car turned into the lane.

'Come on, Liz. Race you to the top of the world.' And they were off, tearing along the border of Five Acre Meadow, over the stile and up the final hill. This was their kingdom, the top of their world.

★　★　★

So the pattern was formed. The only new thread to weave into it was Richard, bronzed and beautiful as he helped gather in the harvest that year. One day he would be a matinée idol, but in that year of 1955 at least one pair of eyes looked on him with adoration.

He was never 'one of the family' as Quentin had become; Richard was too much of a free spirit for that. But he enjoyed his stays at Highmoor, he even thought of the small room at the far end of the corridor as his own. He would need to have been blind not to have seen the way Sylvia watched him; admiration like that was food and drink to him.

'What about taking a punt on the river for the day? My treat,' was one of his suggestions, for unlike the four from Highmoor the McBrides were never short of pocket money. The treat was open to all of them but the proposal was made so that he could show off his prowess with a pole to Sylvia. His reward was in her ill-disguised worship.

And as, stripped to the waist, he worked in the corn field, he saw her open admiration as his just reward. He knew his bronzed and handsome body was feeding her dreams; he knew it, accepted it and saw it as a sure foretaste of what lay ahead of him. Quentin may have been the runt, but Richard was a true son of their glamorous parents.

When his time at Merton finished it was easy enough for him to leave the carefree days on the farm behind; for him they had been no more than an interlude as he waited for the important part of his life to take over. There were plenty more Sylvias ready to worship at his shrine.

3

Seen from the viewpoint of the young, each year saw changes that were exciting and full of promise. While Liz progressed from a daily walk to school in Brindley ('babies' school' as she considered it with her eye always on something better) and journeyed each morning by train to Reading, the others remained one step ahead. First the twins, then Paul, turned their thoughts to what they would do with their lives.

When Christopher announced he meant to go into the army his grandfather was cock-a-hoop with pride; it was the way he'd tactfully tried to guide the boy's thinking. Once the road ahead was decided there was still the need to do well in his school-leaving exams, first O Levels and then, when he was eighteen, A Levels that qualified him for acceptance as a cadet. Sylvia was equally sure of herself, even though her choice came as a surprise to the family. She wanted to nurse and went straight from school to University College Hospital to start her three-year training. She'd always loved the country, had worked on the farm as energetically as the boys; but the call of the metropolis wouldn't be denied; nothing less than a London hospital would suit her plans.

The next to make a decision was Paul. For him the future was clear. As Tim and Sue had always known, Paul would want to farm. In truth

Tim had been looking forward to the day when a bill for boarding-school fees no longer dropped through the letterbox three times a year. But it seemed Paul didn't mean to come straight to work at Highmoor; first he wanted to go to agricultural college.

'I don't see any point,' Sue frowned as they sat on the window seat, both reading Paul's letter at the same time. 'What can he learn there that you can't teach him?'

'A good deal.'

'Rubbish!' Sue defended. 'No one could run Highmoor better than you do. I know we were both pretty ignorant when we came here, but Josh put you on the road. There's nothing some silly college could teach you now.'

Tim's arm was round her shoulder as they shared each sheet of Paul's long letter. He pulled her an inch or two closer, rubbing his chin against her faded fair curls.

'You, my dear sweet lady, are prejudiced. I have learnt how to run a smallish farm efficiently — but Paul will go much further.'

'That's just plain stupid. What would he want with learning about farming rolling acres? One day he'll run Highmoor, when you and I are old and tottery. This is the place he needs to understand.'

'Yes and so he will understand Highmoor. It's for Highmoor that he needs to stretch his knowledge, look beyond. I appreciate that. The farming world is so different now from before the war. Then it was in the doldrums. No one thought of going to agricultural college. But if I

65

were his age — especially leaving school and seeing all my friends going on to train for some career or other, then I'm sure I'd feel just the same.'

It didn't escape her that he sighed as he folded the letter back into its envelope.

'Well, I think it's stupid — and selfish. You could do with the help here.'

'I haven't yet got to that tottery stage you talked about,' he told her. 'It'll be money again though, Sue. More money; just when I thought the fees would be cutting back.'

'Tell him 'No'. There's no point in him learning about forestry maintenance — Tinney's Copse is hardly a forest. And all that rot about land being maintained for vegetables for the freezer factories these days. Like I said, it's stupid and selfish.'

'He loves the land, darling. Imagine if we'd had a son who wanted to go into banking or music or — '

'Of course he loves the land. No one could grow up here and not love it.' She snuggled closer to him, nestling her head against his chest. 'I can hear your heart.'

'Can you hear what it's saying? Sue, a letter like this makes us stop and think. We'd naturally assumed he'd leave school and come home. Well, if he wants to go on to agricultural college, then we ought to say thank God for it. We'll manage, we always have.'

'Oh, we've more than managed, Tim Marshall.' Sitting bolt upright she looked him in the eyes. 'I wouldn't be anywhere or anybody in all the wide world but here and just as we are.' Then moving close again she teased his mouth with her lips. 'Nowhere in the world,' she whispered.

'Nowhere?' he mumbled. 'If I had ten minutes I'd take you somewhere.'

She laughed delightedly, taking his words in the same teasing way as he'd spoken them.

'Aren't we lucky, Tim, you and me. Do you know, when I was just a youngster I would never have believed people could be like we are after more than twenty years. Are we normal?'

'Something we shall never know. My guess would be that our lamp burns brighter than most.'

'Coo-eee,' came a call from the lobby. 'May I come in, Mrs Tim?'

''Course you can. We were just reading a letter from Paul.'

Mrs Josh was as ageless as her husband, assuming that 'ageless' means unchanging rather than looking young. Spotlessly clean, yet her clothes were all so similar that it would be easy to assume she never changed them. The mornings found her enveloped in a floral overall; the afternoons in a dark skirt, light-coloured blouse and a pinafore tied around her waist. Sundays — a day of rest as she called it, although no one ever saw any sign of her resting — she wore a dress instead of a skirt and blouse, and in the morning a pinafore, never an overall. Sunday morning was given to 'cooking Josh's dinner' — as if he didn't get fed for the rest of the week. But look out of the window at ten past six on Sunday evening and the Joshes could be seen leaving their cottage as they set out to walk to Evensong, shoes highly polished, Mrs Josh with her hat freshly trimmed for each season. To the Marshalls they were as dear as any family.

'I had post too,' she told them, beaming with pride. 'That's why I popped across. Just wanted to show you. From Sylvia, it is. See, a picture of the theatre she'd been to. Read it and see. Can't you just imagine her, proud as Punch? He always was her hero, was that brother of our Quentin's.'

The picture postcard she passed for Sue and Tim was from Sylvia. She had been to see Richard play the lead in his first West End production, a farce. And afterwards he'd taken her to supper. Remembering Sylvia's schoolgirl hero-worship of him, Sue imagined her excitement at being singled out, probably taken backstage and finally going on to a restaurant. She's not a child, she thought confidently, she's seen enough of life to be wise to him.

'I bet the student nurses are green with envy,' Sue chuckled, 'Richard McBride is more than just his parents' son. To be as gifted and as handsome is — is — well, it gives him an unfair advantage. He's half-way up the ladder in just one step, while some battle on for years and don't get anywhere.'

'That's the way of things, my duckie,' Mrs Josh agreed sagely. 'Well, good luck to him, I dare say. He always seemed a nice enough lad. Any road, if he's half a man there must be times when he plasters on his greasepaint and thinks what a charade it all is. The other thing I came for was to say, if you can use an extra pair of hands I'm free for an hour, we could get things sorted in the dairy together.'

To Mrs Josh, being free for an hour would never mean there was time to sit down and look at the paper or dally over her elevenses. The pleasure of freedom from one job came from being able to help with another. Brought up on a smallholding near Cholsey, she'd been no stranger to a woman's work on a farm when Josh, then the most junior labourer at Highmoor, had married her in the far-off days before the Great War.

As she and Sue worked in the dairy together, churning butter and skimming the scalded cream in readiness for Sue to take to Brindley, she took up the conversation of the McBride brothers.

'All right for that one, always has been,' she said, 'his sort always fall right side up. It's our Quentin bothers me, always has.'

'Quentin is a dear,' Sue was quick to imagine criticism.

'Oh, he's that all right. Too easy hurt, that's his trouble. Thinks the world of young Liz, you know. It worries me — and, mind, I'm not blaming the child — she's pretty as a picture, full of life. There'll be plenty more young men have an eye for our little Liz, make no mistake. And if she spurns him, then he won't even have us to fall back on. We're all he's ever had to love, with parents like he's got. Like Josh says, all they're fit for is poncing around looking for admiration. Threaten them with a proper day's work and you wouldn't see them for dust.' She stood back and surveyed her large, flat carton of thick cream.

69

'There now, my duckie, I'll just pop a lid on, then this is ready for you to take.'

'Bless you, Mrs Josh,' Sue thanked her. 'They're just children. Quentin's not even finished at school. Dr Kimber has great expectations for him, there seems to be no doubt that he'll go on to Oxford. And, when he does, he'll mix with different sorts of people from us. I know he loves helping in the garden, but according to Dr Kimber he's a true academic. Put him in his right environment and he'll blossom.'

Mrs Josh's only answer was a sniff.

* * *

The 1960s was the decade that was to bring a new freedom to the young. Once a qualified Staff Nurse, Sylvia stayed in London. It was the place to be in those next years; it set the trend, those who were part of it felt themselves to be at the hub of the universe. On the ward she worked untiringly, as untiringly as off-duty she fashion-hunted (as far as her meagre salary allowed) at the newly opened boutiques or danced in some smoke-filled cellar-bar; but while those things went on, the guiding light over and above all else was Richard. When they were together she was sure she was as important to him as he was to her. It was only when they were apart that doubts assailed her. Already he was established on the West End stage; at the flick of his fingers surely he could have attracted any woman he chose, so why should he choose her? From her earliest recollections she had had no secrets from Christopher, in fact usually he understood without being told. But now he was stationed in Germany, letters were all they had and words that would have been spoken easily — or not needed speaking at all — couldn't be written. So she threw herself wholeheartedly into her work and lived to the full every opportunity she had of being with Richard. Apart from the occasional brief visit to Gloucestershire to the Grands, the only time she spent out of London was at Highmoor. For all of them this had always been the place to come with their problems, with their excitements, with their hopes and their sadnesses. Richard fell into each of these categories and yet into none; she could talk about her feelings to no one.

★ ★ ★

'It's my life and I shall do what I choose with it.' It was out of character for Quentin to sound so belligerent.

'It worries me that we may have influenced you.' Tim looked with concern at the young man this 'cuckoo in their nest' had become. He remembered the first day he'd brought him home, the child saying 'I like to see things grow. I like to know about them.' Now here he was, intending to throw away his chance to read classics at Oxford and, instead, go to a horticultural college in Scotland.

'Of course you've influenced me,' Quentin smiled unexpectedly. 'And I'm more grateful for it than I can say. To both of you — to everything at Highmoor — ' The smile had gone, overtaken by a look of embarrassment. 'Anyway, I've made up my mind. I know just what I intend. Honestly, I'm going into it with my eyes wide open. Isn't that right, Liz?' Seeming to have run out of steam, he turned to her for support.

'We've talked about it for years,' Liz agreed. 'Since we were just kids.' And what else was she now? She was enchanting to look at, her hair still a 'honey-gold cap', her build still petite, her dark blue eyes a mirror to her thoughts. 'It seems to me, we only get one chance and it's just plain stupid to waste it doing the wrong thing. Dr Kimber says Quen's so clever — well it wouldn't be *clever* to do what he doesn't want to do. It would be *stupid*.'

Quentin took off his spectacles, polished them furiously in his handkerchief and pushed them back on again. Apart from that he seemed unusually sure of himself.

'Liz is right,' he looked from Tim to Sue then back again, even by his standards his expression serious. 'I know exactly what I aim to do. And thanks to my grandparents there is nothing to stop me. I shall sit my A Levels first of course, but that's simply because having studied for them I need to know I've not been wasting my time. But in the autumn I shall go to the horticultural college. It's three-year course.'

'You'll be twenty-one . . . ' Sue was thinking of what he said about his grandparents.

'That's right.' Then his thin face lit with a smile, 'twenty-one and free. I've thought about it for a long time, this isn't just some wild scheme. That's right isn't it, Liz?' as again he looked to her.

'I told them, just now.' She beamed with pride. Pride in him, or in being looked on as part of his scheme and carried along on the same tide of importance? 'He's going to have a first-rate nursery, Mum — Dad. You ought to see the plans he's drawn up. Show them, Quen. Next time you come, bring your drawings.'

Quentin again looked first at Sue then at Tim. 'You'd be very welcome to see them if you care to. It wasn't that I was keeping them from you, it was simply that it's all a long way off yet. I didn't want you to think they were just a kid's pipe-dream.'

So the following weekend he brought his drawings. Clearly what he had in mind was a far cry from the glasshouse or two of someone starting small and meaning to grow. Quentin had done his sums on a much larger scale; acres of glasshouses, acres of trial grounds.

'That boy never ceases to amaze me,' Tim said as they watched the document case holding the plans being strapped on to the back of Quentin's bicycle. 'How long have you known what he has in mind, Liz?'

'Ages. Years.' She was cock-a-hoop at the stir his plans were causing, to say nothing of her own place in them.

'But you never said anything. You must have heard me say how Dr Kimber planned for him to go to Oxford.'

She shrugged her small shoulders.

'Oh, Dr Kimber. He's not interested in Quen, only in getting a feather in Merton Court's cap. Anyway, you never asked what he really wanted.'

He wondered about Liz. Certainly he didn't intend to throw good money after bad; nothing would ever make an academic of her. As soon as she was sixteen she would leave school. And then, what?

'And what about you, Liz? We've never asked you, either. Sylvia did well in her exams, she was able to nurse. Whatever you decide, you must buckle down and pass your O Levels or you'll — '

'Rubbish! I don't see why I'm even taking the silly things. Dad, I want to work for a florist, learn how to make bouquets and wreaths. Like I said about Quen, you have to do what you want.' She glared defiantly at her parents, prepared to do battle and determined to win. 'So that's it. That's what I'm going to be.'

Tim's slow smile held affection and understanding.

'Is this the plan you and Quentin have hatched?' he said, his smile indulgent.

She lowered her gaze; he couldn't read what was going on in her mind.

'Don't know about that,' she mumbled. It was all very well for him to talk to her as if she were still a child, why couldn't he see that she was behind all Quentin's plans? Of course she was, just like she'd always been the one to decide what they did or where they went.

It was late that night; Tim and Sue were lying in bed, already drifting towards sleep, when she

74

said, 'If she plays with Quentin's feelings I'll never forgive her.'

'They're just children.'

'Being children has nothing to do with age. She's been the axle his world turns on. She's always known it and she's always taken it for granted. But does she ever consider that being loved by someone gives you responsibilities? If she hurts him, even though I love her, I couldn't forgive her.'

Silence between them was usually a comfortable thing. After her words had fallen into the still darkness she wished she could recall them. She could feel Tim's disbelief. Naturally enough they'd often been cross with their children, but never had either of them spoken in that calm, cold voice about one of them.

'Sometimes, Sue, I believe you think more of that boy than you do our own.'

'That's not true. Of course I don't. I love them all, ours, the twins and Quentin too. But Tim, he only has us and no matter how much we care about him it can't make up to him for what he's missed.'

'Go to sleep, lady.' If she believed his light kiss meant that she'd brought him round to her way of thinking, she soon found she was wrong. 'He'll probably fall for a Scottish lassie and build his nursery north of the border. And as for Liz, exams or not, the world's her oyster.'

Sometimes he could be surprisingly blind, she thought as she snuggled more comfortably ready for sleep.

Those who were able to get to Highmoor for Christmas always came. And that was the year when the change in Harold became so apparent. For the first time the Grands came by train instead of in the Black Rover that had served them so well.

'This time of year, they're probably wise,' Tim said. 'I wonder how she managed to persuade him. Do you want me to meet the train, or can you?'

'You'll be busy; they don't get into Brindley until quarter to six. They say they'll get a taxi, but I thought I'd be there to surprise them.'

'Good lady. If Paul gives a hand, we'll have done milking by the time you get them home.'

Highmoor was decked for the festival. Only days before, Paul had returned home, finally finished at the agricultural college. After his years of training he was proud to display his knowledge, and secretly, looking for a chance to make his mark. Quentin was there too for the duration of his last Christmas holiday from Merton Court. The smell of the ceiling-high Christmas tree filled the house, a house decked with holly, mistletoe and evergreen. The fires burnt a little higher into the chimney, cards festooned every available flat space. The spirit was infectious. When Sue set off to meet the train Liz and Quentin had covered the kitchen table with newspaper and were endeavouring to make a holly wreath for the front door.

The train arrived on time and immediately one or two doors burst open; passengers who'd been shopping in Oxford scrambled out into the brightly lit platform. Where were they? Had they missed the train? The guard was already slamming doors, the green flag in his hand. Then she saw Lucinda leaning out of an open window frantically trying to open a door.

'Wait,' Sue shouted to the guard. 'Someone is still getting off.'

'Better buck up about it then. Ain't got all day you know.' There was no attempt to keep his voice down; Lucinda couldn't fail to have heard him. Ignoring him, Sue opened the door and helped her to the platform. At a glance she could see that all wasn't well. Since the twins had grown up, the old summer holiday plans had given way to their making the occasional brief trip to their grandparents, so it was a year since Harold and Lucinda had visited Highmoor.

'The cases are too heavy for you, dear. Oh dear, isn't there a porter?' Lucinda was clearly agitated, feeling helpless and inadequate. 'That dreadful man is going to let the train start before I can get Harold off — and the cases too.'

Get Harold off! That should have warned Sue.

'Don't worry.' She sounded more confident than she felt as she helped Harold down the steep step then jumped on to the train to collect their bags.

It seemed the guard was determined to make things difficult.

'Decided to get off at last, then?' he glowered, his hand on the door ready to slam it closed.

'No, no, please . . . she's getting our things.' For Lucinda it was the last straw after a difficult journey; her mouth trembled out of control.

'Don't worry, Aunt Luce, he's only trying to be a bully.' Then to the uniformed man, not attempting to disguise her anger in a cloak of politeness, 'If there's no porter, it would speed things up if you took the bags instead of standing watching.' He was no match for her. Silently and unsmilingly he did as he was told.

Finally the train was waved on its way and there was time for greetings, but not before Sue had realised that throughout the entire incident Harold had been humming 'The Blue Danube' and tapping his foot in waltz time.

'Have you said hello to Sue? Come on, Harold, think where you are.'

'Umph? Ah, Sue! And what are you doing here? Sue! Bless my soul. Lovely surprise, my dear.'

Lucinda looked on helplessly then, seeming to square her frail shoulders, took hold of his arm and steered him towards the exit while Sue tried to look as though two heavy bags weighed nothing. By that time the guard had seen fit to disappear.

'Are you coming in the front with me, Uncle Harold?'

'Yes, yes. And very nice. Yes, fancy you coming all that way to see us. Good of you.'

With the bags safely in the boot, she opened

both doors. 'In the front then,' she told him.

'That's the way,' he said good-humouredly and immediately got into the back.

'I'd better get in the back too.' Lucinda didn't need to elaborate, but Sue noticed how, once he was comfortably seated, she leant in front of him to make sure his door was locked.

'We'll soon get home. Now that you've arrived we shall begin to think it's really Christmas.' Silly chatter, but she felt she had to fill the silence. 'It's a year since you were here. You ought to come in the summer, you know. Even though the twins aren't home, there's still Tim and me. And Liz.'

'And that young Quentin at every opportunity,' Lucinda made an effort too, while Harold was lost in dancing his Viennese waltz.

'Ta, ta, ta, ta, pom, pom, pom, pom,' he sang.

It was much later, when the warmth of the blazing fires and, even more, the warmth of the love Lucinda was always so aware of at Highmoor, had lifted some of her burden of care. The meal over, she followed Sue to the scullery to wash the dishes.

'How long has he been like this?' Sue went straight to the heart of the trouble. 'Why didn't you tell us?'

'I shouldn't have come. It wasn't fair of me to inflict us on you.' Lucinda kept her face turned away. 'I knew I wasn't being fair — '

Forgetting her wet hands, Sue left the deep porcelain sink and put her arms around Lucinda's stooping shoulders.

'You should have come ages ago. What

happened, Aunt Luce? He was always so bright, so — so vital.'

'Last winter I saw the first signs. He couldn't remember things for two minutes at a time. Kept telling me the same thing, asking the same question. Poor darling. He couldn't help it. He can't help it now. I do try to be patient. But, Sue, sometimes I feel frightened, I can't bear to look into the future.'

Tim came to join them, taking a towel as if it were the normal thing for him to do — which it certainly wasn't.

'He's having a nap by the drawing-room fire. Quentin and Liz are in there. Do you think the journey has confused him, he's not used to trains?'

Lucinda shook her head. 'It's happened gradually,' she said, near to tears. 'But today's no different from yesterday, or tomorrow.'

'You've written to us, yet you've never even hinted . . . '

'Oh, Tim my dear, how could I? How could I sit down and write about him as if he were — well, just anybody. Could you, if it were your Sue?'

Forgetting he was making a pretence of having come to help, Tim put his arm around his adopted aunt.

'No, I couldn't. But we're one family, you two are the Grands to all of us. Troubles should be shared, whatever they are.'

Lucinda gave up the battle and let the burning tears escape.

'So frightened. Not of Harold, never of

Harold, but of what's ahead of us. A year ago he was himself. You remember him wearing the Father Christmas costume just like he always had when it was time for the tree? But every day he grows further away, says things that make no sense to me. Or is it me who's getting silly? Is that it?'

'Perhaps when he sees the costume he'll remember,' Sue tried to sound hopeful.

'It's nearly Christmas,' Lucinda rubbed her face inelegantly with her handkerchief, 'I know it was selfish of me to inflict us on you, but I thought if I could just try and forget for a few days — '

A quick glance between Sue and Tim, then it was he who voiced what both of them were thinking.

'Why just a few days? What is there to rush away for? Stay at least through the winter, see how you feel then. You'll find it easier here, there's always one or other of us about.'

'Please, Aunt Luce. If Elspeth and John were living you'd have told them, you'd not mind having them help you. I think they must be glad to know you're here with us. They'd want us to be together.'

A few minutes later, Lucinda's tears dried and her eyes brighter than they had been for many a month, they went into the drawing room to tell the others.

So Highmoor gathered in its flock. Even after all these years, Quentin marvelled at the never failing generosity of spirit there; it never faltered, never changed. He looked at Sue and Tim, his 'adopted aunt and uncle', and was so aware of the affection he felt for them that it was a physical ache in his chest. Before the next year was over he would be going away to Scotland. Suppose things changed here, suppose when Liz left school and went to be apprenticed at the florist's she grew tired of all they'd planned? He took off his spectacles and polished them so hard that Sue looked at him with a puzzled frown.

★　★　★

Harold accepted his new surroundings without question. As Tim had said, there was always one or other of them about and so the burden of keeping a constant eye on him was eased.

'If you're going outside, let me see you're well wrapped up,' Lucinda would button his overcoat, knot his scarf around his neck and make sure he wore his cap. Then he'd be off to talk to Josh, or even to take a spade and believe he was helping.

Tim had suggested the Grands should stay at least until after the cold weather. But as the days began to lengthen and morning frosts became less frequent, they took very little persuading to stay on. Each week Harold failed more noticeably. Such a short time ago Lucinda had never been called on to so much as write a cheque; now all the responsibilities fell to her. A kindly neighbour re-addressed their post, but it was clear that dealing with accounts — especially income tax — worried her. Thankfully she let Tim guide her. Perhaps it was the fear of being without him and without Sue's constant care that made her so frightened of going home. Just before Easter their house was put on the market.

★ ★ ★

That winter, with Paul home, Tim found himself with a new freedom. The boy had become a man, his years at college had taught him things unknown (and unneeded!) by his father. Between the two of them the companionship had always been strong.

For years Tim had been a member of the local hunt but, on his own, he had seldom found the time to ride out with them. Once Paul was home, all that changed.

'It's just a matter of organising,' said Paul with sure confidence. 'We'll soon get through the early milking if I give you a hand, Dad. After that, well, winter time the farm isn't going to grind to a halt if we play hooky for a few hours each Thursday. Mum's home, Josh is always around, and Fred isn't stupid.'

'A good thing my ladies can't tell the time,' Tim laughed as he fixed the electric machine to the udders of a doleful-looking Guernsey cow on the first Thursday of the new year. 'There you are, old lady,' he patted her rump with affectionate familiarity as he watched the efficient way Paul worked. 'Your mother's getting the breakfast, so as soon as we get this lot done it'll be waiting.'

'You ought to have done this before, Dad, half an hour can't throw them off balance. Mum and Dawson are quite capable of using the cooler and separator. And getting the urns to the gate.'

'Having two of us working makes a great difference, son. You've no idea how glad I am to have you back from that college.'

Paul smiled in satisfaction. How far away those days seemed when he'd been just a kid, doing as he was told. Now they were equals . . . although a silent voice boasted that he was more than his father's equal. Now that he was there, there would be no need for the old man to be tied; he and Mum could go away for a proper holiday knowing that everything would be taken care of. More than taken care of. Already there were one or two things he had in mind to alter. For instance, think of that barn where Mum planned to grow mushrooms. What a daft idea! How much could she hope to make out of the few she'd produce in a place that size? Pin money, that's all it would be. Like the butter and cream she took into Mr Hartley's shop in Brindley. Everything here was small. It was crazy. You had to have ambition, you had to think big. The trouble with Mum and Dad was that that was something they'd never done. They'd been content with the sort of hand-to-mouth exist- ence they'd scratched out of the small acreage they'd got here. Scraping along, having a job to meet the bills half the time. Well, Paul thought, that's not for me. What we ought to do is put out feelers to old Bert Hamilton down the lane. It's time he packed it in, farming isn't for old blokes like that. Add Silverdale's acreage to Highmoor's and you'd have something worth considering. Mr Hamilton could let us have the land

— agricultural land doesn't fetch a fortune — anyway, the bank would back us once they know the things I've got planned. He could sell the house separately, probably get a good price for it. Talk to him the right way, I reckon we could persuade him. Got to persuade Dad first, of course. But I didn't spend two years at college just to mess about here as if I'm another Fred Dawson. Double our acreage and we could have a bigger herd, much bigger. We'd put the lot down to pasture, build a modern dairy, employ people. You never get anywhere with a small mixed farm — all work and precious little profit. Once I get involved with the accounts side — and I will, of course — then I'll be able to make Dad see things my way.

'Nearly done, Dad? That's it then. Let's go and eat, then we'll load up.'

Tim's answering grin held all the anticipation of an excited boy. Wasn't this as he'd always dreamed it would be, with Paul and him working together, riding to the hounds together?

As soon as they'd bolted their large and sustaining fried breakfast, all of them completely ignorant of words like calories or cholesterol, father and son were ready. Sue went to the stable with them, looking on them with pride. How like his father Paul had grown: the same height, the same straight back and broad shoulders, the same rather coarse wavy hair that would with time bleach just as Tim's had. They walked their mounts into the horse box that was already connected up with the Land Rover, Tim's chestnut Titan, and Paul's five-year-old mare

Rosie, recently acquired for him to mark his completion of the college course and start of his work on the farm.

She and Tim exchanged a look of satisfaction as he switched on the engine and she waved them on their way to North Hinton Manor where that week's hunt was to meet. Her feelings were much in line with Tim's; how well everything had turned out. Paul home, a farmer to his fingertips. Had they been able to know Paul's thoughts and ambitions they would have been less happy. So too would he, had he been able to look ahead from the first week of the year to the last, half-way through the next hunting season, and see that despite all his efforts nothing had changed. No, that wasn't quite true, for by the end of the year Sue's mushrooms were cropping and each day she took one large punnet, sometimes two, into Dylan's Greengrocery in Brindley. Pin money perhaps, but it gave her enormous satisfaction.

★   ★   ★

Through that year Sylvia came once or twice, her visits usually no more than a night between duty periods. It was in August that she phoned with the news that she wanted to spend the weekend at Highmoor.

'I have some time off,' she told Sue on the phone.

'Lovely. When will you get here?' Perhaps this time 'time off' meant proper leave. 'Just wait till I tell the Grands.'

'Oh, not till late. He's just the same, is he?'

'I'm so glad they're here, Sylvia. But, yes, just the same.'

'Aunt Sue, will it be all right if I bring someone with me? Well, I'm sure it will be, you know him already. It's Richard. That's why we can't get there until so late, he doesn't even get off stage until nearly ten. And we have to be back in town by teatime Monday.'

'Of course Richard's welcome. He wants to wish Quentin well before he goes off to Scotland, I expect.'

'Scotland? I'd forgotten, our little Quentin must have left school by now of course.'

'Our little Quentin, as you call him, is no longer so little. And he left school with flying colours, better than any of you — including Richard,' Sue told her tartly.

'Sorry, Aunt Sue. He was always a clever clogs and I'm glad I shall see him to wish him luck. But about Richard. I see a lot of him, Aunt Sue. I have done for ages.' She sounded so matter-of-fact and calm; but, then, that's the way she'd always been. That she'd made an idol of Richard McBride hadn't been taken seriously, after all she was one of thousands. That's how his life would always be. But to bring him home . . . not as Quentin's brother but as . . . as what?

'You all go to bed,' Sylvia was saying. 'I have my key and I can make us something to eat when we get there if we're really starved. I expect Richard will have Christo's room, won't he? I do wish Chris could be home. We've always told each other everything and letters aren't the same.'

There was no logic in Sue's strange feeling of unease, she knew there wasn't. If only Sylvia had been bringing some nice young doctor home to meet the family . . . but an actor, especially a McBride . . . During the years since their first visit, there had been one or two occasions when the Marshalls had met Quentin's parents again. There had been the day the famous couple had been asked to open the summer bazaar at Merton Court — a fund-raising affair when the school was keen to build squash courts. Then, on another occasion, Sue and Tim had driven to London to their luxurious apartment to collect thirteen-year-old Quentin after he'd spent a week with them. One look at him had told Sue that the week had been utterly miserable for him, and she'd not been prepared even to consider that it probably had been as difficult for his family.

If Sylvia had to fall in love, why did it have to be with Richard McBride? Sue looked forward to their brief visit with less than her usual hospitality. She wished Sylvia was coming on her own or, better still, that Christopher could have been the second, as it used to be. She even encouraged the thought that it was because he was so far away that his twin clung to her hero-worship of a matinée idol.

Yet when the weekend came it was impossible to dislike the handsome young god. Had Richard spoken disparagingly to Quentin, then it would have been a relief to have something to hold against him. Instead he showed interest in the horticultural college, even led Quentin on to talk about his plans for the future. And there appeared to be no resentment that their grandparents had left everything to the boy his mother so openly called 'the runt'. As for the Grands, they were enchanted with him.

But Sue hardened her heart and reminded herself that he was a play-actor, giving his all to a performance which brought such obvious admiration.

'You do like him, don't you, Aunt Sue?' Sylvia was helping Sue to clear away the Sunday dinner, for at Highmoor the main meal on Sunday was always at one o'clock. 'I know you are always protective of Quentin, but it's not fair if that turns you against Richard because he's Quen's brother.'

'I don't think of them as brothers. Quentin isn't like the rest of them.'

'There! Even the way you said that! The rest of them! As if they — as if they — had the plague or something. Quentin doesn't like them because he was always frightened of them. He's grown up now, I can see that, but he was such a funny, frightened kid when he first came here.'

'And if he was, whose fault was that?' Sue hated feeling angry, but she was angry now.

'Probably circumstances. And that fact that his grandparents were so overkeen on him. You know why that was? The old lady always had poor sight and as she got older she was blind. Anthony — I call him and Elvira by their Christian names, they prefer it — had no problems, neither did Richard. Then along came Quentin, nothing like any of them and, apparently with his grandmother's eye problems. Always moping around with headaches, blind as a bat without glasses even as a toddler — '

'Sylvie, I can't believe you're saying these things.'

'I just want you to understand. I know he couldn't help being different, but it wasn't all their doing that they were so distant from him. Elvira's parents had no time for stage people. She was an only child. They wanted her to live on the estate in Ireland, they fought against her being an actress and her marriage to Anthony was a disappointment to them. Can you imagine having Anthony McBride as your son-in-law and yet seeing him as a disappointment? The trouble was there was a complete breakdown of understanding. Anthony has talked about it sometimes. Anyway, reading between the lines, I think it was to spite him and Elvira that they left everything to Quentin. If Richard had shunned the stage, then he might have come in for some of it. But we are what we are.'

'Is he resentful — about Quentin's legacy?'

'Heavens, no. Already Richard must make more than Quentin's ever likely to with his seedbeds.'

'As you say, Sylvie love, we are as we are. It's not Richard I'm interested in, it's you. Don't let him hurt you. Perhaps I'm old-fashioned and out of touch with things, but — oh, I suppose I just don't know anything about stage people. Except that I don't like the McBrides and I don't care who knows it.' Then, purposely drawing a line under the subject, 'I wish you didn't have to go back so soon. When will you get your proper leave?'

'This is it. I have a fortnight. You've probably read in the theatre notices in the paper, Richard's play comes off at the end of the month — that's Tuesday. It's opening on Broadway for the winter season, but after Tuesday he'll be free for a while. He and I are going to France. Aunt Sue, what you said about me getting hurt. I shan't, I'm sure I shan't. But even if in the end that's what happens, I wouldn't do anything any different. Can you understand?'

Sue turned from the sink and hugged her. Oh yes, she could understand. She wished she could banish her feeling of foreboding. Was there anything harder to bear than being unable to protect someone you loved?

★   ★   ★

And then came the day in September when Quentin was to set out. Liz had started a new term two days before, so by eight o'clock in the morning she had to leave to catch her train.

'I'll walk with you to the station,' Quentin told her.

Had they been older they would have been better able to hide their emotions. Yet watching them while she tried to look as though she were more interested in the morning paper, Sue felt a twinge of suspicion. That look on Liz's face as though she were a tragedy queen, wasn't that a

91

sign that she was enjoying the drama of the moment, thriving on the emotion?

'Yes,' Liz nodded. 'Come with me, Quen. One last time.'

'Oh for heaven's sake, Liz,' Sue snapped, 'he's not leaving the planet. Instead of being at school he'll be at college. It'll be Christmas before you know it.'

'*You* wouldn't understand,' Liz wrung her hands — and were those crocodile tears that brimmed in her eyes? Sue was angry with herself that she couldn't trust the girl, who so often annoyed her. 'You've always got Dad. But what about me? When Quen's gone — what about me?'

Quentin pulled off his glasses, his eyes closed. Then, hardly aware of what he did, he gave them an unnecessary polish and put them on again.

'Come on, Liz,' he mumbled. 'If we hang around you'll have to hurry.'

'Not fair me having to go to school today. I ought to be here. Your last day.'

He ushered her out of the door.

'What she needs is her bottom smacked,' Sue said as she stacked the tray to carry to the scullery.

'The young see everything larger than life, dear,' Lucinda told her placidly. 'Perhaps that's one of the advantages of getting old.'

'Well, she's got no business to make things hard for him. At least I'm glad we'll be relieved of her scenes at the station. His train goes just after four, so we're picking her up at school when she comes out at half past. You'll be all right, you and Uncle Harold. Mrs Josh will be coming in to see to preparing a meal for this evening.'

'You ought not to let her. Here I am, doing nothing. She'll think I'm a silly old woman if I can't peel a few potatoes and make a shepherd's pie.' Lucinda made sure her voice was full of confidence, but it was a long time since she'd catered for more than just herself and Harold. And how much a boy like young Paul could eat after a day in the fresh air she was frightened to think.

'She'll think no such thing,' Sue laughed. 'Anyway, I expect you'll see to things together. She really enjoys coming over here and helping, bless her. It's the company, you know. Josh may not do heavy work on the farm, but he's always out there somewhere.'

If it was company Mrs Josh wanted, then Lucinda was more than glad to supply it. And Harold could come out and sit at the kitchen table and feel part of it.

★   ★   ★

There were nearly ten minutes to wait before Quentin's train was due. All the usual things were being said: 'You've put your ticket where you can get at it easily?' 'Promise you'll eat a good meal in London, you'll have plenty of time before you can board the sleeper,' 'If you get a chance, try and ring us in the morning to let us know you're there safely.' Yes, his ticket was in his jacket pocket, yes, he'd eat a big meal (despite

93

still being skinny, Quentin was usually hungry), and yes, he'd phone at the first possible moment.

'Tell Liz I'll write tomorrow. It may take a day or two, I shall be miles from a town, but tell her I'll definitely write. And tell her — '

They all turned at the sound of someone rushing along the platform towards them.

'What in the world are *you* doing here? You shouldn't be out of school for more than half an hour.' Tim suspected her appearance spelt trouble.

'How could you expect me to stay there? I didn't have any money for the bus fare, I ran all the way. Quen, I was so frightened you'd be gone.' Her huge blue eyes were full of anguish as she looked at poor, helpless Quentin. In her school uniform, with her black velour hat, black stockings and gymslip, small for her fifteen years, she looked such a child. But did he see her as a child? Had she the emotion of a child? Sue looked at Tim helplessly. Not for the first time she was out of her depth with Liz, who seemed to see herself as the lead performer in a drama of departure.

'Here's the train,' Quentin pushed his fingers through his always neat hair. 'Don't be sad, Liz. I've got to go, you know I have. It's what we always planned.'

If he expected that to cheer her, he was mistaken.

'I know. I know,' she cried in a voice of tragedy. She clasped her small hands behind her back as if she had to use all her control to keep them in check as he kissed Sue, then

94

shook hands with Tim.

Then he turned to her, just as the train shuddered to a halt and the carriage doors were flung open.

'Liz . . . ?' He seemed hesitant about this public farewell. Emotion frightened Quentin, it always had.

But not Liz. With a flourish she unclasped her hands and threw herself at him, her arms around his neck.

'I ought to be coming to. We could learn together.'

'We have to do what we planned,' he told her gently. 'You'll soon be here to meet me coming back for Christmas.'

'How can you say that! It might seem soon to you, but to me it'll be an eternity. I don't want you to go.' She clung to his jacket. Around them people were watching. Sue felt sure she was aware of the interest she was causing and played up to her audience.

'On you get, son,' Tim said, putting his hands on Liz's shoulders and hauling her firmly off him. 'And don't worry about this one.'

Gently Quentin kissed Liz's forehead, then climbed up the step into the train. Leaning out of the compartment window he looked at the three of them, Liz's face a mask of tragedy. But was it genuine, Sue asked herself, or was she thriving on every second? The whistle was blown, with a jolt the train moved, and even though Liz ran by his side as far as she could the distance between them lengthened.

'Now then, young lady,' Tim turned to his

daughter. 'How did you manage to get here more than half an hour before the end of afternoon school?'

'I just came,' she mumbled, the drama over and nothing ahead but misery.

'Then our first job is to drive you back to school to explain and apologise.'

Sitting in the back of the car, the tragedy queen had given way to a not-as-grown-up girl as she'd liked to believe herself. Sue heard the quiet sniffing and knew that this time it wasn't play-acting. Whether it was brought about by Quentin or the trouble she'd have to face at school was uncertain.

'You both stay in the car,' she said when Tim drew up outside the main entrance of the school. 'I'll go and explain.' After all it wasn't really a lie to say that Liz had acted on impulse, she'd been so upset that their son — adopted son — was going off to college. It was very thoughtless of her to go missing without consent, but they'd kept her in the car because she would so hate her classmates to see her tearful state. It was surprising how a few words from a caring mother could wipe out all trace of sin.

By the time they left the school, Quentin's train had gone through Maidenhead and Slough and was rushing on towards London. The start of his venture. He looked forward to all he wanted to learn; he strained towards the challenge he'd set himself. But Liz? How much did Liz really care about what they'd promised each other? Today's scene had upset him more than he'd ever let her guess. He knew her so well, he understood her, forgave her faults and loved her as he loved life itself. He wished she'd not made those scenes today. To Quentin drama held no substance. He'd almost felt that she was enjoying her display of grief. Then he was swamped by guilt that he could think such things of his precious Liz.

Leaning against the back of the long seat, he took off his spectacles and went through the habitual ritual. When they'd left Highmoor he had felt quite composed. If only now his head would stop hurting. Suppose it got worse like it usually did. Please, make it stop hurting . . . he closed his eyes.

4

It wasn't the first time Paul had hinted that they ought to acquire more land. As far as Tim was concerned, the suggestion didn't even merit consideration — even supposing he'd had the money. He meant Highmoor to remain as it was. But for more than a year Paul had been home working with him; he deserved this latest suggestion at least to be discussed.

'If the time comes where Bert Hamilton puts Silverdale on the market, then we might consider making an offer for the fields adjacent to our own. But no more than that. Apart from anything else, we'd be hard pushed to manage more acreage than we have already without taking on another man. As we are, we can manage with just ourselves and Fred. We're a good team.' His smile told Paul just how good a team he thought them. 'But the move must come from Bert Hamilton, I'll not try to persuade him as long as he feels he can still cope.'

Paul frowned. 'Who's to say he wouldn't be glad to be given an excuse for packing it in? He's too old for the job, Dad. Don't forget, he has no son to take responsibility off his shoulders. Farming needs someone fit, strong. And, today more than ever, a good farmer has to be forward-looking.' Something he'd heard many times at college. 'I saw him at market the other day,' then, with an infectious laugh that almost disguised the axe he was attempting to grind, 'that's to say I *almost* saw him through the cloud of smoke from that same filthy old pipe he's sucked as long as I can remember. I don't think he was there to sell — and certainly not to buy. For him Wednesday market is just a day out. There he was, surrounded by a lot of old cronies. It may sound hard, but to be honest all that any of them were doing was getting in the way of people who were there to do business. It was a good thing when they pushed off across the road to the pub. Anyway Dad, it's not the bit of land adjoining ours that interests me, not without the rest to go with it. We need more pastureland, much more. If we put every acre of Highmoor down to grass it still wouldn't be enough for what I have in mind.' How young and enthusiastic he sounded. If there were pitfalls in the road he envisaged, he ignored them. 'And we need better buildings, more cattle sheds and a proper dairy, somewhere well equipped where we could employ staff — women would do — full time. Highmoor Dairy could make a name for itself, Dad. Can't you just see it? Not just the odd carton of cream and lump of butter Mum messes about making.'

More than anything it was that that drove the final nail into the coffin of Paul's plans.

'When your mother and I aren't here, then it'll be up to you to do as you like. But I'm afraid, son, that won't be yet — please, God. And while we're here, we do things *our* way.' An echo from a while back came back to him; he seemed to hear Sue's voice, see the way she turned to him, angry on his account that the burden of fees wasn't to be lifted after all. Just plain stupid, she'd called the idea of Paul wanting to go on to college, selfish and stupid. But, of course, that hadn't been true. The boy was probably more capable of running Highmoor than he was himself. But capable or not, Tim's mind was firmly made up. Highmoor had managed (managed? more than managed . . . again he thought of Sue's championship, her loyalty, her never-failing support) all these years, and so it would continue. ' . . . when we're too tottery . . . ' came another echo. Well, that wouldn't be yet, damn it, it wouldn't be for years. The idea of wanting to get rid of Sue's dairy!

On the surface nothing changed between them. Indeed, to Tim's way of thinking the incident was closed, it had left no scar. Paul was always good-humoured, he worked with never flagging energy — and even though there were times when he saw Tim's methods as being old-fashioned, he learnt to say nothing. But the seed of discontent had been sown and it was making strong roots. How could they have expected him to come home from college and be content to be little more than a glorified labourer?

He knew in his heart that he wasn't being fair. Tim had no secrets from him. In the past no one disturbed 'the Guv'nor' when he was in his office. But that rule didn't apply to Paul. Everything was open to him: the milk records, the ledgers, the bills and receipts, nothing was kept from him. Yet, seeing the way the farm was run only added to his irritation. 'Sometimes I wonder the old man doesn't resort to using a quill pen!' he grumbled silently as he sat at the wooden table that served as a desk. What a way to file invoices, speared on a metal prong as if we were still living back in the 1930s. But then, wasn't it in keeping with all the rest? The so-called office was no more than a wooden hut built on to the end of the Dutch barn. Since Tim had had electricity installed in the farm buildings there was at least a light, its unshaded bulb throwing a crude brightness at the touch of a switch on to what Paul considered 'the miserable mess'.

The months slipped by. It was in the early summer, during haymaking, that a small paragraph on an inside page of the daily paper caught Lucinda's eye.

'Oh dear,' she whispered. 'Sue, see what it says here. Sylvia seemed so happy with him . . . Oh dear.'

Sue frowned, that premonition of trouble immediately alive again.

'Read it out to us, Aunt Luce' (us? Harold was sitting across the kitchen table where she was kneading dough, drumming his fingers in time with today's tune), 'is it about Richard?'

Lucinda adjusted her rimless glasses and took up the paper. 'It's headed 'Richard McBride Weds',' she read. 'It was a quiet wedding yesterday for Broadway's handsome idol when he married lovely Drucilla Mountjoy. The only people present at the registry office ceremony were Anthony McBride and Elvira Dereford, parents of the groom. The happy couple first met in Hollywood a few months ago, where it is prophesied that Miss Mountjoy has an exciting future after making her debut in *The Dancing Girls*.''

Hadn't Sue always felt a sense of foreboding? She heard the echo of Sylvia's words 'Even if in the end I get hurt, I wouldn't do anything any different.' How certain she'd sounded. While *he*, as shallow and selfish as his parents, how much had *he* cared as he took everything she offered, then left her, no doubt without another thought as the glamour of Hollywood and all the fuss they would make of him beckoned. Kneading her dough with more force than necessary Sue seethed with anger she wouldn't let Lucinda suspect. Loyalty to Sylvia helped her to speak casually.

'Who's Drucilla Mountjoy? I've never heard of her, have you?' she enquired lightly. 'Now I come to think of it, Sylvia never mentions Richard these days. Perhaps they weren't as close as we thought, Aunt Luce. Anyway, she has promised to come for a whole week at the end of the month. If we've been imagining romance where there wasn't one, then I dare say she knows all about this Drucilla person.'

'Not very likely,' was Lucinda's opinion. 'If Richard McBride has been casting his net in other ponds, he's not likely to make Sylvia his confidante.'

'His parents' play is still on in London; they must have flown to New York especially for the wedding. She might have heard something from them.'

From the way Lucinda pushed the paper to one side and muttered something about wishing Christopher were nearer, it was clear she didn't take Sue's suggestions seriously.

A week or two later Sylvia spent a week with them, seeming to want to immerse herself in the daily happenings around the farm. She and Paul had always got on well; but if she confided in him, he said nothing. It was on the day before she returned to London, a warm morning at the end of June, that she came to help Sue fill her mushroom basket ready to take to Dylan's.

'You know he's married?' It was Sylvia who broke the silence. There was no need to mention Richard by name, he'd been at the forefront of both their minds. Each day Sue had hoped she'd say something, once or twice she'd been on the verge of broaching the subject but something had prevented her. Wouldn't it be kinder to Sylvia's pride to pretend she hadn't read too much into their relationship?

'Richard? Yes, it was in the paper. Did you know beforehand? I mean, you're friendly with his parents?'

'Am I? I was, or I thought I was. They have busy lives — and so have I. If you think I'm going to pine away with a broken heart, then think again, Aunt Sue.' It worried Sue to hear the unnatural hardness in her voice.

'Well done, love. Quentin didn't know about it until he read it afterwards either. You know what

103

I think? I think you're better off without the lot of them.'

'You always thought that. But no.' Sylvia had been bending over the mushroom bed, but now she stood up straight as if to bring home the truth of what she wanted to say. Despite the humid warmth in the dimly lit shed, a cold shiver ran down Sue's spine as she looked at her. 'No. I'll never be better without him. I don't regret one single moment.'

'They live in Tinsel Land, they get dazzled by ambition for fame.' At that moment — and certainly not for the first time — with the exception of Quentin, Sue hated the whole of the McBride clan and all they stood for.

⋆　⋆　⋆

So the summer went on. By harvest time Liz's school blouses had become polishing cloths and her gymslip been turned into a mini-skirt. She still caught the train to Reading just after eight o'clock each morning, but now she hurried to the station with a new eagerness. Her plans were coming to fruition, as she became adept at making bouquets, wreaths and floral arrangements. Each time she took a deep breath, the heady perfume of her workroom carried her forward to the time when . . . There were other women in the workroom, a ready audience when she told them about the nursery that she and Quentin were going to build. How much better this was than wasting her time at school!

Scholastic success had done little for Quentin's confidence; any progress in that direction had come from Highmoor. By the time he returned from Scotland for his second Christmas there was a marked change in him. Physically he would never have the tall, almost military, bearing of Paul; and he would certainly never have the perfect physique of his own father and brother. But gone was the nervous, skinny youth and, in his place, was a young man of certainty. He was almost half-way through his three-year course and, just as he always had, he absorbed knowledge like a sponge absorbs water. But this time was different. Had he been a natural sportsman his years at Merton Court might not have led to the same academic success. Because he'd been useless on the sports field and ashamed of his failure, his way to prove himself had been in book work. Now every new thing he learnt gave him personal satisfaction. Partly, of course, it was because he was laying the road to the future he'd planned so carefully; but even without the golden legacy from his grandparents, his love of what he did would have been the same. With each month his enthusiasm grew stronger, more alive. His twentieth birthday came and went. By that second Christmas holiday he had only months to wait before the inheritance that had been held in trust all these years became his own.

There were no longer any children at Highmoor, but old habits still lived on. Liz didn't start decorating until Quentin arrived; it had always been their job. Tim and Paul brought in the ceiling-high tree and set it up in the usual corner of the drawing room; just as he did each year Tim sawed extra large logs — the Yule logs had a place of importance almost as great as the Christmas puddings, which had been made in October. At Highmoor nothing changed, or so Sue and Tim believed.

The kitchen had always been the heart of the house. Meals were only carried to the dining room when Sue had to put her best foot forward for 'visitors' rather than 'friends'. Those occasions were rare and it was the scrubbed wooden kitchen table, covered for meals by a checked, starched cloth, that had seen all their joys and sadnesses through the years. It was around that table the children had done their nightly homework when they had still been at the 'baby school' in Brindley; then, their work packed away in their satchels, had drunk their nightly cocoa. More recently and with less enthusiasm, Liz had sat there to battle with algebra or Latin while her mind wandered with a will of its own. It was here that Mrs Josh had taught Sue to knead dough and make light pastry. It was here, with an oilcloth spread, the children had painted their first pictures and moulded their plasticine. Birthday parties, christening parties, every occasion that had been a milestone in their lives had been marked around that table. Sometimes there were only Tim, Sue, Paul and the Grands at midday, so they sat Tim at one end, Sue the other, Paul at one side and the Grands side by side at the other. Then in the evening Liz had her allotted place between Paul and her father. When

Quentin was home he sat between Sue and Lucinda. And, that Christmas with everyone except Christopher there, no one had to say to Sylvia, 'You can take that chair.' She knew where to sit, it was *her* space, as comfortingly familiar as the loud tick of the clock on the wall and the sight of the willow-pattern china. Even on Christmas Day no one had to ask where to put the two extra chairs at the table. Josh and Mrs Josh would sit, as they did every year, one either side of Sue.

Tim and Paul had pushed the early milking forward just as they did on hunting mornings. By twenty to eight, with Sue and Sylvia, they were walking across the footpath to St Michael's, drawn on by the peal of bells. Sue slipped her hand into Tim's. Why was it on Christmas morning that the message of the bells always made her want to cry? Not tears of unhappiness, but something she couldn't name. It had to do with having those she loved around her. A bit like taking the inventory and knowing everything is as it should be, she told herself.

'All right, lady?' Tim whispered. Had he read her thoughts? She nodded. Oh, yes, all was right, so right that sometimes she was frightened.

The only thing she didn't like about going to the early service was that there was no music. She wanted to sing 'Oh Come All Ye Faithful' at the top of her voice and have the sound absorbed into the volume all around her. And that's how it must have been for the second contingent, Liz, Quentin and the Grands; for when they came back just in time to get the table ready, Harold was pom-pomming the tune with fervour. Every now and again he'd stop; they'd think — or hope — it had faded from his mind, but a few minutes later he'd start up again.

'That's enough, now, dear,' Lucinda told him as the dishes were brought to the table. 'Time for you to sit to table.' Unerringly he went to the right chair.

'Ah!' he sniffed appreciatively as the huge turkey was put in front of Tim. 'Christmas is it, eh? What?' Then he was off, but this time even the words had come back to him.

' . . . joyful and triumphant,' Liz joined in. Then Paul, then Tim, until before the first verse was over they were all singing at the top of their voices, in tune or out it made no difference. If those choirs of angels could hear them, they must have been gladdened. And surely they wouldn't have been offended that as he sang, so Tim carved and passed the plates. 'Yea Lord we greet Thee, Born this happy morning . . . '

Sue looked at those gathered around the table, her gaze finally resting on Tim, her vision blurred by tears. Still singing, he half-closed one eye in that secret message of understanding.

★ ★ ★

Perched on the edge of her parents' bed, Liz looked enviously at her mother. It was the night of the annual Hunt Ball. Sue had bought a new full-length dress of midnight blue and had borrowed Lucinda's pearls and fur cape.

'Do I look all right?' she turned round for Liz

108

to inspect her and give a verdict.

'I wish I was coming. Yes, you look quite nice. Well, very nice, I suppose really.' To a seventeen-year-old who had been nowhere and done nothing, it seemed unjust that people of her parents' age should be all decked up and going dancing while she stayed at home with the Grands. Not that she didn't love the Grands — although *he* could be trying, but she was getting tired of waiting on the sidelines while life went by.

'Still beautifying?' Tim's voice came up the stairs. 'I'm pouring us a drink before we go.'

'Lovely,' Sue called back to him. 'For all of us, the Grands and Liz too.'

There was an air of party about the old house, as they sipped their drinks and Sue lapped up their admiration.

'Crumbs, is this my Mum? Doesn't she look stunning?' from Paul.

'Very pretty, my dear,' Harold told her. 'Ta-ta-ta-ta, tom-tom, tom-tom,' he sang, holding out his arms as if to lead her on to the dance floor. Obligingly, she circled the drawing room with him, then guided him to his chair by the fireside.

Soon they were gone, the sound of the car growing faint as they turned into the lane. Liz imagined the scene that awaited them, the bright lights, the music, the ladies in long dresses, the men in dinner suits. And here she was with nothing more exciting than watching television with the Grands. By next year Quentin would be home. Home? But what would be the point of his coming back to Highmoor, if there was no land around there for his nursery? It was a problem that returned time and again. If only she were a bit older they could go anywhere. But she'd never be allowed to leave home yet. Her pretty face set in a line of discontent. She'd been left on the edge of life for so long, wearing Sylvia's hand-me-downs skilfully altered by Sue, too young to do this, too small to do that. Now, just because she lived in the country she didn't get the chance of fun. Of course she could ride — and she did at the weekends — but she wanted to dance, she wanted to be taken out to dine, she wanted to wear fashionable clothes. Most of all she wanted some young people to have fun with.

'You look very solemn, dear. I expect you would like to have gone too instead of being left with Harold and me by the fireside,' Lucinda was sometimes uncomfortably perceptive.

'No, I wouldn't, Gran,' Liz lied. 'It looks jolly cold out there. Shall I carry the little table across, then we can go on with the jigsaw.' When she said it, she suddenly saw the image of Quentin and felt sufficiently pleased with herself that, at least for the moment, she had chased the devils off her back. If he were here, this was just the sort of thing he would do, she thought as she set the half-done puzzle in front of where they sat on the settee and pulled her own chair close enough for her to reach it too.

* * *

110

'Who's the redhead?' Sue asked as Tim led her to join the quickstepping throng on the small dance floor of Upley Court Hotel, the regular venue for the Hunt Ball.

'With Paul? I don't know. I've not seen her at the hunt. Someone's wife or daughter, I suppose.'

'Daughter, I hope,' Sue laughed, 'or he'll have a jealous husband after him with his crop. He's been with her on and off most of the evening.' Then Paul was forgotten as the dance came to an end. Everyone applauded but very few couples left the dance floor, they wanted more. 'Isn't this fun. I want to dance every single dance, don't you?'

'It seems I shall have no choice,' he laughed fondly. 'Poor lady, she doesn't get much fun, does she.'

'Stupid, of course I do. But not the dancing kind, all dressed up in Aunt Luce's pearls.'

'And cape.'

'You make me sound like Cinderella.'

By that time they were waltzing, his chin nuzzling against her curls as he whispered, 'No, when the clock struck Cinderella ran home at midnight all by herself. You, my sweet lady, have a lot of night ahead of you.'

The following Monday morning Tim said he would be out for a while, he wanted to go to Reading, there were one or two things he wanted from the agricultural engineer's storehouse in the cattle market. Nothing unusual in that, although Paul felt himself badly used that his father disappeared without giving him the chance of coming too. When the Land Rover returned Sue was in the dairy churning that 'lump of butter' Paul thought of so disparagingly.

'You were quick,' she called.

'Come here and close your eyes.'

She did, holding her face, her lips pursed expectantly.

'What? Kisses too? Is there no satisfying the women?' he laughed. 'No, keep them closed. Turn your back.'

She did as he said, then felt something put around her neck and knew he was fumbling with a clasp. Eyes still closed, she touched the smooth, cool pearls.

'She'll have to go on borrowing the cape, but she shall have her own finery.'

'Tim . . . oh, Tim . . . ' She turned towards him, eyes wide open and suddenly brimming with tears. 'As if I minded borrowing — '

'Go indoors and look at them in the glass.' He sounded as cocky as the children used to when they brought home their first paintings to be pinned to the wall. She nuzzled her head against him. And, not for the first time, she sent up a silent 'thank you' that she was *who* she was, *where* she was, here at the centre of her universe with those she loved around her.

She was still admiring the single strand of pearls when Paul came looking for her.

'Mum, I thought you were in the dairy. Look, Mum, will it be OK if I bring Phil for supper?'

'Phil? Of course it'll be all right, but do we know him?' Mentally she was lining up the young men of their acquaintance.

'Her, not him. Don't you remember, I introduced you at the Ball. Philippa Geary, the smashing redhead.' There was nothing diffident about Paul's approach to what Sue suspected to be his first serious infatuation. 'She teaches the top class at the primary school in Brindley. Poor devil. I remember what we were like at that age, frightfully full of our own importance. I suppose it was harmless, but we used to give Miss Huntley a hard time, one prank after another. But I imagine Phil's really good at her job, Mum, doesn't seem a bit fazed by the little horrors.'

'She's not local is she? Lodgings can't be much fun.'

'She's not in lodgings. She's rented a cottage — well, that flatters it really, she showed it to me yesterday. One of a dreary terrace in Hendred Street. Two up and two down, with the sound of next door's radio thrown in for good measure. Actually, it's even smaller than two up and two down; one of the ups has been converted into a bathroom and the two downs have been knocked into one. But she's got a real knack, you ought to see the way she's got it. Very modish, not a frill or a bit of chintz in sight. Anyway, thanks, Mum. I told her we eat about six, Dad and I are always starving by then. Then if I can borrow the car, I want to take her to Reading to the Odeon. It'll be OK, won't it?'

She didn't doubt it. In fact she was excited at the thought of Paul taking an interest in the striking-looking redhead. A local schoolteacher . . . well, what could be more suitable? Like most women, Sue had a romantic streak and very little control on the brakes of her imagination as she had her son married and living in one of the farm cottages. Exactly which one she didn't probe, for there were only two: one housed the Joshes, the other Fred Dawson and his wife Sheila.

Still in the same frame of mind about the visit, she persuaded Tim to come straight indoors after the teatime milking and change into better trousers and a clean shirt. For herself, she selected slacks and her best jumper. She was tempted to add her new pearls, but at the risk of looking over-dressed, she decided against it. Even so, sitting in front of the dressing table, she held them around her neck. He must have spent more money than he could easily afford, she thought, gazing at their pearly lustre and noting the name of the jewellers on the inside of the case. A smile tugged at her mouth as she moved them to hold against her cheek. Her faraway expression showed clearly that wherever her thoughts were taking her, it wasn't to the ham and egg pie that was in the oven or to the stranger who, this evening, would be given 'Christopher's place' between Liz and Tim.

★   ★   ★

Tall and slender, Philippa Geary was even more striking than Sue remembered. She had the pale, fair complexion of most redheads, although she'd missed out on the freckles that so often go with it.

114

'Nice-looking gal, eh? What?' Harold voiced his opinion loud and clear, earning a withering look from Paul. 'You don't mind me telling you you're a beauty, do you, my dear?'

'That's something no woman ever minds,' Philippa assured him. He was delighted, he liked the naughty twinkle in her greeny eyes; it made him forget that life was such a confusing business these days; it made him fancy he was a young man again, cutting a dash in his uniform and knowing it. He bowed his still handsome head and took both her hands. 'What about a dance, eh? What?' Then, 'Pom, pom, pom, pom, ta, ta, ta, ta,' as he whirled her into a waltz.

'Harold, Harold,' Lucinda tugged at his arm. 'Just behave yourself, Miss Geary has hardly had time to take her coat off. Oh dear . . . '

'Too keen, was I? She how they treat me, m'dear. You just book me a dance or two later, put me down on your card.'

Philippa didn't answer; she simply looked across at Paul, raising her eyebrows in a way that spoke volumes. That was a pity, for the only one in the room who seemed unaware of her expression was Harold. Lucinda saw it and felt mortified that anyone should laugh at Harold, who used to command such respect; Liz saw it and was furious; Sue saw it and was hurt for the Grands; Paul saw it and replied with a conspiratorial smile; Tim saw it, and Paul's acknowledgement as well, and felt a sense of foreboding. And yet perhaps none of them was being fair.

The meal started with home-made cream of

vegetable soup. A basket of home-made bread rolls was passed round, everyone except Philippa taking one. Then followed ham and egg pie, potatoes mashed with butter and cream, spinach and mixed root vegetables.

'A very small portion of pie, Mrs Marshall. They say, don't they, that the nation was healthier when food was rationed. And I don't doubt it. Dairy products are so fattening.' Did she mean to sound offensive? Sue gave her the benefit of the doubt; Tim didn't.

'Lot of tommy rot. Do we look unhealthy? Certainly we don't. If you'd prefer to starve yourself until you're skin and bone, then good luck to you.' Then to Sue, taking the plate she passed down to him and at the same time ignoring her warning glance. 'Thanks, lady, that looks good.'

'How are you enjoying the school, Miss Geary? Oh, I say, can't we call you Philippa?'

'I wish you would, Mrs Marshall. I'm enjoying it well enough. Of course I've little to compare it with, this is only my second school. I was lucky to get a house to rent, did Paul tell you?'

'Yes, he did. Have you lived on your own before?' It seemed no one was prepared to help Sue out. Liz still looked like a thundercloud, Lucinda didn't attempt to find an olive branch, Harold was busy playing the drum on the underside of the table in time with some imaginary tune, and Paul seemed content just to listen with pride to his new-found friend.

'No. After boarding school I went to college,

116

but I lived out, sharing of course. Then I shared again in my last school. This is the first time I've had a proper place of my own.' Her sudden smile transformed her.

Why, Sue thought, she really isn't prim at all; perhaps she's shy. Now we've broken the ice she will be easier.

'I suppose you can eat at school — '

'I could. But I certainly don't. Of course I have to stay through the lunch break, but I make myself a salad.'

Tim snorted. Paul looked at her in open admiration.

When Sue brought a rice pudding from the oven, topped with a golden skin, their young guest murmured a polite, 'Not for me, if you don't mind.'

'All the more for us,' Tim was at his least hospitable. No wonder Paul looked uncomfortable.

'I won't either, if you don't mind, Mum. If we've both finished and you'll excuse us, we'll get on our way. We shall have missed a bit of the short film in any case by the time we've driven to Reading.'

It was a relief when the door closed behind them. When Tim passed his plate back for a second helping — including the edges that were sticking to the pyrex dish, they all knew it was his way of putting two fingers up to Miss Philippa Geary.

★　★　★

117

Occasionally she came to the farm, but more often Paul met her outside.

'I just hope he knows what he's doing,' Tim said as he reached to turn off the bedside light. Night and morning, at the farm they kept early hours.

'He knows her better than we do, darling. And really, there are an awful lot of us here, she must find us a bit daunting. I admit, she does seem a bit schoolmarmish, but she can't be or he would have tired of her.'

In fact, schoolmarmish wasn't the impression she'd made on Tim but, he supposed, men see things differently. Certainly she could do with feeding up on good red meat, put a bit of flesh on her bones. But her thin build didn't detract from her sensuality. Paul was no different from any other young man of his age; she had her own home where no one could unexpectedly walk in on them.

'It's been going on for months. Every evening he's there. You can't tell me she spends her time marking homework.'

'Oh, Tim,' Sue chuckled, snuggling closer to him, 'you sound like a maiden aunt. Seriously, I do believe he is in love with her. He seems so cheerful.'

'Humph,' was the only answer. Not a happy 'humph'.

'Remember before we were married. The only time we ever got to be by ourselves was if you took me to the pictures. Times are different now though, I suppose the war changed the way people thought about the young. Anyway, we needn't worry about Paul. I bet you half a crown before long they'll be engaged.'

'God forbid. You don't honestly think that, Sue?'

'I think he's smitten. But even more important, I think — and I've watched them together if he's brought her here, I mean watched them purposely to see the little things that give a girl away — I think she feels the same about him. And if that's so, then, Tim, we ought to be pleased. What could be better than Paul marrying the local schoolteacher?'

'A lot could be better. He could fall in love with someone gentle, someone sensitive. Can you honestly see her as a farmer's wife?'

Sue couldn't. But she wasn't going to admit it.

'When we married, had you ever thought of me as a farmer's wife?' She wrapped her leg around his, not purposely to distract his thoughts but because she loved the nearness of him. They said no more about Paul, in fact very soon Paul was forgotten, by him and by her too.

★   ★   ★

Through spring and summer Paul worked unflaggingly. His cheerful manner never faltered, it was as if now that his thoughts were so much taken up with Philippa he had forgotten his wild scheme to bring about alterations at Highmoor. To Tim it seemed that this was what he'd looked forward to. As a child Paul had wanted nothing better than to help on the farm, to learn from his father, or from Josh or Fred. Naturally enough,

119

college training had given him a lot of high-flown ideas, but to those were being added the more practical lessons of the day-to-day running of Highmoor.

Between father and son, the friendship never wavered, in fact it seemed to grow stronger in the bond of common experience. Sure that, however involved Paul was becoming with Philippa, she had no power to change him, Tim gradually became less wary of her. Sue had made an effort to like her right from the start; Harold's view was patently obvious, he would have filled her dance card any time; when Lucinda detected no more silent laughing at his expense she was prepared to forgive and forget. So that left only Liz, whose dislike never lessened.

'Paul's no fun any more, Mum. Oh, I know he and Dad work together OK, but he's turning into as big a sober sides as his precious Philippa.' The truth was, Liz was lonely. She loved the work she did, she was proud of the expertise she was gaining and her head was full of dreams of the part she would play when Quentin built his nursery. But it all seemed so far away, it would be ages before he finished at college and even then he had to start looking for somewhere suitable to build. When he found the right place, if it was miles away, how could she hope to get involved? Perhaps the whole thing had been a silly pipe-dream. No wonder Liz was the least happy at Highmoor during that summer.

It was in the autumn that Paul and Philippa announced their engagement.

'Marrying my lovely young lady?' Harold

pumped Paul's hand. 'Lucky young dog you are. And you, m'dear,' to Philippa, 'it'll be nice to have you always here. Eh? What?'

'I wish we had another cottage,' Sue said, kissing her future daughter-in-law. 'But to start with, room is something we have plenty of in this rambling old house. Like Uncle Harold says, Philippa, it'll be lovely to have you always here.'

Philippa looked from one to another; she seemed bemused by the suggestion.

'Here? In the farmhouse? But why would we do that? I have a house already. I know it's only rented, but it will be fine until we decide what we want.'

That ought to have rung their warning bells.

They planned to be married a few days before Christmas, as soon as term finished at Brindley's 'baby school'.

'I'm looking forward to meeting your parents,' Sue said, forcing herself to believe it was true. In fact she considered they must be a very odd couple, for they apparently played no part in Philippa's affairs.

'I wouldn't expect them to come. They split up years ago, my mother is married again. Well, we all have our own tastes, I suppose, but he certainly isn't mine. And my father has been in Australia for years. So I'm afraid you'll be disappointed.'

On the contrary, Sue didn't attempt to hide her delight.

'So the wedding will be from here? Oh, that's lovely. Did you hear that, Aunt Luce? By then Christopher ought to be back from Germany,

Quentin will be home. With a wedding and Christmas to decorate for, Liz and Quentin will make everything look wonderful.' The wedding was still three months away, but in her mind Sue was planning something akin to a banquet.

'I don't want any fuss. It'll be a very quiet registry office ceremony and I thought we'd book a table for lunch afterwards at the Upley Court Hotel.'

'Where you met . . . ' The romantic in Sue wouldn't be defeated.

'No, actually,' Philippa laughed. 'Paul and I had a good nodding acquaintance before the Hunt Ball. It was he who gave me my ticket. But Upley Court is the best place around here.'

'I see.' Sue kept good control of her tone, she didn't mean to let them guess her disappointment. Just about the wedding plans? About the fact that Paul had already had a life outside the farm even before they first met the striking redhead? About the way her suggestions for using Highmoor were brushed aside as so clearly not good enough?

'I'm sorry if you would have preferred us to come here, Mrs Marshall. But we all like to do things our own way. You'll have your Christmas party here with all the family, and I'm sure that will be work enough for you. But the wedding is our day, it's important that we don't get pushed into accepting less than we want simply to please other people.'

'Of course you're quite right,' Sue made a supreme effort. But she couldn't resist adding, 'Liz would love to do the flowers, I'm sure. Her work is a combination of natural talent and good training — '

'I know. Her work is beautiful. But what would I want with a bouquet? The last thing I intend is for us to arrive at Upton Manor looking like a bridal party. Honestly, I want it all to be low key.'

Sue felt as though they were to lose a son and gain nothing. But, even to Tim, she wasn't prepared to put into words the unnamed fear that niggled at the back of her mind as the weeks passed. Harvest was carried, the corn threshed, the stubble burnt and, finally, the cycle was completed with the beginning of winter ploughing. That was a time of year Tim and Sue had always enjoyed, the straight furrows seeming to symbolise the accomplishment of one year and the promise of the next.

'She doesn't know about being a family.' It wasn't so much for Philippa's sake as their own that Sue tried to make the rest of them feel more kindly disposed towards the girl who would so soon be brought into the fold.

As so often happened, Paul had gone out for the evening. 'No doubt making do with a lettuce leaf and a slice of cucumber' could be read in Tim's expression as he looked at his son's empty chair. The rest of them were gathered around the well-laden kitchen table.

'Fine-looking girl,' Harold chortled. 'Nearer the bone, sweeter the meat.'

'Harold, behave yourself,' Lucinda whispered.

'She thinks she knows everything,' pouted Liz. 'And when she really doesn't she makes do with looking as though everyone around her is stupid.

123

I wonder what Christo will make of her. I bet he's had enough girlfriends to be choosy. Put a man in uniform and the girls go down like ninepins. Isn't that so, Grandpa?'

Harold sat a little taller and gave her a saucy wink.

'Let me see now,' he frowned the next second, 'Christopher, you say. Gone off out somewhere, has he? With a girlfriend, did you say? My silly head. Ought to write things down. Did I know?' Helplessly he looked from one to another, his mouth trembling and his eyes suddenly haunted by fear.

'About girlfriends?' Liz laughed, hoping to ease the tension and take that miserable look off Lucinda's face, 'No, we none of us know. I was only guessing. He's so good-looking, I bet he has them queuing up.'

'Hah,' Harold seemed satisfied.

And when Tim told him, 'Not many weeks now before Christopher will be home on leave. That'll be a day of celebration, eh, Uncle Harold?'

'When? When did you say he's coming?'

'I don't know exactly — but not long now.'

Harold seemed content and concentrated all his attention on his plate of roast beef, while Sue picked up the conversation where she'd lost it.

'We have to make allowances for her — Philippa, I mean. Her life hasn't been that easy, it can't have been, perhaps that's why she never talks about it. We must hold back, we don't want to frighten her by looking as though we expect her to be the same as the rest of us. Just

124

wait, by the time she has their first baby, I bet she'll find it easier to be one of a family.'

'I hope you're right, lady,' Tim said. 'But she seems to expect to go on with that teaching job. Being a farmer's wife is a long way down her list of priorities if you ask me.'

* * *

Christopher had been overseas for three years. He'd gone out a 2nd Lieutenant; he came home a Captain. He'd gone out a boy; he came back a man. If they saw changes in him, so certainly he did in them. Paul being only three years his junior, they'd progressed in line with each other. In any case, Paul had developed into exactly the sort of man everyone had known he would. He accepted Tim and Sue as the same now as they had been all his life. It was his grandparents who had been hardest hit by the passing of the years for, even though Lucinda was still as trim, still as smart, she was like a toy with a broken spring. As for Harold, who'd been such a hero in the eyes of the child Christopher had been, except for the occasional flash of understanding the ageing man had gone beyond recall. And Liz? Three years ago she'd been a gym-slipped schoolgirl. In features she'd not changed, even her honey-brown hair was worn in the same cap-like style; still she was short, as slightly built as her mother. But no one would mistake her for a child. Now she was an adult, an enchantingly pretty adult. Perhaps of them all it was the Joshes who remained exactly as he remembered, never young and so never old either; they were simply the Joshes. On the afternoon of his first day home he went the short distance along the lane to their cottage, as sure of his welcome as he'd ever been.

'Now you're home perhaps the old gentleman will get himself better in step. Many an hour he spends along here with Josh and me. As I say, old age can be a frightening thing. Better not to think about it, better just to keep busy then it might pass by without noticing.' Christopher looked at her affectionately, not pointing out that as far as old age went she and Josh must have a good head start on his grandfather. 'Now then, Christo, lad, what about a cup of tea and a piece of ginger cake.' Christopher stretched out his long legs as he sat on the wooden rocking chair by the kitchen range.

'Mrs Josh, you don't know the times I've dreamt of your ginger cake. A big piece, please.' Now he really knew he'd come home!

But before half the huge wedge of cake had disappeared he was hearing Mrs Josh's views on the coming wedding.

'Why couldn't the boy have found a nice girl from around these parts, that's what I'd like to know. Now, you, it would be different for you. Travelling the world is what your job is all about, I dare say. But young Paul, his world is here. Bless his heart, can't you just remember him as a slip of a lad, so set on being a man already, helping Mr Tim, learning, always learning. Oh, it's not for me to criticise, she may be a very nice girl. None of them say a word against her, don't get me wrong. It's just this feeling I have. She isn't one of us. That's the rock bottom of it.'

'Paul isn't daft, Mrs Josh.'

'Ach! Don't give me that, lad. Not a man born who isn't daft when a good-looking girl sets her cap at him. And she's that, right enough — good-looking. Your grandfather comes over here sometimes blithering away about her, fair smitten he is, bless his old heart.'

★ ★ ★

The next day Sylvia arrived with three clear days between shifts. Sensitive to the closeness between the twins, the family gave them plenty of space and no one was surprised when, despite driving rain, they donned wellingtons and oilskins and headed for the Downs. They were almost tempted to take a picnic with them as, whatever the weather, they always used to on the first day of school holidays. But, instead they sat by the fire in the Highwayman, each with a pint of cider and a ploughman's lunch. And it was here that Sylvia talked about Richard.

'Do you hear from him? You never mention him in your letters.' No one but Christopher would have talked to her so freely.

'Only what I read in the newspaper — or once or twice I've bumped into his parents. I don't expect Quentin hears either. They're not exactly a close-knit family.'

'And what do you read?'

'They had a child — less than six months after they were married. The papers left no one in any

127

doubt about that, although Drucilla Mountjoy pulled the wool over everyone's eyes at the wedding. She really looked absolutely stunning in the pictures.'

'Can I get you another cider?' He needed to digest what he'd heard before she told him more.

'Just a half would be nice. There's a scarcity of bushes on the way home.' It was such a joy to be with Christo again. She held her hands towards the blazing logs in the grate, thankful that here was someone she could talk to about anything. She longed to hear herself telling it all — that she and Richard had been lovers, that for ten glorious days they'd been cut off from the rest of the busy world in a *gîte* in Normandy, that . . . that what? That she ought to have known she was no more than a passing interlude, always for Richard McBride there would be women as gullible as she had been. Since him, there had been no one else for her. Would she end up an old maid? That's not what they called one these days, now she would be looked on as a career woman. Well, thank God she had a career she loved.

And just as she knew she would hold nothing back from him, so Christopher came back ready to listen, to understand. In truth, as the story unfolded, he would like to have found the great and glorious Richard McBride and given him the hiding he deserved. But today his was a listening role.

While they sat quietly talking by the open hearth in the Highwayman, there were only four around the table at Highmoor. Not that fewer

128

people meant any change in the seating arrangements, but simply more empty chairs.

'All very mysterious, the way Paul and Philippa went off this morning. In the middle of term, I wonder she could do it,' Sue said as she collected their empty soup plates and put a bubbling and golden macaroni cheese on the table. Lunch was looked on as a 'light meal' — although that wasn't the way Philippa would have described it.

'You know what I think?' Lucinda sounded almost excited. 'I think that when they get back she'll bring her wedding outfit to show us. After all, Sue, who else has she? Poor girl. Every bride needs someone to take an interest.'

'If I were the headmaster of the primary school I'd take an interest, right enough,' Tim said, lavishly spreading butter on a slice of crusty bread. 'What's Saturday done wrong that she needs to go shopping in the middle of the week? You may be sure she's trumped up some cock and bull story of where she's gone. Anyway, it doesn't take two of them to buy a bridal outfit.' He was disgruntled. The last day or two Paul had been quite edgy, then suddenly last night he'd sprung it on them that Philippa had somewhere she had to go today and he was going with her.

A sudden gust of wind brought the rain hitting the window facing the yard, while a gust of smoke blew back down the chimney. Sue got up from the table and opened the damper, then sat down again. It was an instinctive action, one grown from years of knowing the vagaries of the range.

'Those poor children out there on the Downs,' Lucinda said.

'Good for them,' Tim smiled, his ill humour gone, 'nothing like a good stomp in the wind and rain for clearing away the wretched town atmosphere. You'll see, Sylvia will come home with roses in her cheeks and bright eyes.'

'That, Tim my dear, will have come from being with Christo more than braving the elements.' Lucinda had the last word. After all, they were *her* grandchildren.

Tim went back to the yard; Sue lit the fire in the drawing room so that the Grands could doze in the warmth. On the kitchen wall the old clock ticked loudly. Sue might wish the twins weren't out in the weather, she might be slightly uneasy about Philippa's need to take a day off school, but nothing could destroy her own feeling of peace. It wasn't even dented by the need to prepare piles of vegetables for the evening meal. The thought of the young couple on the brink of marriage didn't worry her, in a way she could understand their determination not to be swamped by the family. Give them time and everything would settle down, gradually Philippa would become one of them and would look on them as her family. In a rare mood of warmth towards her soon-to-be-daughter, she decided to make an extra dish for supper, for the steak and kidney pie she'd prepared wouldn't meet with a health fanatic's approval. There was some chicken left . . . her mind was jumping ahead of her as she prepared the leeks. If Philippa knew she'd made a risotto especially on her account,

130

she would stay for supper. It was important on this, the first evening with each of the twins home, that the young people should all get to know each other.

The steak and kidney pie was consumed with gusto, the risotto was kept warm until it looked dry and unappetising. It was late when they heard the car draw up in the yard, then the sound of two doors being slammed.

'Sorry we're late, folks,' Paul said as he ushered Philippa through the door from the lobby. Did Sue imagine it or was his voice just that bit too bright? 'I was frightened you'd be in bed. You didn't save us any food, did you? We had something on the way home. We felt like celebrating. Hello, Sylvia. Gosh, this is auspicious, all of us here to hear what we have to tell you.'

5

Sue's instant thought was of all the evenings the two young people had spent at Philippa's little house in Hendred Street. One look at Tim and she was certain his was on the same lines. A baby! Well, was that so dreadful? Hadn't she always said there was plenty of room at Highmoor — until they could find a place of their own, she added, silently remembering how the suggestion had been received previously.

'Whatever you have to tell us, it's clearly something good,' Tim meant his son to know his family were right behind him.

'Yes, it's good all right. It's great! Well, we think so, don't we, Phil?'

'It's absolutely fantastic. We've been afraid to hope.'

Afraid to hope? Surely, even in these free-thinking Sixties they couldn't admit to being afraid to hope even before they were married?

'I would have told you before,' Paul was saying, 'but I honestly didn't think I had a snowball's chance in hell of it coming off. Now I don't know where to start.'

Another glance between Sue and Tim, suddenly less certain and, without knowing why, both of them feeling a chill of apprehension. But whatever the news, it must be something good, something that had given Paul and Philippa cause for celebration.

'Start at the beginning,' Liz said, 'but first don't let's stay out here in the kitchen, let's go into the sitting room so the Grands can hear whatever it is too.' Her thoughts were flitting from one suggestion to another: perhaps they'd found a house, a proper house not that pokey little place in Hendred Street. But why would that have taken them all day? She led the way through to the sitting room.

Philippa had met Christopher briefly the previous day and, as they crossed the hall to join the Grands, Paul introduced her to Sylvia. Sue touched Tim's hand as if for reassurance, and was answered by one short, tight grip. A brief contact, hardly aware of what they did.

'Paul's got some news for us, Gran,' Liz announced. 'Go on, Paul, you can start now. We're all agog.'

It was Philippa who told them. Her nature wasn't to mince her words, so she came straight to the point.

'Paul's been given a splendid new job. It's in Somerset on the Mendips; he's to manage a fantastic farm, a huge place just like he's always wanted. The title on the job description was estate manager.'

'I was going to start at the beginning,' Paul said. 'But I'll come to that in a minute. Dad, you are pleased for me, aren't you? You must be. You didn't send me off to that college so that I could footle around on your own patch here doing the same as Fred Dawson.'

The silence was intense. Sue swallowed a lump in her dry throat. How could he do it? Why couldn't he at least have told them what he was thinking, given them a warning? This time she couldn't reach out to Tim's hand, she couldn't even look at him.

'Gosh,' Liz said. 'Estate manager. Will you have a house? Are there stables so that you can take Rosie?'

'Dad?' Paul waited.

'Well done, son. If that's what you want — looking after someone else's land and taking a wage for doing it — then it sounds as if you have landed on your feet.'

Paul's smile was broad, it combined relief and excitement.

'Just you wait till you come and see it. I've got all the details, of course. I'll let you see them, you'll find it interesting.'

Interesting? Heartbreaking?

'You might have told us what you were planning.' Small though she was, when she was angry Sue could be formidable. 'When have you arranged to start? You might have had consideration enough to give your father time to engage another worker here.'

Paul laughed good-humouredly. 'There you are, you see, a farm worker can replace me easy as wink. The owner was there today for the interview, I told him when we were being married and what we arranged was that after the ceremony we should go straight there.'

'So you'll get a house?' Liz was still waiting for his answer.

'Vast,' Philippa took up the story, 'compared with my little hovel, and built since the war so it's quite modern. Of course it's not furnished to my taste, but we'll alter what we don't like. I'm glad the bush telegraph hadn't got hold of the story and passed it on to you. As Paul said, we wanted to be sure before we said anything. But of course I'd had to give in my notice at school so there was always the danger of it leaking out.' She smiled at the room at large, 'If Paul hadn't got this job I'd have had to look for another post, or do private tuition. It wasn't *me* who was the doubt, it was whether Paul would be considered to have experience enough. But he talked them round — and of course the college had written the owner a letter giving a fantastic reference. So, Mrs Marshall, there will be two less for Christmas after all.' She laughed delightedly, taking it for granted that everyone else would be as pleased as they were themselves.

'Can't credit it, you know.' Try as he might Paul couldn't get the grin off his face, 'Phil and me in our own home. And that place, there isn't a farm around to equal it. I can do it, I know I can. But, Dad, Sir Egbert Hilton — he's something in the City, mostly lives in town — he could see that I'm up to it. None of that wait till you're older, want more experience, all that baloney.'

Keeping up with events was quite beyond Harold. The twins were talking to Philippa — what a cracker she was, moved with the grace of a tiger. Young Paul going to marry her, that's what they said. Looking at her legs, long and slim; but it wasn't just that. Harold didn't torment his mind chasing after words, leaning

135

back in the fireside chair, he let his imagination run riot. Slim legs, but strong, or yes, strong, supple . . . Agile as a cat, she was. Young Paul going to have her in his bed. He was just a boy, what did he know about how to satisfy a girl like that red-headed beauty? Nothing of the docile wife about that one, she wouldn't lie back and think of England. Nothing of the innocent virgin about her. A schoolmarm, did they say? Plenty that she could teach. He nodded, his eyes closing. If he were younger, if he weren't such a helpless old fool, he'd give her something to think about. Young Paul . . . He was woken by the sound of his own sudden snore. He sat up straight, looking around furtively to make sure no one had noticed that for a minute he must have dropped off. Nice, having the family all here. What was it they were talking about? Something was wrong, he could feel it in the atmosphere. He may not have been able to keep abreast with all the talk, but he was sensitive to atmosphere. Dear oh dear, what was the matter? The young ones were all talking together, they sounded cheerful enough. Lucinda was working at some sort of stitching, but he wasn't happy with the way she kept her eyes on what she was doing as if she wished she were somewhere else. He poked at the fire, expecting that would give him their attention. But it didn't. Tim and Sue — ah, it was Tim and Sue he wasn't happy about. But why?

'All home, eh? What?' he boomed across the room to them, expecting the reminder would banish whatever it was that bothered them.

From behind a cloud of tobacco smoke, Tim made an effort to respond.

'Have you got your pipe in your pocket?' he asked. 'Here, fill it with this and tell me what you think of it. They hadn't got my usual at Hardy's today.' He threw his tobacco pouch to land on the elderly man's lap. Harold forgot he was supposed to be worried about something and filled his pipe, then lit it with a spill from the box on the mantelpiece. This was what he liked, good male companionship, the contentment of a shared smoke. 'Thank you, my boy,' he passed the pouch back. 'Not such a bad life, you know. No, pretty good. Family home, hah.'

★ ★ ★

Sue knew Tim was awake, even in sleep he wouldn't have been so unnaturally still.

'He ought to have told us,' she whispered. 'All these weeks they've known — '

'He didn't think he stood a chance. But I wish he'd trusted us enough that he hadn't felt he'd have to hide the failure of not being selected.'

'I'm so angry. I feel all knotted up with anger — that's what hurts. Oh, not with her, I don't give a tinker's cuss about her. But, Tim, how could he do it?'

Tim drew her closer.

'Don't be angry, darling, not with him. Perhaps it's been our fault, we oughtn't to have expected him to come back here and be content.'

He spoke quietly, his voice was even, yet she knew his aching disappointment. Since Paul had been home she'd seen the two of them as working so happily together; Tim must have thought the same. And, all the time, had Paul been wanting to get away? Or was it Philippa's fault, she with her empty house to entice him to?

'I thought he was going to tell us she was pregnant.' In the night-time stillness even a whisper seemed loud. 'And blow the gossip it would cause, I was excited — for them and for us too. But this . . . '

'It's been my own fault,' Tim said. 'He had plans, he wanted us to take more land, have a bigger herd, build a new dairy. I wouldn't listen. I said I was in charge here, you and I, and he'd have to wait till we were too old to manage. His turn would come, then he could do as he liked.'

'And suppose you'd done as he wanted, what then? If *she* talked him into it, he would have applied for his grand job as estate manager just the same. Then where would we have been?' Her anger showed no sign of abating. 'Who does he think he is, that he can throw in his hand almost without warning? You'll have to take on another man.'

'Replacement for Paul.' It broke her heart to hear the way he said it. 'He probably thinks we're too old already — like Bert Hamilton at Silverdale.'

'Stupid little nincompoop!' Only a whisper but it expressed just how she felt. 'He should never have gone to that stupid college. He always loved Highmoor, if he'd come here straight from school — '

'No, darling. If he'd come straight from school

he would have felt bitter that we'd deprived him of his opportunity. I try to be fair. I try to put myself in his place. If it were you and me, just about to be married, wouldn't we have wanted to branch out on our own? Of course we would.'

'That's different. He's just a kid still. I bet she's older than him, you know. Not much you could tell her about life.'

'Or about anything. But she's the woman Paul wants so, lady, we must accept. We didn't expect your father to organise our lives for us.'

'Well, of course we didn't.' How could he make such a stupid comparison? 'Not that he would have wanted to, he was much too interested in his own.'

'And so, darling, must we be. What was it they called it in the newspaper the other day — the generation gap, I think it was. He probably thinks we're getting old — we know we're not; we look on him as a lad still — he knows he's not. It's a lesson we all have to learn, or we shall be the losers, Sue. He mustn't leave here feeling guilty, he mustn't leave under a cloud of bad feeling.'

'Well, I don't like *her* and I don't care who knows it. She's spoilt everything.'

Tim was so wise, she thought, as she turned round to 'sit in his lap' for sleep. He was more than wise, he was *good*, truly *good*. Of course he was right and they ought to make themselves remember what it was like to be young and life full of promise. But from where they were now, how shallow all those youthful dreams seemed. Their marriage had grown stronger with every

139

year, with every hurdle they'd had to climb together . . . years with good harvests and a few pounds extra in the bank, years with poor harvests when even the school fees had been hard to scrape together, shared anxiety when one after another the children went down with measles, cosy late-night 'second suppers' of toast made on the toasting fork in front of the bars of the kitchen range, then liberally spread with their own butter. Yet when they'd first come here, if they'd been told that they were only at the beginning of understanding and growing together they would have laughed. They'd believed that because they were still in the thrill of those first heady months of marriage, their love was complete. Perhaps you never reach a final goal, perhaps as long as you are together the roots grow deeper and stronger.

He drew her closer.

'All these years, Sue. I never doubted it would all be his.'

'We'll get another man to help, we've got years and years ahead before we need think of that. And I bet you one thing, Tim Marshall, when he's worked a stranger's land for a while he'll know the difference. Let him spread his wings, then when he's ready, he'll fly home.'

★ ★ ★

The train sped southward, the windows of every compartment running with condensation so that it was almost impossible to see the changing landscape. Hour after hour the soporific motion

140

continued, changing only as the train slowed to a stop at major stations. Then there was the bustle of passengers getting off, more getting on, the slamming of doors — and the journey went on.

Not for the first time, Quentin rubbed his hand over the misted window to look out on to the winter scenes that unfolded. He'd been on the train since first light, for hours the glorious countryside had been blanketed in white: frost in the valleys even though on the more distant high ground he knew it was snow. Even south of the border every tree had been edged with frost, the puddles looked hard as iron. By the time they went through the industrial Midlands, afternoon was already giving way to early dusk under the leaden sky. The scene was one of winter at its dullest, and in the lights of the occasional street lamps he could see that a fine drizzle was being blown almost horizontally.

By contrast the atmosphere in the gently rocking carriage resembled a tropical hothouse. The heat control lever was pulled round as far as it would go to ensure a gush of hot air from under the two long seats where passengers sat facing each other. How was it they could all look so chilled? An elderly lady in the diagonally opposite corner pulled her fur collar closer around her neck; the woman next to her took her small daughter on her knee and tucked her plump little legs under the skirt of her overcoat. Satisfied, the child thrust her thumb in her mouth and took up a position of drowsy contentment. Quentin undid the top button of his shirt and loosened his tie. He felt as if dozens of sharp knives were jabbing the back of his eyes, he could hardly bear to open them even in the poorly lit compartment. It was ages since he'd felt like it. Why today? Of all times, why now, the day he was going home? Working in the glasshouses, studying the subject dearest to his heart, there was nothing to upset the even, unemotional tenor of his days. All his life he'd been dogged by nervous headaches. But, reason told him, today nothing can go wrong. You'll be home, everyone will be just the same. Nothing changes at Highmoor. And Liz, Liz will be there . . . Was that what worried him? That constant fear that his lovely Liz wouldn't feel the same about him. All the things they'd planned, would they still be what she wanted? She wrote to him often, just as he wrote to her. But when had he ever poured into his words just how much he loved her? Never. They'd grown up sharing all their troubles, all their triumphs. Eyes closed, he let his mind slide back down the years. With Paul and the twins gone, he remembered how he and Liz had walked behind the binder, determined not to admit to just how heavy they found the sheaves. She was tiny for her age, and four years younger than him, but Liz wouldn't admit defeat. Then he remembered the day when they'd cycled to Christmas Common taking their picnic lunch. She must have been about thirteen, day rides were part of the long summer holidays and they'd done it often enough before. He'd not understood why it was that Aunt Sue had tried to make excuses to keep them at home. But Liz wouldn't listen and off they'd gone. A smile tugged at his sensitive mouth, his headache was almost forgotten as in his memory he heard Liz saying she wanted to rest 'just for a bit'. How worried he'd been; Liz never gave in to being tired. Suppose she was ill. Laying their bikes on the ground they'd started towards a promising-looking spot sheltered by gorse bushes. He'd known something was wrong even before she stopped, bending forward, her hands pressed to her groin. Never in his life had he prayed so fervently. Please don't let Liz be ill. Somehow he was standing close behind her, his arms around her, his own hands covering hers. 'What is it? Tell me. Don't be ill, Liz.' She moved her own hands then to cover his. 'Not ill,' she'd whispered. 'It's never happened to me before. This is my first time. Oh Quen, I do hurt. All across here, and my legs. Didn't know it would hurt like this, the others never told me.' He hadn't immediately understood. Then realisation had come. His beloved little Liz wasn't a child. She was a woman. She was his woman. He'd led her to the mossy path by the gorse bushes and drawn her to lie just as they'd been standing, he close behind her. 'Your hands are so warm. Let's just stay here, Quen, not go on to the Common. Do you mind?' He wouldn't have minded anything, all he ever asked was to be the one to take care of her.

They'd had no secrets . . . No, that wasn't true, he acknowledged, as the miles between them lessened. Perhaps he'd been a fool never to say to her all the things that filled his heart. But it hadn't needed saying, she must always have

143

known. When had he stopped loving her as a child? The day they'd set out for Christmas Common? No, before that even. For him, surely she'd ceased to be a child right from the first time he'd woken in the precious privacy of his cubicle bed at Merton Court, awoken powerless to hold back where his fleeting dream was carrying him. He'd known her and loved her through every stage as she'd come to adolescence. What if she knew now how night after night his fantasies were built around her? Would she understand? Would she be surprised? Would she tell him it was the same for her? No wonder those knives stabbed behind his eyes. Liz's life was so different now. Her letters came as regularly, but suppose she'd outgrown all their dreams and plans, suppose the sort of affection she felt for him was the same as she might feel for Paul or Christopher?

It was nearly Christmas, Quentin was on his way home. Normally he wouldn't have left the college until the following week, but he'd come early because tomorrow was Paul's wedding.

'Are you all right, man?' A gruff voice from opposite him and someone prodded his knee.

'Yes. Thank you, yes. It's just a bit warm.'

'Not out there, it isn't. Are you going far? All the way to London same as me?' His fellow traveller didn't look the sort to talk to strangers, a dapper little man wearing a pinstripe suit and a grey 'Anthony Eden' hat. The truth was he'd been watching the young man opposite him, seeing how even when his eyes were closed the lids twitched as if they were alive.

144

'No. I have to change at Oxford. We ought to be there in a few minutes.'

'Hot in here, did you say?' The lady with the fur collar gave an exaggerated shiver. 'These trains are an abomination, they cook one's legs and freeze one's back. You'll need to wrap up when you get out, young man.'

'I've half an hour to wait,' Quentin told them, suddenly glad that the long silence was broken. 'I just hope the buffet is open.'

He began to gather his things together: two cases and a carrier bag containing uneaten sandwiches given him by his landlady and more than half a Thermos of milky tea. The thought of it made him fear his migraine would end the way it so often did. He was thankful to hear a change in the rhythm of the train, they were slowing, in a minute he'd be in the mercifully cold, night air. Hardly seeing them through the haze of pain, he wished the three — plus still sleeping child — goodnight and stumbled on to the platform. Thank God, he took in the air in great gulps, just for a moment putting his cases down and holding onto a post. He would be all right, he was free, he was in the fresh air.

'Quen!' Was he dreaming? He looked round him, frightened to hope. 'Quen, I've been here ages,' Liz flung her arms round him. 'I've got a surprise for you. Come on. I'll take one of the cases. And what's this?' She screwed her nose up as she looked in the carrier bag. 'Looks pretty reasty, I'll ditch it in the bin over there, shall I?'

He was home. She was glad to see him. Already the knives weren't so sharp.

'Yes, chuck it. Oh, Liz, it's good to be back.'

She laughed delightedly. How funny he was; of course it was good to be back. And he didn't know yet just how good. Wait till he saw what she had to show him. She'd been very secretive about it, not told him a thing all these months.

'We've got a long time before the train, Liz. Are you warm enough out here? It may be crowded and smoky in the refreshment room.'

'Dad's car's outside. But he said I could come and watch for you to get off the train.' There now, she thought with satisfaction, that didn't give him a hint.

It wasn't until they got outside to the empty parked car that she could wait no longer.

'Haven't you guessed? Oh Quen, what a duffer you are! No Dad, no Mum. Just you and me! Now can't you see? Dad taught me to drive — well, sometimes it was Mum or even Paul — although he's so busy being in love that he hasn't had a lot of time. I passed my test last Monday.'

'Little Liz,' he put down his case and tilted her face up to his, 'little Liz driving a car.' He grinned — a rare thing that set her heart racing with excitement. For weeks she'd practised, wanting to drive for its own sake, but always striving towards this moment.

'Proud?' She needed to hear him say it, even that rare smile wasn't enough.

'Prouder than you know.' Opening the boot he put the two cases inside, then opened the driver's door for her. 'It seems I'm the only one still on a bicycle,' he chuckled.

'Oh, once you get home, I'll soon teach you. It's easy as wink.'

'Liz, I do love you.' The words were spoken even as he thought them.

But then so might he have spoken to an excitable younger sister. And was that how he meant her to hear them? Liz peered at him in the near darkness of the interior of the car.

'Do you?' There was a stillness about her. She spoke the two words quietly; silently she waited for his answer.

If he told her the truth, that she was his whole world, that everything he did was with the thought of the future he'd built his dreams on, would it build a barrier between them? Did she love him as a playmate, a brother, someone to bring her troubles to? Or did she long for them to be together, a man and a woman, sharing everything? When she thought of love, was it him she imagined? He tore off his spectacles and groped in his trouser pocket for a handkerchief.

Her hand was gloriously cold on his brow. Did she know how the devils of anxiety hammered his brain? He gripped her hand and carried it to his mouth.

'Yes, I love you,' he whispered, thankful to say the words. Whatever the outcome, he had to tell her. 'Liz, I love you with every fibre of my being.'

She'd been 'the little one' all her life, always left behind by all of them except him. But now she was an adult, she was the same as all of them. She could drive a car, she was learning a trade. But those things were nothing compared with falling in love. This put her on a par with

147

Paul — and Sylvia, who Liz had always suspected, had had a romantic affair with glamorous Richard McBride. Now it was *her* turn. She'd looked forward to this evening, to meeting Quen, to knowing she had someone of her own at home with her. But it was those words 'I love you with every fibre of my being' that filled her universe. In a minute he would kiss her, she knew he would. Not a brotherly peck, but a long, passionate kiss like she'd seen in films. Instead of switching on the engine, she wriggled round on the bench seat, moving as near him as she could despite the uncomfortable pressure of the gear stick on her leg.

'And me, Quen. I'm in love with you, too,' she breathed, her voice soft and beguiling to her own ears. Her mouth teased his, her lips slightly parted. Then, dropping his glasses in his haste, he took her in his arms. There were always people in the station forecourt, but she didn't care. She wanted the world to know. Quentin was in love with her.

They hardly spoke as they drove towards home. Neither wanted to break the spell by talking of anything outside the orbit of their new-found wonder. Just once she asked him, 'How long have you known — about loving me I mean?'

'I've always loved you.'

She was disappointed. Of course he'd always loved her, she'd known that as she'd led the way as they cycled along the narrow country lanes. But that was different. That was child's love.

'I mean — this sort of loving?' she prompted.

148

'Ages.' He swallowed an Adam's apple that seemed twice the size nature intended. 'I think about making love to you, Liz.' Would she understand what he was leaving unsaid? 'Where are you going?' His thoughts were interrupted by her turning the car on to the track of the old Roman road.

'Let's get out, Quen,' she said, braking to a halt. 'Let's stand here at the top of the world in the icy cold rain.'

It was his heart's turn to race with excitement. Who but his darling Liz would suggest such a thing, would know how he longed for fresh air?

The truth was, it wasn't the cold miserable winter night she wanted so much as the opportunity for him to hold her. This was proper, grown-up sexual love. Sometimes in the warmth of her bed she'd known an unnameable ache, a tingling that made her clench her teeth wanting something and not knowing what. But now she knew exactly what it was her body cried out for. And there, high on the Downs, the moonless sky dark under a blanket of cloud, fine rain blowing on them, she pressed herself close to him, her own desires heightened by triumph as with assumed innocence she moved against his erection.

'If it were summer, we could make love,' she whispered. 'I wish it were summer.' But summer was months away. In a few minutes they'd be home, back to a house where Paul was the centre of everyone's attention. She and Quentin would be just 'the young ones'. She wrapped her leg around his.

149

His headache had gone, lifted either by the fresh air or by so much less that filled his mind.

'It's what you want too, isn't it, Quen? Please say it. I want to hear.'

'That I want to make love to you? You know I do. Every night you haunt my dreams, always you, always you.'

Surely, she thought, this must be how all the great lovers have felt.

'Are you going to ask Dad?' Then with a chuckle that sounded just like the child she'd been, 'Not whether you can make love to me. I mean whether he will let us be properly engaged.'

'He'll say you're too young. But Liz, I know and you know, if he makes us wait until you're twenty-one even, there could never be anyone else for us but each other.'

Twenty-one! Three years' wait without even having a ring to wear!

'If he argues, just leave him to me,' she said with confidence. There had seldom been anything Liz had wanted that she hadn't managed to get. 'We'd better go, they'll wonder why we're so soaked.'

It was as they drove the last few miles to Highmoor that an idea came to her.

'Tomorrow, we could leave Mum and Dad and the others at the hotel. We could come on home. Dad will be fidgety about the teatime milking if only Fred is there.'

'Good idea. They mustn't come away until they've seen Paul and Philippa off.'

'No one at home but us. We'd just see Fred

150

was managing — not that he'll need us — and then . . . Oh, don't you see? It's what both of us want. If we — you know — made love I mean — then we'd really belong. And anyway if we told Dad we'd already been to bed, he would be bound to say yes. It would be just plain stupid, then, for him to say I'm too young to know my own mind. Anyway, I would have burnt my boats.'

He didn't answer.

'Quen . . . ?'

'No, Liz.'

'I bet Sylvia and Richard went to bed together — and Paul and Philippa too, always there in that place in Hendred Street. What else would they have been doing?'

'I expect they did. But Liz, this is *us*, not them. I want to love you as my wife, right from the start I want to know that we belong to each other.'

She pouted. It was too dark to see, but he knew she did.

'We'll persuade him, Liz. And by the end of next year I shall have finished in Scotland. We'll find a place together, build the glasshouses, watch all our plans take shape. Both of us, Liz. Always together.'

Perhaps she didn't answer because they'd come to a narrow part of the road and there was an oncoming car with full headlights. Slowing down she kept well to the left, concentrating. She mustn't let him guess her inexplicable feeling of disappointment. Was it simply that he wouldn't be tempted by her idea for tomorrow afternoon?

151

Or was it something to do with that 'Both of us . . . always together'? Somehow the picture it conjured up in her mind wasn't nearly as romantic as that magic hour she'd suggested. Another hundred yards and she turned into the lane to Highmoor. Trying to avoid the deep rain-filled ruts she concentrated, peering ahead.

★   ★   ★

As the following day worked out, her scheme would have come to naught in any case. The registry office ceremony was at half past eleven, so soon after a quarter to twelve they were out of the building and getting into the cars. Tim and Sue's wedding present had been a new car, a new Standard Eight. Not the most suitable vehicle for rough country roads perhaps, but it had been Paul's choice. A Land Rover would go with his new job, but as a second car (he thought of it as Phil's car) it was ideal. He liked to think that his choice had taken into consideration his parents' limited means, something he'd become so used to that it was second nature to him. So after the ceremony they set off to Upton Manor Hotel in convoy, the bridal couple leading the way with Christopher and Sylvia in the back. Next came Liz in the farm saloon, these days a Standard Vanguard, Quentin by her side and the Grands in the back. Following her came Tim and Sue in the well-hosed-down-for-the-occasion Land Rover, with Josh and Mrs Josh in the back, bedecked as if for Sunday Evensong. The family had no idea of Philippa's surprise that the old couple should be invited; it was something that all of them, including Paul, took for granted.

By midday the convoy had left the town behind and was moving steadily (for Paul, too, had one eye on Liz coming behind) along the Oxford Road towards Pangbourne. Then across the river at Streatley and on towards the Downs and Upton Manor. Long before one o'clock they were attacking their first course, if Philippa could ever be said to 'attack' her food. A rum sort of wedding, was Josh's opinion. The nearest to a speech was Tim raising his glass towards young Paul and his fancy teaching-lady and saying 'Bless you both'. Ah well, times changed. The boy looked as though he'd won the pools and, Josh supposed, that was more important than all the trimmings they seemed so set on doing without.

It was just before half past two when Tim signalled that he'd like the bill.

'I say, Dad, that's jolly good of you,' Paul leant across Philippa to whisper. 'We'd budgeted for it. Are you sure?' Suddenly Tim knew he was afraid to trust his voice. This really was the end, any minute Paul would be gone. No more easy companionship on the farm, no more loading the horses and going off to the hunt. He took the bill that was put down in front of him, glad to escape from the table to pay it. But leaving the well-fed party, still the memories came to him: the sturdy little lad who'd been his constant shadow, the lad so proud of his muscles as he'd rolled up his sleeves and taken his place on the tractor. His boy, his son . . . now he'd outgrown Highmoor. ' . . . didn't send me to college so that I could footle around on your patch the same as Fred Dawson' came the echo. So now he was going, he and that scrawny — No! He pulled his thoughts up sharply, she was the woman Paul loved. So all of them must love her, all of them must accept her as she was and not try to shape her to fit into their own mould.

The bill paid, he found they were all coming out from the restaurant. Hiding behind a smile he led the way outside to the car park.

The drive home was more crowded: Sylvia made a third on the back seat of the Vanguard, while in the Land Rover Sue squeezed in between the Joshes so that Christopher could sit in front with Tim. Surely after a wedding there should have been a lingering feeling of festivity. They all tried, but their main feeling was one of loss. Through the years as they'd looked to the future, none of them had ever considered the possibility of Paul leaving Highmoor. It had been just as much home for the twins, but they'd always known they would flit the nest, sure that it was always there for them to come back to. And Liz? Well, she wasn't likely to stay single and at home for ever. Quentin? Not really family, but none of them thought of him as anything less. He had grand plans of his own. But Paul was a natural born farmer. No wonder Tim was so quiet as they drove home.

★ ★ ★

'It's going to put a lot more work on Mr Tim,' Mrs Josh said the next morning when she brought a basket of fresh-picked sprouts to the house. 'Josh would give his eye teeth — well, leastways he would if he had any to give — ' she added with a chortle, 'to be more useful. I'll tell you the trouble with being young, Mrs Tim duckie, it fills your head with ambition. We used to have it ourselves once, more years ago than I care to count. We dreamt of having a place of our own, not taking a wage for what we did. But there you are, we don't always know what's best. I often think, how would it have been if we'd gone out after some smallholding of our own? Lonely, that's how it would have been. There we were, young, dreaming of a place of our own to bring up a family. But it wasn't to be. We weren't blessed with children of our own,' she tipped the sprouts into a bowl as she talked, her expression one of complete contentment with her lot, 'instead you came along and took Highmoor from old Mr Marshall. Life works into its own pattern, and a pretty one it turns out to be. You'll find that, my dear. Don't fret about your Paul. You'll see it's all working to a purpose.'

'Highmoor belonged to him, though, Mrs Josh, or it will do one of these days. Yet he'd rather be somewhere else, paid for his labours, lining someone else's pocket. If he doesn't want Highmoor, what are we doing it for? It's a family farm. Before Tim's uncle there was *his* father, before that his father's father, now Tim — but Paul will never come back to a small farm even if it's his own.'

155

'Now then, Mrs Tim, don't you let me hear you talk in that tone. What are you doing it for, indeed! Not for Paul, no nor for Liz either. You and Mr Tim are doing what you do for each other and because to throw in the towel you'd be failing yourselves. Now then, I've got a few minutes on my hands, duckie. I'll just get these sprouts done so they'll be ready for the pot when you come home from church. Pretty well time you got your hat unless you're going to follow the choir in. Is there anything else you want seeing to while you're out? I see the young ones are outside with Mr Tim, all looking spruce.'

'Bless you, Mrs Josh.' And she didn't mean just because of the sprouts. 'You always make me feel better.'

'Easy enough sometimes, m'dear, to let something throw you. I dare say she wasn't the girl you would have chosen for him — no, don't tell me, best say nothing. You're feeling disappointed at the way things have gone. But don't lose sight of the things that matter, Mrs Tim. Look at them out there, look at Mr Tim and the way they're all around him. They're not going to let him feel put down. For all the world it's as if they're telling him how important he is to all of them. Ah, and that he is. To all of us. So, if young Paul wants to find pastures new, well, there's nowt anyone can do. Except be here for him always to come home to.'

'What would we do without you — you and Josh?'

A throaty chuckle as the old countrywoman set to work on the sprouts. 'Get along with you, child. Go and put your hat on. Now where are they going? The young ones are starting without you.'

'Tim's taking the car. The Grands are coming as well this morning.'

'And quite right too. Our young Paul may not have made his vows in church, but it behoves all of us to have a word with his Maker on his behalf, ask that He'll keep an eye on the boy.'

★   ★   ★

'Sue,' Tim looked into the sitting room where she was leaning over Lucinda's latest jigsaw puzzle while Harold snored gently from his usual fireside chair. 'Can you give me a hand a moment?'

'Is something wrong?'

'No. It's just I need an extra hand,' he lied.

'Yes, I'll come. I'll be back, Aunt Luce, don't finish it without me.' Then, the door closed behind her. 'A hand, Tim? Has the milking machine packed in?'

'No. We're in the office — Quen, Liz and me. The others are still out tramping about somewhere. Sue, Quen wants them to get engaged. She's too young. But you know Liz, when she has her mind set on something.'

'They're both too young. But when you're that age you feel old enough for everything. He's always loved Liz, you know he has.'

'She's all he's known. Anyway, you come and hear what they have to say.'

He ushered her into the unheated office, lit

with the power of the one unshaded bulb.

How young they both looked standing hand in hand, facing the door like two culprits facing a judge.

'Mum, make Dad see sense,' Liz greeted her. 'He talks as though I were a baby. I'm not. And I know what I want. We both do. Don't we, Quen? You tell her.'

'What I want,' Quen said, no sign of nerves in his voice, 'what I've always wanted, is to be with Liz. This is nothing new, Aunt Sue, you know that. Everything I've planned, everything I mean to do, it's all for Liz — she *must* be part of it.'

Sue nodded. How dear Quentin was to her, as dear as her own children. He was so sure of his love, she was sure of it too. But Liz? Was she mature enough to know what she was promising? Suppose they were engaged and then Liz got tired of him, found someone else? Even with your own children, you can have no idea of what goes on deep in their hearts. Look at Paul . . . no, forget Paul, this is Liz you're thinking about.

'Please yourselves anyway,' this was Liz at her most difficult, her parents knew all the signs. 'If you say no, then it won't make any difference. Well, it will. It will mean I don't wear a ring and no one will know there's anyone special in my life — other men, I mean. I want everyone to know that I'm going to marry Quen. And if you say no, it won't alter anything else. You won't always be able to stop us.'

'You've neither of you met anyone else — '

'For myself, I know there will never be anyone

else,' Quentin was as solemn as that owl-like child they'd first taken into their home.

'Neither will there be for me,' Liz took both Tim's hands in hers, looking at him beseechingly with her huge blue eyes. 'Once Christmas is over he will be going back. Please Dad. We've already made our promises so you can't change any of that. So what's the point of making us wait until I'm twenty-one? Would be just stupid. Nothing's going to change, so why not say yes now?'

Tim and Sue looked at each other, sending and reading a silent message.

'There's no one we would prefer for a son,' he said. 'So what do you say, lady? Do we give them our blessing now or make them wait?'

Sue's answer was to go to Quentin, her arms wide.

'I'll take care of her always, I promise you I will.'

Sue didn't doubt it. She looked at starry-eyed Liz and asked herself why she had this feeling of doubt.

'Taking care is a two-way thing,' she said. Then, kissing Liz, 'Good times and bad, make sure you take care of each other.'

'Oh Mum, what a gloomy way of giving us your congratulations.'

Liz had asked for some time off during the following week. But all she'd been allowed was one day, the Monday. Just prior to Christmas she was lucky to get even that. She'd wanted to be free because Quen would be home, but she'd never imagined the day would take the form it did. Beside herself with excitement and importance, she again borrowed the Vanguard so that she and Quentin could go to Reading. He insisted that before they went to the jeweller they would buy the things Sue had written on her shopping list. That done, the day was their own. She found it hard to look casual as the tray of diamond solitaires was brought out. In November Quentin had celebrated his twenty-first birthday, if opening the packages that had come through the post — even including a cheque from his father — could be called a celebration. It had been a milestone. The sole beneficiary of his grandfather's estate, he was a young man of considerable means.

'Which do you like best, Liz?'

'They're all ever so expensive,' she whispered as the assistant turned to bring another selection from the window.

'Good,' Quen told her. 'I want it to be wonderful.'

She swelled with pride. The day was turning out to be even more wonderful than she'd dreamt. They made their choice and she gazed at her hand in pride and disbelief. None of the family, absolutely none of them, had ever had a ring like this. It was hard to keep her face in control and stop her mouth turning into a broad smile as she watched the manly way Quen took out his cheque book and spent a fortune as if he did it every day.

* * *

Never before had the centre of the stage belonged to Liz. Folk from towns might believe life in the country moves at a slow pace — but that couldn't be said of the passage of news of Liz Marshall's engagement. Before she'd worn that beautiful diamond ring for twenty-four hours it seemed there wasn't a person who hadn't heard. The Kimbers drove over from Merton Court to congratulate Quentin and, if secretly they marvelled that he could have won the heart of lively and attractive Liz, their manner gave no hint of it. Bert Hamilton, the elderly farmer from Silverdale, made a point of calling: 'Just the excuse I needed to come and give the lassie a kiss,' he said with a saucy wink. 'And as for you, young man, I hope you realise you're stealing away the prettiest little gal in the district.' The Joshes were overjoyed, to their way of thinking it was a match made in heaven.

Tuesday morning the workroom of the florists where Liz was training in Reading was abuzz with the news. The ring was admired, Liz was led on to talk about their plans for the future. She'd never felt so important. Sylvia had gone back to London to the hospital where she would be on duty during part of Christmas, and Christopher, whose leave would last until after New Year, had gone with her. Only Quentin was left behind at Highmoor, making himself useful where he could but aware of his own inadequacies compared with Paul. Even though Liz would have loved to have been at home on the farm too, the fact that she had to work did have its good side. Didn't it show just how necessary she was? A lifetime of being the youngest, the one expected to tag along in the shadow of the others, had left its scar.

★ ★ ★

If on Christmas Day Paul felt a tug of nostalgia for the atmosphere of home, the smell of the tall tree, the annual sight of the banisters entwined with holly and ivy, he didn't give it room to settle. Naturally enough, as he'd carved their home-bred capon he'd remembered the laden table at Highmoor, he'd almost believed he could hear 'Three cheers for the cook' as his mother brought in the rich pudding, dark with hours of long cooking and an excess of alcohol. He'd loved every hour, each year the magic had been the same. But that was the past. He'd moved on. If Liz felt full of her own importance, that was nothing by comparison.

'I'll give them a call at home, make sure they're behaving without me. Then we ought to go for a long walk,' he said as he dried the last dish.

Philippa shivered. 'Have you looked outside? It's perishing. Why should we want to go anywhere?'

'Don't know that I do exactly want to. I suppose I suggested it because that's what we usually did on Christmas afternoon. What about you? What used you to do on Christmas afternoon?'

'Much the same as any other. Read or maybe watch television but that's never anything very interesting. When you're on your own it's a difficult time of year.' Her greenish eyes were watching him; when he reached his hand towards hers she entwined her fingers in his, rubbing her thumb on the palm of his hand. 'But this year is different. Let's not go out.'

His mouth suddenly seemed dry. Was she meaning what he thought she was meaning? He carried her hand to his mouth and, as he kissed the palm, she slipped her thumb between his parted lips, moving it in a way that set his pulses racing. No, they wouldn't go out.

'Put another log on the fire,' she whispered, then drawing away from him closed the curtains even though it was no more than two o'clock. His phone call was forgotten. The fire blazed up the chimney, the sheepskin hearthrug was their magic carpet.

At Highmoor Liz and Quentin went for the ritual walk, coming back rosy-cheeked (and red-nosed) just before four o'clock. Harold donned the Santa Claus outfit just as he had each year ever since he and Lucinda had first spent Christmas with the family; Tim took the gifts off the tree and told him who to give them to.

Everything had been opened and the screwed-up wrappings collected in the waste-paper basket when the telephone rang.

'Ah!' Tim shot to his feet, a sign to all of them just how anxiously he'd been waiting for the call. They all pretended not to have noticed.

'If it's Paul, call me to say hello before you ring off,' Sue purposely didn't go with him to the

163

hall where the instrument was fixed to the wall. No one spoke after he'd gone, probably because they were all straining their ears to listen. When he said, 'I'll call your mother,' she needed no calling.

'Happy Christmas, Paul darling.'

'And you, Mum.'

'What have you been doing?' It was as well she couldn't see his expression as he heard the question. Or was it? Wouldn't it have reassured her about her son and this woman they saw as cold and unbending?

'I've been telling Dad about everything here. He'll fill you in. Mum, get Quentin and Liz to the phone, will you, I think they need a word from the voice of experience.'

Tim was already struggling into his duffle coat.

'My old ladies are waiting for me. They have no respect for Christmas.' It was already past milking time.

'I'll put my coat on and come too,' Sue said. She hadn't helped with the milking for years, but this afternoon it seemed natural for them to go together. The 'young ones' were talking on the phone, the 'old ones' (the Grands and the Joshes) were dozing by the fire. Pulling the hood over her head she walked by Tim's side to the milking shed.

'You're a good lady,' he told her, giving her hand a brief squeeze. 'With two of us, we'll soon get done.'

'And by the time we get back one of the others will have made the tea. I put the cake out ready — a sort of hint,' she laughed.

Philippa would have been horrified. After the enormous meal they'd eaten at one o'clock, they couldn't possibly have needed Christmas cake! And certainly not the cold home-reared beef and home-cured ham that would follow later in the evening. Philippa had Paul's welfare firmly in hand.

* * *

On the 2nd of January Quentin returned to Scotland and life settled back into its normal routine. It was during the second week of that bitterly cold month, on a morning when Sue was cooking the usual robust breakfast ready for when Tim came back from the early milking session. The Grands weren't breakfast eaters, they took their time getting up and never appeared until Liz had gone for her train, Tim had been fed and evidence of the meal been cleared away.

'You're soon back,' Sue said as she heard the lobby door open.

'Sue — '

At the sound of his voice she turned from the large pan of sizzling bacon. Do hearts really miss a beat? The shock of seeing him was like a physical impact.

'Tim, what have you done?' Fish slice still in her hand she went to him, taking his arm and guiding him as if he were a blind man to the rocking chair by the range. 'Have you hurt yourself? Are you ill?' Words tumbled from her.

'Damned silly. Just couldn't . . . couldn't . . . '
He leant back, closing his eyes.

'Liz! Liz!' She must have run into the hall, for she found herself out there, shouting as Liz ran down the stairs. Then both of them were back with Tim, helpless as they waited for him to tell them.

6

Whatever trouble had come their way, there was a practical streak in Sue that had never failed. Yet looking at Tim there was no logic in her thinking. He couldn't be ill! Not Tim! He'd gone out to the milking shed exactly the same today as every other morning.

'Be better . . . minute,' he mumbled. 'Indigestion . . . can't shift . . . '

She chaffed his cold hand, the left hand, for the clenched fist of the other was pressed against his chest, moving as if he were trying to break the pain that gripped him. They'd eaten nothing since the previous evening; why should he get such dreadful indigestion after all these hours? She wriggled her own hand between him and the back of the chair, working it in an upward movement reminiscent of when she used to 'wind' the babies. Even though he opened his eyes she knew she was no nearer to helping him. It was as if every ounce of strength had left him. Then she saw a change; his eyes closed, his jaw tensed, but there was no escaping.

The doctor . . . she must get the doctor . . .

But Liz was ahead of her. If Sue had been knocked off balance by the sight of Tim, then Liz's reaction was no less. She'd never known her father to have so much as a day's illness. Now not only was something very wrong but almost more frightening was the helpless, lost look on her mother's face. Over the last few weeks Liz had thought of nothing but herself — unless it was herself and Quentin. She'd delighted in her new role as a fully fledged grownup. But in that brief moment as she saw her parents, Tim looking frighteningly strange and Sue, for the first time in Liz's memory, not able to see what had to be done, Liz took a great leap across the threshold into adulthood.

Sue heard her voice on the telephone, she knew it must have been a call to the doctor's house for as early as this he wouldn't have gone to his surgery.

The door from the lobby opened and Josh came in.

'I knew something was up — looked out o' the bedroom window and saw him in the light from the milking shed. Leaning against the doorpost, he was. Couldn't seem to hardly stand. Got my things on quick as I could.' Then to Tim, 'Don't you worry now, old son, we'll keep things going while you rest up.' At Tim's lack of response he felt no more use than Sue. 'Sent for the doctor have you, duckie? Reckon we ought to get him to have a look.'

Sue was ashamed of the burning sting of tears. Josh's protective care of them had never failed.

'He's on his way, Josh.' It was Liz who answered.

'Good gal. Now then, best way I can help is to get back over to the shed and see to the milking.' It was years since the old man had actively helped on the farm. Did he even understand how to use the electric milking machine? 'Don't you worry about the outside jobs,' he laid his gnarled hand on Sue's head as she knelt by Tim, 'me and a milking herd are no strangers. We managed well enough all my days without all these new-fangled contraptions.'

'I'll help you, Josh. I know about the machine,' Liz told him. 'I'll watch out for the doctor's car, Mum,' she added as she dragged her coat on and followed him.

'You'll miss your train. You've not had your breakfast.' Was Sue just making a crazy clutch at normality, or did she really expect Liz to treat the day as normal? Either way, her remark didn't get an answer as the girl closed the lobby door behind her. There was only the vaguest hint of daylight, she could just see the outline of Josh's bent figure ahead of her as she hurried to catch him.

'You don't think it's anything serious, do you, Josh?' She needed her old friend's reassurance.

'We're not up in medical things, my duckie, we must wait and see what Dr Hammond makes of him. Between ourselves, I've said to my Ada more than once, these last weeks he's been working every hour — harder than he need if you ask me. Misses the boy and won't stand still long enough to own up to his disappointment. That would be what I'd say has made his insides make him stop and rest. That's just between you, me and these old milking ladies. Now, you'd better get showing me how to use this modern nonsense. It's al'ays seemed to me, the good Lord gave us people good hands same as he gave cows their udders, nice and easy to get the milk flowing. But not fast enough for today's world. That's the pity, child, everyone's in such a rush these days. Nature ain't good enough for them.'

'You're probably right, Josh. I *can* milk by hand. Well, you remember how I learnt when I was just a kid. But today time really is important. Even if the doctor gives Dad something to take the pain away, I shall phone work and tell them I shan't be in. That's right, isn't it? I shan't go to Reading today, I shall stay here, give Mum a bit of support.'

In part, she was speaking the truth. It took the doctor no time to recognise that what Tim was suffering had nothing to do with indigestion and to send for an ambulance. But it took longer for the ambulance to get to the farm.

'Here, child, put your arms in your coat,' Mrs Josh followed the procession that moved out to the vehicle that stood in the yard, its door open. First the stretcher bearers, then Sue with Liz. Somehow she steered Sue's arms into the sleeves of her coat, Tim was hoisted on board, Sue climbed in after him. Standing in the lobby, wrapped in their winter dressing gowns and looking older and more frail than anyone had time to notice, Harold and Lucinda watched.

'I'll come in the car, Mum, then I can drive you both home,' Liz shouted as the doors slammed shut.

The ambulance moved slowly off, the driver turning into the frost-hardened lane and trying to avoid the ruts. Progress was slow until they reached the main road. From there on he put his foot hard on the accelerator, the bell clanged to warn traffic that an emergency vehicle needed right of way. Sue watched Tim, frightened to hope, frightened not to hope. It was like a nightmare that had no end, no waking up in a dark bedroom with racing heart and the relief of normality. She wanted to pray, but even prayer needed concentration she couldn't grasp.

Liz had said she would follow in the car but before she left home she had phone calls to make. First she rang to explain that she wouldn't be at work. Next she looked in the telephone pad to find Paul's number so recently given to them. He wasn't at home, but she told Philippa what had happened.

'I'm off into Truro,' Philippa said, 'it's an ideal day to go because I know Paul won't be home until late afternoon. But, don't worry, I'll leave a note telling him about Tim' (from Mr and Mrs Marshall they had become Tim and Sue. Philippa had said with her usual outspoken honesty that having managed most of her life without a Mum and Dad she was too old to acquire them now) 'just in case he gets home first. I'm sure he'll ring as soon as he hears.'

Her response had left Liz feeling alone and unsupported. So she put through a long-distance call to Quentin. She knew there was nothing either he or Paul could do, but she needed to hear a voice, to know that they cared as much as she did. Then, ignoring minor details like ruts in the lane, she set off as fast as she could, hoping to catch up with the ambulance before it reached the hospital. Of course she didn't succeed, for she had no bell to clear the way ahead of her.

Over the river at Streatley, on through Goring and Pangbourne, with very little to hinder her. By the time she came to the outskirts of the busy town, the morning traffic made progress slow. But at last she turned in at the gates of the hospital, followed the signs to the visitors' car park. Where would they have taken him? She looked around at her unfamiliar surroundings, not knowing where to start. But today she had to make herself think rationally, it was up to her to do the thinking for her mother. So she went in search of the main entrance, sure that's where she would be given directions.

Calm thinking paid dividends, for in minutes she was by Sue's side in a waiting room.

'Where is he?' How funny it was that you felt you had to whisper, almost like talking in church or in the public library.

'They've taken him for tests or something. I don't know. They rushed him off. They told me to wait here. I don't know where they've taken him.'

Liz was glad she was here even though she could think of nothing to say that would take that bemused look off her mother's face.

'Perhaps it'll be nothing serious, Mum. Perhaps they'll X-ray him and say it's nothing to worry about. He's been miserable about Paul, he's hidden behind working too hard.' The idea wasn't her own, but there was no need to go into details. 'I phoned the boys, Paul and Quen, I mean. I didn't know how to phone Christo. Anyway, I don't want them to think there's anything to get alarmed about. There won't be,

Mum. He probably just needs to rest — or have a nasty dose of something unpleasant to shift whatever's upset him.' For her own sake as much as her mother's she tried to sound bright, to hang on to hope.

'No. Tim's ill. Not just 'not well'. He's ill. Feel so helpless. Can't think , , , '

Liz slipped her hand into Sue's. She wanted the comfort of some sort of answering pressure, but Sue didn't seem so much as aware of the contact. All around them there was activity: a screaming child was brought in, a man with his arm in a makeshift sling and blood seeping through an unprofessional-looking bandage, a pregnant woman who had slipped on the pavement, a motor cyclist brought from an ambulance on a stretcher. Other people's troubles, other people's tragedies; yet they felt they saw it all through the wrong end of a telescope. A nurse told them they could get refreshments at the WVS stand in the vestibule so Liz went to fetch them each a cup of tea and a Chelsea bun.

'That's all they had, Mum. Nothing easier to eat.'

'Liz, what can they be doing? All this time — has something gone wrong?'

'I expect everyone is having to wait ages. Try and eat, Mum. We had no breakfast and Dad'll want to know you've had something.'

Like an obedient child Sue bit into her bun. It was only then that she realised how hungry she was. Their wait wasn't over and it was afternoon before they were told which ward

173

he'd been taken to. Following the coloured line painted in the corridor they found their way and were greeted by a young probationer nurse who said the Sister would like to speak to Mrs Marshall.

'This is our daughter, she can come with me.' Sue's instinct today more than ever was to keep the family together; she ignored the probationer's uncertainty.

'Mrs Marshall,' the Sister greeted them with all the charm of a social hostess. 'Do come in both of you. You'll be Mr Marshall's daughter, perhaps?' to Liz.

Relieved, the probationer scurried off to face her next hurdle. Only two weeks into her training, each day was fraught with pitfalls. That morning she'd been allowed to shave an elderly and difficult patient, not a happy experience especially as she'd managed to let the razor nick his chin. Being an angel of mercy seemed an interminable way off. So far her learning hadn't gone beyond how to push a bedpan under a recumbent body, how to clean it in the sluice room, how to wash dentures and replace them, how to rub backs and bottoms to avoid bed sores. In everything she learnt there was a right way and — always so much easier — a wrong. At least she seemed to have done no wrong in allowing Mrs Marshall's daughter to hear what Sister had to say.

And what they were told, sitting facing the good-looking and charming Sister, was what deep in their hearts both of them had known and yet been scared to suggest. Tim's indigestion had been a heart attack.

'He is very much better — '

'Better?' Sue suddenly sat straight in the stiff-backed chair. 'He's going to be all right?' She held her trembling lip between her teeth, frightened to trust her voice.

'He has been very lucky. Sometimes it happens like this, a mild coronary can act as a warning. Of course we shall need to keep him in hospital for a while.'

'Yes, yes, of course. But he's going to be well again?' She wanted to hear it said, here in the hospital where illness and death were a part of life.

'Certainly he has pulled through this, but we shall keep him monitored for a few days. He needs bed rest and I'm afraid he'll have to adjust his lifestyle. Dr Meredith has been talking to him. I understand he farms, does a good deal of the heavy work himself.'

'You mean he won't be able . . . ' Sue's voice trailed into silence.

'This attack must be seen as a warning, Mrs Marshall. But I've known cases where, with the right diet, the help of medication and, of course, a guard against physical strain, patients can adjust to lead long and happy lives. Today has been a shock, to all of you. But the time will come when you will be thankful it happened, for not every coronary has a happy ending, as you must know.'

'You've been very kind,' Sue heard herself say. 'May I see him?'

'Just for two or three minutes. He mustn't be

allowed to get excited — agitated — you understand?'

'Of course I understand.' As if she would say anything to worry him! 'Is he in the main ward?'

'Oh no, that won't be for some days. He needs one-to-one nursing. But you may have a moment with him on your own. Don't talk to him about the future, not at this stage.' Then with a smile, 'Progress is always quicker and longer lasting if the patient avoids worry.'

'I'll wait in the corridor, Mum. Tell him I'm here to drive you home, but you go in on your own.'

★　★　★

It seemed she had only just settled on the bench at the end of the corridor when Sue reappeared.

'I told him I'd come again in the morning.'

'Does he look better?'

'I must bring his own things. He's wearing a sort of night-shirt that belongs to the hospital. He hasn't been shaved. They said I can come at any time. Any time, Liz. But only stay a few minutes. That'll worry him, knowing they won't let me sit with him. I wouldn't talk. Just be there.'

'Did he look better, Mum?' Liz repeated.

'Sort of nightshirt. Why didn't I think this morning and bring his pyjamas? Got no toothbrush.' She needed to find petty worries, they protected her from the shock of seeing him looking so ill. 'I'll drive home, Liz. I want to. I'd rather.' Of course she'd rather. Driving took her

176

concentration, and that's what Tim would want. She had to be strong for Tim. Later she'd think, later she'd worry about the future. But for the time it took to drive home she could keep her fears at bay.

When they arrived Lucinda was anxiously watching out of the window.

'Has Paul rung?' Liz greeted her. 'Is he home yet?'

'No. But Philippa called. How is he? Are they having to keep him in overnight? Oh dear, poor boy. He won't like that at all. Josh and Fred saw to the afternoon milking. But dear Josh is an old man, Sue. How long do you think Tim will be?'

'Quite a few days, Aunt Luce.' Sue couldn't bring herself to say any more than that. And at that moment she was saved by the shrill ringing of the telephone bell.

'Mum? Paul here. Is it serious? Phil spoke to Gran and she didn't seem to know anything. What did they tell you at the hospital?'

This time Sue hid nothing. Paul was their rock. Perhaps if he'd not gone away this wouldn't have happened.

'I say, Mum,' his concern was apparent as she came to the end of all the Sister had told her, 'that's just about the devil. I wish he'd got someone in before I left. That's what he ought to have done. Even if he decides to pack it in, he can't let the place go to pot while he's looking for a buyer.'

She couldn't believe what she was hearing.

'It's *now* we need someone, Paul. Josh and Fred — '

'Josh! Oh, poor old chap, Mum, he's way past it.'

'No one is past it if they care enough. And Josh certainly cares.'

'Yes, he's great, he always has been. I say, Mum, I wish there was something I could do. But just starting here, well I can hardly ask for time off to come and hold the fort till you can get another chap. You won't need a proper manager, not like I am here, handling accounts and the lot. Once Dad's home, even if he can't do anything heavy, he'll probably enjoy doing the paperwork. But I do feel bad about being so useless. He didn't suggest I could ask for time anyway, did he? No, of course he wouldn't, he'd see how impossible it would be after less than a month.'

'No, of course he didn't. He wasn't actually in a fit state to talk about anything.'

'Crumbs. Poor old Dad. Give him my love, Mum, in the morning, won't you. What ward is it? I'll drop him a line.'

On that day there was no fire in the sitting room, they were all congregated in the kitchen. When she went back from her telephone call all she told them was how concerned Paul was, how he wished he could be there to help. Beyond that, she wouldn't even let herself think.

★   ★   ★

During the night there was nowhere to hide, though. Tim's side of the bed was cold and empty, moving to the middle the expanse of space all round her was even worse. They hadn't told him yet that he had to change his lifestyle; she must be the one to tell him, it was something they must face together. But, there alone, she couldn't bring herself to imagine the moment, to think of the words she'd used to lessen the blow. As if there could be any way of lessening it! What a moment to imagine Philippa and her critical view of the meals at Highmoor. Had she been right? Sue piled the blame on herself, in her misery she had to blame someone and who else was there? She believed sleep was impossible but, in fact, she cat-napped, waking with a start of realisation all too frequently. At about half past five she was woken by something else, yet she wasn't sure what. Listening in the stillness of the house, she felt sure she'd heard something. Yes, there it was again. It sounded as though someone were raking the ashes in the range. Liz must be up, probably thinking she'd go out early to help Fred and Josh. Poor Liz, yesterday had been hard for her too. Easier to think of Liz than remember that sick feeling of disappointment when she'd listened to Paul. Yet he was right, of course he was right. He couldn't possibly expect to be given time off to come and run Highmoor. But 'find a buyer' for Highmoor. This was a family farm, Tim was fourth generation — even though it had been inherited from an uncle — there had been Marshalls at Highmoor for more than a hundred years. Paul's voice echoed, there was no escaping. So she got out of bed and put on her slippers and thick dressing gown. She and Liz would make a cup of tea, they'd give up the pretence of sleep.

There was no need to put on any lights as she crept down the stairs, the last thing she wanted was to disturb Lucinda and Harold. She could see a shaft of light under the kitchen door. Poor Liz, and she'd been so happy these last weeks. Silently Sue lifted the latch of the kitchen and pushed it just wide enough to slip inside.

'I woke you. Aunt Sue, I tried to be quiet. How is he? What's the news?'

'Quentin! You've come home!' She bit hard on the corners of her trembling mouth. He must have been travelling for hours . . . their dear Quentin . . . 'He'll be in hospital for a few days yet.' Soon she'd tell him the whole truth, but seeing him so unexpectedly had robbed her of the armour of control she'd been so determined to find.

Always sensitive, he knew she'd want to be strong. So, giving her a moment to get herself in hand, he turned back to the range and gave the smouldering coals one last rake.

'I know I can't compare with Paul, but I thought he'd not feel so bad at not being able to walk away from his new job if he knew I was here.'

'Quentin, what about your course? What about your own studies?'

'First things first.' Then his face broke into one of his rare, broad smiles. 'We'll keep things afloat for him, don't you worry.' And knowing the 'him' to be Tim, she felt new hope. It was as if a shaft of sunlight had forced its way through the leaden sky. 'You, Liz, me, the Joshes and Fred, between us, Aunt Sue, we'll make sure he knows we're keeping things going until he is fit again.'

She shook her head.

'There's so much I have to tell you. Quentin, you don't know how glad I am you've come.'

For him it was a unique moment. The people who meant more to him than anything in his world were turning to him for support. If during the previous day Liz had taken a giant stride to adulthood, now it was in knowing their need of him that Quentin found the confidence that had always eluded him.

'You must be starved. When did you leave the college?'

'As soon as Liz phoned yesterday morning. I got the first train to London, but it was nearly midnight by the time I got there. I travelled to Reading with the morning papers — and the post I suppose. And the same on to Brindley.'

'And walked from the station at that hour.' Her motherly instinct was to touch him, to hug him as she used to when he was the lonely and insecure child she'd first known. But today she sensed his need to be the one to be relied on. 'Of course you're starved. You must be.'

'Tell you the truth, I am. At that time of night I couldn't find anything open, just chocolate machines, you know. Funny time of morning to fancy it, but I'd love a huge hunk of bread and cheese.' At the thought of crusty home-made bread spread thickly with butter and a hunk of cheese, his stomach rumbled emptily. The one-time scrawny child had grown into a thin and wiry-looking young man despite his more than healthy appetite. Now, while Sue made a pot of tea, he collected his food from the larder, digging his strong teeth into the crust even before he got the plate to the table.

Then, and thankfully, she told him everything she knew.

* * *

With each day Tim grew stronger, the shock of what had happened receding. But the path wasn't smooth, for the more like himself he felt the more he worried about the responsibilities that had been thrown on the others.

'You're in the right place.' Sue greeted him with a laugh and exaggerated shiver as she came to his bedside and bent to kiss him. 'Talk about cold as charity! Quentin had a job to break the ice on the troughs this morning.' Immediately she wished she hadn't said it; she could see his quick, worried frown.

'The boy has his own life. Sue, how long are they going to keep me stuck in here? I'm not an invalid. I walk to the washroom, I sit in the day room if I want to. I need to get home. Things are piling up. Why did he have to leave us?' And she knew he meant Paul.

'We're keeping abreast, honestly, Tim. The ground's too hard for working. You'd be proud of the way we manage your ladies.' She tried to make a joke of it, sick with fright at the agitated look on his face, the nervous tic at the side of his mouth. Always the rock they all depended on, what had this last week done to him? She'd driven to Reading determined that this would be the day she told him that they must make changes, even though she couldn't imagine what those changes could be that would leave him feeling whole. Now she knew he wasn't ready. Perhaps tomorrow . . .

Two days later she brought him home and still the right moment hadn't been found.

It was as they drove along the Oxford Road out of town that he said, 'Dr Meredith gave it to me straight this morning. Sue, I had a close shave.'

'I know, Tim.' She took her hand off the steering wheel and covered his, that lay limp at his side. 'We've been frightened, all of us. But we have to learn to be grateful. That's what Sister Wilkins told me that first day. This has been a warning. Now, if we don't break the rules, it won't happen again. They've given me a diet sheet.' Even without looking at her, he knew her laugh was forced and unnatural. 'You're not going to like it.'

'The farm — he told me I can't go on as I was. He suggested getting a manager. Sue, I don't know what to do. It's as if the bottom's dropped out of our lives.'

'No!' There was nothing unnatural this time in her response. 'No, it hasn't. But it nearly did. Listen to me, Tim Marshall, it's not up to us to grizzle, it's up to us to say thank God. I've never been so frightened — '

'Nor I.'

'But it's behind us now. We'll look forward, make ourselves face what we have to face

— managers, diets, as if any of those things matter. We ought to have advertised for another man before Paul went.'

'My fault. I just . . . ' Just what? She didn't dig.

When they arrived home Mrs Josh had prepared a meal, beef stew, dumplings, mashed potatoes, home-grown root vegetables and sprouts. Surely there was nothing in that to hurt him? Even so, Sue took no pleasure in watching him eat. How much of his troubles had been *her* fault?

Afterwards she persuaded him to go and talk to Lucinda and Harold in the sitting room.

'They've been so worried, poor old dears. It was hard on them because there was nothing extra they could do and feel they were helping you. We others got a sort of kick out of keeping things going.' Sue spoke briskly, some of her characteristic optimism coming back as she saw him in his natural surroundings again. 'Go and give the old dears a few minutes while I clear these things.'

'I ought to go outside and see what Quentin is up to. Sue, it worries me, he ought not to be giving his time to Highmoor.'

She didn't answer immediately and, when she did, he knew she spoke honestly. This wasn't a thought-out answer, made to give him peace of mind.

'It was so dear of him to come. I don't think I've ever been so thankful as that first morning coming down to find him here. But since then I've seen something else, Tim. Helping us has

184

done more for Quentin than any academic achievements could. A bit like Liz. They've suddenly grown up.'

'He's a good lad.'

'He's more than that. Hark! That's the front door. Word must have got around that you're home.' She hurried to answer it to find a delivery van outside. A dozen bottles of malt whisky and a handwritten card: 'A dram a day keeps the doctor away. My thoughts are with you. Richard.' Now how could he have known? Quentin? Sylvia? the question remained unanswered in Sue's mind. As for Tim, he was touched by the thought behind the gift but, lacking Sue's feminine eye for romance, felt no such curiosity.

'I'll go and have a word with the Grands,' he said. 'But later I want to give Quentin a hand. It's not right for him to have to tackle the milking on his own.'

'He'll think you don't trust him,' Sue clutched an excuse from out of the air. But, in fact, when she went to join the others in the sitting room Lucinda signalled for her not to make a noise. One either side of the fireplace Harold and Tim were asleep. That was the customary way for Harold to spend his afternoons. The grey afternoon brought an early dusky, icy rain running down the window panes and still Tim slept. By the time he stirred Quentin had dealt with his ladies. All the animals had been fed and stables, sties and barns cleaned. That each day the work at Highmoor was done willingly and no corners cut was a tribute to Tim and to the affection and respect they all had, from the Joshes and Fred to the family. All the week Mrs Josh had done the dairy work, even ageing Bert Hamilton drove his tractor along from Silverdale to see if they needed any help.

★   ★   ★

Lucinda and Harold went early to bed. He had very little idea of time and she pretended to like an hour or two's good read before she turned the light out for the night. One of the problems of getting old, she considered, was the dread of being in the way. No one would ever hint at it, but this was Tim and Sue's home, they deserved some privacy.

'Mum, come into the kitchen a second, can you? I want to show you something,' Liz said.

'Of course, love. What's this? Something you've made at work?'

But once out of the sitting room and the door closed behind them, Liz shook her head. 'Nothing,' she whispered. 'That was just an excuse. Quentin wants to talk to Dad and I thought it would be easier if we were out of the way.'

'He's getting anxious,' Sue jumped to conclusions, 'he wants to get back to college. Of course he does. I shan't be going to the hospital any more, I can take over the milking. You back me up if your father argues. He's not ready, Liz. I can't let him — '

'Mum, it's not that. Quen will never be a farmer, but we're both really glad that he's here.

186

I wonder who told Richard about Dad,' she changed the subject. 'Quen didn't. I asked him.'

'Sue,' Tim called, opening the sitting-room door. How silly it was to be frightened so easily. How could anything be wrong when he was in there with Quentin?

'Do you want us?'

'I want you to hear this. Don't know what to say. Mustn't rush into things. Hardly come to terms with thinking about a manager. Don't know what to think.' Quick thinking and decisive, he'd never 'not known what to think'.

'What's been going on in here?' she asked, her voice just that bit too bright. 'Quentin? Is it that you feel you should go back to Scotland? My dear, I can understand that. And I've just been saying to Liz that now there won't be any more hospital visits we can — '

'It's the top fields,' Tim said, just as if she hadn't spoken. 'Long Meadow right up the slope and through to the Oxford road. All the arable fields. Pretty well half Highmoor.'

'What about the arable fields? Am I particularly dense or are you really making no sense?'

'Aunt Sue,' Quentin came to her rescue, 'you've seen my drawings, you know what I mean to do. The only thing I hadn't been able to plan was where I should find the land. If it could be here, from my point of view — and from Liz's too — it would be wonderful.'

'The Top of the World, that's what we always called that part of the farm,' Liz looked at her father with her eyes wide in that way that had

187

seldom been known to fail. 'Dad, don't you think it's almost like Fate, or kindly Providence, whichever you prefer. It's the heavy work you've been told you can't do. The cattle wouldn't be that much of a problem and I bet you could get a local man to help without having to look for a living-in manager.'

'Don't say anything yet. There's all the time in the world.' Quentin was more sensitive than Liz to Tim's feelings. He took off his glasses, gave them a vigorous and unnecessary polish, then rammed them back again. 'The land would be ideal from my point of view, but that's not the main thing. It — it's — ' again he raised his hand as if his glasses were to be given yet another shine, then realised what he was doing and stopped himself, 'it's just that, well, being one family is important. There's a lot we can help each other with. I don't mean I'm much use on the farm, I more or less do what Josh tells me, he's the oracle. But when the building starts for the glasshouses, the heating, water facilities, all that sort of thing, it would be good if I could bring any problems to talk over with you. I've got great plans, but the honest truth is I'm just a novice.' Was he really so very changed from that diffident child Tim had first brought home? 'You'd probably see pitfalls that I'd miss.'

The uncertainty in his voice must have reminded Tim of the solemn and frightened child he'd been. He put his arm around Quentin's shoulder.

'Your drawings impressed me, son. But if I can ever give you any advice worth having, nothing would please me more.'

Liz had been so proud that Quen was in a position to save the situation at Highmoor, now here he was humbling himself just as if he were a child! The idea of making their Top of the World the nursery had been so exciting; if Quen bought all the arable land, then her father would be able to manage, there would be nothing but a small herd of dairy cows and the farmyard animals. And Quen would be the one who'd come to the rescue, make it possible for her parents to stay on at Highmoor. No wonder she'd felt so happy as she'd called her mother out of the room so that Quentin could make his proposal. Now just hark at him, 'just a novice,' 'bring my problems to you to talk things over'. She turned away rather than look at them, Tim with his arm around Quen as if he were still a child. Anyway, if there were problems, *she* and Quen would sort them out. Perhaps it was a crazy idea, perhaps they ought to look for somewhere in another county. Paul hadn't stayed at home. No, came a silent reminder, Paul had married a woman determined for them to build their own lives. That's what she and Quen ought to do instead of his crawling to Dad, almost begging him to accept a chance to hang on to something of his old life.

'You need time to think about it,' Quentin was saying. 'I wanted to talk to him first, Aunt Sue, but I'm glad you know now. More than anywhere, it's where I want Liz and me to be, but you mustn't let that influence you. Whatever you decide, I shall understand. And there's no hurry, for the time being I'm perfectly content with things as they are. Josh taught you well, now he's doing his best to make something of me,' he added with a laugh.

'You ought to be back at coll — '

'I'm not going back,' Quentin cut in, 'I posted my letter this morning explaining that I wouldn't be returning. When I left Merton I had time to fill in and I've learnt an enormous lot. These coming months will be a lot of cramming, working for certificates that I'd need if I intended to look for employment. But I don't.'

'I ought to agree straight away,' Tim frowned, facing something he had no stomach for. 'Coming home this morning, I was trying to make myself accept that Sue and I would have to get rid of the farm. Now you make a suggestion that surely means I should be able to keep going — 'at half cock' to use Paul's expression. We ought to agree, Sue . . . ?' He looked to her for help.

'Quentin says there's no rush to give him an answer. Let's sleep on it. And Quen — ' There was so much she wanted to say to him, dear sensitive, loving Quentin. But of course she could say none of it. Fortunately she was saved by the telephone bell. It was Paul to talk to Tim.

★ ★ ★

'I mentioned Quentin's suggestion to Paul,' Tim said as he stretched out thankfully in their own bed again. 'I couldn't give an answer until I'd talked to the boy. When we were working

190

together it was the natural assumption for both of us that one day Highmoor would be his to farm.'

Sue moved close to him, her arms around him, her heart bursting with thankfulness. If the farm were only half its present size, if Paul had no interest in one day coming home to it, as if those things mattered. The events of the past fortnight had given her a true perspective; even if they had no choice but to sell Highmoor, that was nothing compared with what might so easily have been. 'I had a close shave,' Tim had told her. She buried her face against his shoulder, so warm, so exactly the same as if this night were the same as any other.

'Sue . . . ?' he prompted, waiting for her to speak.

'What did he think you should do?' she asked. 'He won't farm Highmoor, darling. We can't make plans for our children. Our parents couldn't have made plans for us.'

'Family — that's what Quentin said, didn't he? What about Liz? Does she want to spend the rest of her days at Highmoor?'

Sue considered the question, but this time he didn't prompt her for an answer. So in tune were they that he knew she was trying to find the truth.

'They'd talked about it together. That's why she got me out of the room. She said Quentin wanted to talk to you about something. So she must agree.'

'Umph,' he sounded less than sure. 'She didn't have anything to say. And that's not like Liz.'

Sue smiled affectionately as she thought of the girl's scowl as she'd listened to Quentin telling Tim it would be good to have him nearby to turn to. Her mind jumped back down the years as she imagined how often, out of Quentin's hearing, Liz had stood up for him to the others, always frightened that they saw him as a weakling. Yet this evening she'd not had the perception to realise why he'd spoken as he had, surely a sign of anything but weakness. How differently someone more brash might have made his offer to buy the high ground of the farm, proud of newly inherited wealth, wanting to be seen as the saviour of the day. Tim, always the strong one, was even now not aware how carefully Quentin had protected his feelings. Sue moved her head so that she could kiss Tim's end-of-the-day bristly chin.

'I'm scratchy, lady. Didn't shave before bed.' For it had been his custom to shave at night because of his early morning start in the milking shed. He drew her still nearer, not in a comfortably tender hold, but so that they pressed close against each other. Both of them wanted that complete union; sex had always been a natural, joyous expression of their love.

She wanted him to make love to her: not tonight did she crave the erotic adventure lovemaking so often was, every part of their bodies alive with sensual excitement. What she longed for was to know the warm weight of him on her, to draw him close as she felt him entering her. There would be no heightening of passion, no straining towards a climax; it wasn't

192

that that she wanted, but simply to be one with him, one flesh and surely one heart and soul in their thankfulness.

'No, no. I mustn't.' He loosed his hold, but not before she'd realised that just as quickly as his passion had been aroused so it was lost. The knowledge frightened her, even though reason told her that there could only have been one end to the path she wanted to take.

'Did you think I was going to rape you?' she whispered, forcing a teasing laugh in her voice. 'Oh, Tim, I'm so thankful. Silly things we worried about, like Paul going away, like poor Uncle Harold being in such a muddle. Those sort of things are just part of living. But you . . . hold my hand, Tim, shut your eyes. Together let's both say 'thank you'.'

Holding hands, they lay side by side in silence.

It was a few minutes later, her disappointment, his fear and both their heartfelt thanks behind them, that she turned her back and sat in his lap for sleep.

'I'll tell him tomorrow, lady. It's not like selling the high ground to a stranger. Being family is important, wasn't that what he said?'

'Will he build a house on top of their world, do you suppose? Or will they live here?' Imagining the changes the future would bring, they tried to find new hope.

★　★　★

It seemed to Liz that if Quen had given up his course, there was no point in her rushing off to

Reading every day. She'd learnt all she was likely to learn at the florist's where she worked. But her father could be very pig-headed sometimes and said no one ever got to the stage where there was nothing else to learn. So each morning she cycled to the station and left her bicycle, then caught the 8.10 to Reading. It really did seem unjust, she ought to have been at home. Quentin was still spending a lot of his time on the farm, but there were other and much more exciting things going on. For instance there were visits to the solicitor for documents to be drawn up for the transfer of the land; there were visits to various building firms with Quentin's plans. When the quotations arrived there was the decision on which to engage to carry out the work. There were catalogues of equipment to be studied. And all the time she was busy making wreaths, bouquets, sheaths or exquisite flower arrangements.

Each day Tim grew more distant from that close shave; and all the while his confidence grew. A young man named Ted Rawlings from Brindley was engaged to come in each day, and with no arable land to occupy him, Fred Dawson took over the milking. The truth was, Highmoor had become little more than a smallholding. Often Tim thought of Paul's suggestion that they should turn it into purely a dairy farm. But who would have envisaged this? That year the high ground was left fallow, for as soon as the sale was completed work would start on building the vast acreage of glasshouses. For Quentin didn't mean to begin small and grow with the trade. In his estimates he had allowed time for seedlings to mature and for a trial ground to take shape. As the months of 1966 went by his plans began to take shape. He foresaw that before the year was out the glasshouses would be complete, water and electricity installed and heating too. Shelves and propagators would be filled with young plants. And by summer of 1967 he would spend out on advertising widely, Top of the World would be in business. Coming from a stage family he might have been looked on as the runt, but where else could he have inherited his flair for the spectacular? And the Grand Opening he had in mind was nothing less.

But that was a long way ahead. Before Tim's illness it could have been looked forward to as 'next year at haymaking' or 'next year at harvest'. At Highmoor time could no longer be divided into seasons of ploughing, planting, haymaking and harvest. Measured in any way, there was a long road to travel before 'Top of the World' could open its gates, and as Tim and Quentin signed the contract changing the ownership of the top acreage they both expected the going would be smooth and the road straight.

7

Half-way up the steep, south-facing slope Tim stopped. Always this had been one of his favourite views, below him his own cattle grazing in his own fields, and higher on the hillside, at this season, the sweet-smelling hay. Not this year though. The barren earth told its own story. Standing alone he felt bowed down by the knowledge of his fallibility. A year ago he'd taken his strength for granted, there had been nothing on the farm he couldn't do. Even now he felt well. And yet . . . and yet . . . Fear was always looking over his shoulder.

Here at what was now the border of his own land he sat on the stile that would lead him on to the southern edge of Quentin's Top of the World, the stile that divided yesterday's life from today's.

'What's the matter with me?' he muttered, not even the cows near enough to hear him or show any interest in his presence. 'Me! When I think how it used to be . . . ' His voice was lost in the silence of the morning, only his thoughts raced on. I fail her. I fail us both. I want it, Christ knows I want it. Horny as hell, even thinking about it. If she walked up that hill now, I feel as if I could jump on her. Then what would happen? You know damn well what would happen. The same thing as always. Prime of life, don't they call these years? Useless, impotent, so scared . . . so hellishly scared . . . If I don't manage it soon I'll go barmy. Reason told him that doing what was natural would be better for him than what so often happened. How could the exertion of making love, the thankfulness and peace of mind he could find no other way, be more of a strain than this? What good would it do a starving man to bring him to a plate of steaming food, let him take up his knife and fork, then whisk the plate away? Would he be less hungry? No, he'd be ravaged with hunger. Dear God, Tim mouthed silently, I try and help myself. For Christ's sake help me. Always the same . . . feel strong as Samson, then just when we both think this time'll be different I'm limp as a rag. Damn it all, it was my heart that played up, just my heart. He ran his fingers through his sun-bleached, curly hair, took a deep breath and climbed over the stile and started on up the steepest part of the hill.

As always Quentin was glad to see him. The work was going on apace. The ground had been prepared for the vast acreage of glasshousing and, in preparation for the time when the buildings would be ready for water and electricity, the supplies had had to be brought underground from the lane by the farmhouse. All that was already completed, now the foundations of the glasshouses were taking shape. If Quentin wasn't to be found in the farmyard, it was a sure thing he was at the top of the hill with the builders.

As he turned to wave a greeting, Tim wished he could have seen into his mind. Oh, not that there was any doubt of the sincerity of his pleasure at Tim's interest. But what did he see as he visualised his dream coming to fruition, the glasshouses heavy with the scent of damp fibre, flowers and pollen?

'They've started on the foundations for Liz's part,' Quentin said, coming the last few yards to meet him. 'Whatever is grown in there will be for her to decide. She's learnt so much, you know, at that place. Are you all right? It's a heck of a climb, isn't it.'

'I'm OK,' Tim panted. 'Yes, it's a pull up, but the view makes it worth while. They're getting on well, son. At this rate the autumn will see you with your hands full.'

'Before then I'll be making a start in the first houses. If we're to be on time with an opening early next summer, I need to be working quite steadily by autumn. And from there on, each year will see more land taken into use. But first we have to concentrate on growing on our first batch of seedlings, getting the foundations of stock.'

It did Tim good to be with Quentin, it gave him some sort of a hold on a future that was so different from the one he'd taken for granted. If any one thing had lifted his spirits over these past months it had been the hours he spent with Quentin, often in the evenings poring over quotations, being turned to for advice. Here, their gaze carried to a far horizon and even a glimpse of the distant silvery thread of the Thames glinting in the May sunshine; there was a feeling of hope.

'I'm glad you came up. There are some packing cases over there, let's go and sit down.'

How peaceful it was up here, just the impersonal sound of the builders further across the one-time corn field, and high above them the cry of a curlew. Taking his pipe from his pocket Tim was as conscious of contentment as, not many minutes before, he had been of frustration and his own inadequacies. He lit up and watched as the smoke spiralled upwards. Didn't Sue always say that when the Lord closes one door, he opens another. In this scheme of Quentin's He'd certainly done that.

'I wanted us to have a talk,' Quentin said. Surely, living in the same house, there was plenty of opportunity. So this must be a *talk*, something of importance.

'Umph?' Tim prompted, something of his contentment in the sound.

'It's about Liz and me. I know she's young. But she's nineteen now, and nothing is going to change our minds.'

'You want to bring the wedding forward? It's what both of you want?'

'Yes, of course. I wouldn't ask you if I weren't sure about what Liz wants. This isn't just *my* project up here, it's hers too. It's important that right from the first she'd be part of everything. You can understand that. You and Aunt Sue came to Highmoor together. Oh, I know we're sort of together, living in the same house and all that. But — '

'You're quite right. If it's what you both want, when had you in mind?'

Quentin smiled that rare, wide smile.

'Tomorrow would do us very nicely. But failing that something during the summer if it can be arranged.'

* * *

They were to be married in August. Out of courtesy rather than anything else, Quentin wrote to tell his parents. He'd seen so little of them over the years that the reply, arriving a few days later in his father's handwriting, came as a surprise.

> Naturally we hope to be present, so I trust you will be able to arrange the ceremony for a Monday, bearing in mind that we are not free agents.

For as long as he could remember he'd schooled himself to expect neither interest nor affection from them; that was the way not to get hurt. Now, alone in the same small bedroom that had been known as his since Tim had first brought him home, he wasn't prepared for the sudden gladness he felt as he read it.

So the date was fixed for the third Monday in August. Liz pretended her delight that Quentin's parents were planning to attend was simply for his sake. But the truth was far more complex. She'd hardly ever seen them, she'd always disliked them on principle because they were, in her opinion, 'rotten parents to Quen'. But just imagine the stir the wedding would

200

cause! And what did it matter if people who gathered outside the church would be there to see the visiting celebrities, nothing could take away the fact that it would be *her* day, *she* would be the centre of all the excitement. Quen had been part of the family at the farm for so long, she doubted whether anyone connected the name Quentin McBride with the famous Anthony, or even with Richard, who'd never had anything to do with Brindley village while he'd been a pupil at Merton Court. Quentin had always been 'the lad they look after at Highmoor', and without the glamour of his parents her wedding would only have interested those who could never resist hanging round the church door at the sight of waiting cars bedecked with white ribbons.

A casual word to the vicar must have been how word reached the grapevine, where it was picked up by the local newspaper. It soon became clear that this would be no quiet family occasion. Sue seldom went into a shop in Brindley without being stopped, often by people she hardly knew, all keen to hear about the arrangements as if by speaking to her they were forging a link with the famous.

Richard's long international cable came about a fortnight after Anthony's letter.

Congratulations — stop — before being invited I offer myself best man — stop — shall fly home alone — stop — often think of Highmoor — stop — may not be adventurous but you would go far to find anywhere with the atmosphere I remember there — stop — my regards to the family — stop — Richard.

If it were needed, that put the final nail in the coffin of a quiet wedding. The next time Sue was stopped for news she was able casually to name the best man, silently laughing at the wide-eyed disbelief. Two famous stage people had set Brindley buzzing, but the thought of no less than Richard McBride taking part in the ceremony brought Hollywood into their midst. The recipient of the tidings could hardly get away quickly enough, keen to be the first to spread the news. There was nothing middle-aged and *passé* about Anthony McBride and beautiful Elvira Dereford, through the last decade they had gone from strength to strength. The stage was their forte, although they had on occasion appeared in films. But Richard's career was following a different track; Hollywood seemed to have become his natural habitat. His handsome face looked down on many a schoolgirl or teenager from its place on the bedroom wall, the last thing to be seen at night and the first to be greeted in the morning — while, in between, he inspired dreams in two continents.

The daughter of a local farmer and the owner of the nursery that was taking shape would have been visited by the reporter of the *Brindley Echo* with his camera. But the presence of the McBrides *en masse* meant the Marshalls found themselves in unfamiliar limelight. The time came when the marquee was erected on the front lawn, a wooden floor laid partly to disguise the mossy would-be grass and partly so that ladies wouldn't get their stiletto heels embedded. By the third Saturday in August the lane fronting the farm became the most popular walk in the district. With its gold and white silk lining, the air heavy with the scent of floral decorations Liz spent the entire Sunday setting up, the marquee took on the spirit of fairyland. One or two Sunday walkers who stood peering in at the gate managed to catch her eye and call their good wishes; it was all so thrilling, she'd never felt so exhilarated in all her life. The well-wishers were invited into the marquee to see and admire, the more practical side of her nature believing that their admiration would be good for her future trade. How proudly she talked to them of the new nursery and of Quentin's brilliance, making sure casually to mention his family as 'my future in-laws', throwing their names in for good measure. If it had been suggested to her that her pride in Quentin's ability had anything to do with his being his parents' son, she would have disputed it. But never had she lived through a period like the days leading up to their marriage.

* * *

'They ought not to both start from the same place,' Lucinda said. 'It's asking for bad luck.'

'Try telling them that,' Tim laughed. 'This is their home — before and after.' His satisfaction was plain to hear. For Highmoor had seen changes over the last ten weeks, local firms had put their men on overtime, every stop had been pulled out to make sure the work was done on time. Liz and Quentin were taking over the entire top floor of the farmhouse. At one time the rooms would have housed servants, for only over recent years was the tall Georgian house run without staff. One of the rooms — and it must have belonged to the most junior of servants — had been converted into a bathroom, the walls tiled, the floor covered with cork; a second, hardly any bigger, was to be the kitchen. Those two were one either end of the building, their ceilings sloping. Their doors opened on to the landing, those and two more leading to rooms of much better proportion. Of these the front, overlooking the lane, was to be their bedroom; the back, with a view over the barns to the top of the hill and the gleam of glass, was to be their own sitting room. For weeks if either of them — or both — couldn't be found, it was a certain thing they'd be at the top of the house. Quentin had engaged a local plumber, cabinet maker and finally a decorator. There was to be no making do with second best for his beloved Liz. They'd gone to Reading together to choose their furniture, dealing with a firm specialising in antique and reproduction, so that everything was (or appeared to be) in the right period for the Georgian house.

For Sue and Tim, who had years of experience of making do, the transformation of their attics was nothing short of miraculous.

'Doesn't it look super, Mum,' Liz looked on their achievement with pride when the finishing touches were in place, matching towels neatly piled on a fitment in the bathroom, counterpane spread and matching curtains hung in the bedroom. Sue was naturally domesticated, she loved to care for her home and cook for her family. Liz had inherited none of her flair for home-making but her sense of achievement in all she and Quentin had designed was enormous. Looking around her at what used to be the cluttered attics, she felt utterly secure in her future. She and Quen stood on the brink of a shared challenge. She looked ahead and saw their way as trouble-free as it had seemed when, long ago, they'd first built their dream. Tomorrow was her wedding day; by this evening the house would be full.

'I can't wait to bring the others up to see what we've done. I hope it won't be too late when they get here, because first we want to take them to the nursery while it's still light.' Tomorrow at twelve o'clock she would walk up the aisle with her father, then home to the reception in the marquee before they drove off into their new life. Only it wouldn't be. It was a sort of break in proper living to have a holiday.

'Did you and Dad have a honeymoon, Mum? I suppose you did, everyone does.'

'We went to the Lake District. He drove a motor bike and I rode in the sidecar.' Twenty-eight years ago, yet it was like looking back at another age.

Liz nodded. 'I suppose it's just me, but it does seem to me a silly time to take a holiday when you really just want to get on with the rest of your life.'

Sue put an arm around her slim waist in a brief hug. 'It's a way of getting off by yourselves, away from guests and family. A good way to start the rest of your life, love.'

'Expect you're right. I wonder what Philippa will think when she sees all the lovely things Quen has bought for us,' Liz took no pains to hide her satisfaction in her one-up-manship. 'Bet she'll be green with envy. We're so lucky that his grandparents thought such a lot of him. Don't you wish you and Dad could have had down-stairs spruced up like this when you came here?'

'Do I? I suppose I must do. But just coming here, taking things as Tim's uncle had left them, that was all part of our new beginning — the beginning of the rest of our lives.'

Liz chuckled, taking her mother's hand in hers and swinging it in a way that seemed to show she was too excited to be still. 'And from then on, all our old junk got stacked up here. Quen's room looks like a storeroom, what with the rocking horse, Paul's old train set, my dolls' pram, and *three* high chairs. Why you ever kept three, goodness knows.'

'Elspeth was so proud of the ones she'd bought for the twins, Christo's with blue padding and Sylvia's with pink; I couldn't bring myself to get rid of them. The other one was Paul's and later yours. Anyway, one of these days you may all be glad to have them.'

'Honestly, Mum, you are an awful old hoarder.' So often Liz had jeered at her mother's squirrel-like tendencies, but today nothing could irritate her.

'Just you wait. The time might come when you want those things. Any one of you,' she added.

'Huh,' Liz scoffed. 'Neither of the twins seem interested in marrying, both much too wrapped up in their careers. I see Sylvia ending up as Matron of some huge hospital. As for Christo, he'll be a General.'

'Chump,' Sue's laugh gave no hint of her nagging worry.

'Then there's Philippa. Can you see *her* as a mother?' Secretly she wondered Paul found the courage — or the desire — to get in bed with her. But she felt it better not to say so to her mother, especially on the day before her own wedding. 'I shall have a family, though, Mum. So you and Dad won't be deprived of grandchildren. Isn't it funny, talking about me having children and knowing it's not just some faraway thing. I hope we do fairly quickly — although I mean always to work. You did, didn't you? You didn't lie around like an invalid when you had Paul and me?'

'Small chance,' Sue laughed. 'Come on, dreamer, best foot forward. Tim's put both extra leaves in the dining-room table and I've put out the best damask cloth and napkins ready. Can you see to the rest? Get the cutlery from the posh canteen. Best everything tonight. The Marshalls are out to impress.'

'And quite right too. We've never had a wedding in the house before. Paul's was such a miserable affair.' Then, giving an exaggerated impression of the sister-in-law she thought so starchy, ''Oh dear me, we mustn't go to Upton

Manor looking as though we're a wedding party.' Silly twit. I want everyone to know that's what we are. Didn't they look gorgeous when they tried on their 'Moss Bros'! My last night of being a Marshall. Change your name and not your letter, change for worse and not for better. Isn't that what people say? How stupid. Listen, there's a car. Two doors slamming. Must be Paul.'

One behind the other they ran down the narrow attic stairway.

'Hello.' They heard Sylvia shout as she came into the kitchen from the lobby. 'I'm home. We're both here.' In the excitement of greeting her Sue almost, but not quite, forgot to be surprised that the other half of 'both' was Richard.

'Richard, this is lovely,' and with the same natural warmth she'd welcomed him when he'd sometimes come from Merton Court, she hugged him. 'We're quite a party tonight. Paul and Philippa are due at any time.'

'And Christo?' Sylvia wanted to know. 'Has he arrived yet?'

'He came yesterday. He's taking the Grands for a drive. This evening the Joshes are coming in too. We'll be quite a party.'

'And here's the gorgeous bride,' the smile Richard treated Liz to would set many a heart racing.

'Hi, brother Richard. How come you have a car? I thought you flew from Tinseltown just for the wedding or the weekend or something?'

'True. I arrived this morning. The car's hired. Like Cinderella's carriage it has to be back by midnight on Tuesday. I return to the States later in the week. Where's little brother hiding himself?' It was a long time since he'd seen Quentin. The image he carried was of a timid boy, on the defensive, retreating behind a book. On the rare occasions the parents had felt duty must be done and had insisted on his spending some of his holiday with them in London, the visits had been disasters. The London apartment had been the meeting ground for their wide circle of theatre friends; Quentin hadn't fitted in and had made no effort to try. Silent and morose, making no attempt to hide his frightened hostility to an atmosphere he'd found alien, what should have been good-natured gatherings of compatible people had ended with Quentin retiring to his darkened room. No wonder the parents had given up listening to their conscience and let him while away his time here at Highmoor.

'Quen's up at the nursery. I'll take you up now if you like.'

'Presently. Where's Tim? I must see him first.' To the family he was Dad or Uncle; to Richard, from Mr Marshall, he'd gone straight to Tim.

'He'll be in soon,' Sue told him. 'He's seeing to the milking.'

'And he's quite well now?' She knew this wasn't polite conversation, Richard really cared. In answer she nodded, touching her hand against the kitchen table.

'He's careful,' she said, 'and, of course, there's much less to do here now that Quen has taken the high ground.'

'It must have been a huge worry. Can I go over and say hi to him?'

Looking out of the window a few minutes later she saw it was Richard who loaded the heavy urns on to the trailer for Tim to drive to the gate for collection.

So the day went by. Paul and Philippa arrived, Christopher and the Grands returned, the Joshes donned their best and joined the party. Conversation never flagged, the pitch of noise was every bit as high as anything Richard had heard in those days when Quentin had visited their parents' London apartment. Yet there was no hiding behind dark-lensed glasses, no retiring to darkness and solitude in his room. Tomorrow's bridegroom was self-assured, completely without nerves.

★ ★ ★

Barefoot, silently opening her bedroom door, Sylvia crept across the landing and down the stairs. She wanted to think it was the heat that made sleep so impossible, but she knew that didn't even begin to be the truth. Perhaps outside in the fresh air she could start to think clearly. Across the hall to the heavy and seldom-used front door where she knew just how hard to tug on the bolt and just how gently to turn the large metal key, then leaving the door wide open she stepped out into the still, night air. Wanting to be certain no one knew she was there, she walked round the marquee then sank to the dry ground on the far side, out of sight from the windows of the house.

Ought she to believe him? Did he honestly think she'd forgotten how easily he'd dropped her for the glamorous Drucilla? And was he being honest with her now? In any case, even if all he told her was true, did he ever consider that she had a life of her own, ambitions of her own? But had she? Were her ambitions nothing more than a need to give herself a goal, any goal?

She felt in the pocket of her silk negligée for her cigarettes and lighter. This matching set, nightie and negligée, had been a wild extravagance, bought to wear when they'd gone on holiday in France. She'd been so sure — so stupidly sure, she added, lighting her cigarette. Since then the expensive garments had been wrapped in tissue paper and left untouched in her drawer. Since the French affair (affair? And for him that's what it must have been) she'd often been to Highmoor, she'd even had one holiday in Norway, but until now she had never considered wearing them. When she'd packed her bag before going to bed on the Saturday night, she'd taken the tissue-paper package and laid it carefully at the bottom of her case. In her heart she knew it had to do with Richard's offer to be best man. He and Drucilla would be at Highmoor.

On the Sunday she'd worked an early shift, from seven in the morning until three in the afternoon. The idea was that, if she hurried, she could change from her uniform and get to the station in time for the 3.55 train. Now, her eyes closed and drawing deeply on the cigarette, she relived the moment when she'd run down the steps of the hospital — and there he was. He'd come to England on his own; he'd enquired about her at the hospital and been told that Senior Staff Nurse Ruddick was on Men's Medical Ward and would be off duty at three o'clock. She'd schooled herself to be ready to meet him at Highmoor, she'd even had her hair done specially when she'd finished work on the Saturday (had it done for the wedding, she'd told herself, knowing that she lied). As she'd hurried down the steps her mind had been on getting to the station, so when he'd stepped into her path she'd crashed straight into him. Caught off guard, he must have seen her reaction.

There wasn't a cloud in the starry sky, the full moon was riding high and by now she was so used to it that she could see clearly. That's how she noticed the movement of a shadow. Someone was coming along the lane! Instantly her mind jumped to every conceivable kind of villain from a sheep rustler (not that Highmoor had any sheep), to a house burglar, to a rapist. With one lithe movement she was on her feet, the burning tip of her cigarette hidden behind her back. Where could she go? One side of the marquee was right to the hedge, the other was visible from the lane — and where she was was almost in the lane! Desperately and with no thought for her tempting night attire, she tried to wriggle between the hedge and the marquee, so that the prowler would pass without seeing her. Or was he a vagrant meaning to use it as a night's shelter? These thoughts crowded in on her in

212

hardly more than a second.

'Wait, Sylvia, it's me.' Was it training in projecting his voice that made the soft words of a whisper carry across the space between them as he came into view? 'You couldn't sleep either.' He took her cigarette and trampled it out on the mossy grass, then held her hands in his.

'You haven't been to bed,' she said unnecessarily, seeing that he was fully dressed, with the exception of his jacket on such a warm night.

'I've been walking — thinking. Don't run away. Did you suppose I was some evil-intentioned prowler?'

'I didn't know. I ought to go back indoors, Richard.'

'Perhaps that's what you think I am — an evil-intentioned prowler. Sylvia, seeing you again . . .'

'Shut up, Richard. This isn't a screen set, you're not playing the romantic lead. We're old friends. We're here for a family wedding. And if we found it too hot to sleep, what harm is there in talking together in the garden? That's innocent enough.'

'It would be, if it were true. Why couldn't you sleep? For the same reason as I knew I couldn't face going to bed.'

'I expect it's something to do with the time change. This time yesterday you were seven or eight hours behind London time.'

'The things I said to you this afternoon — about my marriage. God, Sylvie, it's all such a mess. But there's Juliet. Drucilla says having a child has ruined her dancing career, every time we have a row — and God knows that's often enough — she says she ought to have found someone to give her an abortion. Of course she blames me — and rightly. But Sylvie, don't you think there are times when we don't know best? I mean, take Juliet. If I'd stopped to think of the risks I was taking in those first weeks with Drucilla, then none of it would have happened. I mean, I wouldn't have got her pregnant, I'd have been careful. Yet, now she's here — honestly Sylvie, she's a great little person. I never expected to feel anything for a young child. But — this sounds hellishly wimpish I dare say, but it's the truth — I truly love her, pure, altruistic love. Is that what parents usually feel? Not Drucilla. I realised right from when we were first married, Drucilla resented the child and resented me for what being pregnant had done to her career. I just adore that kid. She follows me around like a shadow whenever I'm home. I've got grounds enough to divorce Drucilla, but you know the way the law leans, and she'd fight for custody even though she doesn't give a damn about the poor kid. Probably make her grow up thinking I'd disclaimed her.'

Sylvia fought against being swayed by what he said.

'It wouldn't boost your ratings either,' she said, hating the cynical tone yet not being able to hide it.

'No. I've thought of that too. You see . . . I am being honest. Then there's something else that bothers me. I remember how it used to be between Quentin and the parents — still is, I dare say. I couldn't guess what's bringing them here tomorrow, whether it's some latent affection or pure curiosity to see what he's making of his life. But Quentin had our grandparents, and he had all of you. Juliet has no one but me. I won't let her down. She is my responsibility. Anyway, I told you, for the first time in my life I know the feeling of selfless love.' He was silent, probably waiting for her to comment. Then, when instead of speaking she felt for her cigarettes, taking one and passing the packet to him, 'Sylvie, just one thing, and I want you to promise to tell me honestly. Have you forgotten how it was for you and me?'

Just for a moment she hesitated as he looked at her in the flame from his lighter.

'No.'

'Is there anyone else?'

'You said just one thing. That makes two. Anyway, whether there's been anyone else or not isn't your business.'

'That's not true. Everything you do matters to me. It always has. Almost always. Even when we were kids on the farm,' he laughed, 'I used to show off atrociously knowing you had your eye on me.' Then, more seriously, 'There was just that one period — and I see it so clearly now, she knew exactly how to lure me. I was heaven-sent for her, a young hopeful being fêted in Hollywood, still wet behind the ears, pretending to be so full of self-confidence. I'm not proud to remember how flattered I was that she was interested in me. Ideals or no, I went to bed with her the second time she took me back to her flat

215

— I rejoiced in it. I knew she was a floozy, but that only added to my feeling of self-esteem. Sometimes at night, sometimes during the day, we would go there over that first week or so — '

'I don't want to hear. You've no business to talk about what went on between you and her. While you were rejoicing in romping in her bed, did you tell her about *me*, about what easy prey — '

'You know I didn't.' Turning her face towards him, he looked at her steadily. 'I need to talk to you, my darling Sylvia. I'm filled with self-loathing, it's as if my soul is scarred. Can you understand? If I were a Catholic perhaps a priest would do. But no, it's *you* I've longed to tell it all to.'

'And now you've told me,' she said quietly. 'And what am I supposed to do? Give you absolution? Richard, face reality. You are at the top of your professional tree; I am starting to climb up mine. We have totally different lives, probably totally different values. Ages ago we thought we were in love — '

'Not *thought* — '

She went on as if he hadn't spoken. 'But life has moved on, perhaps it is that we've grown up. Can't we just accept and be friends? And, after tomorrow, relations too.'

Sitting side by side, she watched him. Was he acting out a part? Was his need of her support real? Could she trust him? And if she wasn't even sure of that, surely what she felt for him couldn't be love — pure, honest, genuine. Suppose she'd been the one to have his child instead of Drucilla. By now he'd probably be turning to some other woman for understanding.

He sat with his knees drawn up and parted so that his hands hung limply between them, so limply that she wondered he didn't drop his cigarette. She tried to stifle a yawn, but not before he noticed.

'You're tired.'

'I was up before six. And tomorrow — today — we have a lot to do, a wedding to go to. We ought to go indoors.' Yet it was strangely peaceful under the starlit sky. She closed her eyes, leaning back against the frame of the marquee. She didn't open them when she sensed his movement, she didn't need to look at him to know. When his mouth found hers she knew she ought to push him away. He'd dropped her last time without a second thought, he'd do it again. But he was here, he was kissing her, holding her. She drew him closer. This wasn't a matinée idol with fan clubs of young girls in two continents, this was the boy she'd idolised when he'd come to the farm from Merton Court, the first and only man she'd ever made love with. Surely he was the only man she ever could make love with. In those seconds there was no Drucilla, no Juliet.

'No!' Reason caught up with her.

'Yes,' he whispered. 'Sylvie, let me. I want you so much. I kept thinking about you, the way we used to be. Forgive me, don't turn me away.'

'We can't. It's different now, it has to be different.'

He moved his head away just far enough that

they could see each other in the pale golden light.

'For us it will never be different. We both know it. I can't make you, I love you too dearly. I just beg you. Let me love you, Sylvie. I'll take care.' Immediately the image of unknown Drucilla was there in front of her, and just as immediately it was thrust away.

'Yes,' she breathed. 'Love me. I want you to.' She spoke so quietly he could scarcely hear, but he knew what her answer must be.

As well the film-struck girls of Brindley were all safely in bed and asleep. A walk down the lane past the farm would have given them a less than glamorous view of their idol, his trousers around his ankles, the moon gleaming on his pale buttocks. The ground was mercilessly hard on his knees, on Sylvia too. The harshness of nature's bed was all part of the miracle. From high in the trees across the lane came the call of an owl and, from afar like an echo, the reply of another. Like us, she cried silently, no matter if he had a dozen wives it's *me* he's come back to.

★ ★ ★

'He's really come along remarkably, our little runt,' Elvira whispered to Anthony under cover of general applause at the end of the groom's speech.

'Not a trace of nerves,' his father agreed. 'Such an odd child, used to make one quite uncomfortable with that owl-like gaze. Today he's done well. I applaud him.'

'And Richard isn't an easy act to follow.'

On that they agreed, Quentin forgotten and his pretty little bride too.

In the warm marquee the perfume of the flowers was almost overpowering. And whatever was that silly old man doing? It seemed Sylvia had noticed Harold at the same time and was making her way to where he was plucking flowers from the trailing garlands Liz had fixed around the supporting poles.

'Pretty aren't they, Grandpa,' she took the little bunch from him and tried to poke them back into the gaps, 'we'd better leave them like this until everyone has gone. Hasn't Liz made it all look splendid?'

Easily distracted from what he'd been doing, he beamed his pleasure to have her coming especially to talk to him. 'And so are you, my dear. Pretty, pretty as picture. When are we to see you with a husband, eh? What?'

'The trouble is, I can't find anyone to compare with you, Gramps. Let's see if we can find a piece of wedding cake, shall we?' Then taking his arm she guided him towards the buffet table which an hour before had been heavy with mouth-watering food. Even now the board hadn't been cleared so, as well as the cake, she piled a few more snippets on to a plate for him. The bulk of the catering had been prepared by Sue and Mrs Josh, at least they had dealt with the cooking. But Lucinda's contribution had been invaluable, and how proud she'd been in the run-up to the big day, as they made their lists and she had real responsibilities of her own. Her ideas and expertise in 'pretty nothings' as she termed the small savouries she produced, came from years as the wife of a serving officer with all the cocktail parties and in-house entertaining that entailed. Add to that Liz's short bursts of excited enthusiasm, and the food for the fifty or so guests was as attractive as it was delicious.

'There, Grandpa, if you sit on this chair at the end of the table, it's easier than standing up to eat.'

'Don't like getting old, Sylvie, child. You stay as you are, young and bright. Now, let me see, do I know any of these people? Good to see the ladies all got up in their folderols, and us men. What do you think of us all, eh? What?'

'I think we all look gorgeous.'

'Here, child, bend down so I can whisper.' She did as he said. 'That brother of Quentin's, an actor or something, film star don't they call it, he's got his eye on you. Don't blame him, mind you. What? Been watching him, yes, I've been watching him and he's been watching you.'

'Must be my new hat, Grandpa,' she laughed.

But Harold's mind had moved on. 'Go and get Paul and that filly of his to come and talk to me, there's a good girl. Never see him these days.' Then, with a wink that made Sylvia feel uncomfortable, out of keeping as it was with the grandfather she'd believed she'd known through and through, 'She'll be a goer, that one. None of your once a week, if I don't have a headache, about her.'

'Grandpa, you're an old rascal,' Sylvia let him see she'd taken it as a joke. But there was an expression on his face as he looked across the marquee at Philippa that was no more familiar than the wink had been.

★ ★ ★

The day was nearly over. Quentin had signed the hotel guest book, Mr and Mrs Q. McBride had been taken to their room, unpacked and gone to the dining room.

'I wish I was starving hungry,' Liz said, reading the menu. 'But I just haven't wanted any food today, not even all those lovely things Mum and the others had made. Too excited.'

Quentin felt ashamed of his appetite. Heightened emotions always made him hungry, and today they'd been heightened as never before. He'd never forget a single second of it, Liz meeting him at the chancel step, turning to him with her huge eyes bright with excited happiness. It had almost been too much to bear. Suppose when he had to repeat his vows his voice failed him, suppose his hands were shaking. But that would be failing her, showing himself to be less than she expected. His voice was clear and strong, his hands warm and firm as he'd slipped the ring on her finger. Mrs Quentin McBride.

'Love you so much,' he whispered looking at her across the small dining table, his lips hardly moving.

Her mouth turned up into a teasing smile. 'And you want to spend hours filling yourself with food!'

His stomach rumbled noisily. She didn't dare look at him, inside she was shaking with laughter. This was her wedding night, she wondered whether it was normal to feel like this. Ought she to be nervous, uncertain? Ought she to feel wildly passionate? Not that she knew a lot about being wildly passionate, but she was sure she'd find out. In fact she was experiencing none of these high-flown emotions, she was just aware how gorgeous it was that she and Quen were on their own.

And while they took what she considered far, far too long to be served and to eat their four-course meal and to drink one tiny cup of coffee, at Highmoor those who remained of the family gathered around the check-clothed kitchen table. Sue served the casserole that had been cooking slowly in the bottom of the range oven since before they'd left home for church at midday.

'Such a shame Sylvia and Richard went back tonight,' Lucinda said. 'I'd quite thought they would have been here until the morning the same as Paul and Philippa.'

'He only had the car until tomorrow, Aunt Luce,' Sue made excuses. 'And he hardly had a chance to talk to his parents today, he's sure to want to spend some time with them.'

'It wouldn't have hurt Sylvie to stay, all the same,' Paul said. 'She knows the Grands look forward to seeing Christo and her.'

Christopher said nothing, but from the tight look around his mouth Sue suspected that closeness between the twins was leaving him in no doubt what was taking Sylvia speeding back to London.

'The worst about all the fuss of this sort of wedding,' Philippa said, no doubt meaning to be affable, 'is that when it's all over and the bride and groom have gone, the whole thing goes so flat.'

'Never let it be said!' This time Tim interposed, piling his plate with Josh-grown beans and marrow, one eye on his daughter-in-law as if to defy her to tell him he should cut down on what he ate. 'How can it be an anti-climax when we have you, Paul and Christo still here? Go into the dining room and see what sort of wine you can find, there's a good chap. Seven of us, you'd better bring a couple of bottles.' Wine with their meals was a rarity at Highmoor, it had the effect of turning a meal into an occasion. He was determined not to give way to the niggling feeling of irritation Philippa always gave him. And nothing, not Philippa, not an unacknowledged thankfulness that the guests had gone, must be allowed to spoil the hours that remained. He'd welcomed their guests with no sign of the strain he felt as he'd got through the most hectic and certainly most emotional day since January. He was tired, his legs felt like lead, his shoulders ached. Pull yourself together, man, what have you done to get tired? Damned all! Not like Sue, preparing food for all that crowd, finding time to see to the chickens just as she did every day, and somehow after all that putting on her smart new outfit and looking the prettiest woman there.

'Great isn't it, Dad?' Paul was waiting for an answer. Great? What was great?

'Sorry, son. I was miles away. What's great?'

Philippa, sitting so straight and erect, put a smile on her face as she turned to him.

'My new job,' she said. 'Paul was describing how I met the head of Higworth Castle, a girls' independent school a couple of miles from where we are. A charming man. When I told him I was seriously thinking of teaching again he snapped me up. So I start at the beginning of next term — in three weeks' time. Now, I have a really good idea. Before term starts, why don't you have a few days with us? You'd like that, wouldn't you, Paul? There's plenty of stabling, you could bring whatever you call your horse.'

Watching Tim, Sue realised just how much he had missed Paul.

'What do you think, lady? No, we can't. It's not fair on poor old Josh, especially now that Quentin has his own place to run. He was wonderful, you know, when I was out of action.'

'I know, Dad. I felt rotten. But you're fine now, I can see you are.' The suggestion had been Philippa's, but Paul knew the responsibility of having the Grands in the house, and he knew even with only the dairy and the farmyard animals, the work that was involved. It must have been some sort of telepathy between Sue and him, for it was she who spoke what was in his mind.

'You go back with them, Tim love. Just for a few days, I mean. Take the Land Rover and the horse trailer. Imagine how pleased Rosie will be

224

when Titan arrives. If I were to come too, honestly I'd only worry.'

'It's us, perhaps we could find a little hotel for a few days — '

'It's not you, Aunt Luce,' Sue laughed, 'it's two dozen laying hens, a shed of mushrooms and a daily dose of cream to be processed. If Mrs Josh thought it had so much as been suggested, she would insist on doing everything. And I can't have that. It would take all the pleasure away for all of us. Anyway,' she ended on a positive note, 'if you're getting your thoughts around a new teaching job, Philippa, you can do without another woman trailing around after you. These two,' indicating father and son, 'they can amuse themselves happily for hours, give them a horse to ride and some land to ride it on.' She felt herself to be something of a heroine — and an actress too.

So it was agreed that the next day when Paul and Philippa returned, Tim would follow behind with the Land Rover and the horse trailer. Before they went to bed they looked out his best jodhpurs and hacking jacket, and his highly polished riding boots. Like a child packing his spade and bucket, Tim was ready for his holiday.

By the time Sue was carefully packing the yellow polo-necked cashmere sweater Quentin and Liz had given him last Christmas (and which had never been worn), the newly-weds had finished their dinner. They walked in the beautiful grounds of the hotel and, finally, decided they could retire to their room without any of the guests guessing that they were honeymooners.

'We've got a gorgeous bathroom,' Liz said. 'I'm going to have a bath.'

Was she suddenly shy of him?

'I could get ready for bed while you're in there if you like.'

She didn't answer. She wasn't sure what she wanted. No, that wasn't true; she was sure, but she didn't know how to tell him without sounding what in her mind she described as 'sort of pushy'. But the bathroom proved even more 'gorgeous' than she'd realised. On the shelf was an array of beautiful-smelling potions: bath salts to throw in the water, body lotion to rub on her body. She pulled off her clothes and admired herself in the long mirror which by the time she came out of the water would be steamed up. Then she stepped in and lowered herself into the warm, pungent water.

We can do as we like. We're on our own. 'Quen,' she called.

'Is everything all right?' he asked from the other side of the door.

'No. I'm all by myself. Come in and see me, Quen.'

His Adam's apple threatened to choke him as he opened the door, only to have his vision lost when his glasses steamed. He heard Liz laugh.

'Did I say 'see me'? Oh, you've got your jimjams on. Take them off, Quen, and get in the other end. It's a *huge* bath.'

He turned his back as he undid the buttons on his jacket, and then the cord around his waist,

226

stepping out of his trousers as they fell to the floor. At the thought of getting in the bath with Liz, his pulses were throbbing. How could he let her see him for the first time looking like this? He must somehow sit down in the foamy water before she realised.

'Come on, slow coach. Put some more smellies in first. I feel like a princess.' Mostly what she felt was enormous relief. Here she was, naked, sitting in a tub of frothy warm water that smelt like lilies of the valley and she felt no sense of self-consciousness.

'Quen, turn round. We mustn't be shy with each other. I mean, why should we be? There's nothing we can't share, you and me, surely.'

He turned towards her, his embarrassment and shame gone. Nothing they couldn't share, she had said. So why should he not want her to see how much he wanted what must surely follow so soon?

She not only saw, but she raised her hand and touched him.

'I sort of knew, well of course I did. But I didn't know it would be quite like that. And me. Am I like you expected? I want us to know everything.'

'I only know that I can't believe what's happening. You and me here, all our lives ahead of us to share.'

'Quen, look, it's got small.' She was peering at him. 'Does that mean it's not going to be able to — you know — make love? Is it me? Seeing me?'

He reached forward and took her hands. 'No, my darling, darling Liz. It's the bath water.

You're lovely, beautiful.'

'And that's without your glasses,' she chuckled, delighting in his words and in the situation. 'Perhaps we ought to have gone to bed dirty. But it would have been a shame to waste all these nice things they've put out for us. There's body lotion too. I'm not sure if it isn't a bit sissy for you, but I'm going to smell wonderful.'

A few minutes later he got out, then held a large towel for her to step into. On such a hot night they didn't waste much time drying; anyway Liz was keen to try the complimentary body lotion. She carried the bottle with her to the bedroom, then passed it to him. With her back to him she faced the bed as he gently massaged the lotion on to her soft skin. Her back, her stomach, her breasts, her legs; and when he pulled her back towards him she knew he had recovered from the warm bath. She'd been brought up on a farm; she certainly wasn't ignorant of sex. She'd watched the bull serving the cows, and October time she'd seen the fun the ram had had in the field at Silverdale. But suddenly she felt out of her depth.

'Quen, I'm not sure how we do it. Not properly sure.'

In truth, neither was he. But nature was helping them. And long before the first cockerel crowed they had left innocence behind them and both felt they had a new maturity.

* * *

And in London, in her one-bedroom flat in a converted terrace house in Finchley, Sylvia lived out the dream she'd carried these last years. But like all dreams it couldn't last. For just one more day he'd be with her and then he would return to Hollywood, to that other life where she had no part.

8

Tim stayed nearly a week with Paul and Philippa. If anyone had suggested to him that being away from home, perhaps especially away from Sue, would help him take a big stride towards forgetting his fears, he would have discounted the suggestion. Yet, for various reasons, that was exactly what it did for him. There was no manual work for him on the great estate, but plenty to fill his mind as he and Paul slipped back into that easy natural companionship they'd shared in the time they'd farmed Highmoor together. Sometimes they went astride Titan and Rosie, and what memories that brought back! Sometimes Paul drove the estate Land Rover. Whatever they did over those few days, the one thing that never varied was the pleasure they found in each other's company.

He was only there from Tuesday until Saturday but each evening he and Sue spoke briefly.

'This is quite a place, Sue. No wonder the boy was so keen.' That was Tuesday, when he'd had time for no more than a drive around the estate.

'They're happy, Tim? You know what I mean.' Of course he knew. Loyalty to Paul had stopped them fully acknowledging their misgivings about his choice of a partner, yet both had felt the other's niggling doubts.

'So it seems.' Not very enthusiastic.

By Wednesday his voice rang with pride: 'Paul is entirely on top of his job. I wish you could see him with the men, you can feel their respect and yet he's — well, he's just Paul, I don't have to tell you — always friendly, interested in everyone.'

At home she was adding his tasks to her own — with Josh's never-failing help. Although Highmoor was little more than half its original acreage, there was work enough to keep all three of them busy. Fred's day started with the early morning milking; it finished when the urns from the day's teatime session were deposited at the gate for collection. It was he who kept the cowsheds clean and the equipment sterilised. Normally care of the pigs was a shared responsibility but, with Tim away, Sue knew that Fred made a special effort to stretch the minutes of each hour. For months now it had been Tim who had driven the herd in from the lower fields and dealt with teatime milking; Fred's offer to do it while he was away was made willingly, but Sue felt it important that it was *she* who did Tim's work; adding it to her own daily tasks made her feel more part of his short holiday. If only she could have gone with him, seen where Paul lived, seen what sort of a wife Philippa was proving.

By Thursday she could sense a change in Tim's manner.

'You sure you're managing all right, lady? Do you remember the figure when you fill in the milk records? Well, never mind if you don't, I'll soon be home.' This was her own Tim, she could hear a new ring of purpose in his tone.

And Friday: 'I'm taking them out for a meal

this evening. Just the three of us. There ought to have been four. I'm glad I came, it's somehow lifted the shadows if you can understand what I mean. Just one thing marred it all: you should have been here too. I'll get on the road after breakfast tomorrow.'

He was ready to come home and, even more important, she could tell just how much good his break away from Highmoor had done him.

★ ★ ★

Saturday evening, the sun disappearing behind Top of the World, Sue and Tim strolled up the incline of the lower slopes and climbed to sit on that same stile where Tim had been filled with such failure and frustration a few months before.

'Tell me — I don't mean about the estate, I mean about *them*.'

'So good to be home,' as if she hadn't spoken he followed his own thoughts, easing her gently closer and holding his arm around her shoulder. 'A thousand things I want to say.'

'You've said it all, darling. You're home. Not just living here at Highmoor — but *home*.'

'I don't understand it, I don't know why seeing Paul there where he's a paid employee, seeing him married to a woman I disliked right from the first — yes, I can say it now — it's,' he hesitated, groping for the right word, 'it's cleansed me.' She moved closer, nuzzling her face against his neck.

'You're bristly,' she whispered, still nuzzling.

'I'll shave later. And Sue — God, this is hard

to say — Sue, it's going to be all right. I was wrapped in fear, it was warping me. Now all I know is thankfulness. It will be all right again for us — ' She knew what he meant and this time the fear was hers. Could fear alone really have done that to him? Supposing his new-found confidence was stripped from him? Wouldn't that be even worse for him than what he'd suffered all these months?

'It always has been all right for us, just being together, loving each other, understanding each other . . . ' She drew back far enough to look directly at him, her wide blue eyes serious.

'I'll rephrase that.' It was so long since he'd spoken to her in that tender, laughing voice. 'It's going to be like it used to be.'

'And very nice too,' she went back into her nuzzling position. Would it be like he wanted? Like she wanted? She mustn't doubt, doubting showed lack of faith. Please, please, make it work for him, for us both. Please, don't hurt him again. 'Now I want to hear about Paul and her.'

'I think I was wrong. There's a side to Philippa I hadn't seen. And, Sue, she was most hospitable, she tried hard to unbend. I suppose we are all the product of the way life has used us. Anyway, first I want to tell you more about the boy. Watching the way he handles things — and the responsibility is enormous — Sue, I wish you could have been there. I've never been so proud of him.'

Through the months of that year pride had played no part in Tim's view of life. So that was one thing that helped restore him to being the man he used to be. Another was more subtle. It had to do with Philippa and the nagging worry he'd had that Paul had made a mistake. In the honest recesses of his mind he knew he'd never liked the iceberg he'd gained for a daughter-in-law. He'd seen her as cold, been disappointed that Paul could have married a woman so different from Sue or even Liz. But, during the days he'd been with them, he'd discovered she was far more complex than he'd imagined. Now he tried to explain his feeling to Sue.

'That hair of hers, tight off her face in that bun thing on top of her head like some ballet dancer. I believe that's partly why we saw her as so frigid.' The reddest hair he'd ever seen, but not coarse and frizzy. 'It's long, you know. Right down her back, shines like silk. Not my cup of tea, a woman coming down to breakfast like it, but that's what she does. Some sort of a silk dressing gown thing, that pale face of hers without any make-up, yet — hard to pinpoint what made me so sure — under that cool front she puts on, she's a highly sensual woman. Seeing her from a new angle killed off a lot of my worries. And I had been worried, I can tell you. If you ask me, it's a good thing he's a young man with abundant energy.'

'You don't surprise me,' Sue answered. 'I never thought she was sexually frigid. And you ask Uncle Harold, he's got her sized up.'

'Beats me. Things seem to have been going over my head. Any news of Liz and Quentin?'

'Darling, they've only been on their honeymoon for five days. Can you remember spending your time writing cards?'

'No. But they aren't like other people. One blessing, lady, we don't have to worry about those two. You won't have had time to look in on the work up the hill, of course. Tomorrow I'll go and see how the painters are getting on so that I can tell them if they ring. The sun's going down, time you and I went home.'

Walking back towards the farmhouse it seemed their troubles were behind them.

'You know what I think?' Sue said idly.

'I'm just going to be told. What is it? Something profound?' With hands linked they walked side by side down the narrow track that edged the field.

'I think it's so easy to take happiness for granted, as if we have a right to it, that worries are sent to us to make us take stock. To take stock and be grateful, Tim.'

'I am grateful, my sweet lady, grateful for you, for the family, for each and every precious day. But you're right. Until that happened to me last winter I was never as aware as I have been since. There's not a day that I don't thank God for giving us this second chance. Why do you think I'm so docile and obedient? It's because not trying to prove my strength is a small price to pay.'

She nodded. They came through the gate into the farmyard and saw Lucinda and Harold watching from the window.

'Poor Aunt Luce,' Sue said as she waved.

'Poor him, I should have thought.'

'No, it's she who suffers. It tears her to pieces.'

235

As they came through the lobby into the kitchen Harold greeted them with a beaming smile.

'We watched you coming,' he told them, bending to kiss Sue. 'Fancy you coming all this way to see us. Come in, come in, my dears.'

Lucinda turned away but not before they'd seen the stark misery of her expression.

'So Uncle Harold, how about you and me going in the other room and leaving the girls to talk while we have a drink together?'

But Harold's mind had cleared, he couldn't be sure what he'd said, but he knew this wasn't his own home and he'd been making a fool of himself. His gaze darted from one to the other, his face worked. 'Silly old fool you must think me . . . just confused for a moment . . . don't remember . . . let me see now, what was I saying?'

Tim put his arm round the stooping shoulders. 'It was me who was saying something, I suggested you and I go and see if we can have ten minutes men-only time and a tot of whisky. How would that be?'

'Yes, yes, that's the way. Something though . . . something I said . . . '

'You said you were glad to see us home. We've been out a long time. Sue wanted to hear all about Paul — '

'Paul. Ah, yes, that's it. Paul, he was here a bit ago. Where's the boy gone?' Tim guided him out of the room.

Later, the waning moon casting its magic on the familiar shapes and shadows of their bedroom, Sue and Tim lay close in each other's arms. A few hours before, skirting the edge of the cattle field, they had talked of thankfulness and gratitude. Now they knew its full meaning.

'Hold my hand,' she whispered. 'Both of us say it.'

He didn't need to ask what she meant, good times and bad they'd always known where to turn. He took her hand, they closed their eyes. They were together, the wood they'd travelled was behind them. Their thanks were silent, a surge of gratitude from the depths of their souls. Lucinda and Harold's troubles cast a dark thread, but in a way they neither of them analysed, even drawing that into the pattern only enriched it.

★   ★   ★

So life at Highmoor entered a new phase, one in which the way was smooth. Of course there were minor hiccups, how could there not be when daily Harold became more confused?

Watching Liz and Quentin settle him into the back of their car to drive him the road way to Top of the World, Lucinda was ashamed that her own feeling was one of humiliation — not for herself, but for him.

'They're such dears,' she said and, without looking at her, Sue knew how near to tears she was. 'I *do* appreciate their kindness. But that's what's so hard, Sue, so desperately hard. To feel gratitude for people's kindness. All of you — I don't know what would have become of us if we hadn't come here.'

'Now you're talking poppycock, Aunt Luce. Of course you came here. Families are here for each other. Quentin has always felt like family, but it's lovely now to know that's what he really is. One of us for always.' It was a futile attempt to steer Lucinda's thoughts in a happier direction.

'He used to have everyone's respect. That's what hurts so much. Now we all give him our love — yes, my dear, I'm sure you all do — but it's a love based on pity not respect. My poor Harold. You didn't know him when he was young. After the first dreadful war when we were in India, oh, Sue you should have seen him. Proud as a peacock I was — or I suppose a peahen, but they're such dull birds compared with the males. I suppose that's how it was for us really, it was he who was the handsome one, the centre of every gathering. Now he can't hold two thoughts together at a time, can't hold one even sometimes. My poor Harold.'

'Your poor Harold will be having a very good time up at the nursery, you can be sure of that. There's nothing he likes better than to be with the young ones. Now listen, Aunt Luce,' in an exaggerated appearance of sharing a secret, Sue lowered her voice, 'promise not to spread it around and I'll tell you a secret.'

'Yes? Of course I won't say a word, dear, you know I won't.'

'That's why I'm going to tell you. You see, it's not my own secret.'

Lucinda's anxieties were pushed to the back of her mind as she waited to hear.

'I was collecting up the eggs when Quentin went off to the nursery this morning and, unusually, he was on his own. Just casually I called out to ask him where Liz was, expecting any minute she'd come bounding out and chase him up the hill.'

'What a pair of children they still seem sometimes,' Lucinda smiled indulgently. 'Well, little Liz really, I suppose. Quentin has always been more of a sober sides. But, go on, you were telling me . . . ?'

'He said he'd made her go back to bed for a while. There was a merchant of some sort calling at about nine so he had to go on up to the nursery, but she'd promised to stay in bed until he got back. I assumed it was a nasty period, sometimes she used to get a lot of pain.'

'Such a wisp of a thing,' Lucinda said. 'Usually marriage puts an end to those sorts of troubles. Poor little Liz.'

'I didn't probe. I don't think he would have been embarrassed, but you never know.'

'Well, dear, you mustn't worry. Bright as a button when she suggested Harold might like an hour with them.'

'I went up to see her, took her a hot water bottle for her to cuddle. But I was wrong. It certainly wasn't a period. Her last one was in October.'

'November, December, and here we are into January. You mean she's expecting? Oh, but that's wonderful. They are pleased?'

'Need you ask! She said they wanted to be absolutely sure before they talked about it in case they courted bad luck. But there's no doubt.' Sue remembered the empty room when she'd tapped on the door with her hot water bottle, then the unmistakable sound of retching from the bathroom at the end of the landing.

'Most mornings it only happens once, then I'm better,' Liz had told her as she came limply back to the bedroom. 'I expect because I wanted us to be early, I hurried too much. Quen said I must stay in bed. Were you sick every morning, Mum, with Paul and me? Purposely I told Quen everyone is. He's such a worrier.'

'Yes, I was. But it won't last.'

'Even now, it doesn't. I get up extra early so that I can get it over and be ready to go with Quen. Only, this morning it seemed to sort of hang about. It's finished now, I can tell. I'll have a bath and get dressed. So Mum, you and Dad are going to be grandparents. About the end of July or a bit after I expect. What do you think of that?' What a child she'd looked, sitting on the edge of the bed, waiting for praise just as she used to if she brought a good end-of-term report back from school.

Forgetting any remaining feeling of delicacy Sue had hugged her.

'I think it's wonderful. I want to tell the world.'

'I think the world can wait a few months,' Liz had giggled. 'Tell Dad if you like. And I'll tell the Grands and bit later the Joshes. I know it's silly, but I've quite liked no one knowing except Quentin and me.' Then with a chuckle of one-up-manship, 'I wonder what Paul will think.

They've been married all this time, over a year, and all she thinks of is that silly school.' No longer was she of no consequence, tagging long behind the others!

'I must go down, I was seeing to the chickens. You sure you're all right now?'

'Fit as a flea, Mum. There's something awfully degrading about being frightened to stand out of bed because you know another minute you'll have your head down the lavatory. But there you are — 'tis woman's lot.' And clearly she was a woman who was pleased with her lot.

Leaving her to get dressed, Sue went back to the yard to collect her basket and go on hunting in the usual places where the hens hid their eggs. Looking across towards Tim's office at the far end of the barn she saw the light was on; the egg hunt stood no chance against the pull of that.

★　★　★

Winter gradually loosened its grip. The future was bright, even the memory of the clouds that had darkened the earlier months of the previous year receded. Paul continued to make a success of his stewardship; Christopher wrote regularly from his new posting to Gibraltar, sometimes to the Grands, sometimes to Tim and Sue. As for Liz, tiny and almost childlike in build, yet, the early months over, she was going through her pregnancy with complete naturalness. For herself, Sue looked forward to the future with never a doubt; only at the back of her mind was one worry, a worry that had no positive

241

explanation and yet one she couldn't put out of her mind, and that was Sylvia.

On Whit Monday Top of the World was to be officially opened. Staff had been engaged some six weeks before that, for the place had to be eye-catching in the glasshouses and outside.

'You can't make a garden in a few months,' Quentin had said, 'not unless you buy in established specimens. What we show at Top of the World, we shall grow at Top of the World.' Even so, the previous autumn he had worked as hard as any farm labourer, ploughing, harrowing, raking and finally planting the sloping ground below the glasshouses. By spring the young and tender grass was through, ready for its first light trim in time for the opening. Behind glass on a notice board was a sketch of the proposed plans for the site, the position of the beds, the names of trees and shrubs that would one day turn the open grassland into a beautiful garden.

Midway between Easter and Whitsun there was a picture in the daily paper of Richard arriving from the United States, a little girl striding purposefully at his side. There was no sign of his wife and no mention of her in the short paragraph: 'Richard McBride arriving at Heathrow Airport yesterday with his four-year-old daughter Juliet. This is the child's first visit to his homeland and, from his expression, it is a moment of pride he has been looking forward to. The McBrides are to be well represented on the London stage in the coming months. Not only are his parents, Anthony McBride and Elvira

Dereford, keeping audiences enthralled in *Days of Winter*, but Richard is taking a break from his glittering Hollywood career and will be playing the lead in *Russian Roulette* which is due to open at the end of May.'

'Have you seen this?' Sue said as Quentin and Liz arrived back from a long day at the nursery. 'Your big brother's in England, Quentin.'

Heads close, the two read it. 'Your niece, Quen. She looks cocky, just her and her father.'

'Perhaps his wife's following, or already here. She's not a name like he is, the press wouldn't waylay her at the airport. But Liz . . . Richard here . . . do you suppose he'd do it?'

Why is it, Sue wondered, that those two can talk in riddles and always understand each other?

'Your parents would know where he's staying. We'd have to get his number from them.'

'Difficult,' was Quentin's opinion of that suggestion.

'But Quentin,' at least Sue believed she'd understood his reason for 'difficult', 'they came to your wedding. They were keen to be here.'

'What? Yes, I know. Oh, you didn't follow. We were thinking of asking Richard to open Top of the World. I wouldn't like to get his phone number from the parents, it's tantamount to telling them his name is a bigger draw than theirs.'

'Which,' Liz, the practical, put in, 'it is.'

'Perhaps he'll telephone you,' Sue suggested it, but she believed the chance was slim.

In the event, it was Sylvia who phoned that same evening. She said she was calling to see how everyone was, to make sure Liz was well, and how about Grandpa? And Sue threw in a few questions too, even though she was sure they were both skirting round the thing that was uppermost in Sylvia's mind. How was she getting on with her new promotion? (For Sylvia had been made Ward Sister.) What was the latest she'd heard from Christo?

'Aunt Sue, listen, I don't know what you're going to say. But please, *please*, try and understand. It's so important to me that you and Uncle Tim know what I'm doing is right.'

'It's Richard, isn't it.'

'It always has been. Tell me I'll get hurt — well, isn't it better to *live* even if you know there will be pain; it must be better that just existing. He came home yesterday morning.'

'Where's his wife? I saw the picture, just Richard and the little girl.'

'Juliet. He adores her. I know that. I haven't any illusions, Aunt Sue. I know his most honest, pure love is for Juliet. I know that I'll never be part of that life he lives in Hollywood, or even amongst his stage friends in London. All I can be is a sort of secret, important — honestly I *know* that — but a secret part of his life, kept hidden.'

'Sylvie, you're worth more than that.' Sue kept her voice low, the hall seemed such a public place to carry on a conversation. Even though Harold and Lucinda had been in bed for some time, if they heard she was talking to Sylvia, they'd be downstairs like a shot.

'How many of us get what we think we're worth? Anyway, without him I'm not worth

244

anything. Listen, Aunt Sue, and please try and understand, please don't feel disappointed and think I'm making a mess of my life. Richard is buying a small flat. When I say he's buying it I mean he's paying for it. It's to be in my name. We found it this afternoon, a top flat in a converted Regency house.'

It was as if that niggling worry that had prodded Sue in her quiet moments suddenly burst into life. But what could she say? To condemn Sylvia would hurt her (and who knows how much hurt was already lying in wait for her without alienating her from her family). And anyway, did she wholly condemn? What sort of love puts self-interest first? Was that what she wanted for Sylvia?

'Am I happy for you or sad? Honestly, I don't know. Happy I suppose. Except — call me old-fashioned and I expect you'd be right — but he has a wife. You say how much he cares for Juliet, then surely he ought to be thinking of her and putting his marriage before everything else, even you. That sounds cruel, I don't mean it to.'

'I know that. Do you think I can ever forget he has a wife? I'm like some star-struck kid, the way I flick through all the movie magazines on the newsagents' racks looking for pictures — the two of them together at film premières or guests at some glamorous and unreal sort of party. I know people would say I'm being a fool — except those who would write me off as a scarlet woman. But, Aunt Sue, you and Uncle Tim aren't just people, you're the ones who have given me the principles I live by. I want your blessing.' Then, more defiantly, 'Nothing will change what I do, it's as if I have no choice. Try and understand. I know it's hard. You and Uncle Tim didn't have an easy time, both of you young when you married, then all us lot to look after. Romance must have got blown out of the window.'

Sue frowned. If that's what Sylvia thought, then was she really mature enough to go into the sort of relationship she intended?

'Of course you have my blessing. And, Sylvie, the dearest thing I can hope for you both is that it lasts all your days,' then with the hint of a laugh, 'even when romance has got blown out of the window.'

Later she related the conversation to Tim, prepared to fight his disapproval and stand up for Sylvia. In the event he heard her through in silence.

'He's not the first man to get swept off his feet by some glamorous and easily available woman. The child's mother, I mean. I remember the first year he came across from the school to help carry the harvest, Sylvia could hardly take her eyes off him.'

'That was just a schoolgirl crush.' Immediately Sue wished she hadn't said it.

'Let's say please God this isn't, and please God she will always be the secret he can't exist without.' Tim didn't condemn, he didn't so much as consider the social stigma Sylvia was inviting. Relief flooded over Sue; his attitude gave her freedom to condone the sort of extra-marital relationship that was outside her

246

own experience. 'Didn't you say earlier that the youngsters wanted to ask him to open the nursery? Did you remember to get his telephone number from Sylvia?'

'I'll call her back. No — better than that. You speak to her, Tim.'

He did. Purposely Sue busied herself in the kitchen, she didn't want to be tempted to eavesdrop. The outcome of that call was that on Whit weekend Highmoor buzzed with life and activity, every room was filled.

'We'll need both leaves in the dining table,' Sue told Paul, home for the nursery's big day.

'Let's eat in the kitchen, Mum. I'll carry the table down from the playroom to put on the end of this one. 'Home' is the kitchen, not the dining room as if we were all visitors. Or is it because Richard McBride is too swanky these days?'

'Richard is no such thing,' she defended. 'Yes, we'll eat out here. The heart of the house; that's what Mrs Josh used to call it when you were all small.'

'Hey, lady, don't start talking in that tone as if you were Old Mother Time. I'll get the table. Philippa is doing some marking, she'll be upstairs for a while yet.'

She turned away so that he couldn't read her thoughts. Marking, be damned! If she were the wonderful teacher and organiser she liked to let them believe, then she need not have brought the excuse of a pile of exercise books away for the weekend. More likely she thought herself too intellectually superior for the rest of them! With her mouth set in an unusually tight line, Sue plunged her hands into a bowl of water and started to trim the stalks of a huge pile of asparagus Josh had cut fresh that morning.

'Wanting a hand with anything, duckie?' Mrs Josh appeared in the open doorway.

'Not if you're busy. Otherwise, it would be a nice idea if you made some elevenses for you, me and the Grands. Put enough water in case Paul wants a coffee too.'

'Just Paul? Where's *she* then?'

'She has some school work to see to.'

'Huh,' and a sniff was clear expression of Mrs Josh's sentiments. 'What time is Sylvie bringing our celebrity? Funny, isn't it, that brother of Quentin's being the sort of idol the young girls make such a song and dance over. Rudolph Valentino — was the same with him, you know, when I was young. Couldn't see what they went so silly about myself, give me a man with a bit of brawn, someone who would be on hand to change a washer in the tap or unblock the sink. Poofy lot, some of them.'

Sue laughed. 'Not Richard, no one could call him that.'

'Nice enough young man, I dare say. Looked pleased with himself in that picture with his little girl. But it's not natural, not for real proper people like you and me, duckie, a man coming all that way with a child and no wife. What's she up to, back there in that make-believe world? Faces plastered with make-up, half-naked bodies, bosoms pushed pretty well to their chins. If the Lord had meant a woman to have breasts turning upwards, that's the way he would have fashioned them. Silly lot they are, if you ask me. Three dessertspoons of coffee be enough, you reckon? Maybe I'll put in a fourth. If her ladyship takes her nose out of her books she might come down and we wouldn't want her to think we didn't know how to make a good strong cup.'

'Richard adores the little girl, so Sylvia says.'

'Ah, very likely. Poor little soul. What sort of fun can it be for a child, tagging along like some sort of showpiece? Never mind, we'll have to see to it she enjoys her weekend. Our little Liz never flags, does she? But then, she always had her own share of energy and someone else's too. There, we'll give that five minutes to brew then I'll give the old dears a call.'

* * *

'I've put Richard in the end room, and put the little camp bed in there for Juliet,' Sue told Sylvia. 'You're across the landing in your own room.' She looked as uncertain as she felt. Would Sylvia see it as an expression of disapproval?

'That's fine, Aunt Sue.' Then, seeing how Sue relaxed, 'Funny lady you are,' she laughed.

'It was because of the Grands . . . and Philippa, she's so toffee-nosed — '

'I mean funny lady for worrying,' Sylvia put her arm around Sue's waist and hugged her.

Richard seemed equally relaxed. On the Saturday afternoon the two of them took Juliet up the steep slope to the nursery.

'Here, lady,' Tim called to Sue as she came out

of her mushroom shed, 'what do you make of them?'

She joined him. Leaning together over the five-barred gate that led to the first of the cattle fields they watched as Richard climbed the stile that divided Tim's land from Quentin's. Then Sylvia helped Juliet up, so that he could lean across and lift her over.

'I wish it were different,' he said. 'But who are we to say? I wish we could watch them and have no — no — shame? Is it shame, Sue? That child deserves two parents. Sylvia deserves better than she will ever find with him.'

'I'm schooling myself to stop worrying about any of them.'

'Liar,' he laughed. 'Come on, I'll give you a hand with the hen houses.'

* * *

The advantages of having Richard to perform the opening ceremony were twofold. Even before that weekend he had let it be known to the press where he and his daughter would be. In turn the press did their homework, recalled how the previous year he had been best man at his brother's wedding and took up the story from there. All of that was free advertising beyond anything Quentin could have hoped for. Add to that the crowds who would flock merely for the sight of Richard McBride and the sound of that glorious speaking voice that earned him such renown, and the opening was an assured success. A field was opened for car parking, Paul put himself in charge of the amplifier hired for the occasion and, when the speeches were over and Top of the World officially open, he made sure that soft music relaxed visitors into staying. Richard mingled with the visitors, he let himself be seen buying plants (what could he do with plants?), other people followed suit. The cash till rung.

'Have you seen Harold?' Lucinda tugged Sue's arm to attract her attention.

'He was here earlier. He was here when Richard was talking. He'll be all right, Aunt Luce, what harm can come to him up here?'

'Silly of me, I just don't like not to be able to see where he is. I'll ask the others. Perhaps he's helping Paul with the music.'

But he wasn't. None of them had actually missed him until they were asked, yet neither had any of them seen him.

'I'll walk back to the house and see if he's there,' Philippa offered. 'He probably wanted to get away from the crowd.' Certainly it was what she wanted.

She found him in the farmyard, surrounded by doleful-looking cows. It was only then that she realised the gate leading to the field had been left open.

'Ah!' he greeted her, standing a fraction taller, touching his cravat to make sure his appearance did him credit. 'They're all off out somewhere. But come along in, my dear. Let me see now, you'll be Paul's filly, eh? What?'

'Never mind that. Look what you've done. And the gate to the lane is open too. Thank God

I got Paul away from this madhouse. Here, give me that broom and you stay where you are.'

Docilely he did as she said. That extra inch he'd gained when he'd stood purposefully straight was lost, his face was a mask of misery.

'Done something wrong . . . ' he muttered. 'Silly old fool I am. Time I was gone.' He leant against the side of the barn, his mouth working yet having no real idea of how he'd disgraced himself. Looking down he noted he was wearing his best linen suit. Must be some reason. Ah, because the pretty filly had come to see them. Yes, that would be it. Forgetting his instructions, he followed her round to the front of the house and out on to the lane. Lucky dog, young Paul. Just a bit of a boy, what would he know about keeping a goer like that one happy? Good legs, ah, right up to the round little arse.

'I'll give you a hand,' he called as he came towards her. By gum, he'd like to give her a hand too. All talk, that's your trouble, Harold Ruddick. No, oh no, I'd be as good as any man if I could get my hands on that one for five minutes. Spirit's willing, by gum, yes, so it is. I'd give her a hand, right on that little arse . . .

Philippa ignored his presence as, waving her broom, she rounded up the five cows who were contentedly munching the grass on the verge of the lane. Born and bred in the town, with neither love for nor interest in the ways of country living, yet she drove the cows as efficiently as she did everything. The front gate closed, she turned her attention to getting all of them back in the field where they belonged.

'You and Paul,' close behind her Harold's voice startled her, 'he's just a lad you know. Things he doesn't know . . . a girl like you . . . ' His brain may have been feeble, but his hand moved fast enough to take her by surprise as he lifted her short, flared skirt and dipped into the elasticated top of her knickers.

'Why, you dirty old bugger,' she kicked backwards, the heel of her sandal striking his shin.

'Didn't mean . . . didn't know . . . don't tell . . . silly old fool I am . . . useless . . . don't know.'

'Shut up your drivelling nonsense and get out of my way.'

'Yes.' He'd done something to upset her badly. Oh dear, if only he could think. What was it he'd done? Anything? Nothing? Did he really remember the feeling of smooth, warm flesh? Or had it been just his imagination? It was what he thought about every time he looked at her. Good breasts, get his hand under one of those, feel it warm and heavy. He ought to apologise to her, but he was so confused he wasn't sure if he'd actually touched her at all. Good-looking gal, by gum, if he were younger he'd give her a good seeing to. He didn't like it that she was angry with him. He wished he knew what he'd done to upset her. Had he told her the things he'd like to do to her? He didn't think he had.

He cleared his throat and made a supreme effort. In that moment he felt he was still the man he used to be in those far-off days in India.

'We've got them all back in their field, my

dear,' he said as she shut the gate between the farmyard and the grazing pasture.

'Now you'd better start clearing up the mess they've left in the yard, it was you who caused it. I'm going indoors, I have some reading to do. And don't you get ideas and start following me upstairs.' She turned away, muttering something to herself. To Harold there was no doubt what it was, 'useless old half-wit, how do they put up with him?'

It would have broken Lucinda's heart if she could have seen the way his face crumpled as he turned his back on Philippa's retreating figure. Taking the broom he started to sweep the yard, spreading what had been three individual cow pats over a wide area and clogging the tough bristles. Can't do it . . . making it worse. Josh'll help me. Josh'll know what we have to do.

Dropping his broom he went round to the front of the house and out into the lane, again leaving the gate open but this time it didn't matter, now that the cows were safely back in the field. Most days he walked along to see the Joshes, he even believed they looked forward to his visits as much as he did.

'All right for me to come in?' he called, opening the door, certain of his welcome. Then, when there was no reply, 'You there, Mrs Josh?' from the bottom of the stairs. Disappointed, he looked out of the window on to their tidy patch of garden. Perhaps he'd sit down and wait a while, they'd be pleased to find him here when they got back from wherever they'd gone. Funny where everyone was this afternoon.

By this time all knowledge of the opening of the nursery was lost to him. But some things needed no active memory to penetrate his understanding, things like the fact that at Highmoor, whatever the weather, a fire always burnt in the kitchen. There it heated the water, so he supposed the fire in the kitchen range at the Joshes' cottage must do the same. That the range was cold, all that was left in it the well-sieved and unburnt coals from last time, didn't change the direction his thoughts were going. Neither did the fact that there was a perfectly good gas cooker next to the porcelain sink.

Harold thought of his friends, imagined them returning home to find him waiting, a warm glow behind the bars of the range. He'd go outside to the shed and find a few slithers of wood to get it going. It was a long time since he'd had a fire to build, the task carried him back to better days. He hummed as he filled the scuttle with small, quick-to-burn knobs of coal, then collected a good bundle of twigs and tinder wood. Next thing would be matches. Now where would Mrs Josh keep her matches? 'The Blue Danube' was getting a good airing as he hunted, moving from mantelpiece to drawer in time to the music. No matches. Never mind, he'd make some spills and light them with his cigarette lighter. His failure in the farmyard vanished from his memory, he was delighted with the prospect of the pleasure he was going to give the Joshes. That the spills were made with the gas bill that had arrived that morning and been put behind the clock on the mantelpiece didn't come into his scheme of things. Twirling to the waltz time of his favourite 'The Blue Danube' and seemingly hypnotised by the flickering flame of the spill he caught his foot on the hearthrug and almost stumbled. As his fingers burnt he dropped the flaming paper, but he didn't lose the rhythm of the dance. While his shallow concentration had been on lighting a fire for his friends, he had rolled up the centre pages of the morning's newspaper to make a nest for the tinder wood he arranged on top of it in the grate. The remaining pages had been discarded and left lying on the hearth. Now as he dropped the burning spill for a second it caught in the turn-up of his trouser leg before he waltzed free and it landed on the unwanted pages. The dance and the vivid scene in the Mess that had been part of the life he'd loved filled his mind; in that first minute he was unaware that the material of his trousers was burning. Then something stung his leg, stung it again and harder. Looking down he saw the yellow tongue licking at the material of his trousers and, beyond that, the flames were leaping from the fast disappearing newspaper. The scene in the Mess vanished, the music was silenced and the dance stilled. He was alone and frightened. He shook his leg as if that would free him of the fire, then he picked up the remains of the burning paper. Trapped in pain and terror he hadn't known what to do. The flames from the paper leapt high; that's when he dropped it on to the table, where it started to devour Mrs Josh's neat pile of darning.

At Top of the World champagne had been handed around (champagne brought from London by Richard) to the customers. Sales had been far higher than expectations; visitors whose object in coming had been to see a real live film star were gradually departing while Quentin was happily talking to the genuine horticulturists.

'I think I'll walk on home, dear. Unless you'd like an extra pair of hands with the glasses,' Lucinda said to Sue, who, with Mrs Josh, was washing the champagne flutes hired from Richard's off-licence.

'Won't you wait, Aunt Luce? You mustn't worry about him, Philippa must have found him or she would have come back.'

'Yes, yes, dear, I'm sure she must have found him.' And for some inexplicable reason it was that that worried her. She'd noticed the way he watched the girl. He wasn't really capable of — well, of doing any damage, she couldn't bring herself even to think the unthinkable. But she could read his mind, and she'd known him too long to be mistaken. 'What about you walking home with me, Juliet? Shall we go together?'

The little girl turned the idea over in her mind, looking seriously at Lucinda, whom she saw as extremely elderly and frail.

'Sure, I'll come along with you. You can hold on to me if you like, going down the hill. I'm tough as old boots, that's what Dad says. Why do you suppose old boots are tough? I'd have thought they were thin and worn out.' Like you

257

are, she added silently, but her jolly smile gave no hint of it.

'I expect you grow out of yours long before they get worn out,' Lucinda struck just the right note to earn Juliet's liking.

'Yep. I'm growing 'normously tall. Like Dad I expect. He's tall and strong too, that's what I'm going to be.'

'I shall be glad of your help at the stile,' Lucinda pandered to her ego, knowing that it would be nearer the truth that she would have to be the one to give a helping hand.

The little girl smiled delightedly at her, then held up her hand for Lucinda to take.

'Look at that, Grandma,' she said as, the stile safely behind them, they turned the bend towards the farmhouse and the cottages.

'Oh dear, Juliet, we'd better hurry. You know what I think? I think he's lit a bonfire. Can't turn my back two minutes . . . '

9

Before they came to the farmyard where the discarded broom had been dropped amidst traces of recent bovine occupation, Lucinda realised the smoke was coming from further along the lane, shielded from view by trees. She had heard Tim say that once the morning milking was done Fred and his wife were going to spend the Bank Holiday with their married daughter in Swindon. But how unlike Josh to light a bonfire and leave it to burn while they were both out.

'Let's go and find Grandpa and Philippa. They must be indoors.'

'OK.' Juliet agreed obligingly, although she wasn't enamoured with the prospect. Grandpa, as she'd been told to call him, made her feel uncomfortable and the lady with red hair hadn't shown signs of being any fun at all. A sigh escaped her before she could remind herself that she was meaning to be very good so her father would be proud of her.

'Harold! Harold, are you there? Are you upstairs? Harold! Philippa! Oh dear, wherever can they be? Perhaps she's still looking for him.'

'I'm up here, Mrs Ruddick. I found Mr Ruddick. The cows were all over the place, he'd left the gates open. He's down there somewhere, I left him clearing up the mess they'd made.'

'You mean you left him by himself? Oh dear,

we never do that. He's not come back to the nursery.'

'He must be around.' So much for gratitude! Coming back to the farm, chasing after those wretched cows the old idiot had let out, and fine thanks she got for it. But leaning over the banisters she looked at Lucinda and forgot to be angry. Poor old dear, being saddled with that smutty old bugger. What would she say if she knew how he'd been pawing me with his hand down my knickers? If he belonged to me and got himself lost, I'd let well alone.

'There's smoke along the lane. Fred's away for the day. Would Josh have lit a bonfire, then gone out? You don't think . . . ?'

Philippa's mind was full of anger but it was overruled by her heart as she looked at Lucinda's helpless anxiety.

'We'll walk along and see, shall we? If it's out of hand, I'll throw some dirt on it. Does he like fires? I mean, why would he want to light a bonfire?'

Lucinda shook her head. 'Don't know.' Then, hating to read Philippa's expression, 'He wasn't always like this. A fine man, courageous, quick-witted. It's as much an illness as any other, but so much harder to watch.'

'Come on, Mrs Ruddick, let's go and see what he's up to. Coming, Juliet?'

'Sure, I'll come.' A bonfire sounded more promising. She put her hand into Lucinda's, a reminder that she was here to give support, then strode out in the direction of the lane and, she hoped, adventure.

'Oh my dear Lord,' Lucinda breathed. 'The smoke, it's coming from the back door, the kitchen door.'

Now what was the idiot doing? Yet, even thinking it, Philippa didn't hesitate. 'You and Juliet stay here, I'll run on.' An illness it may be, but Philippa's anger towards Harold grew by the second. Why couldn't he try and consider his poor, worrying wife once in a while? Well, it had to be up to her, there was no one else to go in and get the old imbecile out. But perhaps they were misjudging him, perhaps old Mrs Josh had left airing too close to the fire. Perhaps sparks had spattered on to a hearthrug. All these thoughts crowded one on top of another in her mind as she ran towards the open back door. Perhaps . . . she clutched at straws as she came to the open doorway. Already the black smoke was stinging her eyes, smoke so thick that through it she could see nothing except yellow tongues of fire licking on what was in truth the chenille table covering (but from that distance Philippa didn't know that).

Just briefly she looked back to the lane and, if she'd needed anything to boost her courage, she found it in Lucinda's expression. So what to do? He must be in the cottage somewhere. If he'd started the fire, more than likely he would have hidden from it up in the bedroom. Barmy as hell, there was no knowing how his mind would have worked. Used to be different, that's what the old lady had said, used to be a fine man, quick-witted. She shivered despite the heat. Guided by instinct, she was tearing open the buttons of her blouse and taking it off. The water in the butt was stale, but this was no moment to consider hygiene. She dipped her blouse in the water, then tied it across her mouth and nose. The smell was horrible, but at least it might help her to breathe. Then, dropping to her knees, she started the crawl across the smoke-filled kitchen. The smoke was filling her throat and her lungs; making a supreme effort she shouted.

'Are you upstairs? Stay there, I'll come and get you,' she choked. Her eyes stung and watered so that she could hardly see. That's how it was that she was almost on top of Harold before she realised. Frantically, she looked around as if inspiration would come like a genie in a cloud of smoke. Then, using all her might, she started to roll him, backwards and forwards, over and over. What the flames had left of his best linen suit was a blackened wreck. But the flames were out. That's when she tore her blouse from her face and wrapped it round his singed hair. All the time the image in front of her was Lucinda, waiting, trusting . . .

Crawling backwards she dragged Harold towards the fresh air. In the kitchen the fire was dancing merrily, reaching out to the curtains, the cushions on the wooden fireside chairs, even starting to eat into the wallpaper.

'Ring for the fire engine,' she yelled. And from outside, even before she brought Harold into view, they heard her.

Juliet didn't like it at all. She felt frightened and didn't understand why. 'I'll go and get Dad.' Her relief at the thought was overwhelming. 'I know the way. I'll get Dad.' And she was gone, thankful to get away from the old lady with such a funny dazed look as if she didn't know where she was. The red-haired one had said something about a fire engine, but the Grandma one was just standing there as if her shoes were stuck to the lane.

Just as Harold had an hour or so before, Juliet left the gate open between the pasture and the farmyard, but this time the cows stood watching her benignly as she made manfully for the hill that her short legs felt to be a mountain. The stile wasn't easy, but she wasn't one to give in and she managed.

'Dad!' she shouted using all the breath she could muster, 'Dad! I've come to get you. The lady with red hair said get the fire engine but Grandma is just standing there. I don't think she knows how to do it. And I don't know either.'

By that time Quentin was seeing the last of the visitors into their car, the boxes of seedlings carefully stowed and a large order left for delivery in another month or so. He was the only one who didn't see Juliet's arrival. As he turned to walk back from the car park he met the family literally running towards him *en masse*, all of them except Liz.

'What's happened? Where's Liz!'

'She'll explain,' Tim answered. 'Sue and I will take the Joshes, you others pile in with Richard.' Even as he spoke he was in the car and the engine started. The road way was much longer than cutting through the farm but he drove fast, not even slowing down as they went over the rutted ground of the lane. Just inside the gate to Highmoor he stopped and they all piled out.

'It's either Josh's or Fred's. You send for the engine, Sue, we'll go straight down there.'

They were met with the sight of Philippa, her wet and filthy blouse discarded, her hair tumbled from its usual ballerina-like coiffeur, her eyes bloodshot, her face, shoulders, arms, in fact all that was visible, smeared with black streaks. But they hardly noticed her as they saw the form lying on the verge. Harold had been taken to the nursery looking handsome and debonair in his light linen suit. Now the suit was unrecognisable, in fact most of it was no more than charred remains; with his smoke-blackened skin and singed hair they would not have known him.

By that time Richard's car had arrived. In one glance he took in the scene and decided it was no place for Juliet. No one seemed to notice him as he picked her up and carried her back to the farm. Carried her? Juliet was never carried, she prided herself that baby days were long gone. But as he lifted her she wrapped her arms around him and buried her face against his neck. She didn't want to see that man lying on the ground, she wanted it not to have happened.

'You and I have a job to do,' he whispered. 'Some of the cows have got into the yard, do you think we can persuade them back where they belong?'

'Um,' she nodded, 'we'll do it together, Dad.' With her head still nuzzling against his neck and her eyes closed, she didn't see Sue hurrying from the lobby, anxious to get back to the others.

'Sue, it's not good. Sylvie's there now, but we ought to get an ambulance. It's Mr Ruddick. I don't know how he is, but he'll need help.' Sue knew he kept that light note in his voice on account of Juliet.

As house fires go, the damage to the cottage wasn't extensive. The damage to Harold was far more serious.

★   ★   ★

Tim and Sue drove Lucinda to Reading to the hospital. Purposely he didn't try to keep pace with the ambulance they followed; Lucinda had had shock enough without the clanging of the bell orchestrating her misery. Once in the waiting room of the casualty department, memories crowded back on Sue. She slipped her hand into Tim's and felt the answering pressure. Remembering it all from this distance in time, Sue realised just how far the terror had receded.

Perhaps Bank Holidays bring more than their share of minor accidents, perhaps most of those waiting were here for nothing more serious than cuts or sprains. Yet she knew so well the feeling of helplessness she recognised on the faces of those waiting on the long wooden benches. They'll look back on it, she told herself, just like we do now; once they are healed the horror will go. And for Aunt Luce, please help her, make things good for her. Perhaps the shock might sort out the tangles in his mind, perhaps like the trip switch on the electricity meter. If only it could be like that and she'd have him given back to her, the *real* person.

For two hours they sat there before a nurse came across to Lucinda and, in a hushed and gentle voice, told her the Casualty Sister would like to speak to her. Sue and Tim went with her.

★   ★   ★

None of them talked as they drove home from the hospital. By the time the formalities had been dealt with the evening was over. Once or twice Sue turned to look at Lucinda, so still and quiet that she might have been asleep. How could she remain so composed? Even as they'd listened to the Sister telling them there had been nothing they could do, he hadn't regained consciousness and had died peacefully, Lucinda had shown no sign of emotion.

Arriving in the lane to the farm they could see the fire engine was still outside Josh's cottage. The still air was full of the smell of burning, and although the fire was out the engine would stay until there was no fear of it finding somewhere to take hold again.

Tim parked near the lobby, then without waiting for the others went straight indoors. So by the time Sue and Lucinda went in the news had arrived before them. Liz had never come face to face with death before; the nearest had been when Tim had been rushed to hospital but he'd recovered and seemed so fit that she'd relaxed back into that childhood feeling that tragedies only happened to other people. When she put her arms around Lucinda she didn't

266

even ask herself whether she was giving comfort or looking for it.

'There, child, you mustn't be upset,' Lucinda told her. 'She ought to be in bed, Quentin, she's had a busy day.'

Seeing the Joshes standing there with Quentin and Liz made Sue realise how the fire was changing all their lives.

'The others all had to go, Mum,' Quentin told her. 'Except for Richard, they're working tomorrow. I promised we'd phone them when you got home. Shall I do that?'

Sue nodded, then with her back to Lucinda and speaking quietly she told him what the Sister had said. Then turning to the Joshes, 'Liz has sorted you out? You know which room is to be yours?'

'Mrs Tim, duckie, by tomorrow we'll start drying out. I told Liz, even tonight upstairs would be all right for us at the cottage.'

'Go to bed and get a good night's sleep, we'll think of all that tomorrow. And you, Liz, you ought to be in bed like Aunt Luce says.'

So they were left alone, just the three of them.

★   ★   ★

'I don't need tablets,' Lucinda pushed them away. 'I don't want to be sent off to sleep. Not tonight, my dears.'

'You need your rest,' Tim laid his hand on her shoulder. 'Swallow them down with your Horlicks.'

'Rest is more than sleep, Tim. How long is it

since my mind has been able to rest? My poor Harold, awake or asleep I was alert. Of course I was. Just like when Tim was ill, Sue, you tried to take over his jobs; Harold's mind was ill, I had to think for both of us, I had to watch out for him. This afternoon I didn't. I forgot to watch him.'

'There were so many people milling about.' It was the first excuse Sue could pull out of the air.

'For more than fifty years we were together.' If only she'd weep, Sue thought. But there was something uncannily calm, almost peaceful, about the old lady as she sat at the kitchen table, her cold hands gripping her mug of Horlicks. That she was cold on such a mild night was the only hint that she was in shock. 'I can't find the words to make you understand. Only God in his heaven can know that it's because Harold was — is — so dear to me that I feel as if a great burden has been taken from me. No — I've said it badly. I knew I would.'

'Drink up while it's warm,' Sue realised that that too was a senseless remark to make. It wasn't a sleep-inducing drink Lucinda needed, it was someone to listen to her rambling thoughts.

'He's not muddled any longer, Aunt Luce.' It was Tim who understood. Lucinda turned to him, this time her eyes brimming with tears that a minute before hadn't even threatened.

'Dear Tim,' she muttered, digging in her pocket for a lace-edged and inadequate handker-chief. 'You do believe that, don't you? You're not trying to comfort me?'

'Aunt Luce, the real man never changed. Our bodies may fail, but nothing destroys the true essence of what we are. That's why he was so often frightened, he knew he was out of step and he couldn't straighten things out. But now all that's behind him. His soul is the same now as always.'

'Always and forever,' she whispered, blinded by tears. 'You see why I won't take those tablets. Tonight I can talk to him, tell him things and he'll understand.'

Sue kept her back to them, making an excuse of raking the fire and banking it up for the night. Twenty-four hours ago the old house had been alive with the sound of young voices, except for Christo the whole family home. Not just the family, for Richard and Juliet had been there. She wished she could dispel that niggling doubt, that fear that Sylvia was courting trouble. But all that belonged to last night. Tonight so much was changed: Harold gone for ever, the young ones rushing back to be caught up in their own busy lives. Only Highmoor stayed the same. Not for the first time Sue found herself aware of generations of Marshalls who had lived and died in the old house. And tonight, perhaps because she was more shaken than she realised by the events of the day, she let her thoughts go to Liz. Before many more weeks were passed there would be another generation, another thread to weave into the pattern.

'Come on, lady, are you going to kneel in front of that range all night?' Tim hoisted her to her feet. 'Time we all went to bed.'

* * *

269

Had Philippa been many minutes later it would have been impossible for her to get through the flames and recover Harold's unconscious body. By daylight the cottage was a desolate sight. Worst of all was the kitchen, of course, but no one would ever discover what he'd been doing that could have started a fire. Mercifully, the next morning when Tim, Sue and the Joshes stood in the water-soaked, charred remains of the kitchen none of them knew how the poor, broken one-time soldier's waltzing fantasy had ended as he'd fallen, screaming, to his knees.

'Upstairs wasn't burnt. We'll have to get working on cleaning up all the downstairs mess, but upstairs wasn't touched,' Mrs Josh turned to lead the way up the narrow staircase. But, of course, upstairs was smoke-blackened, the acrid smell of the fire was everywhere.

'We'll get Hunters in,' Tim said, naming the local builder who had done most of Quentin's work at the nursery and the conversion of the top rooms in the farmhouse. 'The whole place must be done right through. Insurance will take care of it,' he added, seeing their concern. 'Meantime you must bring what you can of your own things over to us. The house is large enough for all of us; we'll sort things out so that you can have your own sitting room.'

No one, not even Josh, had ever seen Mrs Josh cry. But she cried now.

'Poor old gentleman,' she excused her weakness. Not for the world would she let anyone guess that her tears were for the place that had been home since she'd come there as a bride of eighteen.

★ ★ ★

Quentin was looking out of their sitting-room window, his gaze drawn to the nursery buildings, the glass glinting in the rays of the setting sun. He heard Liz coming up the second flight of stairs, stopping to listen as someone from downstairs called to her.

'Sorry, Mum, say it again, I didn't hear,' he heard her shout back.

Soon the baby would be here, and as he listened to Liz and her mother's shouted conversation a worried frown clouded his thin face. If they were downstairs how would they ever hear a small baby cry? They wouldn't. Of course there was no reason why they should be downstairs, these rooms were their home. But Highmoor wasn't like that, you couldn't live here and feel yourself separated from other people. Had the idea of converting these rooms been a mistake? Ought he to have dipped further into his legacy and had a modern bungalow built next to the nursery? A modern bungalow? No, not for Liz and him . . . Liz, him and their family. He wanted their children to be brought up in this changeless place. There had been Marshalls here for two hundred years. He wasn't a Marshall, neither would his children be Marshalls; but they were part of the clan. This is where they would belong, just as he did.

Later, lying in bed, he put his suggestion to Liz.

'The Joshes' cottage? At the moment it's the most ghastly mess, but if we were having it we could get it done just as we wanted. Yes, Quen, let's do that. We'd have a garden of our own — you'd like that. A proper home of our own. But what about these rooms? I suppose it would be quite useful for Mum and Dad to have the extra space now that their rubbish has been cleared out and they're habitable again.'

'I thought the Joshes might move in here. It's not for me to suggest, I mean Mum and Dad would have to like the idea and suggest it to them. But before I mention it, what do you think, Liz? It would be better if we were downstairs again while the cottage is got ready, this is too far away for us to hear a baby.'

'I think it's a gorgeous idea. Give me your hand, Quen. Feel him, I think he thinks he's a Morris dancer tonight.'

In the dark, Quentin rested the flat of his hand on her swollen body. His jaw ached, his heart was thumping, he was weak with love for his precious Liz as he felt the squirming movement of their child.

The next day he went in search of Tim and found him in his office checking the bill he'd just received for animal feed. Coming straight to the point, he put forward his suggestion.

'It's been the Joshes' home far longer than I've owned the farm,' Tim pointed out. 'I can understand your wanting a place of your own, you and Liz, and perhaps the top of the house isn't right for a baby. But Quentin, the Joshes' views must be considered.'

'But of course.'

'Their cottage went with his job. That was years ago when he was no older than you are now. Whether he can still work or not, as far as I'm concerned it remains their home — full stop. If we put your suggestion to them, they may feel they have no choice but to accept. I won't have them made to feel they have no right to the cottage.'

Quentin pulled off his glasses, digging for his handkerchief. They were treated to a polish so vigorous that it was a wonder he didn't damage the lenses.

'But you know that's not what I meant. Forget the whole thing if that's what it looks like.'

Tim looked at the young man who had been like a son to him for so long. Poor confused Quentin, his one fault was that when he cared, he cared too deeply. Getting up from the table that tried to pretend it was a desk, Tim put his arm around him.

'Josh is out in the yard, we'll get him over. Keep the ladies out of it for the moment.'

Josh had taken Quentin under his wing from his first day at Highmoor; even as a child there had been little the elderly man hadn't understood about the nervous boy. So, hearing the proposition, he had no thoughts of being pushed out to suit Quentin and Liz's convenience.

'But those posh rooms you've just had done, lad, you can't mean you want to hand them over like that. Anyway, the big house, that's up to Mr

273

Tim here. Ada and me, we're grateful to be there till the cottage has a bit of new paint on it. That's what we'd thought. But if you and Liz want the cottage, then me and Ada, we'll find — '

'Please Josh, don't even say it.' Off came Quentin's glasses, his eyes tight closed, then as if he realised what he was doing he rammed them back on again before they were treated to a second unnecessary polish in not many more minutes. 'You know it's not that.'

Tim moved to sit down again, watching his old mentor, who seemed never quite able to forget that he'd come to Highmoor as a young farm worker.

'We both know it's not that, Quentin,' Tim said reassuringly. 'Tell Josh everything you've told me.'

So, looking directly at Josh, Quentin did just that. Had he been talking to Barbara Kimber, his solemn owl-like expression would have made her uncomfortable just as it used to when he'd been a pupil at Merton Court; Josh knew him better. He heard how Quentin was worried that if a baby were put to bed at the top of the house, unless one of them was up there its cries wouldn't be heard. He gave Josh an easy loophole to avoid being pushed into anything he didn't want, by talking about the alternative of building a bungalow on part of the ground belonging to the nursery.

'There's only one thing I'm absolutely determined about,' he said, talking now to both of them, 'and that's that this baby, and any other children we have, will be brought up amongst all this. I know what it meant to me when I used to come here. That's what I want for our family, to know that we're all one unit. It's Highmoor, and it's even more than that; it would be the same wherever we were if we were all of us there for each other — and that means you and Mrs Josh too.'

'Bless the boy,' Josh muttered, not quite looking at either of them.

'Don't say anything Josh, not yet,' Tim drew a line under the conversation. 'Talk to Mrs Josh. As far as I'm concerned, and I know this goes for Sue too, nothing would please us more than knowing you two were making your home in the quarters Quentin and Liz sorted out.' He knew Mrs Josh's independent streak and it had always worried him that if the time came when she was without Josh, she would go to the council and ask to be housed. As Quentin had said (and surely as only Quentin could say it, with honesty and tightly reined emotion) the Joshes belonged with the family.

'Talk to her, Josh. But promise you won't try and persuade her into anything she doesn't want. The cottage is yours; I had a cheek even to suggest we swapped. Promise me.'

'Aye, lad, I'll give you my word. But I recall well enough how she cracked on about that kitchen you had put in for your Liz. And the view. You sure you want to give all that up and go to live in a labourer's cottage?'

★   ★   ★

275

The upshot of it all was that Quentin and Liz moved down to the first floor while the work to the cottage continued, and the Joshes were installed in their own so-called self-contained apartment at the top of the house. Self-contained or otherwise their entrance was through the kitchen and the lobby, and except that they were all under one roof life went on much as it had before the fire.

The new arrangement suited Lucinda well. Time had been when Harold had always been sure of a friendly welcome at the cottage. Being with the Joshes had somehow made him less bothered by those dreadful thoughts he could never untangle. Now it was Lucinda who took to climbing that top flight of stairs. There was something soothingly companionable about sitting by the sitting-room window with Mrs Josh, usually both of them knitting for the coming baby.

Still Liz went to the nursery each day, for by July 'her' glasshouse combined with the outside area planted for her use gave her a riot of flowers. On the day of their opening she'd taken orders for bridal bouquets, and since then there hadn't been a funeral in the locality for which she hadn't been asked to make at least one wreath. It was a small beginning to what she envisaged, but in the first season it was all she wanted. Later, when her body was her own again and she'd had time to work a routine combining flowers and babies, she would take a trainee. But not yet. At that stage, Top of the World belonged just to her and to Quen. Her workroom was mercifully out of the sun, the roof well insulated and blinds at the south-facing windows so that she looked out, not at the farm pastureland, but across what had been turned into an entrance drive to the car park. She'd hated having to refuse a wedding for the first Saturday in August, but she was ever practical and although she meant to be working again a fortnight or so after the baby arrived, she knew the date wasn't in her hands.

As they came to the second half of July she had to fight her corner to get to the nursery at all. To rest wasn't in Liz's nature, although for the last month or so she and Quen had driven to the nursery each morning instead of walking up the steep track skirting the cattle field. And secretly she was thankful that she'd given up her smart kitchen to Mrs Josh, for by the time they came back home at the end of the day the thought of her none too expert efforts at making a meal held no appeal at all. Back in her own seat at the kitchen table she ate the food Sue cooked, thankful that the conversation went on with no help from her and, apparently, no one noticing her silence.

'I've persuaded Liz not to come in with me today,' Quentin told Sue when he came down to breakfast. It was the last Friday in July and, according to Dr Hammond's calculations, just six days before the date the baby was due.

'Quite time she stayed at home,' Sue said briskly. 'You did well to persuade her, Quentin, I know just how pigheaded she can be.'

'I'm a bit worried actually, Mum. She didn't

seem to need any persuading. You don't think there can be anything wrong?'

'I think she's more tired than she's been prepared to admit. But by anything wrong, if you mean anything unnaturally wrong, then no I don't. Eat your breakfast, Quentin love, and when you've gone I'll go up and see her. I'm just glad she's agreed to stay where she is for an hour or two.' Then, passing him his coffee, 'But I wouldn't mind betting that before you've had your first half-dozen customers she'll be borrowing the car and chasing after you.'

Reassured, he dug his teeth into his fried breakfast.

'Dad not back yet?'

'Any minute he will be, I heard him taking the churns out to the gate.'

The pace of life never varied. No more was it dictated by the seasons, as it had been when Tim had run a mixed farm. But one day followed the last, prepared the way for the next, the cycle went on. And just as Sue used to pack food for those who worked in the fields at haymaking and harvest, so recently she had been getting a hamper ready for Quentin and Liz, who stayed all day in the nursery.

'Take your food anyway,' Sue put the small hamper on the table. 'Very likely by then Liz will be there to help you eat it.'

'It's not like her to give in. If she isn't there I shall come back to see her.'

'No, don't! Quentin, you'll make her frightened to rest if you flap each time.' It was a rare thing for her to speak so sharply to him. 'Of course she's tired, you'd be tired too for goodness sake. And she's such a little thing — she looks as big round as she is high.'

Quentin pushed his half-eaten breakfast away.

'So worried . . . is she too small? She will be all right won't she?'

'Having babies is natural. If she doesn't go into labour by the end of next week Dr Hammond is taking her into hospital. But perhaps she won't keep us all waiting that long. Go to work, love. Oh good, here comes Tim.'

So the day moved on a stage: Quentin drove off to the nursery, Tim came home from milking, Sue cleared the meal then went up to see Liz. From the landing window she saw Tim taking the pails of rich milk into the dairy ready. Friday was always a busy day: she had butter to churn, she had cream to scald and skim, she had mushrooms to weigh into punnets. All that must be done this morning and taken into Brindley ready for the weekend.

Turning towards Liz's room, she saw Mrs Josh coming out of it.

'Was just coming down to you, Mrs Tim. I just popped in to see the child, well you go and look to her, that's the best thing.' Then, whispering, 'Don't know if it might be the start of things. You'll soon know. And listen to me, Mrs Tim duckie, Friday or no, you leave the dairy to me. Not much I'm any use for, but I can still churn good butter, ah, and see to the creaming too. Forget all that. Mr Tim'll take the things to Brindley. Best you stay with our little Liz.'

Sue must have heard her, but she didn't wait

to answer. Already she was in Liz's room.

'I'm all right now, Mum. Don't look so scared.' And except for her higher than usual colour, Liz certainly looked well enough.

'Mrs Josh said she thought the baby had started. I don't know, Mum. I didn't tell Quen, it hurt so much that I couldn't stand having him getting in a state. He's gone, has he?'

'Yes. When did you get the pain?'

'The first time was when he was in the shower. I went to get out of bed. Mum, I've never felt anything like it. Do you think something's gone wrong?' She'd seen many a calf being born, sometimes she'd even thought that the cows' loud, unnaturally pitched mooing was a sort of song of triumph. But there had been nothing triumphant about how she'd felt.

'By the time he came back from his shower I was OK again. I almost told him, but then I thought that if I did he'd panic. I know he can't help it, but I don't think I could cope with him if it was hurting like that again. I didn't mean to call out when it came again, it was so sudden — Mrs Josh heard me. But it's gone now.'

'I'll wait up here with you. When it happens again we'll check the time and we'll see how long it lasts. We don't want to send for the nurse too soon.' Then, trying hard not to let anxiety show in her smile, 'Looks as though today's the day we've all been waiting for.'

'So hot, Mum. Can you open the window a bit more.'

But even at its widest it made no difference. There was no movement in the sultry air.

280

Leaning out, Sue looked down on the farmyard where Tim was cleaning out her hen houses. Even as early in the day as this she could see the back of his shirt was damp with sweat.

'We need a storm,' she said to Liz. 'Poor Quentin, up in those glasshouses.'

'Mum — coming again, just starting, getting stronger — Mum — '

'All right, love. Grip my hand.' Sue checked her wrist-watch as Liz clenched her teeth, fighting to arch her body as if that way she could escape the pain.

'That's about ten minutes since Mrs Josh was in here with you. I think I'd better call Nurse Watson. Liz, it's going to hurt like hell. Try and sink into the pain. Keep telling yourself, this is natural, this is the baby pushing to get born. Help it, push with it if you can.'

Limp and weak, her flushed face shining with perspiration, Liz nodded.

'I'll try. Want to get it born quickly. Then you and Dad can go up and tell Quentin once it's all over.' Sue's confidence must have boosted her, for with the pain gone at least for the moment she was ready for more, excited how to show that anything one of her father's herd could do, she could do better.

Sue telephoned Nurse Watson, who arrived from Brindley to coincide with Liz's next contractions. Highmoor was a flurry of excitement; of them all only Quentin didn't know what was going on. Mrs Josh turned the handle of the old-fashioned butter churn with as much vigour as she would have fifty years before; Tim, feeling useless in the house and unable to be idle, hosed and scrubbed the yard; Josh filled the mushroom punnets; Fred sterilised the milking machine and everything else he could lay his hands on. Only Sue stayed within calling distance of the nurse, ready to fetch, carry, bring water, take away soiled sheets while Lucinda, thankful to be playing a useful part, shelled the bowl of peas Josh had brought in the previous evening, then turned her attention to scraping potatoes.

'What memories it brings back,' she said as Sue came through the kitchen on her way to report to Tim. 'Poor child. Silly isn't it, how knowing what's happening brings it all back.'

Sue nodded. 'I've never believed it. But it's true. Aunt Luce, I wish I could bear it for her. She's such a mite. Supposing — supposing — ' No, don't say it. Don't let yourself think it. Liz, even now she so often seems like a child playing at being grown-up, making circles round adoring Quentin, taking his love for granted. But this she has to bear alone — make it easy for her, please help her.

The morning passed, contractions followed quickly one on another. Drawsheets soiled with blood and water must surely mean it would soon be over. But by mid-afternoon the only change was that Liz was getting weaker. It had only been about seven hours, not a long time for a first baby, but this one seemed no nearer.

Nurse Watson decided the doctor should be called.

Tim had taken Sue's deliveries into Brindley. It was three o'clock, normally Quentin wouldn't be home for at least three hours. But they had no right to keep him in ignorance. Sue decided that as soon as Tim came back she'd ask him to drive up to the nursery and ask Quentin to close up and come home.

'Of course he ought to be here. But, Sue, she's going along all right? Nothing wrong?' Like all men, and perhaps especially all fathers, he felt helpless.

'Yes, of course she is. But it's not right for him not to know what's going on.'

'Wish it was over. So damned hot for her too. Hark, was that thunder?' And, as if to answer his question, there was a brilliant flash of lightning, a pause of a second or two, and a loud roll of thunder.

She watched Tim reverse the car and start towards the lane, then hurried back indoors just as there was another flash of lightning. The day had been hot but overcast; now as the wind suddenly gusted, heralding the storm, it was so dark she turned on the lights in the house. Huge individual drops of rain splodged on to the farmyard Tim had so recently hosed. Then, as if the taps of heaven had opened on them, the storm broke. From room to room Sue went, shutting the windows.

'I'll bide with you downstairs, duckie, till it's over,' Mrs Josh came down the steep stairs from the attic rooms. 'Never could get on with storms. Turn me right upside down they do. Hope Josh has sense enough to stay in the dry. And where's Mr Tim? Not back from Brindley yet?'

'He's driven up to get Quentin. There's no one

283

in the yard, Josh must be in the sheds.'

'Oh dear, oh lawks, did you see that flash? And there's our poor Liz wrestling away in there. Hope that nurse has pulled the blind down.' A countrywoman all her days, Mrs Josh could look a rat in the face without a qualm, wring a chicken's neck if she had to, skin a rabbit, chase away a marauding fox, but a thunderstorm seemed to turn her bones to jelly.

'We'll go down and make a pot of tea, Mrs Josh. Aunt Luce will like that too.'

'And when poor young Quentin gets here, best we put a tot of something in his, he'll be in that much of a state. Reckon he'd rather be having the bairn himself if nature would let him.'

* * *

At the nursery Quentin had been surprisingly busy. Even without customers there was always more work than there were hours in the day. When the storm broke he switched on the lights and went on with what he was doing undeterred. Hearing someone come into the main 'shop', as they called the large covered-in area where indoor plants were displayed, he left what he was doing and went to serve, to advise, to try and look busy while he waited or just to talk according to what was required.

'Dad! Why, you're soaked through! You haven't walked up the hill in this?'

Out of breath Tim sank on to a chair.

'Came to tell you,' he panted. 'Liz has gone into labour.'

'Oh God, is she all right? I ought not to have left her — '

'Nothing we men can do. The ladies like it better if they don't have us to worry about. Yes, she's doing well. Can you shut up here and come home?'

'Of course I'm coming home. Why didn't you drive?'

'I did. I started in the car. Bloody thing stuttered and stopped. Nothing I could do in this weather. I pushed it on to the lay-by and legged it.'

'Why the hell they can't buck up and get my telephone installed I don't know. Let's get cracking.'

'Are you properly locked up, the vents seen to for the night?'

'Yes, yes, let's get home. How long do you think she'll be? Is the nurse there?'

'And the doctor.'

Quentin swallowed, he couldn't ask the question that was at the front of his mind; to ask it was tantamount to losing faith. Dear God, help her, help her. Some women die — no, don't even think it. Dear Lord and Father of Mankind, the words of his favourite hymn sprang into his mind, dear Lord and Father, take care of her, don't take her away, when we get home make them say it's over and she's well. Please, please, dear Lord and Father of Mankind . . . Over and over the silent words echoed. By his side Tim sat, his eyes closed. But as Quentin drove towards Highmoor he thought of no one except Liz.

'You go on in. I must get the cattle in,' Tim

said as with a screech of brakes the car came to a standstill.

The afternoon milking must be done. Routine can't be held up by thunderstorms (and by this time this one had cleared the air and seemed intent on turning itself into a wet and cooler evening), or for babies. Tim called into his office to change into his Wellington boots. Then from where he kept it propped in the corner, he took the stick he used to guide, prod and steer the cattle towards the milking sheds.

★   ★   ★

'Is it over? Is she all right?' Quentin burst into the kitchen.

'The nurse said ages ago that the head was engaged.' Sue could understand why Liz hadn't wanted him there. His face was working uncontrollably, he ran a trembling hand through his hair, he was even too overwrought to find solace in the usual pantomime with his glasses.

'Liz,' he closed his eyes, 'help her, please help her,' he mumbled. Then as if he'd just realised Sue's presence, 'Why the doctor? Something must be wrong. I'm going up. They can't stop me.'

'Quentin, she's better alone. She'll worry if she sees you're upset . . . ' But she might as well not have spoken, already Quentin was taking the stairs two at a time, meaning to burst straight into the bedroom. But just before he reached the door, it opened and Nurse Watson appeared.

'Ah, there you are. I was coming to see if

you'd like to be with her. Sometimes it helps.'

Downstairs Sue, Lucinda and Mrs Josh looked silently at each other then at the teacups and saucers, the pot covered with its 'cosy' to keep it warm, and the whisky bottle brought out ready to give Quentin Dutch courage. Their long vigil continued.

'The car isn't back yet,' Sue said, not anxiously but more to break the silence, to bring back normality.

'I expect Tim's stayed on at the nursery to close up for Quentin,' Lucinda supposed.

'Good thing if he does,' was Mrs Josh's opinion, 'the lad looked as if he didn't know if he was on his head or his heels.'

Sue opened the kitchen door and listened. Soon, surely soon, they must hear that glorious new-born cry.

Josh came in from the yard. 'No news yet? I see Quentin's car's in the yard. No sign of the guv'nor yet.' Then with a chuckle, 'I wouldn't mind betting he's got stuck there with customers he can't rid himself of. What a day, eh? Come on now, little Liz, keeping everyone waiting so.'

'He'll be getting anxious about the teatime milking,' Sue said as she passed the cup of tea she'd poured for him.

'Thank you, Mrs Tim, m'dear. No, he won't worry, he'll know Fred will see to things. Especially today of all days, he'll be ready to take over.'

How the minutes dragged. Rain beat steadily against the window, the only sound except for the loud, regular tick of the clock. Then, into the near-silence came the cry they'd waited for. As if they were on springs, all four of them stood up from the table and at the same second Fred burst in from the lobby.

10

'Put this round your shoulders,' Fred grabbed the first coat from those on the row of hooks on the lobby wall and threw it round Sue's shoulders. 'You run on over — I'll get the doctor across to take a look at him.'

It was like living a dream. A dream — or a nightmare that she'd never had the courage to face. Please don't let it have happened all over again. Let him have just tripped on something and fallen, knocked himself unconscious. Perhaps he's come round already. When he hears about the baby . . . a boy or a girl? She didn't know. Another hour and she'd look back on this as time past, a moment of terror receded into a pale memory. Please let it be like that, let his eyes be open . . .

Not yet six o'clock on an evening in high summer, yet the eerie light, and still the distant echo of thunder, fed the fear she was too frightened to face. Fred hadn't touched anything in the office, he'd taken one look and rushed to fetch her without so much as closing the door. She noticed the wet patch just inside, and even though she went straight to fall on her knees beside Tim, her mind clutched at the thought that that was the way the rain was driving. It clutched at anything, *anything*, except the thing she dreaded beyond all words.

Yes, his eyes were open. Thank God. She took

his hand. 'No, oh please no,' she breathed, chafing his hand between hers. He was so cold. That's because he's unconscious, she told herself. 'Tim, wake up, Tim. Help me, help me.' Desperate to find some reason for his fall, she looked at the floor. Nothing, nothing he could have tripped against. Anyway, if he'd knocked himself unconscious, wouldn't there be some sign on his head?

There was nowhere to hide from the truth. All these months they'd lived in a fools' paradise, they'd believed last year's heart attack had been a warning and with a lighter workload it would never come again. She tore at the buttons on his shirt, remembering what she'd read somewhere about massaging a patient's chest, pumping life back.

'Let me see him, Mrs Marshall.' Bag in hand Dr Hammond got to his knees, his presence easing Sue out of the way. He listened with his stethoscope, he took Tim's cold wrist in his hand, he shook his head. And finally, he closed the open, sightless eyes. Sue still knelt, watching, too numb even to pray. Her mind knew the truth her heart couldn't accept.

★ ★ ★

Liz opened her eyes to find Quentin sitting at the bedside. It was all over. They had a son. Her hand reached out towards his.

'Where is he? Justin?' (Justin for a boy, Justine for a girl, they had decided months ago, naming the baby after Quentin's grandfather.) 'He's so beautiful. Where is he, Quen?' She felt deliciously peaceful. Like coming out of a dark and terrifying tunnel into the sunlight. She remembered how — could it have been only this morning? — she had wanted to get rid of Quentin before he realised the baby was coming. Yet how thankful she'd been to have him with her through the final interminably long hour. Now she held her arms to him, wanting to hear the things she already knew: how wonderful she was, how she was his whole life, how brave she'd been.

'Quen?' Was this his reaction? If anyone had anything to cry about surely it was *her* for all she'd suffered. But this! Quentin had torn off his misted, dark-lensed glasses and dropped them uncharacteristically on the floor, then, his head on her breast, his whole body trembled convulsively as he sobbed.

'For goodness sake,' she scowled. 'It's me who had to go through it not you, and I managed without making a fuss. You're being stupid.' He wasn't behaving a bit as she'd imagined. 'Quen, stop it.' She shook his shoulders.

'Liz, didn't want to tell you. Not yet. Mum said don't tell you tonight.'

Pushing him off her, she sat up. 'Tell me what? There's nothing wrong with him, I saw him, I held him. What's happened to him?'

Without his glasses, and through his tears, he couldn't see her expression, indeed he could see little more than a hazy shape. His head felt full of red-hot pokers.

'Dad,' he kept his jaw clenched as he tried to

291

tell her. 'Collapsed. Gone.'

'Not Justin . . . ' Then as she took in the enormity of what he'd said, 'Dad's dead, you mean? He can't be. What's the time? I want to see Mum.'

'She'll be in bed. In the morning, darling.'

'If you won't get her, I'll go myself.' On the opposite side to where he still knelt, she pushed the bedcovers back.

'No, Liz. I'll get her. Promise you'll stay there.'

It was little more than eleven o'clock but, except for Liz's room and the small one that used to be Quentin's which now Nurse Watson was sharing with the same crib that had first been Paul's and then Liz's (before being stored in the attic), the house was in darkness.

'Mum?' Quentin called in a loud whisper as he tapped on Sue's door.

'You may come in, Quentin.' How calm she sounded. He was ashamed of his own miserable failure. He ought to be a tower of strength to them, but what use was he? Grateful for the darkness, he went into her room.

'I told her Mum . . . couldn't not tell her . . . couldn't talk as if there was nothing but joy about the baby . . . couldn't . . . ' He sank on to the side of her bed, thrusting his glasses into his pocket and rubbing his eyes with the heels of his thumbs. 'She wants to see you, Mum. I'm sorry, I tried to make her wait.'

'Listen, there's the baby. I think he's being taken in to her.' She ought to be glad Liz wanted to talk to her, she ought to be glad Quentin cared. Turning her back on the dark room she went back to where she'd been before he came, looking out of the window, seeing the outline of the farm buildings, seeing Tim, seeing him everywhere. But he was gone, the undertaker had come that evening and carried him away. Away from Highmoor, away from her. 'All right, lady?' Did she really hear it, or was it only the echo of all their yesterdays?

'Poor little Liz,' she heard her own voice, cool, calm, distant. 'Tonight she deserves just to be happy. And you, Quentin. You've been a tower of strength, Tim must be so glad.'

She heard his stifled sob. She even envied him his tears. Screams, gnashing of teeth, anything would be better than this unearthly, numb sensation as if she were on a different planet. She'd go and see Liz, she'd do what she could for her. But she'd come back. She wanted to be by herself, how else could she find him?

Going into Liz's room from the darkness, they were hit by the brilliance of light. And she was hit by something she only half understood. Sitting up in bed, Liz was holding the new-born child to her breast.

'That's it, he'll soon get the hang of it.' With the experience of seeing more than twenty years of Brindley's babies into the world, Nurse Watson nodded approvingly. Then seeing Sue, she backed away. 'Here's your Mum come to see him. I'll fetch him off you presently.'

Passing Quentin, she tut-tutted as she went out. What an outlook for them all! That nice Mr Marshall taken from them so suddenly and only this miserable creature left. True to say, this afternoon he'd been good as gold, helped his wife no end with her hard battle. But look at him now! Gone right to pieces. No wonder it was the woman had to have the babies. Of course his people were all arty sorts, what could you expect? But surely there was no need for him to wear those dark glasses as if he were on his holidays in the sunshine!

As if Quentin read her thoughts he pulled them off and pressed finger and thumb of one hand against closed eyes that sent shafts of agony through his head. Then, lurching out of the room and almost knocking the retreating nurse off her feet, he rushed blindly past her and into the lavatory at the end of the corridor, letting the door slam behind him. Shaking her head, she turned her thoughts away from him. Babies, now babies and the trouble they sometimes caused getting themselves born, those she could understand. But nerves, never! And that's all that was the matter with that young man! And in Nurse Watson's opinion, to give way to them was selfish indulgence; more to his credit if he thought more about the others and less about himself. Going back into her room she closed the door firmly behind her, took a cigarette from the packet and sat by the open window to enjoy it. She deserved ten minutes' peace; it had been a long day.

'Mum,' Liz held her hand out and felt it taken in Sue's. 'He didn't even see our baby.' Her eyes shone with unshed tears. Sue wanted to say something to comfort her, but her mind wasn't working, she could think of nothing.

'A new life,' she heard herself mutter, her hand gently touching the tiny down-covered head. 'It's like us being carried on a conveyor belt. Tim's journey ended, this little one's started.' That only half-understood sensation began to take shape and even to find a crack in her armour of numbness. 'If Tim's life had to end today, at that hour, that moment perhaps, his soul and this innocent one might have touched.' She hadn't meant to voice the sudden thought aloud. Realising where her rambling thoughts had carried her, she forced a smile she was far from feeling and put her armour firmly back in place.

'Where's Quen? He's in a state tonight, Mum. I thought he was over all that.' There was less sympathy than disappointment in Liz's tone.

'Poor darling. He's been wonderful, he did all my telephoning, everything. Paul will be here tomorrow. They will all get home. Sylvie had a call to Christo, he's promised to get leave.' All of them coming home, the house full just as it had been for every celebration. Coming home this time for Tim. Even her thoughts shied from 'Tim's funeral'.

'Oh, Mum.' Liz was never lost for words — well, almost never.

Pale, empty and weak from the bout of sickness that had shamed him, Quentin came back into the room. Sue didn't repeat what she'd said about Tim leaving life's conveyor belt just as Justin started his journey on it, yet surely of them all it would have been he who would have understood. His own thoughts must have been following something of the same course, for it was he who said, 'Tomorrow I must drive to town to register the baby.' Unsaid was the fact that he would be driving to town to register Tim's death. Perhaps it was that that prompted his suggestion, looking at Liz for her approval.

'A new Marshall at Highmoor,' he said.

'But he's McBride,' Liz looked at the miracle in her arms, she felt his mouth toying with her nipple. Her heart ached with such a mixture of joy and sadness that she clenched her teeth, it was almost too much to bear.

'Liz, I want to register him as Timothy Justin Marshall McBride.'

Sue turned away. Dear, dear Quentin, of all the children none had cared more than he. A new Timothy, a new soul on life's conveyor belt. She heard Liz's eager agreement, she knew their grief. Yet she'd never felt more alone than she did standing watching the three of them, Liz, Quentin and Tim's namesake.

★   ★   ★

Hearing their car draw up outside the house, Sue went outside expecting to greet Paul and Philippa. But Paul had come alone. Getting out he enfolded her in a bear-like hug. His likeness to Tim went further than facial resemblance, the set of his shoulders or his tall, strong frame. As he held her, she felt vulnerable as if, in his strength, she was aware of her own weakness.

'All right, lady?' Did he say it purposely, as if somehow he could fill the void?

She nodded. 'Have to be all right, Paul. For

his sake, I *have* to be.' Then, determined not to give emotion a chance to beat her. 'You must have left home early. Is Philippa not coming?'

'It couldn't have happened at a worse weekend.'

'During the long holiday? I should have thought he'd timed it very conveniently for her.' Whatever was the matter with her that she could speak like it? As well, perhaps, that her acid tone passed unnoticed.

'You'd think so. But today the school is open to prospective pupils — well, to their parents, I suppose, and, of course, they like to meet the staff. Then tomorrow she's promised to be there to help receive another lot of parents at a lunch party. The principal seems to put enormous trust in her. Well, she does the school great credit. Some of them are so dyed in the wool, but she's smart, bright; you can sense how efficient she is just from meeting her. These parents are coming to collect pupils returning from an overseas trip to North Africa. Honestly, the places kids get to see these days, provided their parents have deep enough pockets. She said to tell you she was sorry, but she's promised she'll definitely be here for the funeral — do you know when yet?'

'That's good.' Good? Good that she'd promised definitely to be here for Tim's — Tim's — say it, Paul said it — you say it too. Tim's funeral. This morning the rector had been to see her. Sue Marshall, always full of energy, always to be relied on to help at the church functions, make cakes for the bazaars, collect jumble for the annual fund-raising sale, sometimes even to iron the church vestments. Yet this morning she'd been given a different role to play: a bereaved member of his flock, her name to be on tomorrow's prayer list as he petitioned that she might be given solace. He'd told her that old Ted Huggins, the grave digger, had been instructed where to prepare the ground . . .

'Mum? Would that be best, or is there anything special you have in mind?'

'What? Sorry love, I didn't hear what you said.'

'I said I'd get my working togs on and have a word with Josh. He'll know where I'll be most useful. I expect Fred copes with the herd.' With his arm around her, he turned towards the lobby. 'What about this baby, then? Fine fellow, is he?'

She nodded. 'Perfect.' She tried to say it just as she would if yesterday had been nothing more than the day the baby was born, as if Tim were standing here in the yard, his eyes full of pride in his son. Her wits couldn't manage a whole sentence, it was all she could do to say the one word and fix a smile on her pale face.

Paul stopped walking and turned to look back across the yard to the lower slopes of the pastureland where the cattle grazed.

'Later on, Mum, you and I'll have to have a talk about all this. I know Dad hadn't done much since that business last year, but he'd always been here. This really must put a different complexion on Highmoor's future, I suppose.'

'You mean that now, now that it's too late to matter, you might come back?' As soon as she'd said it she knew she'd misunderstood him.

'Here? I didn't mean that. It was never big enough to be a real challenge, not even in its heyday. I'm not knocking Dad, you know I wouldn't do that. But he'd be the first to admit, he came here with no knowledge. The fact that it was small and he was prepared to learn from old Josh's experience, that was fine. For him, I mean, it was fine. Then, of course, after last year, Quentin bought him out of so much of it. Why, it could hardly be looked on as a career move for me to chuck up what I've got, to look after what's left of Highmoor.'

Anger, frustration, misery, all fought a battle in her gut. She wanted to scream at him, to tell him that she wished that hole Ted Huggins was preparing could be for her too. The years ahead were no longer a challenge, they were a threat. She looked forward to nothing.

'I know it won't be an easy decision, Mum. Perhaps it's too early even to talk about it. But a farm needs daily attention, it's not the sort of thing you can shelve until you get over all this. Josh is past it, Fred's a good man but without Dad keeping an eye on things it could easily go to pot. Still, for today we'll not think about it, eh? Cheer up, lady. Come upstairs and show me your new grandson.'

So the days went by. On one occasion Sue noticed Lucinda and Paul on the patch of would-be grass in front of the house. What was under discussion she didn't know, but it took her back years to see that chastened expression on Paul's face. Whatever Lucinda was laying down the law about, she meant him to know that it was for her to talk and for him to listen.

'Mum,' Sue heard Liz's call, 'here a minute.'

That was the following Tuesday, her grandson was four days old. Quen was at the nursery, Paul was outside working as hard as any man could, Lucinda was in the kitchen putting the decorative finishing touches to a trifle she'd made for the evening, Josh was in the mushroom sheds, Mrs Josh attending to the dairy. So the routine of life was forging its way ahead; only Sue seemed out of step. She made herself cook, even though the thought of food revolted her. But she must overcome that, she must make a pretence of living then, surely, she wouldn't be beaten.

'You're up!' The surprise of seeing Liz sitting in the old nursery chair, Timothy sucking steadily as he fixed his unblinking stare on her, pierced her wall of misery.

'Nurse Watson is going today. When I said I wanted to get up she seemed keen to be off. She has another baby due any day apparently. When I told her Sylvie was coming home today on leave she jumped at the chance of getting home. So Mum, I'm in charge now. I bathed him without her watching this morning.' He'd stopped sucking and let his head flop, a trickle of milk escaping his mouth. 'Full up, Timfy?' She passed him in Sue's direction, 'Here you are, Mum, see if you're still any good at getting his wind up. Do you think Timfy is a bit sissy for him? Timothy is such a mouthful and Tim — 'well, one day perhaps, when he's older.'

'Timfy,' Sue murmured, holding him up and

gently tapping his back, 'little Timfy.' Little he may have been, but he brought his wind up with such gusto that his admiring audience's laugh was spontaneous. 'You little angel,' she rubbed her cheek against his silvery-fair down. A new spirit amongst them, this one sent to them and her own Tim taken. But how could he be taken? She turned towards the window so that Liz couldn't see her face as she closed her eyes, conjuring up the memory of the night Harold had died, of Tim's certainty that death would have ended his body's frailty and let his soul find freedom. If only she could believe that; if only the ice would melt around her heart and she could start to think and to feel instead of going through her days like an automaton.

'Are you coming downstairs later?' she asked, determined that her bright manner should fool Liz.

'You bet I am. I'll get him in his basket first, then I'll come down for elevenses. You don't think I've squeezed into my clothes to sit up here where no one can admire this new me. I'd begun to feel I would look like Henry the Eighth for the rest of my days.'

It was a charade, they both knew it. But it helped.

★ ★ ★

The last to arrive was Philippa. Paul drove to Reading to meet her train early on the Thursday evening. The previous day Sylvia and Christopher had come in the car he'd hired for the week

301

of their leave. What an unnatural atmosphere pervaded the house: its welcome as warm as they'd come to accept without question, the pleasure they all found in being together as great as always, their delight in seeing Liz and Quen with a baby adding a new dimension, and yet nothing seemed real. Had Tim been there, his presence would have been no more than part of the familiar scene. But because he had gone from them, they were aware of him everywhere they looked.

'Aunt Sue,' Sylvia said as the two of them started to lay the table for the first full family meal, 'how do you want us to sit?' It was something that would never have been asked until now. Who was to move into Tim's place? Then, before Sue had a chance to answer, 'Can't believe it. I keep expecting to see him come in.' She'd always talked so easily to Sue, now she spoke her thoughts before she had time to realise the cruelty of her words. 'Of course I do. And so do you. Aunt Sue, I shouldn't have said it.'

But this time there was something of the old warmth in Sue's expression as she looked on this niece she'd always been so close to.

'Yes, you should have said it. And I'm glad you feel like that, Sylvia. I do too, I expect him to walk in from the lobby, I expect to hear that 'I'm starved, lady. I've come home for a crust of bread and cheese.' I expect to hear his step on the stair — ' They both heard the dangerous croak in her voice. She bit hard on the corners of her mouth and put a pile of knives and forks on the table with clatter. 'You're all home, even

Christo's come all that way.' She spoke clearly, winning the battle and determined Sylvia should know she wasn't going to break. 'There's just one thing, Sylvia. We all have our own places. I don't want his to be empty, I don't want to move anyone else into it. Don't know what to do.' Helplessly she looked at the pile of cutlery.

Sylvia had to think quickly.

'If we're all down here at the table, there's bound to be a lot of noise. We probably wouldn't hear Timfy. Why don't we suggest to Liz that she lets us carry his crib and the stand down. That would take up all that space and we should know he was safe. His first appearance at the table. What do you think?'

Sue nodded. 'Lovely idea,' she managed, before she turned her back, taking a long time to sort out the table napkins. Anxious to get on to safer ground, she asked after Richard and Juliet.

'His play is a sell-out. He and I, well everything is just the same. I live in the posh flat he bought for me, he visits when he's free and I'm free. Juliet has a nursemaid, of course. She has no home life, though; it's not right for a child, but her mother seems content to be without her. He works every evening, but my shifts vary. If I'm on a late shift he comes round in the mornings. Sometimes he looks in after the theatre. If I ever get a Sunday free, which isn't often, we take Juliet somewhere. But we have to be careful. If he were a bank clerk or a car salesman or something it wouldn't matter a damn, but stage-struck girls hang around the stage door, follow him when he comes out of the

303

theatre. The press would just love to get hold of it. Richard McBride, the hero of stage and screen, proud to pose for photographs with his daughter, leaves her to the care of a nursemaid while he wiles away the hours (hours, some hope!) with his mistress.'

'But would you mind so much to have it known you're his mistress?' Sue was disappointed; if what Sylvia felt was genuine love, untinged with excitement and glamour, surely she would have been proud for the world to know?

'I couldn't do that to him, Aunt Sue. Don't you see, if Drucilla got hold of the story she'd make great play of it. And even though she isn't a scrap interested in Juliet she'd see that he didn't keep her here in England. And who could blame her?' She shrugged her shoulders helplessly, 'If I were the cause of his losing Juliet it would kill any feeling he has for me. He could never love me, not me or any woman, as he does her. I know that and I accept it.'

They looked at each other in silent sympathy. In that moment Sue wasn't afraid of the pain of looking back. Looking forward was a thick fog of despair; memories would always be her comfort. But what was there for Sylvia?

'The play's opening in Broadway in October. His part will be taken by someone else in London and he'll go back to the States. I suppose Juliet will return to Hollywood and be with her mother. I don't know. It's such a mess. No different from lots of other marriages.' She looked straight at Sue, 'I have no illusions. If he goes back to their home, then he'll be with her. I know that. I think he'd even like it to work out, for Juliet's sake.'

'I don't understand. How can he . . . how can you . . . '

'I'd be there for him no matter what. Perhaps I'm a fool. But if I am, then I don't want to be cursed with wisdom. It isn't just that I'm some woman for him to come to for sex when his wife isn't there. I can't explain what's between us, I don't want to try.'

Sue slipped her arm around the girl's waist. 'I should think not. As long as you understand and he understands, then thank God for the happiness you find in each other. Hark, someone's coming down. I expect it's Aunt Luce.' Their moment was over.

Over the years Sue had often thought how strange it was that she could talk so freely with Sylvia, they saw straight into each other's hearts. Yet with Liz there was a barrier, they never met on a flat plane, the generation barrier was always there. Dear Liz, often pig-headed, equally often selfish, always determined and optimistic. It was nothing to do with the qualities of their characters that made it difficult to find understanding. Perhaps it was because for so long there had been Quentin. With the sort of love he had given her even when they'd been no more than children, she hadn't needed closeness and support from her parents. Had Tim been aware of it too? She would never know.

★ ★ ★

'I'll help you clear away,' Philippa said to Sue after the meal. Perhaps it was her way of saying she appreciated that she'd been made a vegetable pie and saved the necessity of refusing steak and kidney. In fact it had been Lucinda who had made it, glad of the chance to feel useful, but Philippa didn't know that. Then, when Sylvia moved to the sink, 'No, don't you bother, Sylvia. You go off with the others. I've hardly had a chance to speak to Mrs Marshall yet.'

As soon as the crib and its stand had been carried back upstairs, Lucinda followed Liz to watch the ceremony of putting Timfy to bed. The Joshes climbed a further flight to their own quarters, where they'd added their own pictures to the walls and their own ornaments and trinkets to every available space on shelves and windowsill. The others went out through the yard to climb the hill to the nursery where Quentin, having listened to the weather forecast, wanted to alter the ventilation.

'Now then, would you like me to wash or dry?' Philippa was clearly making an enormous effort.

'You dry, dear. Pile the things on the table, I'll put them away later.'

'OK. I'm glad to see you're coping so well. Paul was worried that you wouldn't.' Then with a smile aimed at showing solidarity, 'He underestimates the stamina women have. Has he talked to you — about the future, I mean?'

'Not particularly. There's nothing that talking is going to solve.'

'I told him that would be your attitude. All the talk in the world doesn't get you anywhere

306

without action. It's action you're going to need. I've been making a lot of enquiries, Mrs Marshall. That's why I didn't rush straight here after the weekend. When we've done the dishes I'll show you some details I've collected.'

'What sort of details?' There was no logic in Sue's frightened, trapped feeling.

'I don't know how deeply rooted you are in this area. I always thought of you and Tim (I got used to calling him that when he stayed with us) as not having much of a social life, you both always seemed so wrapped up with the farm. So don't you think that once that's gone you'd be wiser to make a completely fresh start in a new district?' Then, again with that smile Sue was sure was meant to show kindness, 'And where better than not too far from us?'

'Gone? Highmoor gone? But that's nonsense. Paul hinted at something the same. Philippa, Highmoor is my home, it's where all my memories are. This is where I belong.'

'You don't have to forget the past just because the future must be different. And, it must be different Sue (I can say Sue, can't I, like I said Tim?). Paul was saying the other day, this place can hardly be viable since Tim hadn't been able to farm it properly. But all that's over.'

'I don't need Paul to tell me what sort of a living we make here.'

'I've put it badly. I've offended you. I'm sorry. Just listen to what I have to say, think about the good side of what I'm suggesting. I told you there were things I had to do, that's why I didn't come until today. I looked at lots of places, some quite promising, some useless. But the best was only about a mile from us. A very pretty close of bungalows, only just being constructed. I understand they are being taken by people in your sort of position, perhaps some of them older, of course.' The words came at Sue like hammer blows, she heard them yet they conveyed no image. 'But all of you would be widows, all with a need to make a fresh start.'

'I don't know what you're talking about.' She was suddenly frightened. If they dictated to her she could argue, but Philippa was speaking with unusual gentleness.

'Paul says that even with the reduced acreage you'd get a good price for Highmoor.'

'Stop it, Philippa. Highmoor is my home. I don't give a damn what Paul says or you either,' her voice rose ominously.

'You're still in shock. I can understand that, honestly. But surely you and Tim must have talked about this happening. After last year you must have both realised — '

'When we've done this we'll go and meet the others,' Sue cut in as, the washing-up finished, she started to put away the dried crockery. She had to be busy, she had to work noisily, the clattering of plates drowning Philippa's words.

'We're going home on Sunday. Why don't you come with us for a few days? I'm still on holiday and it would do you good to get away. Quentin seemed to manage to help on the farm last year and I'm sure he would again in an emergency. Anyway, even when you see the wisdom of what we're advising it will be weeks — months perhaps — before you're free of the work here. I hope you get some applicants from the advert Paul tells me he's put in the *Gazette*.'

Paul put an advert in the *Gazette*? Had she known? Purposely she'd shut her ears and her mind to so much he had said to her. Sue was ashamed that she could have so lost track with what was going on.

'I expect I shall,' she made herself sound positive; that had to be her defence.

'The trouble is, if you let Liz have the Joshes' cottage, you have nowhere to house a man.'

'I shall manage. The right person will apply I expect. Look, I see the walkers are nearly home; they're coming towards the gate from the field. Let's go and meet them.' She had to get away. Surely the others would support her. Paul wanted her to go and live near him . . . she ought to be thankful he cared . . . Philippa had gone to a lot of trouble, all of it was meant kindly. But why couldn't they see, why couldn't they understand? Tim, they can't tell me what I should do . . . Highmoor is *ours*, it always will be . . . Tim, can you hear me? Do you know what they're saying?

Without waiting for Philippa she hurried out through the lobby, she wanted to get to the safety of the family. Ah, but she must be wary of Paul; Paul said she ought to sell up; Paul was planning her life. Her life? Years of loneliness, years of pointless battling. And again that feeling of utter desolation swamped her. That afternoon she'd gone alone to the Chapel of Rest, she'd looked for the last time at Tim. Thinking of it now in the fading evening of a hot summer's day, she shivered; she found no comfort in the memory. They had made a stranger of him, his face smoothed of expression, his body clad in a white shroud. She'd touched his cold, stiff lips; she'd closed her eyes and tried to imagine that half wink she'd known so well and his 'All right, lady?' She wished she hadn't gone, the image was at the forefront of her mind, coming between her and the person he'd been — the person who'd been so sure his soul would live eternally.

The twins were walking together, Paul and Quentin coming behind. But when Paul saw the two coming from the house he went to meet them. Seeing him working in the yard these last few days had been so natural yet now, after what Philippa had said, Sue was frightened to be with them. She mustn't let them dominate her, she must make them see she was capable of standing alone, that they had no need to worry about her. If only it were true! But it *must* be true, from somewhere she must find the courage. Like a cornered animal she looked around her at the familiar farmyard. Hanging back from the others she waited while Quentin shut the field gate.

Somehow the next day passed. But then so, somehow, had the days of the week passed. Seeing so many people in church as, with Paul at her side, she followed the pallbearers up the aisle, brought home to Sue how respected and well liked Tim had been in the neighbourhood. A governor of the local school, a member of the Parochial Church Council, a sidesman and regular reader at the morning service, so many people had their own memories of him. She could find no comfort in the knowledge that the neighbourhood was sharing her loss. Looking colourless and expressionless, wearing the black suit Sylvia had taken her to Reading to buy, she walked, she knelt, she stood, she sat, she heard the words of the service, she heard Maurice Kimber give the eulogy, she heard Paul read the lesson. The choir sang the Nunc Dimittis; she followed the cortège out to the newly dug grave: Lord, now lettest Thou thy servant depart in peace, those words came nearer than any to piercing her merciful numbness. As the coffin was lowered, she felt Paul's iron grip on her arm. Tomorrow and tomorrow and tomorrow, she screamed silently, how can I bear it? Joy, sorrow, anxiety, despair, time has no respect for any of them; the seconds tick on, the minutes pass, hours turn into a day, one day to the next. So at last merciful night came; she could shut herself in the solitude of her room, *their* room.

With the curtains still open, and the window too on such a warm night, she undressed without putting on the light. Naked, she knelt by the open window, closing her eyes, breathing in air full of the scents of country. With her eyes used to the darkness, every shape in the yard was familiar. Beyond the barn was his office, the moonlight glinting on the small window. For the whole of the week she'd avoided it, as if the horror was waiting for her. Now, though, it wasn't that afternoon a week ago she saw in her mind's eye. She saw the image of the door

311

opening, Tim walking out into the yard, then looking up to the window and seeing her there. She found herself on her feet, leaning far out of the open window, her hand raised to let him know she was watching him. Of course there was no logic in her thinking. Logic would have told her that if he were on the other side of the yard she couldn't possibly have heard his voice speaking to her, any more than she could have seen the love in his eyes as he said softly, reassuringly, 'Talk to me, lady. You know I hear you.'

As suddenly as a dream dies, the moment was lost. The sound she heard wasn't Tim speaking, it was her own strangled sobs. Reality hit her and with it the reminder that every room in the house was occupied, the 'children' were all anxious for her, listening, wanting to help her. Pushing her clenched fist against her mouth she stumbled to the bed. She mustn't make a sound, 'Poor Mum, we must go and comfort poor Mum.' As if they could! Couldn't they see the way they watched her stifled her? Gritting her teeth hard together, and despite the sultry hot night, she got into bed and pulled the covers over her head. She couldn't fight any longer. In her misery she wanted to scream, to beat her breast, to shout her anguish. Instead she buried her head against Tim's pillow, her body shaken by sobs.

Tears must have helped, for weak and spent, she was carried into merciful sleep. When she woke the first pale colours of dawn hadn't even started to light the summer sky. No one would be up for hours. She was free; she could move without any of them watching, worrying 'Is Mum all right?' Silently she pulled her clothes on then, carrying her shoes, crept downstairs like a thief in the night instead of mistress of the house. Once into the lobby she put her shoes on then set off across the yard, through the gate to the track that skirted the lower edge of the cow field, over a stile, along another farm track, over another stile that took her to Church Lane. She had no need of a torch, she'd walked these tracks thousands of times. It didn't occur to her that some people might have been frightened to be alone in a churchyard in the middle of the night.

When the family came down in the morning there was nothing about her to suggest she hadn't spent the night in her bed.

⋆　⋆　⋆

'This is the only chance I have to help you, Sue,' Philippa had knocked, then put her head around the door of the bedroom where Sue was sitting in front of the dressing-table mirror, adding some artificial colour to her pale face. 'That's good. Nothing like a bit of make-up to make one feel better.'

'Come in, Philippa. Yes, it's a shame you can't stay longer.' She sought safety behind a coolly polite manner. But, cool or otherwise, it appeared to be lost on Philippa.

'But really, you know, it's much better to get unpleasant things dealt with quickly, isn't it? I thought you'd need someone to help you sort his

313

things and it would be easier for me than any of the others. As I say, it has to be today, that's the only chance there is.'

Sue caught sight of her own reflection, her mouth open in disbelief.

'Things?' She must mean for Paul, yes. Tim would be glad. There were his best riding boots, hardly worn; his hacking jackets would fit Paul. Into her mind sprang the image of the two of them setting off together for the hunt. All this week the nearest to exercise for Titan had been alone in the paddock. They ought to take the horse trailer back with them, let Titan live with Rosie. It took no more than the bat of an eyelid for the thoughts to crowd in on Sue. 'For Paul. That's a good idea. I'll bring him up to have a look when he comes in from the yard.'

'Paul? Oh, we can manage better without having a man underfoot,' Philippa said confidently. 'Anything that's too worn, of course, wouldn't be any use. But there is a new charity shop opened — very near the bungalows I was telling you about — they're raising money for animal welfare. Tim would approve of that, wouldn't he?' There was something almost vacant in the way Sue was staring at her; it made her quite uncomfortable. 'A beastly job for you, I know. I'll do it by myself if you'd rather. Yes, that might be best. Just tell me which were his drawers and wardrobe.'

Something in Sue snapped.

'Leave me alone, can't you! You and your bloody I-know-best interference.' Sue heard herself scream the words, heard it as if she were listening to a stranger.

Philippa jerked back as if she'd been struck. And at that second Paul, who'd been on his way up the stairs when he'd heard the near-hysterical outburst, appeared in the doorway.

'Hey, lady, that won't do. What's up?'

'It's all right, Paul. She didn't mean it. Look, Sue, we both want to help you. Why do you think we're here?'

'I can't imagine. You don't need to be, not for *me*. You none of you need to be.' She mustn't start crying. If she did how would she ever stop?

'I was going to help her sort your father's things. For the shop at home, I thought.' Philippa despaired! And this hysterical woman tried to make them believe she was capable of running a farm. She couldn't run an ice-cream stall!

'Yes, good idea, Mum. I'll give her a hand. Maybe one or two of his things might do for me at work, eh?' Paul's smile almost begged her to come half-way to meet them.

She made a supreme effort, even managed a shame-faced grimace supposed to be a smile. 'I know you want to help, *both of you*,' she made herself include the daughter-in-law she was never comfortable with, 'but I'd rather everything was left as it is. I'll be the one to sort Tim's things.'

'Such a mistake,' she imagined Philippa must use that tone to her pupils, 'it's like having a shadow on your life. What you need is a clean slate, a new start.'

'What I want, for God's sake, is space.'

Paul lowered his gaze; it frightened him to see that wild look in his mother's eyes. 'Right you are, Mum. We won't say any more about it.'

It was during the evening that she said it worried her that there was no one to ride Titan. He was a big horse; he needed a man, a man who rode well.

'You wouldn't want to sell Dad's horse, Mum? I say, what about if I take him? He stands taller than Rosie, it might be a good idea if instead of our looking for something else for Philippa (we were saving up for something, her lessons are going well), she got used to riding Rosie and I had Titan. I reckon Dad would be pleased about that.'

That time Sue managed something far nearer a smile. 'I reckon he would, Paul.'

The next day when they packed the car, Paul put two hacking jackets and Tim's best jodhpurs and riding boots on the back seat. From the kitchen window Sue, Liz and Quentin silently watched as Titan was walked into the horse trailer. She liked to think she'd made her feelings plain; nothing would persuade her to leave Highmoor.

'When we've gone, promise to think about that development near us,' Philippa said as she bumped her cheek against Sue's in what was supposed to pass as a kiss. 'I've left the brochure over there on the dresser. You'd be so much more comfortable — '

'Take them!' Sue thrust the printed sheets into Philippa's hand. 'I told you *no*. I may have lost my husband but that doesn't mean I've become everybody else's property.'

'Give it a week or so — '

'Leave it, Phil, why can't you?' None too carefully Paul grabbed his wife's arm and pushed her towards the lobby.

Trying to pretend there was no uncomfortable atmosphere overshadowing their farewells, they all went out to the gate to wave them off. It seemed Philippa had been determined to the last, for going back indoors they found the details of the bungalows left on the kitchen table.

'Don't want these, do you, Mum?' Quentin picked them up.

Sue shook her head. 'I expect she meant to be kind. She just doesn't understand.' It was as if a weight was lifted as she watched him screw up the papers, lift the lid from the range, and thrust them into the flames. Perhaps that was the moment when she took her first step towards the life she had to make for herself.

★　★　★

Paul's advertisement brought two applicants. One had recently married a Brindley girl and was living with his in-laws until he could find somewhere to rent. The other was single and seemed prepared to look for lodgings. The first had worked on a market garden, the second was employed at a farm near Henley. Steeling herself, Sue interviewed each of them in Tim's office, promising to write and let them know within the next day or so.

'I ought to take the one with farming

experience,' she said to Josh. 'So why don't I?'

'Well, Mrs Tim, m'dear, ain't for me to tell you your reasons. It maybe that one looked you straighter in the eye than the other. On the other hand, it could be that you're remembering when you and the Guv'nor came here, neither of you knowing about farming. But did that stop you finding out? If it's the lad who's just got wed — much like you and Mr Tim when you came that weekend to look at the place, remember? — and if he shows signs of being keen and quick to learn, then me and Fred'll put him on the right track. And you, not much about this place you couldn't teach him.'

That was how it was that Paddy Dimmock came to Highmoor. And he'd not been there many weeks before they all wondered how they'd ever managed without him. He looked after the pigs, he learnt to do the teatime milking, and whatever jobs he took on he carried out with responsibility. And before those weeks were over, there had been other changes too. The time had come for Quentin to take on staff at the nursery. In his case, he wasn't looking for experienced horticulturists, he was looking for keen, receptive minds that he could train. This first year had been a beginning; he was determined that through each one that followed Top of the World would become more established, that people would come from farther field. And it wasn't only the products of Quentin's labours that would bring them, nor yet just for his own expertise. Timfy was three weeks old when Liz took on two girls whom she would teach everything she had learnt herself at the florist's in Reading. Having a baby didn't deter her. Each day his crib was put on the back seat of the car so that he could accompany his parents. It was easy enough, Liz said; she didn't even need a picnic lunch for him. The McBrides spent their days there, Quentin's private office used for baby-feeding, parent-feeding and nappy-changing.

It was while he and Liz were eating the home-made soup Sue had given them in a flask that he made his suggestion.

'I was thinking about the cottage, Liz.'

'No hurry, is there? Once we're on our own I won't be able to be up here so much.'

'I was thinking . . . what about if we suggest to Mum she offers it to Paddy and his wife? They're stuck with his in-laws — what are you laughing at?' But then Highmoor had been his home for so long, when had he ever thought of Tim and Sue as in-laws?

So when the work was finished on the cottage, the Dimmocks moved in. On the surface Highmoor was back in step again.

11

As the first months after Tim's death dragged by, Sue battled with each day. No one could share her grief; she dreaded any hint of sympathy. If there was any outward sign of change in her it was that the colour in her cheeks owed more to make-up than nature and the optimism in her voice was contrived to hide the ache in her heart. She still went to church on Sunday morning but instead of walking as she used to with Tim, now she drove Lucinda. It was her 'thinking time'. The rector might have felt he was failing had he been able to read her wandering thoughts as he preached. Yet much of her strength came from those quiet moments as she looked around at the ageing congregation, some still coming as couples, but more than one partner gone. They were the same people she'd known for years; written letters of condolence to when one or other of a couple had died. But it was only now that she recognised their courage, their will to accept. If they could carry on with life, then so could she.

Battling with each busy day, she got through the months. Summer over, a short and wet autumn threw them into winter. In December she offered to run the cake stall at the Christmas bazaar just as she always had; the following March she went out in the Land Rover collecting jumble for the spring fund-raiser just as she

320

always had. She ensured the cheerfulness in her thanks forbade sympathy. 'Isn't she wonderful,' the more understanding of her acquaintances said; but there were others with a more jaundiced view, 'That one soon picked herself up. Be looking for another man before you can say knife.' Another spring . . . another summer . . . Timfy started to toddle after her as she fed the hens or collected the eggs.

If on the surface *her* life continued unchanged, the same couldn't be said for Quentin and Liz's. Top of the World went from strength to strength. Keeping no more than the one grazing field for her small herd, Sue agreed to sell off the rest of the land to them. His vision knew no bounds. From the first he'd earmarked land for trial grounds, but the gardening industry was booming as housing developments changed the face of much of the countryside, each property with its patch of garden. A century before, row upon row of small terrace houses had been built, many of them back-to-back, others with narrow walled areas where sunshine had little opportunity to warm the earth. Even between the wars when the working man was often able to attain his dream of owning his own home (or looking forward to owning it some twenty-five years hence when his mortgage was repaid), the two-bedroom and a boxroom estates were usually set out in straight rows and the gardens seldom the result of anything more imaginative than a lawn flanked by flower borders. What Quentin intended was to design and plant a garden filled with shape and colour, enhance it with a rustic building and garden furniture. He was a pioneer in a field that was to flourish over the next decades. At that stage he hadn't thought beyond the visual effect of the building; it was Liz who decided on its use.

Poring over the plans with them, Sue wouldn't have been human if she hadn't been infected with their excitement.

'That's for me and my team, Mum,' Liz told her.

'A workroom away from the glasshouses. Set in a garden. What a lovely idea.'

'Not just a workroom,' Quentin took up the story. 'Let's show you this plan we've roughed out for the building. Three rooms, plus a bathroom, of course. Completely wood-clad, with shingle tiles for the roof. Two steps up to the loggia right along the front.'

'The loggia will have planted-out tubs, and hanging baskets,' Liz threw in.

'With doors in the centre of that leading to Liz's studio.'

'Studio?' To Sue a studio was somewhere an artist painted or, at a pinch, where a photographer took pictures. But flowers?

'I thought of calling it that, Mum. Doesn't it sound grand!' In her imagination Liz saw it all.

'Grand, indeed,' Sue laughed. 'So that's one room. But you said three, Quentin?'

'Yes, well to the left of the studio will be the workroom for the girls, and to the right the kitchen and the cloakroom. What do you think?'

'I think it sounds wonderful. But Liz, if that

one is the workroom what's the point of a separate studio?'

'I shall have a desk in there, and some nice chairs for clients so that they stay long enough to smell the gorgeous smells and get carried away to spend a lot of money,' Liz giggled. 'It'll be full of blooms. The room has to be really eye-catching. And it will be. When I haven't clients, I shall be with the girls in the workroom. I want to oversee everything, be sure that it's up to McBrides' high standard, eh, Quen?'

Laughing, he put his arm around her waist. 'Now I've shown Mum this, don't you think it's your turn to hand out some news?'

'I bet she's guessed already. Haven't you, Mum? By September Timfy won't be an only child any longer.' That was in the January when Timfy was a year and a half old.

That year, 1969, they saw the rustic building take shape, looking every bit as attractive as they'd imagined. The land for the garden was pegged out, the soil of its planned borders prepared and the planting begun.

'Quentin, I wish we could persuade Liz to stay at home.' Sue was watching Liz playing Timfy's version of football with him, kicking the ball carefully in his direction and staggering (blundering? waddling?) after it as, with shrieks of glee, he sent it on its merry way aiming anywhere except towards her. 'She's got three months to wait and look at her! Poor little love.'

'You think there's something wrong?' Immediately he was thrown into panic. 'I know she gets tired, although she won't admit to it.'

'When does she see Dr Hammond again? She hasn't been to him for ages.'

'The week after next. That'll be three months since last time. He did suggest it might be a good idea if she didn't stay at home for the birth this time. But you know Liz, she wants it born here the same as Timfy. You have a word with her, Mum, about taking things more easily. What if you suggested you were finding it a bit much looking after him for so long each day?'

'Oh, I couldn't do that.' There must have been something superstitious in her nature that warned her against tempting fate. 'But I'll do my best.'

Out of breath, still laughing at the excitement of their game, Liz brought the young footballer in from the yard.

'He beat me,' Liz swooped her son off his feet to be rewarded by a huge hug, 'although if we'd called it cricket instead of football I would have made more runs. Time for your tub, young man.'

'I'll do him,' Quentin relieved her of the child. 'You stay and keep Mum company, this is a boys' own.'

Hearing them going up the stairs, Quentin's pace to suit the child's (for stairs were one of Timothy's favourite things — he'd not allow himself to be deprived of the pleasure of using his own two feet), Sue's mind jumped back more than fifteen years to the owl-like nervous boy he'd been. From there it took another leap, back to when she and Tim had been the young parents. The twins had been small like that when Elspeth had been killed, she and Tim had had them and Paul just a few years younger. The sound of the slow climb up the stairs brought so much from those years back to her. Memories, how easy it would be to let them make her discontented with what her life had become. And yet she'd known so much happiness, and even now how blessed she was that Liz and Quentin were still here.

'Phew!' Liz gave a huge sigh. 'I think I'll have to teach him tiddlywinks instead.'

'You do too much, Liz. Those girls can work without you supervising them all the time. You ought to think of the new baby and make yourself rest.'

'That's more than the baby does. Honestly, Mum, I'm sure I must have my dates wrong. Look at me! How can I possibly go on another three months? Henry the Eighth has nothing on me — I'm more like Falstaff this time. Yet I feel so well. Stay home, you say? But why? I'm fine. If Timothy is too much for you when you're so busy, he can always come up to the nursery more. There are plenty of us there to keep an eye on him, he'll potter about quite happily.'

So they gave up the battle to keep her at home. When she went to see Dr Hammond he reminded her that there were twins in the family and arranged the tests.

*　*　*

The night they knew there were to be twins, Sue felt restless. It was the sudden change in the weather, the night hot and still. Naked, she sat

325

on the edge of her bed, forcing her thoughts to the future. Again there would be three children in Highmoor, three new people to grow up here for whom Tim could be no more than a picture in a frame. Had she been wrong to refuse even to look at the bungalow Philippa had suggested? What if she and Aunt Luce had gone there, done what Philippa wanted and made a new life for themselves? Because she was still here, mistress of Highmoor, was that depriving Liz and Quentin of a chance of making a home in their own way? Could she and Tim have lived in someone else's house, no matter how dear that someone might have been? The answer was No. But a bungalow in a close, with a lot of widows, she and Aunt Luce . . . Such a cold, harsh word, 'widow'. In her mind it had always conjured an image of age, kindly, withered, dried, woman-hood gone. How many others feel like I do? Or is it just me? Dried up? Withered? Her small hands cupped her naked breasts, their nipples hard between her fingers. Believe it's him, she whispered, her teeth clenched. Do they all feel like this, all those women she'd bracketed together as 'ageing widows'? Or does time take away this ache? No, don't let it ever dim, don't let the need die. She lay back on the bed. She knew what would follow, what must follow. Tim, stay with me, don't leave me, don't stop, close, closer . . . She'd wanted it to last, in those moments she was sure of his presence until suddenly the wonder exploded and was gone. Lying breathless and alone she let her gaze wander round the familiar outline of the furniture, she moved her arms out to her side mocked by the emptiness of the bed. Widow . . . like all the others . . . No, I'm not, I'm a wife. I'm Tim's wife. Nothing can take that from me.

Climbing into bed she threw off the counterpane and pulled the sheet and one blanket over her. Tim's wife. She smiled in the darkness. Always she'd be Tim's wife and tonight she'd been with him. She'd never get old and withered with the years, always she'd want him and always he'd be there for her.

Along the corridor were Quentin and Liz, the full pageantry of nature woven into their days and nights. For a moment Sue was embarrassed to imagine what they would feel if they could have seen her. They were so young, so sure. They knew nothing of loss or loneliness. Give them long years, she begged the silent night, let them know all the wonder that was Tim's and mine.

     ★   ★   ★

'We'll have to knit twice as fast,' Lucinda said contentedly to Mrs Josh as they sat by the open window, their needles clicking. 'My, but it takes me back nearly thirty years to when Elspeth was expecting Sylvia and Christopher. Thirty years . . . where do they go, Mrs Josh?'

'Reckon we don't notice them slipping past us because we've come down right side up, here at Highmoor. Al'ays been like that with Mrs Tim, ah, and him too, God rest him. Now then, Mrs Ruddick, do you think that's about square, or ought I to do another eight rows of pattern?' She spread the shawl she'd been knitting on Lucinda's bed. 'Reckon I'll leave it at that and get set into the fringe for the edges.'

Most afternoons, once the midday meal (which was only a snack these days) was cleared away, the two kept each other company. Sue would be outside, always busy. Paddy kept the pigs in as tiptop state of cleanliness as pigs could be, he drove the cattle in for afternoon milking, separated the milk, measured the quantities and left Sue a note on the desk so that she could fill in her returns. These days Mrs Josh seldom helped in the dairy, it seemed to suit everyone better if the two older women looked after things indoors and Sue — often with Timfy's help — occupied herself in the yard.

'I see there was a letter for Quentin from some television company this morning.' It was a statement of fact, but from the way Mrs Josh said it Lucinda knew it asked a question.

'I noticed it waiting on the hall table, my dear. Perhaps they've got something being filmed down this way for one of their plays. I wondered if that's what it might be. I dare say his people know some of the folk involved with organising these things. Not that we see much of them here at Highmoor, but they may well have put Quentin's name forward if they need flowers for something, don't you think?'

'Don't see much of them, you say. Never have done, not even when he was a mite at that school. Glad enough to leave him here and wash their hands of him.' Mrs Josh's needles worked

328

furiously as she cast on the stitches for the fringe. From her expression she would gladly have been digging them into the glamorous duo. 'He was better off without them, you may be sure of that. The few times he had to pay them a visit up there in London, he used to go off looking as miserable as sin. Selfish life they lead, that's my opinion. Granted they've been here once or twice since they've had a grandson — humph! But they made sure they let the newspapers know, if you recall, so that there were pictures taken. Our Quentin wouldn't take kindly to that sort of thing. Never was like the others.' Mrs Josh enjoyed her friendship with Lucinda. Two women with backgrounds so different, yet that never put a barrier between them. Perhaps they'd both lived long enough to know what was important. 'Still, Mrs Ruddick, if they've put a bit of business Quentin's way, then that's no bad thing. And very likely you're right, that's what we shall find the letter is.' For it didn't enter either of their heads to doubt that, once the letter was opened, any exciting news would be shared by one and all.

The proposal contained in the letter was very different, although it did stem from a conversation between a producer and Anthony McBride. In truth, though, the thought had been in Anthony's head from the time of his most recent brief visit to Highmoor and the nursery.

'That boy never ceases to surprise me,' he'd said to Elvira as they drove Londonwards in their sleek, silver sports car. 'That place he's setting up is going to be quite spectacular. And

Liz is an attractive asset as long as she doesn't spend her life pregnant. Children or no, I can't see her turning herself into a household drudge. She has too much talent — and too much common sense.'

'To say nothing of a very useful mother,' Elvira had laughed. 'But you're right about Quentin. There's more of *us* in our runt than I would have believed.' And for her, that had been the end of the matter.

But the embryo of a scheme had been developing in Anthony's brain. To say it was based on his desire to help the young couple would have been partly true; certainly the role of kindly benefactor pleased him. But it wasn't as simple as that. Like it or not, Quentin was a McBride; and whatever the McBrides did had to be seen to command acclaim.

The following Tuesday Quentin went to London to discuss with the producer the project that was suggested. And the outcome was a contract for a weekly series to be filmed immediately for transmission during the dark evenings of winter. Entitled simply *In Quentin McBride's Garden*, it was planned to encompass the work of the nursery and the planning of the new garden. This latter would have to be filmed carefully, for the planning had taken place long ago and the outline of the garden was already taking shape. But such is the way with programmes designed to represent a long period and such is the wonder of television that from a view of Quentin's sketched plan the camera focused on a part of the field still left barren.

From there, and to be transmitted in the following programme of the series, Quentin was to be seen pushing in pegs (which had been removed in readiness) until, finally, one small corner would be shown with the first of the perennials (already *in situ*, but who was to know that?). Towards the end of the summer, one programme was to give people the opportunity to visit the nursery where, before the cameras, they would bring their queries to be answered by Quentin. In years to come there would be many such programmes, but in 1969 the concept was new.

'There must be more of the actor in him than we thought, Mum,' Liz said when she came home having seen the first day's shooting. 'He wasn't a bit fazed by it, he just carried on as if it were a normal day.'

'Doesn't he have to talk, explain what he's doing?'

'Oh yes,' Liz chuckled, today having sent Quentin rocket-high in her estimation, 'he sounded just the same as he does when he's training the staff. Honestly, my tummy had a million butterflies — to say nothing of a couple of babies — and I was safely out of the way. But he was cool as a cucumber.'

'And quite right too,' from Josh, who had just come down from the top of the house to check everything in the yard was safely shut and out of danger of any marauding fox in the night. 'Why should the lad be nervous when he's as sure of his ground as he is? Not much Quentin doesn't know about horticulture. He understands the lot, from growing the early tatties, to all those fancy Latin names he gives things. Not surprised they want him for the telly. Shall look forward to that of a winter evening.'

'And think what they're paying him!' There was nothing reticent about Liz; in her pride she would like the whole world to have known the generous terms of the contract. 'When you consider how much work goes into making a tray of cream, Mum, isn't it incredible? He'll get more for those programmes than the profit from the nursery for the whole season by the time he's paid all his expenses.'

Sue's mind leapt to a day years ago: Tim worried how he was going to get the money together to pay for the school fees. But there was no resentment in her, no jealousy. She was as proud as she knew Tim would have been. Of course, the series wasn't filmed one episode at a time. Once the members of the film crew were established at Top of the World they stayed in the area for a few days. Only the last of the series, for which local newspapers and hoardings would carry notices to attract gardeners sufficiently keen to see themselves on 'the telly' that they were prepared to bring their failing or blight-infested specimens, was to be filmed towards the end of August. The date chosen was Friday, the 24th, a momentous date for the McBrides for more reasons than simply the stir caused locally by the filming.

Assuming that all babies came into the world at about the same rate and requiring about the same degree of effort and discomfort as Timfy, the events of that day took Liz by surprise. The twins weren't due for another fortnight, but she'd finally given in and for the last week had only driven to the nursery for an hour or so in the afternoons. On that morning she was tempted to drive up and see how many people were coming to Quentin's filmed 'surgery'; the only thing that stopped her was that she thought it would distract him to have her there. So, while Sue was busy in the dairy, shadowed and 'helped' by Timfy, and Mrs Josh 'lent a hand with the bedrooms' with Lucinda, she started to make the coffee for elevenses. It was then that the pain hit her with force enough to take her breath. This time she knew immediately what it was and, as she gripped the side of the porcelain sink and waited, she knew too that it would soon pass. What she wasn't prepared for was that almost as it receded, so it came again and with it the warm trickle as her waters broke. It hadn't been like this last time!

'Mum! Here a minute, Mum!' Sue heard her shout, and looking out from the open door of the dairy saw her standing outside the lobby. 'Here a minute, Mum!' It wasn't the words, it was the urgency in the way she shouted, that warned Sue. Josh must have heard it too from where he was working amongst the vegetables.

'Hello then, lad,' he appeared, bowl in hand. 'Just the one I was looking for. You and me, we've got to collect up the veggies so the ladies can see to cooking.' Then, with a wink Timfy had come to understand, 'Boys' jobs, eh.'

Timfy fell for it, and happily went off with him.

Back in the house, Sue helped Liz up the stairs, then rushed down to telephone to Nurse Watson; Nurse Watson wasn't at home; another phone call, this time to Dr Hammond's surgery.

'Mrs Hammond's getting a message to him — and she's promised to find Nurse Watson. They won't be long, Liz.'

'Not going to wait,' Liz panted, breathing deeply, sweat running down her face. Her fists were clenched as she moved her position, an instinctive movement in the moment they both knew the birth was imminent. 'We'll manage, Mum.'

'Hold tight to my hands,' and what an effort it was for Sue to keep her voice even and confident. Nights in the barn with Tim when nature hadn't gone smoothly during calving, had they been in preparation for this? Help me, please help me to help little Liz, her heart cried out to him. Then as Liz gripped her, her face almost puce with effort and pain as the new baby's head appeared, more memories flashed through Sue's mind. Small, resentful at being left out of things by the older children, a drama queen to her fingertips, who would have believed then that Liz could have developed this sort of stamina? Even as memory brought the question, so it supplied the answer. Liz had no need to fight to be noticed, she was the most important person in Quentin's world — Quentin's successful world, the truth nudged her, could that play a part? — and with that had come the sort of confidence that has no need to battle. Amongst Sue's jumbled prayers for help came one of thankfulness, thankfulness that as with one enormous effort the head was through, thankfulness she shared with Tim, who had been part of her prayers.

'One more big push, love,' she whispered. 'We can manage without them, we'll show them!' If only she felt as unworried as she made herself sound. This wasn't a single birth, it was twins. Help her, help me . . . With an unearthly bellow Liz strained, forcing her tiny frame to yield to accommodate the baby's shoulders. 'That's it, that's it Liz, now it'll come . . . ' And this time when Liz strained, Sue's hands were there to take the tiny form, to ease it into the world.

'Here I am. Let's see how we're doing,' came Nurse Watson's voice as she plodded heavily up the stairs. For a second Sue and Liz looked at each other in triumph, drawn together by an indefinable closeness.

Timfy had a baby brother, and his sister was in a rush to follow him. The first pains had come at about a quarter to eleven. Before two o'clock, two perfect babies were bathed, dressed and laid in cribs (again Sue had been able to prove the use of her squirrel instinct); Liz was sound asleep.

That same August day not only saw the birth of Russell and Rebecca McBride, it was a day of high excitement at the nursery, where all day people queued with their problems, hoping theirs might be one of the items screened. Quentin, unaware of what was going on in the

335

farmhouse, explained the causes and advised on the remedies. Coming towards the end of their filming time, the producer called him aside. Together they walked back to that ornamental garden that still left much to the imagination, where they stood talking. Quentin nodded his agreement and at a wave from the producer the film crew started to get their cameras ready to be transported to what, in another year, would have gone a long way towards becoming a garden.

'Give me ten minutes,' Quentin said, 'I still have some people to see.' As Liz had said, for him the cameras were of secondary importance. His mission was to answer the problems of these people with their ailing plants.

But when he got back, what had been the tail end of the queue had become no more than one more-genuine-than-most lady horticulturist. Seeing the filming was over, the remaining few stragglers had decided to call it a day.

'I dare say it would need a miracle to give this a future,' one had said, indicating a sad and woody-looking lavender bush in a pot. 'Darned heavy too. I'm going to let the bonfire have it.'

'I really only came because the kids wanted to tell their friends I was going to be on telly,' someone else had dug in her pocket for a carrier bag and put a wilting African violet into it.

So one by one they'd gone, leaving just the one elderly and green-fingered lady.

Ten minutes later Quentin rejoined the producer. The cameras were trained on him and, with the ease of someone talking directly to his audience instead of to a lifeless lens, he said, 'By next spring, when I hope you'll visit me here again, you will see how far we've got with establishing the garden. As you know, so far not all the glasshouses are in use,' then, imagining the next stage and smiling at the thought, 'but by then they will be. Here in the garden, too, the beds will be planted out, the lawns — which we shall seed in the autumn to let them get a good hold during the winter months — will be established. But before you go, there is one last thing I want you to see. Follow me to the top of the slope. There, you see it? This is where you'll find my wife Liz and her team. You haven't seen her this year,' then even taking himself by surprise that he should announce it to the viewing public, 'that's because she is shortly to add twins to our family. I won't show you where the work gets done; she'll want to do that herself when you come back after the winter. But we'll just take a quick look at the studio,' he stood back so that the camera could be taken inside the room Liz cared for with such pride, focusing on a beautifully inscribed sign: Floral Displays for all Occasions by Liz McBride at Top of the World. The displays in the studio were advertisement enough, then as the camera backed away for a final shot of the wooden cabin, the loggia a riot of summer colour from hanging basket and tubs, the filming was complete.

Once Liz was comfortably sleeping and Nurse Watson (who'd been tracked down by the doctor's wife chattering in the High Street) was in charge, Sue didn't hurry to carry the news to

337

Quentin. She knew how important a day like this was to the nursery, and she knew too how he'd want to drop everything and come home to Liz. So she waited. And by the time she arrived the visitors had vanished and the film crew were about to follow suit.

'You go on home, Quentin,' she said, after she'd carried the news to him. 'I know how to close everything for the day. I'll stay till six o'clock as long as you're at home in case the Joshes or Aunt Luce have any trouble with Timfy.'

'No, Mum. Yes, I mean.' Quentin, so composed, so unfazed by the filming, yet the joyous news had thrown him completely. 'Listen everyone,' he shouted down the length of the glasshouse, only then realising there was only one lad there, 'Clem, here a minute. You can go and tell the others. I'm closing early. The twins have arrived, a boy and a girl. Cause for an early night for everyone.' His thin face couldn't stop smiling. Even taking off his glasses for their usual ministrations did nothing to calm him.

'Off you go, Quentin,' Sue urged him. 'I can cash up for you and see the vents are right for the night.'

'You'll see everyone out OK? Yes, of course you will. A boy and a girl. Russell and Rebecca — she'll soon be Becky. Born hours ago and I never knew. I'll go then. You're sure? I say, Mum — ' The smile that had been fixed to his face changed as his mouth started working. She could see the way he clenched his jaw as, once more, off came the poor suffering glasses. 'Been frightened, you know — she's so tiny — dreaded — ' Jaw clenched, a whole sentence would have been beyond him.

Her hug was spontaneous.

'And thank God it's all over and she's fine,' she whispered. 'Go on, love, home you go and meet your new family. They looked pretty good to me.'

His moment had passed, he was back in control. 'We McBrides seem intent on filling up your house for you.'

'And quite right too. Now, away with you.'

She watched him get in the car and set out for home. How different from the day Timfy had come into the world. Not much more than two years ago, the day that had changed everything at Highmoor.

The 24th of August hadn't done with the McBrides yet. But then in Hollywood it was still morning, most of the day was waiting.

★ ★ ★

It was seven years since Richard had been swept off his feet by Drucilla Mountjoy. Newly arrived in Hollywood to star in his first epic film, he'd indulged in the excitement, he'd been fêted, photographed and flattered. His sights had been firmly on his career, or so he'd believed. Drucilla had been part of that scene but, more than that, she'd been like no woman he'd known in his short experience of romance. Beauty alone wouldn't have attracted him, in that glittering city he'd been surrounded by glamorous women.

339

He'd been only twenty-three, five years her
junior. But he'd neither known nor considered
her age as he'd been led down lanes of sensuality
new to him. No wonder, in surroundings so
different and with a woman of Drucilla's
combined determination and eroticism he'd
been lost. What he'd not suspected was how
she'd seen in him the missing piece of the jigsaw
that made the picture of her life. From a chorus
dancer in Broadway she had come to Hollywood, where she'd gained work in the chorus for
one or two musical extravaganzas. By the time
she was twenty-eight she had been faced with
having to acknowledge that she would never rise
above the chorus and, even there, there was
constant competition from those who were
younger. That's when Richard had come her
way, a 'wet behind the ears' Englishman; but so
manly in form and face, combined with elegance
and grace. Even then, there had been no doubt
of the heights to which his career would carry
him. By the cold light of day she'd made her
decision; in the dimly lit seductive surroundings
of her apartment she'd led him to temptations
beyond his will to control. That she'd become
pregnant so soon had been her intention. She
had been patently delighted. He'd married her
and the name Drucilla Mountjoy had disappeared without trace. From then on she was
Drucilla McBride, wife of a star whose future
was assured. That is something that can seldom
be said of an actor; there are few whose names
outlast their careers or even their lives. From
early days it had been clear that Richard

McBride could be among that elite — and Drucilla had been determined to be part of that aura of fame and fortune. She'd hung up her dancing shoes, without regret, and turned her attention to entertaining in their newly acquired Beverly Hills home. She loved the pace of life in Hollywood, and had chosen to stay there no matter where his career had taken him. But always when he'd returned she'd been the same sensuous lover. He'd played Samson to her Delilah. What husband wouldn't? Physically she'd satisfied him, she would have satisfied any man. Yet the image he carried through the years was of another woman, her voice with the pure tones of his own country, her clear blue eyes telling him the secrets of her heart just as they had since he'd first gloried in their transparent adoration in the halcyon summer days of their adolescence.

He'd only been to London once in the past two years, a trip under the pretext of being part business and part pleasure. He'd come alone for, young though she was, the idea of Juliet's training being disturbed simply so that she could visit her grandparents had been frowned on by Drucilla. In her mind she'd envisaged another McBride ('from that famous acting fraternity and with dancer Drucilla Mountjoy for a mother, no wonder Juliet McBride is both talented and beautiful' the magazines would proclaim) with the glittering career she'd once hoped for herself. On that visit Richard had paid a brief visit to his parents in London and had then vanished into the hills of Wales to a cottage

Sylvia had rented for the time he was home. A few short but wonderful days when they'd strode together across the hills, eaten newspaper-wrapped fish and chips on a deserted golden beach; a few glorious nights when lovemaking had been so much more than sexual gratification.

On that 24th of August as the sun went down over the horizon at Highmoor, it shone with relentless heat on California.

'Juliet, it's time for us to go. Come out of that pool, now, right away. I wish I could have had the chances at your age that you get.'

'Not chances,' six-year-old Juliet glowered at her mother, then hurled herself off the springboard into the water. 'Don't want your beastly chances,' she spluttered as she surfaced. 'Go take a running jump at your chances. Hate dancing. Other kids don't have to dance every day.'

'Other kids would be glad of your opportunities,' Drucilla tried to keep the anger from her voice. She'd had many a battle with Juliet and she knew it was easier to guide than push her. 'Just once up the pool and back again, honey, while I go see to my hair. Then we'll be off. OK?'

'Not OK,' Juliet muttered under her breath. Then she noticed Richard going towards his car. 'Dad!' she yelled.

'Hello, Jules,' he wandered over to the water's edge. 'Aren't you going to Madame Hélène today?'

The child sensed that in him she had an ally.

342

So she made a quick decision and scrambled out of the pool.

'I never want to go again.' Dripping wet she stood in front of him, her small hands clasped shoulder height, her eyes full of pleading. 'I hate dancing. Hate it, hate it. Why can't I have fun like other kids?'

Squatting down in front of her he took her clasped hands between his own.

'Perhaps it's because you've been given a greater talent than most other children. Children, honey, not kids. We get good reports from Madame Hélène. Hop indoors and get ready, and tell Drucilla I'll give you a lift in if she likes.' For Drucilla was of the school who liked to be known by her Christian name.

Juliet turned dejectedly towards the house. No one cared. Why couldn't she be just ordinary, have a Mom who cooked their dinner like she'd seen on telly programmes and a Dad who came home from work every teatime? Lonely and miserable, she made for the house. To some she might have been seen as a typical poor little rich girl. But not to Richard as he watched the stoop of her shoulders and recalled the way she'd wrung her hands, the mask of tragedy queen on her young face. Let Drucilla try and make a dancer of her if she liked — the discipline could do nothing but good — but he didn't see Juliet as a dancer, he saw her as an actress, a true McBride.

Juliet stripped off her wet costume and left it on her bedroom floor, then pulled on her shorts, shirt and sandals. With her leotard in her hand

343

she went out to the car. The drive into town was busy; neither she nor Richard spoke until she was coming near the end of the street where Madame Hélène had her dance studio.

'I can walk from here, Dad.'

'Keep on the sidewalk.'

'Sure.' Then, taking him by surprise, she threw her arms around his neck. His response to the unexpected embrace was to hug her in return, glad to see that she had got over her short-lived rebellion. Then he pulled away, his thoughts already on the day ahead.

That must have been at about the same time as Sue was fixing the vents for the night and making sure Top of the World was safely locked up; about the same time as Quentin was bathing his first-born, his heart full of hope and thankfulness; the same time as Sylvia was coming off duty and hurrying in the rush-hour crowds towards the underground station on her way home to her lonely apartment.

During the evening Sue phoned Paul and Philippa. It seemed she had ostrich instincts as well as squirrel, for that night she knowingly buried her head in the sand and wouldn't admit to her feeling of disappointment. Of course they'd been pleased to hear Liz was all right and the babies safely born, she told herself. And of course they were interested and pleased to be told what a success the filming had been. Philippa hadn't meant to be unkind when she'd talked about the advantages of having parents in high places, after all she'd said it with a laugh. And yet . . . and yet . . . Sue wouldn't let herself dig deeper for fear of what she would find.

Next call was to Sylvia, who'd just arrived home.

'That's absolutely wonderful. Aunt Sue, I'll try and get down next week, I'm off on Sunday and Monday.' Always, talking to Sylvia ironed out life's wrinkles. 'Now *I* have some news. Richard is coming over in about a fortnight. He's signed for a film, the studio isn't too far out of London, although a lot of it will be on location in Scotland. But he'll be here, not just for a day or two but for months.'

'Is he coming alone?'

'Juliet is going through the mill, she's being trained by some fancy ballerina with a foreign name. He sounded a bit worried about her when he phoned, said she is getting difficult in the house. Apparently the sparks fly between her and Drucilla.'

'Poor little love. It's an unnatural life for a six-year-old. Do you remember how miserable poor Quentin was? Some children aren't cut out for that sort of life.'

'I know that — but I'm not sure that Richard does. After all, he had no problems with fitting in with his parents. Anyway, Aunt Sue, all being well I'll be with you late Saturday night. Will that be all right?'

'More than all right, it'll be wonderful. Drive carefully, Sylvie.'

Highmoor had come to a smooth patch; if they'd needed evidence, then surely that 24th of August gave it to them. If Sue's conversation with Paul and Philippa cast a shadow, she tried

345

to believe she'd imagined that in their tone she had heard a note of jealousy. Could they resent Top of the World being filmed? No, she wouldn't let herself believe that. So, was it because Liz and Quentin had a family? Yes, that must be why there was such a strained atmosphere. Poor darling Paul, how hard it must be for him to think of Liz with three children and he and Philippa still with no sign of a baby. Let that be why it was so difficult talking to them, don't let it be resentment. Jealousy makes people so miserable. Please bless them with a family. The trouble is I can't picture her with babies. But it's not what *I* can imagine that counts, I know I mustn't ask questions or interfere. So I'll have to trust and leave it to You. As she talked silently to her Maker she prepared the breakfast table, then bolted the back door and turned out the light.

★　★　★

'Sylvia!' It wasn't quite half past seven the following morning when Sue hurried into the hall to answer the telephone. 'Are you at the hospital already? Don't tell me your days off have been changed!'

'Aunt Sue, have you seen the morning paper?'

'It hasn't arrived yet. You forget we live in the sticks. Is it about Richard's film?' For what else could it be?

'Listen, I'll read it. It's only a short item. It's headed 'Richard McBride Joins Search for Young Daughter. Police were alerted soon after midday when Mrs Drucilla McBride, wife of the screen

346

idol, Richard McBride, called to collect their six-year-old daughter Juliet from her morning's dancing instruction and was told that this morning the child had not arrived. Her father was alerted and confessed to having put her down from the car and allowed her to walk the last part of her daily journey alone. This afternoon' — that's yesterday, remember — 'a search party is scouring the area, while alarm grows that she may have been abducted for ransom.' That's all it says. I feel so helpless.'

'Poor little mite. And Richard.'

'You know how much she means to him. He must be in absolute hell — and I can do nothing.' Sylvia never cried, hers was the sort of personality that would be scarred by tears. But Sue heard an ominous crack in her voice.

'Have you tried to telephone him?'

'How can I? I've told you how he is about Juliet. Drucilla is her mother, perhaps this will draw them together. And what am I? What can I ever be? An outsider.' Sue could picture her so clearly, she knew from her voice that she had won her battle for control. 'I expect I'm a coward, but I couldn't bear it if I phoned him and could tell from the way he answered me that that's all I am — an outsider.'

'You know that's not true.'

'I feel I don't know anything. But it's not *me* who matters, it's Juliet. Wherever she is, she must be terrified. If only we could help them search — do something — anything.'

'Of course we can help, Sylvie, all of us. Pray. That's all we can do. All? No, that's only half.

Sylvie, we must pray and trust.'

This time Sylvia made no attempt to hide her tears. 'Pray and trust that he finds her,' she wept, 'and while he's searching, that he knows I'm with him.'

It wasn't until much later in the day that they realised their prayers had already been overtaken by events.

★   ★   ★

'Hello, Sylvia Ruddick speaking.'

'Thank God you're home at last.' There was no mistaking Richard's voice. 'I've been calling your number for hours.'

She could feel the wild beating of her heart. He'd been calling her, he'd not shut her out, he needed her. 'Have you found her? Say yes. Tell me, Richard.'

'Yes. Thank God, yes. But there's so much more to it than that. Sylvia, can you come out here? I mean, can you come as a nurse?'

Her first surge of thankfulness was still there, but so was an emotion she wasn't ready to face. 'A nurse?'

'She's hurt, Sylvie, badly hurt.'

'But she's safe? She'll be well?'

Then he told her. Even he didn't know the whole story, for Juliet hadn't recovered enough to tell him all that had led up to her fall. While every outbuilding and every swimming pool in the district was being checked, while the police were putting out radio messages with her description, Juliet was lying unconscious on the seldom-used stage at the dancing school. That's where they'd found her, late the previous night.

Her school had been preparing a show for the following week and during the day one of the stage hands had taken the key and, approaching from the outside stairs, gone to the scenery loft. He'd found the door unlocked but, since he was the only one to use it, had supposed he'd neglected to lock up last time he'd been in there and decided the less tetchy Madame knew about that the better. Below him the stage had been in darkness, so he'd carried out the work he'd come to do then turned out the loft light and left the way he had come. They'd none of them known the working of Juliet's imaginative and unhappy mind, not even Richard had suspected.

'How badly hurt is she?' Sylvia hoped her professional tone would help him.

'She was still unconscious when she was found. But she came out of that. Sylvia, her leg is badly smashed, broken in three places. I saw the bone. She was lying there, white as death, blood everywhere. They've operated, leg, ankle, even the bones of her foot showed to be broken on the X-ray.' She heard the break in his voice. 'She didn't want to go to the class, for weeks she's been fighting it. I didn't listen. I put her down at the end of the street, if I'd handed her over myself she couldn't have done it.'

'Children mend more easily than the elderly. But, Richard, you won't send her back there?'

'Christ, no. Drucilla's in a hell of a state, she'd set such store on the glowing future that seemed inevitable. In fact, she told me tonight that she'd

349

got a screen test for Jules for some starring child role. Can't make her realise how none of that matters. She's got to be well, Sylvie.'

'What did the surgeon tell you?'

'He says her leg will mend. I think her foot and ankle give more concern. No more dancing, as if dancing matters a damn.' Sylvia heard what went unsaid behind his outburst and knew that Drucilla had been the driving force behind Juliet's training. 'Sylvia, I beg you . . . you will come? Give up your job. She's going to need nursing — '

'Richard, there are plenty of nurses out there. I can't live in your house — Drucilla's house — and know I'm no more than a nurse.'

'What are you saying? You know exactly what you are to me. Sylvie, I need you. Jules and I both need you. I want to get her out of this place. You know I have to be in England, I shall bring her with me. If you travel with us we'll manage.'

'And Drucilla?' How could she bear it? Yet for his sake she could bear anything.

12

Whatever image Sylvia had created, it was certainly nothing like the woman who greeted her when she arrived at the white and pretentious-looking house in Beverly Hills. Or was she being unfair when she saw it as pretentious? Facing the truth, she had to admit that it was in keeping with the others in the neighbourhood, a beautifully designed house with its huge terrace, its sweep of lawns and its kidney-shaped pool. From the edge of that pool a woman waved to her as the driver of the hire car came round to open the door for her and to lift her luggage on to the drive-way. A tallish woman, from that distance it was impossible to guess more than her height and the colour of the dark auburn hair which hung long and loose.

'You must be the nurse,' she called, coming towards Sylvia as the car drove away, leaving her standing amidst her luggage. 'Nurse — oh, I forget your name, although Richard did tell me.'

She shouldn't have come, she'd known from the start it was a mistake. She ought to have stood out against him.

'My name is Sylvia Ruddick. And you must be Mrs McBride.'

'I guess it's best you get used to calling me Drucilla right from the start. Bring your bag and come in.' With a large case, a holdall, an 'under the seat' hand luggage case and a handbag,

Sylvia struggled to keep up with her, feeling clumsy and at a disadvantage. Only when they were indoors and had reached the top of the shallow curved stairway did Drucilla say, as if in surprise, 'Why, gee, I ought to have carried some of your things. You look like you've come for quite a stay.'

'I had no idea how long. Is Juliet home yet?' Sylvia heard her answer as nervously correct. How was it that American voices managed to make the simplest sentence informal while, by contrast, the English sounded unfriendly? Or was it just *her*, was it because she was talking to Richard's wife?

'Richard seems to have tied things up so that you get here first. She's coming this evening. You must be melting in all those dreadful warm clothes.' The remark made Sylvia feel even more travel-soiled that she had before.

'I am rather. But travelling, it's the easiest way to carry a coat.'

'Me, I don't travel. This is where I like to be. Once you've lived in California you get to feel like that.' She stretched her arms high above her head, there was something feline in the movement and it left Sylvia in no doubt that under the loose-fitting floral ankle-length garment she wore absolutely nothing. The material wasn't transparent, yet every curve of her body was apparent as she stretched. 'I'm going to leave you to unpack and get into something thin. Maybe you'd like a swim.'

'It sounds tempting. Perhaps later.' Again Sylvia heard her answer as prim, over-correct.

What was there about this woman that made her react like it? She'd expected Drucilla to be sophisticated, over-glamorous, expensively dressed, elegantly made-up; she was none of these things. There was something more akin to Romany in her appearance. Yet she couldn't be called 'natural' either, for the picture that sprung to mind then would be of someone like Liz, the same now as she had been as a schoolgirl. There was nothing girlish in Drucilla, hers was the naturalness of the animal kingdom. 'I'll come down when I've unpacked. My room is lovely.'

Drucilla shrugged. 'It's nothing special. This is one of the smaller rooms, but it's right next door to Juliet's. Your bathroom is through that door. I like large rooms, lots of space, myself. I'm off for my swim.'

Sylvia unpacked, her clothes looking lost in the huge closet. Next she had a shower in the sumptuous bathroom that was apparently just for her. With a bath towel wrapped round her she was looking out on to the pool where Drucilla was swimming with long sure strokes. She ought to put on her swimsuit and join her. Richard's wife . . . Richard's home . . . She shouldn't have come. She'd been so sure he would have been at the airport to meet her. Instead there had been a stranger holding a sign with 'Nurse Ruddick' written on it, and a hire car waiting outside. Why should she expect them to arrange their day around the time of her flight? If, to Sue, she'd spoken of herself as an outsider, now she had proof of it.

Well, it's no use sitting here sulking and feeling

sorry for yourself, Sylvia Ruddick — Nurse Ruddick — put some clothes on and go out to the pool and be pleasant to his wife. But still she stayed by the open window wrapped in the towel. She watched Drucilla climb out of the pool. The shroud-like garment she'd worn earlier could have covered a multitude of sins, but clad in the briefest of bikinis it seemed it had done no such thing. She had the sort of figure every woman dreams of. Perhaps her breasts were on the large side, but her slender hips, her flat stomach and long legs, made Sylvia feel frumpy and unattractive. Go for a swim, Drucilla had invited her. Should she put her swim-suit on? A navy blue one-piece, worn for cover not enhancement. No, she'd wear a dress. Supposing Richard came home to be confronted by the two of them in their swimming things? Two women, two bodies, one of them so bronzed and perfect. So she dressed in a simple cotton frock and went outside.

'Tell me about Juliet,' she said as she sat on the grass next to where Drucilla was spread-eagled in sun-worship.

'Not a lot to tell. Perhaps this will have frightened her into behaving herself.'

'I don't understand.'

'That morning Richard put her down at the end of the street. Cunning as hell, she is. 'I can walk from here, Daddy,'' she lisped in a poor pretence of mimicking a child's voice, ''I'll stay on the sidewalk all the way.' If he'd taken her all the way she wouldn't have had a chance to go and hide herself in the Scenery loft. Apparently, the day before, she'd stolen the key to the loft, undone the lock then put the key back. Like I say, she's cunning as hell. She'd got it all planned. She meant to lie-up there until all the classes were over, then when the chap who looks after the stage went home she'd be hiding in the back of his truck. He lives some miles away — don't know where and neither did she. But she thought it would be too far for people to be looking for her. Not a thought about the trouble she would give people. Oh no, not her. All she cared about was not being sent to classes. Serve her right that she didn't know the loft wasn't floored right across, there were gaps for scenery. So down she went.'

'She might have been killed.'

'Well, she wasn't. She's been riding for a fall for months. She's never had a bit of appreciation about how lucky she is. I've seen kids being brought to the studios for audition, keen, dedicated kids some of them. But usually the most they can hope for is a two-liner. But her — I'd got a screen test promised for her for when Richard's away. Martin Leipmann, you've heard of him, you must have, he's a well-known producer, well, he's an *extremely* good friend of mine.' Briefly she paused, as if to allow time for her remark to be digested. 'He was organising it. He has a real big production coming up about a waif, a gutter snipe, who dances. It would have been the making of her. She would have landed the part, he'd as good as promised me. And, like I told you, he and I are *very* good friends. But now look what she's done.'

'Thank heavens it wasn't a lot worse. But why was she avoiding her classes?'

'You tell me! Stupid child. Lately she's been so difficult, sulky, bad-tempered, disobedient. And I'll tell you something else.' She peered around as if she expected eavesdroppers to be hiding in the flowerbeds. 'If you're here as her nurse you ought to know, although it makes me ashamed to say it. She's started to pee the bed!'

'Pool little soul.'

'How can you say that? She needn't do it. She's not a baby. Good grief, she has her own bathroom, for Pete's sake. Tamara, the house girl, told me. So since then I've made sure I'm first one in when she wakes in the mornings. It's got to the stage there's never a morning when she's dry.'

'I expect she's glad you sort it out for her without the maid knowing.'

'I what? Not likely, I don't. I make her do it herself and carry the bedding down and put it in the washer. No wonder she snivels, when morning after morning they see her carry her soiled linen out to the washroom. I guess you think it sounds unkind, but there's no better way of making her realise she has to stop it. It's not necessary. It's disgusting and the sooner she realises I won't put up with it the better.' Then, turning to lie on her front and seeming to ease each muscle into her new position, 'I hope they enjoyed it in the hospital.'

'It happens to lots of children, Drucilla. They won't let it faze them. More often than not it's a subconscious cry for help or attention.'

'Attention! What else can we do for her, for Pete's sake? She goes to the best dancing coach in the place, I'd fixed the screen test for her.'

'Does she like dancing?' Sylvia didn't remember her mentioning it when she was in England two years before.

'Of course she does. Is there a small girl who doesn't? But she's got luck on her side too, she's *good*. And whether she inherits my genes or Richard's, she must be a natural performer. If the best performance she can give is bed-wetting then I wash my hands of her. Listen, there's a car. That'll be your uniform. I waited until I'd seen you so that I could decide what size you were before I telephoned. They said they'd send right away. There are two or three sorts, I don't care what you wear so choose for yourself. If you're here as an official nurse, it's important you look the part. When you decide, I'll get them to collect the others and send some more of the one you want. You must have plenty. Nothing looks worse than a person wearing yesterday's overalls.'

' . . . important you look the part' ' . . . a person in yesterday's overalls' . . . and the way she'd talked about Juliet, without sympathy or understanding . . . Richard's wife . . . she ought to have refused him, she ought not to have come. What did she have in common with this creature who'd probably never done an honest day's work? The answer bounced back and hit her before she could stop it: what they had in common was Richard. They both loved Richard, they'd both been to bed with Richard. Yes, but

357

Drucilla was his wife, while *she* was a second string to his bow for when he was miles from home.

'There's another car. This time it must be Mr Wonderful,' Drucilla said, her head buried in the crook of her arm and making no sign of moving. For all the wretched thoughts Sylvia had not been able to hold away, she could feel the thumping of her heart. She tried to look cool, composed. She reminded herself that he hadn't even bothered to come to the airport.

'Sylvie, I tried to get away earlier. I'm so sorry I wasn't at the airport. Drucilla didn't have any trouble recognising you?'

'I didn't go,' Drucilla said. 'It was really too hot, I couldn't drag myself all that way. But it was all taken care of, I saw she was met.'

Sylvia noticed the way his mouth tightened, just as she noticed the look he threw at Drucilla's back as she lay recumbent.

'I've been looked after splendidly,' she told him, feeling uncomfortably aware of the atmosphere and ashamed that she could be so glad. 'Drucilla tells me we ought to be able to fetch Juliet home this evening.'

'How's everyone? How's home and High-moor?'

'Where's Highmoor?' Drucilla stirred herself to enquire. 'Is it the district you live in, Nurse Ruddick?'

'I wish you'd call me Sylvia. No, it's the farm where I grew up and where Richard used to visit sometimes in the holidays.'

'I think I'd rather call you Nurse. It shows

more respect, don't you know? I wouldn't want people to think you were just a friend.'

'No,' said Richard. 'Not just a friend,' his eyes smiled at Sylvia. She remembered the very first time he'd looked at her like that, years ago at haymaking time. She'd been helpless then, she was helpless now. 'Where is Highmoor, you asked, Drucilla. It's on the Berkshire Downs. A small, working farm. There's no one at Highmoor who doesn't work. It's the nearest thing to Paradise this side of death. Isn't that so, Sylvie?'

'It always has been. I thought when Uncle Tim died things would have to change, I didn't think she'd be able to hold it together. But I was wrong. Quentin has taken over another field, bit by bit he's acquiring most of Highmoor. But she has as much left as she can cope with. And, yes, it's still the nearest thing one can find to Paradise.'

'To each his own,' Drucilla laughed without much humour and reached for her cigarettes.

'What time are we going to get Juliet? Oughtn't we to get dressed, Drucilla?'

'We? Not me. I detest hospitals and anyway she and I aren't desperate to see each other at the moment. I have a thing or two to say to that young madam.'

'Drucilla, we don't want a post-mortem about what happened. She's suffering enough as it is. And your disappointment doesn't come into it.'

'I'm off to get into my uniform,' Sylvia interrupted, stopping short when he gripped her arm.

'Uniform? You won't need a uniform, you're just as good a nurse without decking yourself out like that.'

'I don't mind wearing it, honestly. And Drucilla's taken a lot of trouble.'

So she escaped indoors and chose the most austere uniform she could find: a stiffened white linen dress with a wide white belt, a head-dress the like of which hadn't been worn in England since the war, white shoes and white stockings.

'Gee, that looks really professional.' Still wearing her bikini, Drucilla gave her approval.

'Do you intend to be here to see her come home?' There was no smile in Richard's voice.

'That depends how long you are. I'm going in to get dressed in about ten minutes. I expect I'll be gone. She won't grieve.'

Together Richard and Sylvia adjusted the seats in his estate car, leaving only one in the rear and with that pushed as far back as it would go.

'That should give her leg plenty of room. Right, then, in you get.' He held the passenger door for her. Without talking they drove away from the house, a house she still saw as utterly out of character for the Richard she knew — or had thought she'd known. But this was Hollywood, he wasn't likely to find a Highmoor or a cottage like the one they'd rented in Wales, nor yet an apartment in a converted Georgian house.

'She'll be excited by this time, knowing you're on your way,' she broke the silence with a remark that she could have made to a casual acquaintance.

'I've been in and out often, it's you she's excited to see. She was only four that time when she came over with me, but she remembers everything. She talks about it — not just because she knows you're going to look after her — but before that, before the accident.'

When she felt her hand taken in his she told herself she should stop him, she should remind him that she was here to do a job. But just to be near him seemed to cast a spell on her, she had no resistance, her fingers clung to his. He carried her hand to his lips. Ten minutes ago they'd been with Drucilla by the pool, she reminded herself. She looked down at her white uniform, another reminder.

'No,' she snatched her hand away. 'I've come here as your friend, someone you've known since you were at school. Because you're paying me a wage to do a job doesn't give you the right to pick me up and put me down at your whim.'

They were within sight of the tall chimney of the hospital, another minute or two and they would be with Juliet. Surely that would make it easier, anything must be easier than this. But instead of finishing the journey, he drew to the side of the road and stopped the car.

'If all I'd wanted was a nurse for Jules, I'd have engaged one here. Sylvie, when this happened to her — I had to see you, I needed you with me. You're so sane, so caring — '

'Such a mug, is that what you mean? I have a career too, or had you forgotten? No, that sounds dreadful, as if I didn't care about Juliet. And I do care, poor little love. If I can help her, not just look after her until her leg is mended, but listen to her troubles, find out what it really is she was running away from, then I'm glad. But *you*, you're a different thing altogether. Don't give me the 'my wife doesn't love me' thing. Your wife is an extremely attractive, extremely sensual woman. She may not be much of a mother, but as a wife I doubt she sends you away hungry.'

'Shouldn't there be more to a marriage than that?'

'Oh, you poor dear,' she mocked him, 'is there nothing more in your life? Richard McBride, you are at the top of your career, you've got a wife men would die for, you have a beautiful daughter — and you have me. I'm not proud of the fact, the truth is I'm a weak fool. There are times when I think you must be the most arrogant man.'

'And other times?'

She turned her head away from him.

'I really shouldn't have come. If in a week or two you'd arrived in London, you could have come to me like you have for years. Your part-time mistress.'

'You didn't answer me. Sometimes you see me as arrogant, and other times . . . '

She shook her head helplessly. 'I see you as a sort of drug, something I don't think I could live without. If I had any pride I wouldn't tell you.' Her honest blue eyes held his gaze. 'Whether you're near me or on the other side of the world, you're in my life. You *are* my life.' She sat straighter, seeming to realise exactly what she'd said. 'There! I told you I was a mug. But I'm not

362

some sort of whore, even if I do live in an apartment you paid for, even if I'm always there ready and waiting when you have time for me. But that's in London. Just because I'm working for you doesn't give you the right to expect sneaky favours behind your wife's back.'

His eyes were sparkling with merriment as he bent towards her and laid his mouth lightly on hers.

'Friends since school days,' he laughed softly. 'Sometimes, Sylvie my darling, I don't think you know me at all.'

'I think I know you better than you'd wish for. But I mean what I say. As long as I'm here as a nurse for Juliet, that's what I'll be. Just that.'

'With any luck the mighty Victor Eikmann, her consultant, will soon say she's fit to travel. Once we get to London I'll find the finest orthopaedic man in town to take her case.'

'Don't pin your hopes on her going back to her dancing.'

'Dancing! That was just Drucilla's idea, she was pushing the child unmercifully. There are more important things in life than dancing.' This time she turned to smile at him spontaneously, this was the Richard she loved. It's a pity he had to spoil it. 'I'm not going to spend the rest of my days out here making films, you know. In fact, when I come back to England this time I may well go back to the stage. In London I mean, not return to Broadway. I've been thinking about Juliet and the battles she and Drucilla were having about her dancing. She needs to go to a proper school, but what I intend is to find somewhere where the emphasis is on acting. You know, Sylvie, I've seen it so often in her, she has a natural aptitude for bringing out the drama of a situation.'

'Poor little devil,' Sylvia glowered at him. 'A mother set on making her a dancer, a father assuming the alternative is to be an actress. And you wonder I call you arrogant! Does it ever enter your head to find out what Juliet thinks? She may want neither.'

'Oh, come on,' he teased, restarting the engine and moving slowly towards the hospital, 'of course she will. She's a McBride, isn't she?'

'So she may be, but she doesn't have to be a sheep following blindly. What about Quentin, he's a McBride.'

'Think what he was like as a kid. The parents could hardly build their hopes on his talent, now could they? You must admit he was an oddity.'

'There are other sorts of talent and we see plenty of evidence of that,' she told him coldly.

'Talent for producing children, I give you that.' Richard laughed. It seemed nothing she had said had so much as dented his certainty that he was always right.

★ ★ ★

For the first five days that Juliet was home, her presence made it easier to be in Richard's company. The consultant had agreed that as long as she took a wheelchair and had a nurse in attendance she could make the journey to England.

Richard was in the bedroom, looking out of the window to where she had her chair pushed to the garden table and was busy colouring, while Sylvia watched her and chattered. How peaceful it looked. Sometimes all he wanted was for the whirlwind that called itself life to stop for five minutes, to have time to find peace without the constant thought that he was on a treadmill. Each morning he was at the studio by six o'clock to go through the routine costume and make-up. Then, when filming started, there would be long periods of waiting, then hour after hour would be spent repeating the same small scene. Even worse was the fact that filming had no respect for the story, the scenes in any one set would all be filmed together, irrespective of their position in the finished production. There was no continuity; he felt like a robot reciting meaningless lines. Thank God today had seen the last shot filmed; it was over. Oh, the film that would finally be released would be hailed as a glorious success, a box-office triumph. But he longed for the legitimate stage, to take on the personality of his character and to live within it from curtain rise to curtain fall. Imagine doing that, night after night, then going home to Sylvie. She made no demands, yet being with her was exhilarating and wonderful; she made him feel whole.

Until she spoke, he hadn't realised that Drucilla had come into the room. 'I thought you came up to shower and dress. Oh, you're watching your — now what was it you told me — friend, was it?'

He didn't bother to argue.

'Drucilla, I spoke to Victor Eikmann today. He is happy for Jules to travel, so tomorrow I shall arrange our flight. Are you coming with me to England?'

She didn't answer immediately. In her expression, was it mockery he read? Or laughter? Or was she putting a brave face on the fact that she knew he didn't want her with him?

'What would I want with your grey and miserable country? I never go with you, you know that. I wait for you here.'

'What if I don't come back? Drucilla, I want Jules to be educated in England.' Then when Drucilla's only answer was to shrug her shoulders, 'Have you no interest in her at all?'

'Only the other day, I was wrong because I'd interested myself too much. You said I'd pushed her, not taken into account what she wanted. I suppose that was your friend's view, was it? You'd never mentioned it before. And Richard, I do wish you wouldn't call her Jules.' She decided to let the question of how long he meant to stay in England drop. Coming close behind him she wrapped her arms round his waist, at the same time undoing his trousers. 'Time for you to change into your tuxedo. Time for me to dress too.' He could feel the warmth of her body through today's loose-fitting single garment she called being dressed.

'Too hot for that — ' he pushed her arms away and in the same second that he turned to move towards the shower his trousers fell to his ankles. 'Damn it, woman, just go and get dressed.'

'Plenty of time,' she cooed in that voice of seduction that had brought him under her spell seven years before. 'Don't pretend you don't want it just as much as I do. I can see you do. Shut your eyes and pretend it's her you're on top of, pretend it's her legs wrapped round you.'

'I've told you to leave her out of it.'

'Aw, heck, honey,' she cooed, her eyes two green pools of mischief, 'I'm only trying to help you. If you pretend it's her you might manage better. Does she know about your little problem, huh?' Then, her own desire overcoming her need to mock him, she pushed his underpants to follow his trousers to the floor and gripped him in her warm hand. 'Would she do this for you? Or this?' She dropped to her knees.

He wanted to be free of her, he cast a frantic glance out of the window to the two in the garden. His marriage to Drucilla gave him nothing, nothing but her endless appetite for sex. How had Sylvia described her? 'A wife men would die for.' He looked down at the glossy auburn hair, the caress of her hot eager mouth seeming to devour him. How could his body respond while his mind was filled with revulsion? Perhaps it couldn't. He pushed her backward where she lay sprawled on the cream shag carpet. Breathing heavily he looked at her, disgusted at her insatiable need for sex, a need with no regard for love, and disgusted at himself that he could feel nothing but loathing for the woman he'd married.

For a second or two she lay there, her body tense, putting him in mind of an animal waiting its chance to spring. Against his will passion had stirred in him, surely it would have in any man Drucilla set out to seduce. As he'd thrown her off him, so it had vanished. His whole body felt weak, his hands trembled, his legs might have been made of cotton wool. She was quick to notice, her mocking smile seeming to make her the victor.

'Mr Wonderful, what a heart throb he is. If your fans could see you now . . . or *her*, your friend downstairs. Does she know how you are, or is she in for a disappointment?'

'You've plenty of men ready to entertain you, you won't be starved.' He pulled his trousers up, and with them restored some of his poise.

'And what if I have? You ought to be married to a nun, one who's taken vows of chastity. About all you're fit to cope with.'

He walked past her and into the shower room.

The last moments had shaken him more than he wanted to admit. His little problem, she called it. A problem that he didn't want to touch her, that her near-perfect body repelled him? Under the shower he lathered himself vigorously. Another forty-eight hours and he would have left this place, left his wife. For he knew with certainty that for them, this was the end of the road. England, the soft rain, the mist, earth that was never parched with the sun, the humour of the London cabbies, the stoic endurance of homebound workers as they queued in the rain for a bus that was running late. All of that — and Sylvie. For them love had always been complete, wonderful and perfect for both of them. So it would be again, so it always would be. What if there was truth behind Drucilla's taunts, what if the fault was in him? It was months since sex between them had ended in anything but failure. Supposing it were Sylvia ... With a towel wrapped round his waist he went through the bedroom to his dressing room. He had no stomach for the evening ahead, the première of a film from his own studio, something he had promised to attend simply because one of the cast was his own countryman making his debut on the silver screen. As for Drucilla, she liked to see and be seen at every important occasion.

Dressed in his tuxedo, he was ready to face the barrage of cameras that would be waiting outside the movie theatre.

'There's my pretty boy,' Drucilla turned with a smile as he came in. 'Washed all your frustrations down the plug-hole, honey? Oh yes, Mr Wonderful will make them swoon this evening.' Then, dropping her mockery, she turned around for his inspection. 'Will I do?' It was said with complete honesty, she might have been his sister wanting to look her best.

'You look very good.'

'Oh, but how boring! Sounds more like your — '

'Come on,' taking her arm he pushed her ahead of him out of the room.

The next day he arranged the flights and by the afternoon of the following one he was looking down from the plane on to his last glimpse of California. On the other side of the aisle Sylvia sat next to an excited Juliet. Left

369

behind, neatly folded in a pile, were the specially purchased uniforms.

★ ★ ★

'Read all about it,' the news vendors yelled, while the placards varied from 'Film star abducts daughter' or 'McBride flits nest' to 'Actor and daughter flee Hollywood'. The newspapers enlarged on the theme with variations and flights of fancy. Their hints and innuendoes might cast different lights, all intent on titillating their readers, but the basic story was the same: shortly after his daughter had suffered serious injury in a fall, he had ignored his wife's pleas and had brought the child with him to England, where they were staying with her nurse.

The first person Sylvia telephoned was Christopher, her second self.

'Is he using you right? I'm not talking about what the moralists would say but, Sylvie, don't live in some fool's paradise and lay yourself wide open to getting hurt when it's time for him to go back to the States. If that's the way his career takes him, then that's the way he'll go.'

'He's done with Hollywood. He means to stay here. Anyway, all that's incidental. Christo, I've never been so happy, didn't know I could be. Say you're pleased.' His opinion mattered.

'That you're happy? Of course I'm pleased, Sylvie. But if he treats you wrong, by Christ I'll kill the bugger.'

He sounded as if he really meant it, so why was she laughing?

370

'Christo, you're a star.'

Sue's attitude was exactly as she'd expected. 'What does poor little Juliet make of it all? First to be so badly hurt, then to be brought away from her home and her mother — does she see you as a nurse? As a friend? As — whatever children think when one of their parents finds a new wife or husband? Oh, Sylvie, what a mess it all is, love. Does she have to be in London for treatment? I was thinking, why don't you come down here? All of you if Richard can manage it. Why don't you and Juliet stay here while he's working in Scotland?'

'We'll come, we both want to. The nearest place to Paradise, that's what Richard calls Highmoor.' Secretly Sue thought the expression was a sign that on or off stage he remained an actor. 'But when he goes on location to Scotland, Juliet and I will be going too. That's what he wants — and I'm so — so — *thankful*. He wants me to be part of his whole life, not just someone on the edge.'

'If you're thankful, then Sylvie darling, I'm thankful too. You know that. Thankful for both of you. Poor Richard, he's never had any real, solid home life. But with you, he will.' After she'd said it, Sue pictured how 'real, solid home life' might be interpreted: meals on time, a mother to iron the shirts and darn the socks, a father to take a boy fishing, two proud parents at every school event. She smiled at the thought, knowing Sylvie would see beyond all that. Those things gave security, but 'home life' was something that defied description.

Hanging the receiver back on its stand she looked around the hall. Home . . . a far cry from the scenes depicted in the glossy magazines where the rooms of old farmhouses were invariably furnished with antique oak, beautiful displays of flowers, Chinese rugs with their neatly combed fringes and oak beams adorned with highly polished copper. Home . . . Highmoor the nearest thing to Paradise. Her mouth relaxed into something akin to a smile as she looked around her. What would a photographer from a glossy magazine make of the hall at Highmoor with its old-fashioned hall stand cluttered with coats deemed too good to be hung in the lobby, its highly coloured ceramic tub containing all the umbrellas and with Timothy's baby tricycle left at the bottom of the stairs? Forgetting the question even before she asked it, she let her gaze go to the pictures on the wall. No valuable oil paintings here, but framed photographs of the family through the years. There was Tim leading Titan from the stable . . . Sylvie had taken it the last time she had seen him . . . for Sue it had been a surprise. It had been after his funeral, when Sylvie was about to set off back to London, she'd kissed Sue goodbye and whispered, 'I've left something for you on your bed. I thought you'd rather see it on your own first.' Just that, no hint of what it was. Dear Sylvie, she understood so much without being told. Please God don't punish her for loving someone else's husband. Sanctity of marriage, it's always been our code. But then for us it was easy. It is, You know, when you know everything is right. But people make mistakes. Richard made a mistake. And that woman he married, he's been with her for years, please help her too. Imagine how she must feel. But You must know how she feels, it's just me who has to guess. Sylvie is such a darling, she deserves all the love he gives her. Yes, but does he? Or is he using her because she's too honest and doesn't hide from him how much she cares? If only I could help. But I can't. No one can. Except You. And I don't even know how You can manage it without any one of them being hurt. Poor little Juliet, fancy being dragged away from her mother . . .

★ ★ ★

The first few days in London found Sylvia and Juliet alone most of the time, for Richard had lunch engagements, appointments with his agent, visits to the studio prior to the start of filming on location in Scotland. She was surprised at the interest his parents took in Juliet — very little in *her*, but plenty in their granddaughter.

'You'll enjoy watching the filming, Juliet,' Anthony said, assured that what he said must be right.

'I don't like watching,' the little girl told him with no hint of a smile in her voice, her pretty mouth drooping in a pout.

'Good girl,' Elvira laughed. 'Watching is no fun at all. A chip of the McBride block, you want to be part of all the fun.' Juliet didn't

answer, but the pout got even more pro-
nounced. 'I expect you're disappointed about
your dancing, when you were showing such
promise. But never mind, sweetie, I dance as if I
have two left feet but it's never held me back.'
After they left it had taken a walk to Regent's
Park, where Sylvia had bought her an ice cream
and made plans for their trip to Highmoor, to
restore Juliet's good humour.

They'd been in London five days when the
morning post brought two letters, one addressed
to Richard and one to her, and both of them
from Drucilla's lawyers. They read them in
silence, conscious of Juliet busily spreading
peanut butter on her toast. Drucilla was
petitioning for divorce, citing Sylvia and claiming
that Richard had taken Juliet out of the country
illegally.

'Leave it with me,' Richard held out his hand
for Sylvia's letter. 'I'll get legal advice.'

If only he'd said he was glad it was out in the
open. Of course, she told herself, it must be
because he didn't want to discuss the break-up
of his marriage in front of Juliet that he was
silent. But surely a message could be conveyed
by a glance, an expression. Into her mind came
the memory of the way she'd sometimes seen
Tim took at Sue; the room might be full of noisy
children or on rare occasions a gathering of
locals, then without a word his eye would half
close in a second of intimacy. Her own gaze held
Richard's, with all her might she willed him to
give her just some sign, any sign. Folding the
letters, he put them in the inside pocket of his

jacket. As soon as breakfast was over he left the apartment.

By the time evening came and she was at last settling Juliet comfortably (or as comfortably as one can settle with a leg plastered from toe to thigh) in bed, her natural optimism had regained control. He was waiting for her in the living room, she strained towards the moment when she shut the door on the rest of the world and they were alone. Then he would tell her the things she longed to hear.

'I think she's tired. We didn't take the chair this afternoon, she walked a long way on her crutches.'

'I'll fight her all the way, Sylvie. She's got no proof of anything. She agreed that we could bring Jules here. I swear I'll do anything, *anything*, to stop that bitch taking her away.'

'Did you see the solicitor?' She gave not a sign of her disappointment. She tried to hang on to the belief that the only reason he didn't tell her of his thankfulness that soon he would be free, was that there was no need to put into words what they both knew.

'He asked what sort of evidence she had. Proof of adultery, I mean. Of course she has none. You were paid a wage, you're a professional nurse. And there was never any question of her objecting to Jules coming to England. Even when I told her I'd had enough of Hollywood, she didn't try to prevent me bringing her home.'

Sylvia turned away from him and started to pour drinks. In a minute she'd escape to the galley-like kitchen and start assembling some sort of a meal. The thought of food or drink revolted her.

'Say something, why can't you?' Richard was drumming his fingers on the mantelpiece.

'What can I say that you haven't said already? I just want to get the facts straight, Richard.' Her voice was so calm that it seemed deprived of all expression. 'You mean to deny you've ever been my lover — '

'Oh Christ, Sylvie, what else can I do? What other way is there? If a man goes off with another woman and takes his child, takes her out of the country even, then the divorce court will come down on the side of the mother. In some cases that may be right — but not in ours. I won't let her go back to that. Drucilla has no more maternal instinct than a cuckoo, she's never cared except for having her trained to dance, giving favours to bloody Martin Leipmann for promises to get her into films when she ought to be out playing.' He ran his fingers through his hair; without realising what he did he moved his head from side to side like a trapped animal looking for escape. 'If I don't fight, then the divorce will go through, Jules will be sent back to her. Without me there to help her . . . I can't do it to her . . . I can't lose her . . . ' Sinking into a chair, he buried his head in his hands.

Sylvia forgot her own wounds and thought only of his. She put their drinks on the table so that her hands were free, then knelt in front of him, her arms around him, her head against his chest.

'I'll play it any way you want, you know I will.'

He raised her head so that they looked directly at each other. 'What can I do?' he whispered. 'I can't lose you, Sylvie, my precious Sylvie. Suppose I fight her, suppose I go back to that sham she makes her Mecca and take Jules with me. Would you come out there, be somewhere where we could be together, somewhere where I could come to find my strength and sanity? By then Jules won't be needing a nurse, no one would know you were there. Sylvie, say something. What else is there for us? That or nothing.' Perhaps all actors are emotional, the thought surprised her as his mouth trembled out of control.

'Be practical, Richard,' she stood up, reaching for their glasses and thrusting his into his hand. 'If you want to go back and live as her husband, then I ought to say God's speed to you. For Juliet's sake it must be better than you splitting up.'

'That's not true. She's a thousand times better off without Drucilla. That's why I can't risk her gaining custody. I thought when we came home, the three of us, everything would be so different. Don't know what to do . . . can't bear it.' The man who was hero of thousands was a broken reed. Unashamedly he wept. Perhaps his life had always been too easy, when trouble came he was unprepared.

The evening wore on. Neither of them wanted the food she brought to the table and yet they needed to make a semblance of eating, it was the only way to restore some sort of normality. The one thing neither of them could do was mention the morning's letters. They even made a poor attempt at the crossword in the daily paper. By common consent they went to bed early. Officially they each had their own room, and although Juliet was always asleep long before their day ended, the outward show was for her sake as Richard played the nightly charade of undressing in his own, then pulling back the covers, before going across the small hallway to join Sylvia. Until that night they'd never seriously imagined the child being questioned about the sleeping arrangements of her father and her nurse.

Drucilla's blatant and crude attempts to arouse him had sickened him. ' . . . your little problem . . . ' she'd sneered when his spontaneous desire proved short-lived. Repelled by what with her had seemed unnatural, yet with Sylvia nothing was outside the gamut of their lovemaking, between them was complete fulfilment. He'd believed the time would come when Drucilla's image wouldn't stand between him and the complete, uninhibited union that was so right with Sylvia. But that had been before the letter from the lawyer.

'If I have to go back to America I'll come to England as often as I can,' he whispered that night, holding her close, 'Sylvie, that's all I can do. I'm no use to you, I wreck your life, I can offer you nothing — nothing except my love.'

A second-best love, a silent voice whispered in

378

her ear. Second best to a dependent child who needed his protection, was that so dreadful?

'At least we have now,' she whispered. 'No one ever knows what tomorrow has in store. Now has to be everything.'

★   ★   ★

First in the States and, within hours, in England the newspapers got their teeth into the scandal. There was nothing the gossiping masses enjoyed more than the misdemeanours of the great and famous. Drucilla made the most of every opportunity; her story would have melted a heart of stone.

Reporters came to the house where they found her surrounded by an aura of sadness. She told them how for seven years she'd been married to Richard McBride. It was true he'd married her because he'd made her pregnant, but she'd believed them to be a happy couple, she'd never suspected he was leading a double life. Sometimes he'd worked in England, but with a young child she'd stayed at home and never complained. How was she to guess that he had a paramour waiting for him in London? Then when their daughter had had an accident he'd seized his opportunity and brought his mistress to their house; a trained nurse, she'd come to care for their daughter. Until she saw them together innocent Drucilla hadn't suspected that Nurse Ruddick was anything but a family friend. 'But when you love someone, you're sensitive to atmosphere,' she'd explained

379

at each interview, her green eyes shining with unshed tears. 'He didn't want me, didn't need me. I was cast off like a worn-out garment. I begged him . . . he wouldn't even touch me,' and she knew just how to say it to set every male interviewer's pulses racing. 'He was offered a new contract here, but he said he's had his fill of Hollywood. Oh yes, it's made him a rich man. But I couldn't persuade him to think again. Of course he didn't want to take me with him. But he took Juliet. It was *me* who bore her, *me* who gave up a dancing career to be a mother to her. Cast me off, hasn't telephoned me, hasn't written to me. But of course he hasn't. Our marriage is over, I know it is. I've tried so hard, but . . . ' And at that point, or somewhere near it, her words would trail into silence and the interview would come to an end.

The story broke in London with the early editions of the evening papers. Seeing the placards, Richard bought copies and brought them back to the flat where he dumped them in the bedroom before going in search of the others. But they were out, so on his own he read every word, the accounts varying very little between each paper. No right-minded person would see him as anything other than the villain of the piece, but only he knew the entire truth. Drucilla was acting out a part for her own reasons. And he had a very good idea of what those reasons were.

Taking his diary from his pocket he found the number he wanted, then picked up the telephone receiver. That was at about three o'clock. By the time his solicitor's secretary put the cover on her typewriter soon after six, a letter was written, signed and ready to wing its way to a certain lawyer in Los Angeles.

13

Secretly, Drucilla was delighted when her lawyer explained to her the terms Richard was prepared to offer in exchange for an uncontested divorce. Why should she care that there was to be no fight in the divorce court when, by accepting Richard's desertion and his taking their child to live in what to her was a foreign country, the terms were everything she could have hoped for? The house in Beverly Hills was to be hers and, with it, a monetary settlement. Those things alone were every bit as much as she could have gained by airing all their differences in the acrimony of a courtroom, even supposing there had been no digging into the true facts of the life they'd shared in their marital home. But more than that, with a sympathetic press as her mouthpiece, she was able to tell her story to the tabloids. Such a glamorous, desirable woman, there was nothing in her appearance to hint at the delight she took in her power to destroy Richard's image. With tears she told her tale. Like a fool she had believed their marriage to be good, happily she had walked in his shadow, their child had meant the world to her. Perhaps she'd been a simple-minded fool but she had never suspected that through all the years they'd been together he'd been leading a double life and had had a mistress in England. But she loved him too well to stand in the way of his happiness — if his happiness truly lay with a sweetheart from his childhood. Even her little girl had deserted her, always preferring her over-indulgent father to a mother who showed her love by kindly discipline and training. The picture of martyrdom, she told how fairness to Juliet had influenced her decision to give him sole custody, for surely it couldn't be right to send a child back and forth across the Atlantic, living first with one parent and then with another. And that's how it would have to be for, after all the years he had been in Hollywood, after all the friendship shown to him in the States, he had made it clear to her that the country meant nothing to him, he never meant to work there again. (That little gem gave her enormous pleasure, for there was nothing more certain to lose him the affection of the American public.) So, only one stage removed from a saint, she was prepared to relinquish all the natural claim of motherhood. Her battle now must be to carve a new life for herself out of the emptiness of a world she had believed secure.

How the newspapers loved it; how the readers lapped it up. Handsome, talented, fêted, idolised by millions of star-struck women, Richard was at least temporarily toppled from his pinnacle. And that, to Drucilla, was a reward almost as dear as the financial security she gained at his expense.

In England the story was much the same, only given a kindlier slant because of what was seen as his love of his own country.

'It'll be a nine-day wonder,' Sue tried to reassure Sylvia when she phoned from Scotland.

383

That was the day the news had been splashed across the front page of the tabloids and printed in a double column inside the broadsheets. 'Richard is too fine an actor to be brought down by personal scandal, false or true. From what they say of the settlement he won't be the wealthy man he was.'

'I suppose not. But that doesn't matter. Is it *my* fault? Have I done this to him — blighted his career?'

'Sylvie love, an actor's career can't be made or marred by gossip like this. Give him a year, a year of happiness with you and Juliet and all this will have faded as if it hadn't happened. Only you and he — and Juliet — know what things were really like.'

Give him a year, Sue said. It took rather less, before the film he'd come home to make was released with a fanfare of publicity, before the press photographers took a kindly interest in his new marital status and before, at least this side of the Atlantic, he was hoisted back on that plinth of success. And by that time he was already in rehearsal for a return to the London stage.

But all wasn't well in the Marshall family. It was afternoon on a wintry day the following January that Sue came out of the dairy to see Paul's Land Rover turning into the yard.

'Lovely surprise!' she called, running to open the driver's door in her eagerness to get at him.

'Hello, lady,' he climbed out and she felt herself taken in his bear-like hug.

'On your own? Has Philippa started back to school already?'

'Yes, I'm on my own Mum, I have to talk to you. Let's go across to Dad's office' (which showed just how long he'd been away, for to him it was still Dad's office), 'I'll talk to the others later but I don't want us to be disturbed.'

Do hearts miss a beat? She could feel hers thumping, her mouth was suddenly dry. But why should she assume that his wanting to talk to her meant he had bad news? Perhaps it was something wonderful he'd come to tell her. She tried to imagine that he'd brought tidings that Philippa was expecting (and about time too, in Sue's opinion), perhaps he wanted them to share the news together before they told the others.

The little office was cold, hardly any warmer than the yard. But he closed the door and leant against it as if to ensure their privacy. Then, in the light of that single, unshaded electric light bulb, they looked at each other. She waited, forcing herself to keep hope alive, but how could she when one look at him told her whatever his news, it wasn't going to be anything she wanted to hear.

'I'm going to leave my job, Mum. I have to leave — get away from the area.'

'Have to?' she whispered. But Tim had said how well he was doing, how the men all liked and respected him, how capable he was. What could he possibly have done? 'Why? You mean you're sacked? You can tell me. If you've done something wrong, Paul, that's what I'm here for.'

She thought she'd steeled herself to hear anything. But she wasn't prepared to see the way his mouth worked before he gripped the corners between his teeth, or the way in that instant his eyes were bloodshot with unshed tears.

'Paul, love, whatever it is, we'll get over it together.'

He turned away from her, burying his head in the crook of his arm as he leant on the door. As if the floodgates had suddenly opened, he couldn't stem his tears. Even as a child she couldn't remember him crying like it; but then these were men's tears, they came from misery deep in his soul.

'She's leaving me, Mum. She's gone to that bloody schoolmaster. I ought to have seen it coming, I ought to have known. Always busy, always at school. And I was proud, Mum, I thought how dedicated she was.'

Into Sue's mind came a kaleidoscope of memories: Paul, a lad no bigger than Timothy following Tim, Paul the schoolboy trying to work like a man, Paul in love with the frigid-looking Philippa. Then Tim, reassuring her, both of them relieved to believe they'd been mistaken and that what seemed like cool arrogance was a shield to hide from them that she was a sensuous woman, the sort of warm-blooded partner they wanted for their son. And now, this! Sensuous, warm-blooded, unfaithful, preferring another man. Shaken by rage, Sue blurted out her truc feelings.

'Bitch! Gives herself airs and behaves like a slag! Why, Paul? Why? Things were so good between you. In the beginning Tim and I were worried — but he told me things were good. Oh Paul, love, don't cry like that.' Coming close to stand behind him, she put her arms around him. 'If only Tim were here, he'd know how to help you.'

' . . . wouldn't. How would he know? You've never come home to him and told him you prefer some other bloke. Supercilious, academic bloody twit, that's what he is. She's with him now, Mum. Every day she's with him. Nothing to do with the school, term doesn't start for another week. But every day, just the two of them.'

'Paul, you said you had to leave your — '

'My job? Christ, Mum what's the matter with you? You don't think I can stay there with her only a mile or so away in bed with that spineless weed? Better in bed than you, that's what she told me. Mum . . . all over . . . ' Even a sentence was beyond him.

'Come and sit here, love.' She pulled two chairs to face each other across the table that served as a desk where she still kept her receipts on that spike that had so offended him. 'There's still a drop of brandy in the drawer, Tim always kept it — just in case . . . ' She didn't finish her sentence, she didn't need to. But it was those unspoken words that reached to him.

'You were left on your own. You had to bear it, Mum.'

Oh, but she'd not been left, not like this. Help me, Tim. Help me to say the right thing. Our darling Paul.

'Don't know what to do, Mum.'

'There's always Highmoor,' she said gently. 'If ever a farm needed a master, this must be it. We could try and buy that land you talked about to your father, increase the herd like you wanted. What do you say?'

Certainly the suggestion penetrated his misery.

'Come back here? You must be joking, Mum. No good ever comes of going back.' He scrubbed his face with his handkerchief then blew his nose as if that drew a line under his show of emotion and her suggestion too. 'It was because of what I suggested that all this came up with Phil and she told me how things were. I met a New Zealander up at the Manor, he was staying there. He owns a farm — not like our piddling farms over here, Mum. He made me an offer I'd be a fool to turn down. That's what really hit me — he knew how keen I was but, of course, it's not the sort of decision you make on your own,' his voice croaked threateningly then, as if he couldn't resist the pain of torturing himself, he repeated, 'on your own. Oh blast,' he groped for his handkerchief again, 'blubbing like a kid. Can't help it, Mum. I never knew, never gave it a thought that anything was going on between them. How would you feel if it had been Dad?'

Tim? Didn't it show how wrong Paul's marriage was that he could even suggest such a thing? If either she or Tim had been tempted away by anyone else (the idea was ludicrous!), then the other would have known. They'd been like two limbs belonging to the same body.

'Perhaps it was the thought of emigrating that scared her, Paul. She's been happy where you are.'

'Too bloody right she has. As if she'd be

scared of a new country! When we were first married she would have jumped at it, somewhere right away from our past, away from all of you. You don't know her, Mum, you never tried to know her. Perhaps that's why it all went sour, perhaps it was because she felt rejected. You never thought of *her* feelings when you were so beastly to her about those bungalows. You and Grandma could have lived there together — but you were so pig-headed about keeping this place going. Too late now to change your mind, I shan't be there and even if she'd been willing to keep an eye on you at the time she suggested it, all that's over.' His voice was getting stronger. His world had fallen apart, he needed someone to blame and Sue was his whipping boy. While she looked at him, momentarily dumb with surprise, he proceeded to whip. 'You never gave a thought to either of us — not even to *me*. You weren't the only one to be miserable about Dad dying like that, but you were too wrapped up in what it would mean to you and the farm to give a tinker's cuss to anyone else.'

'That's not true, Paul.'

'Come off it, Mum. If you'd cared about *me*, would you have been so damned beastly to Phil when all she'd done was try to help you?'

'What sort of help was that? This is my home, *our* home, yours too, Paul, only you don't want it. And that's another thing — did you ever care how much you hurt Tim when you made it clear this wasn't grand enough for you?'

'What a rotten thing to say!'

Tim, help me Tim. This is Paul and me

389

talking, quarrelling, hurting each other. As if he isn't hurt enough by what that bitch has done to him, without me shouting at him. Please help me, please God, oh Tim, help me to say the right thing. Don't let us be torn apart by spiteful words. Whether she spoke to God or to Tim she didn't ask — and perhaps in her mind there was very little difference as she begged to be guided by some nameless divine hand.

'If she wants to get you away from your family then, surely Paul, she has the ideal opportunity.' Her voice was gentle, it seemed to plead with him not to look for solace in anger.

'I told you, it's too late. She's been having — you know — sex — with her precious Dr Hugh Harvey for months, that's what she's told me. Tender, aesthetic, sensitive, that's just some of the things she says about him. I could say a few more too. God, Mum, he's a right old woman. Wears a Panama hat in the summer, and a deer stalker in the winter. If he came within ten yards of a deer you wouldn't see him for dust. A classics man, that's what she tells me. How can he give her what I couldn't?' Again his voice croaked dangerously. 'In bed, I mean. Oh, he can talk book talk, if that's what she likes. But, in bed, gives her a better time in bed. That's what she says. I thought it was all right for us, honestly I did. Why couldn't she have told me where I was going wrong?'

'I don't know, Paul. She ought to have been able to tell you. Maybe she was going wrong too — and you ought to have been able to talk about it to each other. If I say to you that one of these

390

days you'll find the right woman, you'll think I'm talking rubbish. But what you've just told me about her letting you think everything was all right when, for her, it wasn't — that must be your answer. If you'd been right for each other, of course she would have told you, together you would have laughed your failures away, together you would have learnt. Sex should be such a happy thing.'

His nose blown and the handkerchief again thrust back in his pocket he touched her hand lightly.

'Funny, talking to you about things like that, sex — all the marriage stuff, you know — I mean, you're my mother. I expect I ought to feel embarrassed. But, just to talk, you've no idea what a relief it is. Wish Dad was here.'

She smiled. 'Oh, but he is,' she said silently. To say it aloud might be a step too far.

'So tell me all about this offer you've had,' she tried to change the subject. 'And one thing more: is Philippa still living with you or has she moved in with Dr What's-his-name?'

'She's living in the house with me — but she doesn't sleep with me. She's gone into the spare room. We sort of each look after ourselves, meals and that sort of thing. Don't know what to do, Mum.'

'I'll tell you what *I* think. You don't have to take my advice but I'll give it anyway. Give her the choice, she lives with you as your wife or she packs her bags. Tell her that if she's prepared to make a fresh start, then you'll give up the New Zealand idea if she doesn't want to go there, and find something else in this country — somewhere away from that wretched school. But if she won't live as your wife, then she must clear off to Mr Deer Stalker. And, something else — I have to say it even though you won't like hearing it — I'd say good riddance to her, stupid, supercilious know-all that she is. Oh Paul, what have I said? I spoke first and thought after. I'm sorry, love.'

But this time, despite his bloodshot eyes brimming, he was laughing.

'Mum, I'm going to miss you like mad in New Zealand.'

She sighed. 'One thing I've learnt: distance has nothing to do with miles, it has nothing to do with the veil that divides this world from the next. It has everything to do with opening your heart to the ones you've loved — and will always love.' Then, she sat straighter, her chin high. 'Now then, young fella-me-lad, I want to hear all the details. If you're giving up that fine place in Somerset, then the bait must be very tempting.'

Despite the cold they sat in the office for another half an hour or more while he repeated everything he knew about the farm he would be managing on the other side of the world. By then his face had relaxed into a normal expression, even his eyes were only vaguely pink.

'Gran,' Timothy's piping tones interrupted them as he hammered on the door with the flat of his palms, 'Gran, I can't reach the handle. Open the door.'

Paul got up to let him in.

'Goodness,' the four-year-old's brows shot up

in surprise, 'you're my Uncle Paul.'

'So I am. Have you come to get my Mum?'

Timothy (the baby abbreviation of his name had died as he'd progressed towards the maturity of four years) nodded. 'I came by myself from the Top of the World, Mum said I could. I can do the stile easy as wink. Gran, I've come to help you do the hens. Come on. Mum said I had to hurry or I'd miss you doing them. You haven't, have you? I ran all the way.' And to prove it he gave a great puff.

'Bit of a slave driver, is he, Mum?' Paul laughed.

'He's my No. 1 helper. You go indoors and talk to the Joshes and Aunt Luce. He's let himself be persuaded to stay in the warm since that bout of bronchitis a few weeks back. You'll find him changed, Paul.'

'He can't stay the same for ever. He ought to have been retired off years ago. What's the council for if not to house people like that.' She felt shocked and disappointed by the reply that at any other time would have brought forth a sharp retort. Today she bit her tongue, she told herself it was his own pain that made him want to lash out at those around him.

So all she said was: 'Be gentle with them, Paul. Don't tell them anything that will worry them.'

'Hurry up, let's get working, Gran. Lot to do.'

As Paul walked towards the house, she took Timothy's cold little hand. In appearance he was nothing of a McBride, he was Marshall through and through. As he strode out by her side towards the hen houses, into her mind sprang the memory of Tim leading an enthusiastic Paul off to help in some job or other.

Up in Liz's garden house at the nursery, safely in a specially made larger than normal playpen, the twins amused themselves with their favourite teddy bear, a doll, a drum, a soft ball, and anything else Liz scooped up from the playroom on her way out of the house in the morning. But as they played — and sometimes grizzled or even fought — they must have absorbed something of the atmosphere of the workroom where Liz and her three assistants created bouquets, wreaths, displays of summer flowers they'd dried or even those made of silk. The weeks leading to Christmas had been hectic, and even in January the orders still kept them busy. The new trend was to bedeck the foyer of offices with pedestals of flowers, even the dentist in Brindley had a fresh arrangement each Monday morning. And something of the steady way they worked to produce such beauty must surely subconsciously have made an impression on the almost-babies. Of course, what they liked most about accompanying their parents to the nursery was that the staff made such a fuss of them. The girls in the workroom adored them and even the nurserymen who worked for Quentin seldom passed the window without tapping on it to attract the babies' attention. If Timothy was a Marshall, the twins were certainly McBrides. They might be raging at each other for possession of some toy or other, but the instant they heard a tap on the window the actor in them would come to the fore. They would smile, they would wave, they would jump up and down with excitement or sometimes dance a jig, knowing it would be appreciated. No wonder Anthony and Elvira were enchanted with them. They never ceased to marvel that Quentin should have fathered these two delights, while Richard's daughter remained an enigma to them. Good-looking certainly, but defensive in her manner, sometimes almost hostile.

It seemed to Paul that nothing ever changed at Highmoor. He'd been warned that Josh had become frail but, to his eye, the old man looked much as he always had. Certainly he was old, but then Paul had never thought of him as anything less. Although he spoke regularly to Sue on the telephone, he seldom visited. On Philippa's account he never pressed the point. Now all that would change. Staying at his present job was out of the question; when Sir Egbert Hilton realised that Philippa had left him to live with a man only a stone's throw away he would realise why he had to go. But he could always look for something else in England . . . or he could always come back to Highmoor like his mother had suggested, try and buy some of the grazing from old Bert Hamilton. Imagine coming back here to Brindley where everyone would know his marriage had broken down, where he'd be looked on with curiosity or, worse, sympathy. No, New Zealand was a challenge, a new start. Was it so different from what Richard McBride had done? He'd left a successful life — to say nothing of a gorgeous-looking wife who, according to the newspapers, had been broken-hearted at his desertion — in America and come to make a new life with Sylvia. With Sylvia — not on his own. That was the difference. Paul looked to the future, he told himself challenge and excitement waited for him. Yet he felt like an empty shell. Excitement, like pleasure, is nothing if there is no one to share it with.

*   *   *

He sailed on the last day of March. Farewells in public places are so difficult, he knew within the next few moments he must go aboard. There were a million things he wanted to say, yet he could think of none of them. Two cars had come from Highmoor: in one he'd driven with Sue and Lucinda. In the other had been Liz, Quentin, Timothy and the Joshes. The twins had been left in the care of Liz's three adoring florists. At the front of his mind was the thought that he was alone, that he'd already petitioned for divorce, that Philippa hadn't even said goodbye to him.

Then he looked at Sue, small, courageous, and he thought of what she'd said about miles not being able to separate you from the people you loved and who loved you — not distance nor even death. Dad, do you know what I'm doing? If you do, try and understand. I've made such a bloody mess of things, but this gives me another chance. I'll always write to her, and, Dad, I'll think of her and she'll know. That's what she said. Better start saying goodbye, people are going on board. Good thing when we've sailed.

396

Got to say goodbye to Mum. Perhaps I'll never see her again.

'I'll come on holiday, Mum,' he whispered. 'If I save, I'll be able to fly home when I get a break.'

'Yes, yes of course you will. Paul — Paul — ' But what was it she wanted to say? So much and yet there were no words.

He started his round of farewells. Grandma — she was ancient, like the Joshes. Goodbye. A handshake for Quentin, funny, nervous Quentin, yet Paul thought, he's made a better success of his life than I have. Well, it won't always be like that. I'll show them what I'm made of. A hug for little Liz. Then it was Timothy's turn, his face held up for a kiss and his hand outstretched like his father's in case that was what was expected of boys who weren't babies any longer.

'Paul! We got here! There was an awful hold-up with road works and we were afraid we were going to get here too late.'

The tension of those final moments was broken by Sylvia's surprise arrival as she rushed ahead of Richard and Juliet. She brought with her the feeling of excitement he needed. But even so, the moment came when he held Sue in that familiar bear-like hug.

'Be good, lady. Don't work too hard. I'll write and tell you everything. Mum — you will be all right, won't you? I mean, you've got Quentin and Liz.'

'I've got all of you, Paul love. You know I have.'

He turned and hurried towards the gangway. He felt her eyes on him as he climbed upwards.

But it wasn't only hers he was aware of. He wanted to rush back and tell her that he understood now what she'd meant about the veil that divides life and death.

'I'll make a go of it, Dad. You'll see,' he promised silently.

★ ★ ★

By late summer his divorce was through and by that October of that year of 1972 he received the decree absolute. But for Paul that was only the beginning of the next chapter. It was another two years before in a letter to Sue, he wrote casually: 'Did I mention before that I've met a girl called Trudie Dinsdale? She's great. Not the glamorous sort — but that doesn't mean she isn't attractive, because she is. I've never known a girl with such energy. Great on a horse, well, she ought to be, she's ridden all her life which, by the way, is nine years shorter than mine. She's twenty-two.' Then, in his next letter: 'Trudie and I had a day's sailing. I'd never sailed, but she's really ace. Did I tell you what she looks like? If I did you can jump this bit. She's just higher than my shoulder, slim but certainly not thin, quite a strong-looking build. Her hair is light brown, bleached with the sun a bit like mine has become. She's a gorgeous brown, not just sunburnt like you get in England so that the undersides of your arms never get tanned, but she's the same nut-brown everywhere — well, everywhere that shows anyway.' About four months after that a telegram arrived at

Highmoor: 'Uncork a bottle — stop — Trudie has promised to marry me — stop — just wait till I bring her home to meet you — stop — you will love her — stop — I do — stop — Paul.'

By that time he was thirty-two; there was little in him of the boy whose first infatuation had led him to marriage with Philippa. Although she'd never met Trudie, Sue felt happy about her. She wrote welcoming her into the family and she received a friendly reply. They would be married in New Zealand but, as soon as they could, probably the following year, they would come on holiday.

But it never does to look ahead and make plans with any certainty. By the next year Trudie was expecting; they would wait and bring the baby. Distance doesn't hold people apart if they love each other and think of each other. Sue had been so sure, indeed she would never admit to being less than sure. And yet as the years went by, Paul became more deeply involved in the life of his new country and his new family. When she wrote and told him of Josh's death his only response was 'So the old chap's hung up his saddle. She must be ancient too.' That letter wasn't shown to anyone, Sue screwed it up and put it on top of the burning coals of the old-fashioned kitchen range. When Lucinda died he did say he was sorry to hear, adding that 'She was lucky to get taken in at Highmoor all those years.'

The truth was that with every change he read of in Sue's letters, the more distant he felt from the old life at Highmoor. He and Trudie had two children, the children had two ponies, two hamsters, an aquarium of tropical fish, and the household kept three dogs and a cat. Holidays became no more than short camping expeditions, to visit England as unlikely as visiting the moon.

And so the years slipped by, years that carried them through the closing decades of the century.

* * *

The farming scene had changed, the European Union had brought in rules and regulations that pointed to the inevitable even before the cattle industry was decimated by BSE, the disease that was to bring despair to dairy farmers. Determined not to be overtaken by events she couldn't control, Sue made her plans, asking no one for advice. Perhaps that wasn't the complete truth, for only she knew how many sleepless nights she'd spent silently communing with Tim as she saw the curtain falling on the life they'd known. Through all the years he'd never failed her. To her he was as ageless as she was herself as her spirit reached out to his. Age shall not weary them nor the years condemn . . . but what of her? Slightly built and agile, she carried her years well. But they were just as long as everyone else's. Mum to her own family, Gran to the next generation — and nowadays to the one after that too. Only when she communed with Tim did time have no meaning. Still and always to him she was his 'lady'.

It was in those quiet watches of the night that

the idea came to her, and that's when she 'discussed' it with him. For years Quentin and Liz had borne most of the household expenses. Gradually their positions had reversed; she had become the Gran, and Liz the mistress of the house. One day the wheel would turn again, she would have gone, Liz would be Gran, Timothy's wife Jessie would be mistress of Highmoor.

Pulling her thoughts into line, Sue mentally drew up her plans. That was early in 1998, the year of her eightieth birthday. The herd was sold (for a pittance, for the price of cattle was rock bottom), and the builders were called in. The implement barns, the cowsheds, her mushroom sheds, hen houses, pigsties and even Tim's office were all part of the conversion that became a row of four holiday cottages. It took more money than she could afford, but she had no qualms in spending, the project gave the future a shape. This was part of today's world; all over the country farmers were having to look outside to make a living. Some took in paying guests, some produced and packaged their own goods. Some did part-time jobs elsewhere, some admitted defeat and moved out. The days of living from a small farm were fast becoming history. But 'defeat' wasn't in Sue's vocabulary, she preferred 'diversification'. The Marshalls had been at Highmoor for too many generations to give up easily.

Timothy's great love was horses, just as it had been since he first sat on a pony. The nursery had never appealed to him, always he'd preferred helping on the farm. Once he left school he found work in one of the racing stables on the Downs. Not an ambitious thing for the grandson of the one-time famous Anthony McBride and Elvira Dereford to do, nor yet for the brother of those two rising television actors Russell and Rebecca McBride! And not what might have been expected of the eldest son of the lad Tim had brought home to Highmoor, the child with such a terror of riding. But then Timothy's genes had been inherited more from Marshalls than McBrides.

By the time he was twenty-eight he was a trainer, and his sights were on one day owning racing stables of his own. That was the year he married Jessie Edwards, or to give her her full title, Dr Jessie Edwards, who had recently joined the medical practice in Brindley. There was plenty of room for them in the farmhouse, that top-floor apartment Liz and Quentin had seen as so well equipped, was empty these days and looking very much part of yesterday's world. But Timothy wanted somewhere of their own. Only the cottage that had been the Joshes' was still in use, so the other, which had been Fred Dawson's until he retired and he and his wife moved to Southsea, had been modernised and decorated for them. That was at about the time Sue made her decision for the future of Highmoor.

By summer of the following year when the first visitors came to Sue's newly converted accommodation, Highmoor's cattle fields had become the site of a stable block and yard with grazing land beyond, and the first horses put into Timothy's care. Those who saw Timothy as unambitious clearly didn't read his mind and know the future he was working towards. To start with, jockey and stable lad lived in Brindley, but Timothy's sights were on a time when he would build more accommodation, bring in more staff to be housed on the site. Once again Highmoor had a future, the Marshall-McBride Stable would make a reputation in the racing world.

So the old century, the old century ticked on its way towards its end.

★ ★ ★

'Mum's out there in the cold. She ought to have a thicker coat on,' Liz looked down from her bedroom window to where Sue was leaning on the five-barred gate dividing the one-time farmyard from the one-time cattle meadow.

'I'll take her a wrap in a minute,' Quentin said, looking appreciatively at his wife. Her hair still the same honey-brown, not a strand of grey and scarcely a line on her face. His darling Liz, sometimes it frightened him that everything had always gone so well for them. If there was a fair distribution of happiness, then what could the future have waiting for them? 'Liz,' he held his arms towards her and, just as he'd wanted, she came to him, nuzzling her face against his neck. 'Another ten minutes, darling, and we'll be in the twenty-first century. So many things I want to say, but — Liz, my Liz, I think you know them all.'

403

She nodded. 'We've been so lucky. Shut your eyes, Quen, and remember when we used to ride our bikes, when we were children. You were so good, you always applauded all my showing off,' she laughed.

He smiled, remembering. 'It was the same then, so much I didn't know how to say.' So, just as he would have done all those years ago, as he had done all his life in moments of emotion, he took off his glasses and gave them an unwanted polish.

'Then I'll say it. Just to prove that deep down I'm still the same show-off,' she chuckled. 'The old year, the old century, the old millennium, all of it that we've shared has been so good, Quen. Work, home, family, just being *us*.'

'Liz.' He held her close. He who through so many of those years had presented regular television programmes without a moment's nervousness, yet he was as tongue-tied now as he had been as a youth when he sought the words to tell her all that was in his heart.

But being Liz she understood him without being told. 'I'll get Mum's wrap,' she said.

'No need. There's Timothy out there with her, he's put a blanket round her shoulders. I hope he brings her in, it's almost time to uncork the champagne. I wish Becky and Russ could have been here, all of us home together.'

She laughed. 'They'll be fine, partying like mad I expect.'

Outside, with the blanket warm around her shoulders, Sue was prepared to stay and watch the stars.

'Where's Jess? Did I hear the car go out?' she asked.

'She had a call. The Phillips boy. His parents had found him with an empty bottle of some sort of tablets, Mrs Phillips was in a state when I answered the phone.'

'On New Year's Eve and this special New Year too. It'll soon be midnight. Oh Timothy, I hope she gets back in time.'

'I hope so. But Gran, what a New Year for the Phillips. And the boy. How can anyone do that? However black things may seem, surely there's always hope?'

In the dim light of the starry night, how he brought the past alive for her. A Marshall like her own Tim, like their Paul — as if he'd been sent to prove that Tim's genes would still be here. Tim's and perhaps hers too. Looking up at the stars she shivered.

'Come on, Gran, time we went in,' Timothy kept his arm around her as he turned her towards the old house. 'I was sent to get you, they're all in there waiting for us. Sylvia and Richard, and their youngsters, Juliet and Jim — the kids are in their pyjamas but they're determined to stay awake, Mum and Dad, Christo and his bunch, they've all come over. Not every family can have space for a reunion like this. Listen Gran, there's the church clock chiming. The last seconds of the millennium. A happy new one, Gran,' he stooped and kissed her cheek. Over his shoulder she looked at the sky, the stars seemed brighter as if they knew the moment was important in the march of time.

'Our century nearly over, Tim,' she whispered silently, 'stay with me in the next. Into all eternity, Tim.' Then, smiling up at Timothy, 'I hear the pop of champagne corks. Let's join the others.'

THE END

EATERS OF THE DEAD

Michael Crichton

In A.D. 922 Ibn Fadlan, the representative of the ruler of Bagdad, City of Peace, crosses the Caspian Sea and journeys up the valley of the Volga on a mission to the King of Saqaliba. Before he arrives, he meets with Buliwyf, a powerful Viking chieftain who is summoned by his besieged relatives to the North. Buliwyf must return to Scandinavia and save his countrymen and family from the monsters of the mist . . .

THE SAVAGE SKY

Emma Drummond

1941: Rob Stallard, the unworldly son of a farmer, leaves war-torn London for a Florida airbase along with a group of RAF pilot cadets. He quickly develops a great passion and talent for flying, but is not so happy when he encounters US cadet James Theodore Benson III, son of a senator. Rob is instantly averse to a man who appears to regard flying as merely another string to his sporting bow. For his part, Jim sees Rob as a 'cowpoke from Hicksville'. Personal dislike rapidly extends to professional rivalry, and a near-fatal flying incident creates bitter enmity between them that will last more than a decade.

THE UGLY SISTER

Winston Graham

The Napoleonic Wars have ended as Emma Spry tells her fascinating story . . . One side of her face marred at birth, Emma grows up without affection, her elegant mother on the stage, her father killed in a duel before she was born. Her beautiful sister, Tamsin, is four years the elder, and her mother's ambitions lie in Tamsin's future, and in her own success. A shadow over their childhood is the ominous butler, Slade. Then there is predatory Bram Fox, with his dazzling smile; Charles Lane, a young engineer; and Canon Robartes, relishing rebellion in the young Emma, her wit, her vulnerability, encouraging her natural gift for song.